Praise for the
Dragonfire Novels

Flashfire

"Deborah Cooke is a dragon master of a storyteller.... Lorenzo fills the pages with enigmatic glory only rivaled by his mate, Cassie, and I did not stop turning pages until the firestorm had ended."

—The Reading Frenzy

"Cooke's long-running series continues to be a sexy and thrilling winner!" —*Romantic Times*

"Thrilling and unpredictable ... *Flashfire* is another great addition to one of my favorite paranormal romance series." —Paranormal Haven

Darkfire Kiss

"Quick action, engaging prose, and hot sex."

—*Publishers Weekly*

"Deborah Cooke's Dragonfire novels are impossible to put down. *Darkfire Kiss* is no exception."

—Romance Reviews Today

"Another book not to be missed!" —Fresh Fiction

"An action-packed, fast-paced romantic read."

—Reviews

continued ...

Whisper Kiss

"Truly dynamic."

—Fresh Fiction

"Bursting with emotions, passion, and even a real fire or four, I count myself lucky not to have spontaneously combusted! Don't miss this sizzling addition to Deborah Cooke's Dragonfire series—it is marvelous!"

—Romance Junkies

"Cooke aces another one!"

—*Romantic Times* (4½ stars)

Winter Kiss

"Beautiful and emotionally gripping . . . sizzling-hot love scenes and explosive emotions make *Winter Kiss* a must read!"

—Romance Junkies

"A terrific novel!"

—Romance Reviews Today

Kiss of Fate

"An intense ride. Ms. Cooke has a great talent. . . . If you love paranormal romance in any way, this is a series you should be following."

—Night Owl Romance (reviewer top pick)

"Second chances are a key theme in this latest Dragonfire adventure. Cooke keeps the pace intense and the emotions raging in this powerful new read. She's top-notch, as always."

—*Romantic Times*

Also by Deborah Cooke

The Dragonfire Novels
Kiss of Fire
Kiss of Fury
Kiss of Fate
Winter Kiss
Whisper Kiss
Darkfire Kiss
Flashfire

The Dragon Diaries Novels
Flying Blind
Winging It
Blazing the Trail

EMBER'S KISS

A DRAGONFIRE NOVEL

DEBORAH COOKE

A SIGNET ECLIPSE BOOK

SIGNET ECLIPSE
Published by New American Library, a division of
Penguin Group (USA) Inc., 375 Hudson Street,
New York, New York 10014, USA
Penguin Group (Canada), 90 Eglinton Avenue East, Suite 700, Toronto,
Ontario M4P 2Y3, Canada (a division of Pearson Penguin Canada Inc.)
Penguin Books Ltd., 80 Strand, London WC2R 0RL, England
Penguin Ireland, 25 St. Stephen's Green, Dublin 2,
Ireland (a division of Penguin Books Ltd.)
Penguin Group (Australia), 250 Camberwell Road, Camberwell, Victoria 3124,
Australia (a division of Pearson Australia Group Pty. Ltd.)
Penguin Books India Pvt. Ltd., 11 Community Centre, Panchsheel Park,
New Delhi - 110 017, India
Penguin Group (NZ), 67 Apollo Drive, Rosedale, Auckland 0632,
New Zealand (a division of Pearson New Zealand Ltd.)
Penguin Books (South Africa) (Pty.) Ltd., 24 Sturdee Avenue,
Rosebank, Johannesburg 2196, South Africa

Penguin Books Ltd., Registered Offices:
80 Strand, London WC2R 0RL, England

First published by Signet Eclipse, an imprint of New American Library,
a division of Penguin Group (USA) Inc.

First Printing, October 2012
10 9 8 7 6 5 4 3 2 1

PUBLISHER'S NOTE
This is a work of fiction. Names, characters, places, and incidents either are the
product of the author's imagination or are used fictitiously, and any resemblance
to actual persons, living or dead, business establishments, events, or locales is
entirely coincidental.
    The publisher does not have any control over and does not assume any respon-
sibility for author or third-party Web sites or their content.

ALWAYS LEARNING   PEARSON

*With many thanks to Kerry Donovan
for her editorial expertise and her enthusiasm.*

Chapter 1

O'ahu, Hawai'i—Friday, December 9, 2011

Despite the time of year, the *Slayer* Chen was not feeling festive. He sat in the beach bar on the north side of the island, sipping a glass of pineapple juice and watching his prey. Even though he had donned his favorite form, an elderly Chinese man, and the waitress had underestimated him, his mood was sour. The bar was decorated for Christmas, the walls thick with jingling bells, ribbons, and posters of that jolly old elf laughing in his Hawai'ian shirt. This did absolutely nothing to lighten Chen's mood.

His plan was not coming together and time was slipping away. The year of the dragon would begin on January 23, 2012, less than two months away, and was his chance to ensure his ascendancy over all the dragon shifters. It should be the year that Chen claimed his destiny.

Except that nothing was going right.

It burned that his own choices were at fault. When he had loosed the ancient force of darkfire from the crystal that had held it captive for centuries, he'd been thinking only of confounding the *Pyr*. He'd been thinking of his own advantage and been certain that the darkfire would provide the necessary distraction for him to move his plan forward.

Instead, the darkfire—as unpredictable as it was said to be—had ruined everything. His brand, the one he had used to mark other dragons and enslave *Slayers* to his will, had been first broken and then destroyed. He had been cheated of the harvest of Lorenzo, the one *Pyr* who was within a whisper of turning *Slayer* and the one who could have been a useful ally to buttress his affinity with water. Viv Jason had appeared, whatever she was, and vowed to deliver the *Pyr* Thorolf to Chen to fortify Chen's affinity with air. But Viv was not keeping her promise, at least not so far, and the darkfire seemed to be on her side. Everything had gone wrong because of the release of the darkfire.

That Chen had been the one to free the darkfire in the first place was just salt in the wound.

He, Chen, should be the master of all dragon shifters. He was the strongest, the smartest, and the most ancient of all the dragon shifters. He was the one who still remembered dragon magic, and he was the most cunning. It was his destiny to rule, to be the lord of all. It was his right to command.

His plan would continue as designed, despite recent setbacks. He watched the young surfer ride his board to the beach and shout to his friends, and his anticipation rose.

This part of Chen's scheme was proceeding well.

Yes, he would secure his hold over Brandon and that *Pyr*'s affinity to the elements of earth and water. Brandon was nearly in his thrall. The moon would be full on this night and there would be an eclipse. Some *Pyr* somewhere would have his firestorm, and the prickle of energy in Brandon's vicinity gave Chen new hope.

Could he be so lucky that Brandon would be the one to have a firestorm?

If so, the tide could turn in Chen's favor. The young dragon would be vulnerable in love, caught between his noble impulses and the dark urges that Chen had fed to him. It would be enough to push him over the edge, to make his dragon ascendant for good.

Which would put him in Chen's thrall.

Chen, after all, already possessed three of Brandon's scales. One more scale, and Brandon's dragon would be Chen's, courtesy of the old dragon magic. All of the young *Pyr*'s energy would be merged with Chen's own—plus Brandon's corpse would provide a new supply of Dragon Bone Powder. Chen was so close to claiming him completely, though the young dragon was too stupid to see what was happening to him.

Brandon even thought Chen was his friend. In fact, he thought Chen was the only one who understood the realities of his dragon nature, and he trusted Chen. Even if the *Pyr* came racing to the firestorm, Brandon wouldn't believe anything they told him. They were allied with his father, after all, which was a crime in Brandon's eyes.

That prospect of triumph cheered the ancient *Slayer*, as did the friendly wave that Brandon gave him as he entered the bar. "Hey, Chen! How's it going?" He was still gregarious, easygoing, and confident— when his dragon was safely managed. Chen yearned for the vigor of his youth.

He'd have it soon.

Yes, Chen could almost smell the flicker of the firestorm's flames, courtesy of his own greater powers. This *Pyr* would have his firestorm, and it would spark between him and his destined mate on this night.

Perfect!

"My old friend!" Chen replied, making sure he sounded feeble. He let his arm shake as he hailed the young dragon and was deliberately unsteady on his feet when he rose to greet him. He clutched Brandon's strong hand like a lifeline. "I had to see you one last time," he confessed, letting his tears rise.

"Are you sick, Chen?" Brandon slid into the chair opposite, his gaze bright with concern. "Was the trip from Beijing too hard for you? You know, you've got to take care of yourself, Chen."

"I know. I know." Chen patted the *Pyr*'s arm. "But I cannot change that I am old. It does me good to be here with you, even if the journey is long." He raised a hand when Brandon might have protested. "Enough of the trials of an old man. I have a gift for you. I came to give it to you."

He produced the silver vial of Dragon Bone Powder, the very last of his stash. On the one hand, Chen was reluctant to surrender it. On the other, he knew that doing so was a good investment in his plan. He offered the vial, his hand trembling by choice.

Brandon winced, then leaned over the table to whisper. "You want another trade? I'm not sure I can do it today." His hand passed over his chest. "Each one hurts more, and I want to be in good shape for the competition."

Ah, so the removal of the scales was troubling Brandon. Some of his dragon sense remained, which was useful to know. In the interest of the greater good of his plan, Chen chose to be gracious and cement their relationship.

Before he struck the young dragon down.

He knew he'd get the scale when the firestorm ignited.

"No, no," Chen insisted. "This is a gift from me to you, because we have been friends for so long. I know you like it. It is important to me that you have it." He placed the vial in Brandon's hand and closed the young dragon's fingers over it. He smiled, his heart beating a little faster at his growing sense of the approaching firestorm. "Use it well, my friend. I regret only that there is no more."

"Wow, and you gave it to me. Thanks, Chen."

Chen was surprised when the young dragon caught him in a tight hug and thumped his back.

Surprised, but satisfied that all was coming right.

A group of surfers who were passing the table congratulated Brandon on his wild-card slot in the current trio of competitions, and on his performance in the first two. Chen watched Brandon joke with his friends, the young *Pyr*'s confidence drawing the gaze of more than one woman. Brandon appeared to be oblivious to the young blonde who was openly admiring his muscled physique as he rolled the silver vial between his finger and thumb.

Chen smiled to himself. Brandon would be his to command shortly; then he would move forward with his plan and his destiny would be secured.

Chen could hardly wait.

"You want another juice or something to eat?" Brandon asked. "It's the least I can do when you give me something like this." He flashed the vial, then shoved it into his pocket.

"Just your company is good," Chen said with a nod. "Tell me of your surfing today."

Brandon grinned and started to explain the way the surf had broken that day, his enthusiasm and passion clear. Chen basked in his presence and the strength of his affinities to earth and water. Even undeveloped, they were potent.

In Chen's grasp, they would ensure his victory.

The prospect made the old *Slayer* smile.

*   *   *

Liz felt as if she'd arrived in paradise.

There was no better place to make a fresh start.

Maureen had picked her up at the airport, as planned, and they were driving away from Honolulu. The warm temperature was a welcome change from the snow of New England. It amazed Liz that she'd shoveled her driveway for the cab that had taken her to the airport just fourteen hours before.

Instead of being tired from her trip, she felt invigorated.

Maureen had the windows open on her ancient turquoise Mercedes and the wind blowing through the car felt like a warm caress. The flowers in Liz's lei, which Maureen had bought for her, were yellow plumeria and smelled like heaven.

This place might just be heaven.

Liz felt a tight knot within her loosening, and she knew the stress and tension of the past year was easing out of her body. She was excited at the possibility of making connections at this symposium to access the Papahānaumokuākea Marine National Monument and continue her research there. No wonder she felt so energized. Also, she was ditching a lot of garbage that had been wearing her down.

She smiled, recognizing a thought her mother would have expressed.

Maureen tossed Liz a smile. "Are you relaxing finally, or is it just jet lag that's made you quiet?"

"Probably a combination of both, but it feels good."

"That's the magic of this place," Maureen said. "It

feels so good. Stay a week and you'll never want to leave."

Liz had a feeling it wouldn't take a week to convince her to stay.

Maureen was in her fifties and a ferociously clever marine biologist who had been Liz's mentor and doctoral adviser. She'd always been stern and somewhat daunting on the East Coast, but the woman who had picked up Liz at the airport could have been Maureen's wilder twin sister. She'd cut her hair since coming here to continue her research two years before and had stopped coloring it. It blew around her face in flattering silver waves. She looked less careworn, though Liz imagined that she was still a perfectionist when it came to reports.

"It looks as if it suits you to be here," Liz commented.

Maureen laughed. "They'll take me off this island when I'm ashes in a jar and not one moment before." She winked at Liz. "Since you and I are two of a kind, inviting you here for this seminar is part of my diabolical plan to tempt you here for good."

Two of a kind? Liz supposed that she and Maureen had been similar. She certainly had always liked the older woman and intuitively trusted her. There was a lot that Maureen didn't know about Liz, though, and Liz was going to keep it that way.

Liz saw the entry to the tunnel looming ahead, a porthole to darkness. She suddenly had a bad feeling, like someone walking over her grave, and shivered.

What was going on? She didn't have a fear of darkness.

Maureen must have noticed Liz's reaction because she hurried to reassure her. "It's not a very long tunnel, and it's the quickest way home. Next time I'll take you around Diamond Head for the view. I figured you'd be tired today and quicker would be better."

They were swallowed by darkness before Liz could answer, the headlights of the car illuminating the road ahead.

Firedaughter.

Liz's eyes widened when she heard the whisper. It was a mere breath of sound, like a wisp of smoke on the wind, gone as soon as she perceived it. She couldn't tell if it had been whispered in her ear or had resonated in her thoughts.

Either way, she hadn't been called that in years.

Fourteen years.

She glanced at Maureen, who was apparently oblivious. "Did you hear that?" she asked, already guessing the answer.

"What? Oh! The engine has a little tick. It's funny how it seems louder in the tunnels. It's nothing to worry about." Maureen smiled. "This car will be running long after both of us are gone." She patted the steering wheel with affection.

But it wasn't the engine Liz had heard.

It had been in her head. This was not good.

"Just another minute," Maureen said cheerfully. "This old volcano is high but not that broad. I'm sorry.

I didn't know that you didn't like tunnels. Next time we'll go around."

Then Liz understood what was happening. No matter how extinct it was, this volcano had a connection to the lava of the Earth's core. She was closer to the molten heart of the planet than she'd been in a while. Had something recognized her?

She looked around the car carefully, but she and Liz were alone.

Firedaughter. Liz really didn't want to think about the last time she'd heard that word. Those were memories best forgotten.

To her relief, they shot into the sunlight a moment later and she could forget the whispered salutation. In fact, Liz gasped at her first view of the windward side of O'ahu. It was gorgeous, all azure bays and lush greenery.

A Garden of Eden.

This, not a whisper in the dark, was real.

"So, you have a scheme to tempt me here for good?" Liz asked, encouraging Maureen to elaborate. Liz had hoped that she might find more opportunity in Hawai'i than just a guest spot at a symposium. She was interested, though, in hearing why Maureen thought she should move. "What makes you think I'd leave New England?"

"Why not leave? You've no family, no husband, no boyfriend. You don't even have a cat."

Liz took the role of the devil's advocate. "But it's where I live. I have tenure."

"It's where you *have* lived," Maureen countered with her usual pragmatism. "You could have tenure here, too. Might not take as long as you think."

Tenure, and soon. It was almost too good to be true.

"Besides, New England's not a place that continues to be good for you."

Liz glanced at Maureen in surprise and was shocked to see a brilliant pink aura dancing around her friend. She hadn't seen auras in years, and this one was as glorious as a tropical sunset. Liz blinked and the aura was gone.

No. It must have been an illusion. A trick of the light.

Shaken, she looked out the window, trying to hide her reaction from her observant friend. First the whisper, now a glimpse of an aura. How could her lost powers be reappearing? It made no sense. They'd been sacrificed forever.

And good riddance.

Liz forced herself to continue the conversation. "Why not?" she asked, sensing that Maureen was waiting for her reply.

"Rob, of course!"

Rob dumping her was the least of Liz's concerns, but she didn't correct Maureen.

Instead, she stole another sidelong glance. No aura. That was a relief. She must have imagined it.

Maureen, characteristically, wasn't so easily put off when she had something to say, and for once Liz was glad of it. "What does it serve you, seeing him every day in the lab, knowing he's having sex every night with *that* woman?" Her disgust was clear. "How can you possibly move on and find your own future if you stay in the same place?"

Liz knew that her failed relationship with Rob wasn't an issue.

"I don't think it's a problem. . . ."

"Nonsense!" Maureen shook a finger at Liz. "You're just in denial." She clicked her teeth in disapproval. "Only a man could imagine that you two could still work together as a research team after he did something like that."

"But then, you told me not to date him in the first place," Liz observed with a smile.

Maureen chuckled. "Well, I had been there and done that. Something about him reminded me of my ex in those early days."

It was startling to have something else in common with Maureen. Liz realized she wouldn't mind driving around Hawai'i in a vintage Mercedes in twenty years. That thought made her smile.

Maureen turned off the road, then got out of the car to punch a code into a locked gate that secured a parking lot. Once back in the driver's seat, she continued as if there'd been no interruption. "After the divorce, coming out here was the smartest thing I've ever done—never mind that it's the only thing I've ever done for myself." Maureen parked the car. She fixed Liz with a stern look and her eyes were the vivid blue that indicated she meant business. "It's about time you did something for yourself, Liz. Do it sooner than I did."

"Is that an order?"

Maureen grinned. "Maybe it should be."

Liz smiled. "Maybe you won't be surprised to find out that I accepted the invitation to the symposium, hoping that it might lead to a more permanent connection."

Maureen smiled triumphantly. "Excellent! I'd been afraid I'd have to waste the week arguing this with you." She winked. "Let the bastard miss you, in the lab at least."

Liz felt like a fraud for letting Maureen believe that Rob was the reason behind her choice. On the other hand, Maureen could facilitate her move. There would be lots of time to sort out the truth—if she ever did confess it.

Liz glanced around with interest. "So, where are we?"

"Lilipuna Pier on Kane'ohe Bay, where we get the shuttle boat to Coconut Island. You're going to love it." Maureen exuded enthusiasm. "The Institute is the only thing on the island—no cars are allowed—and you're surrounded on all sides by a magnificent coral reef. Best location possible for research, even if it is a bit inconvenient. Look—here comes the shuttle boat, right on time. We'd better move it. They keep to schedule."

Maureen got out of the car and Liz did the same, taking a deep breath of the ocean breeze. She loved the idea of a research lab that was remote from other people. Solitude was best for good work.

Liz stood by the car and surveyed the island, an outcropping of coral reef with research facilities perched on it. She heard the rumble of the sea, then felt the way her body tingled in response. She felt a familiar quickening, one that she'd managed to avoid for a long time, and was glad that the Institute was surrounded by water.

Water kept fire at bay.

She refused to think any more about that whisper.

Maureen continued to lecture as she hauled Liz's bags out of the trunk. "It's such a fabulous facility for marine research, and particularly good for the study of coral reefs. You, of all people, know that Hawai'i's reefs are younger than other Pacific reefs and—"

"Biologically distinct," Liz concluded, taking refuge in the discussion of her work. "I'm looking forward to seeing more. There must be some great data collected here."

Maureen shook her head as she slammed the trunk of the car. "There is data, but you'll want to get out into the field for a change. Gather your own samples. See the reef with your own eyes. Here's the chance to get away from the computer!"

Liz pretended to shudder in horror. "It's safe in the lab. No need for sunscreen. No sharks."

"Pshaw! With that innate sense of yours, you'd make ten times the progress if you got out into the

reef. You'll make your name here, Liz. Trust me."
Maureen glanced at Liz, expectant, but Liz just smiled.

She was not going to get out into the field. She
was not going to immerse herself in the sensory influence of the earth and the elements. That would be
a losing battle. She'd be casting circles again before
she knew it.

Science was her refuge. Nice, logical, neat science.
No magic or curses came with the occupation of marine biologist, and that worked for Liz. She'd get out
to the preserve, then send a grad student diving to get
her samples.

"I like the lab. It's predictable and controllable."
Liz claimed her own bag from the older woman,
knowing it was heavy, as they walked briskly toward
the pier. "So, over to the island, then early to bed?"

Maureen grinned. "Better than that." She checked
her watch. "You'll just have time to unpack a few
things before all of us go out for dinner. The regulars
want to get to know the new arrivals before the symposium starts, so I chose a local favorite for our first
night out. The seafood there is terrific."

Liz immediately tried to decline. "But I could use
some sleep...."

"Nonsense! It'll be fun." Maureen cocked a finger
at Liz. "That *is* an order."

Liz stood on the dock and watched the shuttle boat
draw steadily closer. She didn't want to mingle with
strangers, not tonight.

That whisper had spooked her.

The aura, too.

Maureen put a hand on her shoulder and squeezed. "You'll do fine," she said with encouragement. "I know you're not much of a party girl, but it will be fun. Order a drink when we get there and drink half of it before the food arrives."

Liz laughed despite herself. "You want me to get drunk?"

"I want you to relax and enjoy yourself. If you need a little sip of something to make that happen, it won't hurt anybody. I promise not to let you drive."

The shuttle pulled into the dock and a young man leapt to the dock to tie it up. The engine kept running as he reached to give Maureen a hand. He flashed a warm smile at Liz, his gaze assessing in a way that Liz had almost forgotten. He offered his hand to help her, and Liz caught a glimpse of a deep purple aura around his fingers.

She blinked and it was gone.

Liz ignored his outstretched hand, then stepped into the boat herself. She stumbled a bit in her haste, and he caught her elbow to steady her.

"Wait till a rough day," he said with a smile.

"Maybe I'll stay ashore then," Liz joked, sitting down quickly.

What if her gift was back?

How could that be? It had been absent for fourteen years. As much as Liz savored the renewed sensitivity to the elements surrounding her, she didn't want the burden of that responsibility again—much less the conviction that she would be tested.

Science. That's what she wanted. Not juju in the dark. No spells. No voices or auras or mystical doings in the night.

Maureen sat down beside her. "You just need to realize how attractive you are," she whispered, misinterpreting Liz's reaction. Liz chose to let her mentor think what she wanted. The engine roared and the shuttle pulled into the bay.

Liz kept her gaze fixed on the scenery. But she was afraid that something unusual was going on here. She wasn't born of a family of witches for nothing. Maureen was right—Liz's intuition was infallible.

And she was spooked.

The sun was setting over the ocean, painting the sky in rich shades of orange and indigo. Brandon had the vial from Chen in his pocket and his fingers couldn't leave it alone. It was some kind of powerful aphrodisiac that his friend shared with him, although Brandon had no idea what was in it.

Just blowing some of it into the air made him ready to go all night long, and it seemed to have a power over women, too. It made them notice him, look at him, smile at him in a way that was completely addictive. He was astounded that Chen had shared the last of his stash with him, and determined not to waste it.

It was more than that, though. Recently things had started to come together for Brandon on the surfing front. He was meeting the right people at the right time, catching the right waves, being seen doing what he did well. He'd earned a wild-card slot in the Triple Crown this fall and had made a good showing in both of the first two competitions. He'd earned money and attention. If he nailed his performance at the last competition, he hoped for a place on the sponsor's team.

This could be the beginning of everything. Despite all his hard work, Brandon intuitively attributed his recent successes to Chen.

Or maybe because of this weird powder. He didn't want to question it much, just ride the wave to success.

This week would be his big chance: the third and final competition was the Pipeline Masters at 'Ehukai Beach. The break there, the Banzai Pipeline, was the break Brandon knew the best. Tonight they were celebrating his recent success and burning off some adrenaline— but this was it. After tonight, he'd be training.

Hard.

The funny thing was that even a taste of success was changing Brandon's plans. He wanted more—on every front. His ambition was stirring to life and, with it, a desire for more from relationships than casual sex. The notion that someday, one day, he'd commit to one woman was feeling a lot more like anytime now. He was ready to have it all.

As a result, Brandon was thinking he should give this vial of powder back to Chen. His old friend used it as some kind of general restorative, and Chen wasn't looking that good. On the other hand, it had been a gift and he didn't want to insult Chen by returning it.

Also, he didn't want his luck to change just yet.

He wasn't sure what to do, so he toyed with the silver vial, rolling it between his fingers in his pocket. He wasn't going to use it, but he liked the weight of it in his pocket.

He and the guys had driven to Kaneʻohe on impulse, wanting to go somewhere other than the usual haunts. This restaurant, although it was part of a small chain, was very different from the casual bar of the same name they knew in Haleʻiwa.

This place was fancy. Serious. Romantic. There were families eating here and couples on dates, and the gardens surrounding the balconies seemed exotic. It was a little bit outside of town, away from the hustle and bustle. Brandon could hear fountains tinkling in the darkness and smell the damp greenery all around them. He could see the stars overhead, too.

So they were debating their choice in the parking lot.

"Let's go to that sushi place," Dylan said.

"Or the Chinese one we went to last time," Matt said. "Huge servings there."

"Awesome spring rolls, too," Dylan agreed, turning back to the Jeep.

"You and your spring rolls," Brandon teased. Dylan could eat more of them—and more hot sauce with them—than any four people he knew. He glanced at the restaurant, unable to shake a feeling that they should stay. It was like knowing that the next wave would be the one even before it rolled in, and he trusted his sense. "It looks good, though. We could call it research. You never know when you might have someone to impress."

Dylan nodded, considering the entry. "The food does smell good."

"Looks like a place women would like," Matt ceded.

Brandon realized he was still toying with Chen's silver vial and pulled it out of his pocket to look at it. He leaned back into the car and put the vial in the pocket of his hoodie, then straightened to find Dylan watching him.

"What's that?"

Brandon shrugged. "Nothing important," he lied.

Dylan's eyes lit with curiosity. "It's that stuff you get from that old Chinese guy, isn't it? What's in it?"

"It's some medicine he takes. He asked me to keep it for him tonight, and I've got to take it to him in the morning."

"Bullshit," Dylan said, his gaze sliding to Brandon's hoodie. "That's some kind of fancy pillbox. Is that shit legal?"

"Well, it's not mine so it doesn't matter. I'm just doing him a favor."

"Why?"

"He's my friend. He's been good to me." Brandon jabbed Dylan in the shoulder and changed the subject. "Unlike you two."

Matt growled, as if taking offense, and they mock boxed.

"Stay or go?" Dylan asked.

"Stay," Brandon said with resolve.

Just then, four cars pulled into the parking lot. The guys turned as one, curious about any new arrivals, and watched the group spill out of their cars.

About half the people of this group were in their thirties, but as conservatively dressed as Brandon and his friends were not. They were also a lot more reserved. Many of them didn't know each other, judging by their body language, and they exchanged a lot of polite smiles. More than half of them had glasses.

The rest of the group was older and had a scholarly look about them. There was one older woman with gray hair who seemed the most gregarious of them all; she was wearing a bright pink Hawai'ian shirt and urging the others to hurry. She put her arm around a dark-haired woman who could have been the youngest of the group and shepherded her toward the restaurant.

Brandon noticed immediately how pretty that woman was. She was wearing a lei of yellow plumeria, black capris, and a white top. He guessed from the lei that she had just arrived on the island. The woman in pink must be trying to make her feel welcome. He smiled at that and noted that she needed a pair of flip-flops to even begin to blend in.

And a tan.

The younger woman was slim with curves in all the right places, taller than most, and had delicate hands. Her hair was long and thick, with just a hint of wave to it. He thought it might curl more in the island breezes. She walked with confidence but looked like she'd rather be elsewhere. She would be stunning when she got a bit more color, and he wondered whether she'd brought her bikini.

He wished she'd really smile.

"Fresh bait," Matt teased, as crude as usual.

"Maybe we *should* stay," Dylan said, watching them pass.

Brandon gave Matt a poke. Matt was a good surfer but a jerk with women. "Don't be a pig. It's not just about sex."

Matt and Dylan laughed. "What *is* it about, then?" Dylan demanded.

Brandon shrugged, watching the woman. "I don't know. Romance. There's got to be more going on to make it special."

"From thirty feet away, it's about sex," Matt concluded, then finished the beer he'd been drinking on the drive down. He was cocky, the way he usually was when he'd had a couple of beers and wanted to show off. Matt was competitive and he hadn't scored a wild-card slot this year; Brandon had known that a few beers would prompt his friend to challenge him. It was predictable but not serious. "Tell you what—let's square it off between sex and romance. Let's see who gets results first."

"What are you talking about?" Brandon asked, although he already could guess.

"Let's go for your brunette. She can choose sex or

romance. Whoever gets lucky doesn't have to buy tomorrow night." Matt stuck out his hand. "Deal?"

Though he'd expected a challenge, this one annoyed Brandon. He had been raised to respect women, and something about the brunette's quiet manner made him feel particularly protective of her. "You really are a jerk, aren't you?"

"Either that or you know you're going to lose," Matt countered with a grin.

Dylan started to laugh. "This place is more interesting than I'd thought."

"Why don't we just get something to eat?" Brandon suggested.

Matt waved off the idea. "Boring," he said, dragging out the word. He watched the other party wait at the entry to the restaurant.

The older woman in pink bossed people around in a genial way. She took charge of the arrangements, from the sound of it, bossing around the hostess, as well. The brunette seemed amused and affectionate. She glanced over her shoulder, and Brandon impulsively smiled at her. She blushed and averted her gaze, apparently fascinated by the discussion about seating.

Brandon knew he wasn't going to leave without learning more about her. He sensed her awareness of him and it made him smile.

"She's not going to know what hit her," Dylan commented.

"I'll order her an extra-large mai tai," Matt said

with satisfaction and headed for the entrance. "On me. It'll smooth the way."

"This I've got to see," Dylan said and continued after Matt.

"Wait a minute. You can't just target her," Brandon objected, striding after his friends. "That's not right."

"Right?" Matt seemed to be amused by this idea. "Look at her. She just got here. For all we know, I'm exactly what she wants on her vacation. All those mainland girls are looking for action." When they got close to the entrance, Matt preened a bit and smiled at the brunette.

She was even prettier than Brandon had thought.

Her eyes widened slightly and she shook her head, as if disinterested in Matt's attention. Her gaze flicked to Brandon again and he rolled his eyes, as if despairing of his buddy.

She smiled then, a real smile, one that brightened her features and made her look young and even more attractive. Brandon's heart thumped, and Dylan chuckled.

"You're on," Brandon murmured to Matt.

Brandon didn't even know this woman, but he was annoyed by Matt's behavior. He was going to defend her from his friend, whether she was ultimately interested in him or not.

It was just the right thing to do.

One fact was inescapable: the men were gorgeous in Hawai'i. Liz couldn't believe how many hunks she'd seen already. They were everywhere—at the beach, in town, on the streets, at this restaurant. There had to be one at every table—never mind the three in the parking lot. They were all tanned and handsome, completely built. She'd never been in a place so filled with incredibly sexy men.

In fact, everything was gorgeous. This restaurant was perfect and romantic. She noticed the couples dining together and didn't doubt that this place had seen its share of proposals. The balcony extended into the open air, the lush velvet of the night pressing against the glow of soft candlelight. She could smell the plants growing in the gardens and hear the splash of fountains. It amazed her that they could drive from that perfect beach where they parked for the shuttle and in five minutes be surrounded by lush rain forest and comparative quiet. It was almost overwhelming to be so closely surrounded by the pulse of nature.

Maybe that was what was feeding her ability to see auras. They were getting brighter by the minute, the people in her group surrounded by glorious hues of light. It almost hurt Liz's eyes to see so many auras, all throbbing and vibrating with energy. The other guests were nervous and their auras were agitated as a result. The table generated a light show that made her dizzy.

Liz glanced toward the bar where those three guys were having beers. Their auras were dimmer, more relaxed, and drew her gaze over and over again.

"Surfers," Trudy confided with a sniff. She was a contemporary of Maureen's, but apparently Hawai'i hadn't made her relax. Her dark hair was tightly pulled back and she spoke more quickly and decisively than the others. "Completely self-indulgent," she added, then sipped her mineral water.

Liz looked at the auburn-haired guy again, the one who had smiled at her a couple of times already. Unlike the others, he didn't seem predatory. She found his confidence appealing, and she sensed that he was comfortable in his own skin. She liked the steady hum of indigo that was his aura, despite her distrust of the reappearance of those auras. Her interpretation of them was intuitive. This aura told her that he would be loyal and dependable.

She didn't want to use her ability to see auras to judge people, but couldn't shake the impression.

His dark-haired friend had an aura of pulsing green. He, too, was loyal to his friends, but competitive and cocky.

He was like Rob.

The third guy, the blond one, had an aura like golden honey. He'd be a good friend, easy to spend time with, relaxed but unambitious. He was the kind of guy who could do nothing with his life and not worry about it.

No, the auburn-haired guy was the keeper. There was a tattoo on his chest, although Liz couldn't fully see what it was, and she glimpsed part of another on his arm. He was drinking beer, chatting with his friends. She liked the rich sound of his laughter. His eyes twinkled when he caught her looking, and he toasted her with his beer before he took a swig.

Probably thinking that he knew what she was thinking. Liz developed a fascination with the menu, fighting a smile. Wouldn't he be surprised if she confessed to comparing auras?

"The shrimp is good," Maureen said, as dictatorial and kind as ever. "They're farmed locally."

Before Liz could answer, the waitress put a large drink in front of her. "With the gentleman's compliments," she said, gesturing to the dark-haired surfer. His smile had a roguish tinge that confirmed her earlier conclusions.

She wasn't interested in just sex.

She told herself that she would have known the kind of guy he was even without being able to see the auras.

Liz pushed the glass away with her fingertips. "Thanks, but no. Please give the gentleman my thanks."

"You sure?"

"I'm sure."

"It's the jumbo mai tai. House specialty."

"I'd just like a glass of white wine, please."

The waitress shrugged. "Suit yourself." She picked up the drink and the guy at the bar scowled. Liz peeked and the auburn-haired guy was debating something with his blond friend, as if he hadn't even noticed. He turned and gestured to the sky beyond the roof over the balcony and she admired the breadth of his shoulders, the unruly tangle of his hair. It was long, long enough to tempt her to touch it. And that tan . . .

A gorgeous keeper.

She didn't know anything about him and she wasn't going to rely on auras. That part of her life was over. Liz took a gulp of her wine as soon as it arrived.

She finished the glass before the food arrived, and Maureen ordered her another before she could argue.

It tasted even better than the first one. The auras got brighter, but the wine made Liz worry less about them.

She told herself that it was the wine that made her feel vital and excited, but deep in her heart, she feared otherwise.

She feared that her powers were back.

Even if she didn't understand why or how.

Chapter 2

The brunette's party relaxed as it got later. They didn't drink much, Brandon noticed, but what they did drink loosened their inhibitions. They laughed more and were obviously having fun. The brunette kept glancing his way, but he wasn't in that much of a hurry to make a conquest.

She seemed different from the women he usually met. She looked like she was a bit older than him. She also looked like she had a job, like she had it together in a way that the girls who hung out at the beach seldom did. But then, he wasn't in a bar; serious people came to restaurants like this one.

Brandon missed serious people. Sometimes he tired of his surfer friends and their inability to look beyond the next wave, the next meal, the next pleasure.

The brunette looked as if she had goals and direction, which was something he didn't see often. She wasn't interested in Matt, she'd made that clear, which also made her different.

He wondered what she was looking for in a guy.

He wondered whether he had any chance of delivering it.

He, after all, also had a goal and direction. Maybe they had more than that in common.

Brandon had felt a new optimism lately. The shadow that haunted him—and the truth of what he really was—seemed to be a more distant threat and maybe one that could be banished forever. It was a good feeling to be almost able to forget the dragon— like catching the perfect wave early—and he wanted to hold on to it for as long as possible.

When her group spilled out into the parking lot in the wee hours, he trailed behind them. He made some excuse, which didn't fool Dylan, and left his friends in the bar.

"I tell you, we'll be able to see the eclipse," insisted one guy, tapping his watch. "It'll start any minute now."

"Three and a half hours' duration," added another guy. "Are we going to stand in the parking lot all night?"

"Let's stay here for a few moments. There'll be less light pollution than back toward town," the older woman said, making her suggestion sound like an edict. "We can watch the beginning."

The others did as they were told.

Brandon remembered that there was supposed to

be a total lunar eclipse on this night. The night was clear, the dark sky filled with stars and the glowing orb of the full moon. He stood and stared at that radiant moon. The warm wind tousled his hair and he could smell the plumeria in the brunette's lei. His heart was filled with an affection for this island where he had chosen to live, and the promise of the future.

By the end of the week, he could have his future secured.

And something to offer a woman like this one.

"Here we go!" cried one of the women, and Brandon saw the first increment of shadow slide over the full moon. The group stared upward, enraptured.

Brandon would have happily stared, as well, but a strange sensation distracted him from the view. His hand was warm but tingling. He glanced down to find orange sparks dancing over the fingers of his right hand, the hand closest to the brunette's group of friends.

At first he thought his eyes were deceiving him, but the flames grew larger, becoming a radiant orange glow that outlined his entire hand. It looked unreal. The fire slid up his shoulder, and he knew it wasn't an illusion because he could feel its heat spreading over his skin like a bonfire. At the same time, a warmth filled his body.

Brandon glanced around himself, but no one else had noticed the fire.

And no one else had the same corona of flames around his body.

What was going on? Matt and Dylan had come out of the restaurant and were arguing about who would drive. The brunette's friends were fixated on the moon.

But the sensation kept getting stronger. When the flames danced down his side, Brandon felt himself become sexually aroused. He was on fire, filled with lust and desire, simmering as he never had before. He spread his hands, looking down at his feet as they were illuminated by the strange orange fire; then a spark leapt from his fingertip.

It cut a blazing arc through the air, one that spewed sparks as it scorched a trail through the night. The spark collided with the shoulder of the brunette. She jumped as if the spark had singed, then turned to look for its source. Her gaze locked with Brandon's and he was shocked that her eyes seemed to be filled with light.

She was glowing, her skin appearing golden and luminescent. There were sparks flying off the tips of her hair and her face was flushed.

What was going on? Her eyes rounded in surprise and her lips parted. Brandon felt another simmer of sexual desire and saw an answering heat in her eyes. Their gazes held across the golden glow of light, and the brightness intensified. Sizzling. Crackling. Demanding. Brandon felt as if they were alone, standing outside of time, as the light brightened between them.

For a moment, he didn't think about the flames. He simply saw the pretty brunette looking at him, *really* looking at him.

Without using Chen's powder.

He sensed her interest as keenly as he could smell the flowers in her lei. His dragon senses sharpened in that disconcerting way, but for once, he was glad of the detail. He heard her pulse leap and felt her inhale quickly. He could smell her body's natural perfume, almost disguised by the smell of the flowers. He saw her flush a little and he knew that she was attracted to him.

Just him.

He hadn't had to encourage her with that powder of Chen's. That was so special that Brandon wanted to be even closer to her.

He had to know more.

Brandon took a step into the golden halo of light, liking how her eyes widened a little in awareness, liking that he could now see just how blue they were.

His heart was pounding so hard that he felt dizzy—no, he felt dizzy because his heart was matching its pace to hers. He could hear her pulse and his own and felt them synchronize. It was a powerful and overwhelming sensation. The beat resonated through his body, pulsed through his veins, made him sharply, keenly, utterly aware of her. She was the center of his world. His sun.

When she smiled, he wanted to be hers.

That was when Brandon realized what was happening. He was having his firestorm. He was meeting his destined mate, the one woman in his entire life who could bear his son.

He'd heard about the firestorm, but only vaguely,

from his parents. He'd never really thought it would happen to him—or that if it did happen, it would be centuries from now. But as he stood and felt the burn of the firestorm, he experienced a new clarity of thought.

This woman had seemed special and different to him because she *was* special and different. This was destiny. She was his destined mate. It wasn't Chen's powder that had brought him good luck lately; it had been the promise of the firestorm. This was his chance to do something important and to do it right. He had been ready for an opportunity to make a lasting relationship, and here was his chance. He had a duty to fulfill the firestorm, which meant he had to pursue her.

Without spooking her with his truth.

This was his shot, in more ways than one. Everything hung in the balance. He could do better than his father. Brandon had to believe it.

All he had to do was keep his dragon in check.

He would romance her. He would woo her and he would win her, and he would conquer the dark force within himself forever—with her help.

His dragon shifter nature had always been a dark secret, an embarrassment, an obstacle to close friendships. He'd resented it, blamed it for his feeling alone in a crowd, wished he'd never been cursed with it.

But the sensation of the firestorm was wonderful, exhilarating, powerful. It was the only good thing about being *Pyr*, and it was happening to him.

To them.

He smiled and stepped toward her, offering his hand. The sparks danced and crackled, as if a bonfire burned between them. She stared at those flames, glanced at her friends—who were so busy staring at the moon that they hadn't noticed anything odd— then took a bold step toward him. Her eyes danced and her smile broadened. Brandon felt like they had a secret, a magical connection, because they did.

The firestorm.

Her hand was in his, the flames crackling between them, the heat filling his blood. The light spread over her skin, dancing over her, making her eyes sparkle. She would have asked a question, but Brandon didn't want to risk the loss of the magic.

He let instinct rule.

He tugged her so that she was against his chest. Her hands fell on his shoulders and she looked up at him, his own desire mirrored in her blue eyes. That was all the encouragement he needed to bend his head and claim her lips with a kiss.

And the firestorm surged through his veins, filling him with hope and desire, persuading him that it knew best of all.

Liz felt that spark electrify her.

Firedaughter.

The word resonated in her thoughts as the old fire surged through her veins. Her power *was* back, against all rhyme and reason. She couldn't explain it, but the evidence was irrefutable. And magic was like that—it played by its own rules.

This was why she'd felt more alive than she had in fourteen years. Arriving here had somehow jolted her awake from a long sleep and rekindled her powers. She was immersed in the sensory power that had once filled her days and nights, and it felt so good and so right that Liz had no desire to throw it away again just yet.

Maybe she was drunk.

Maybe that was why she didn't care.

But she wanted all the sensation that she'd denied herself for the past fourteen years. She wanted to wallow in it, savor it, and enjoy it.

Just for a few moments.

In this moment of moments, making out with the most irresistibly sexy guy she'd ever met suited her just fine. She didn't even know his name. She didn't need to know his name. It was one soul-searing kiss, and after that, she'd never see him again.

Liz wasn't impulsive about sex. She wasn't someone who lost control. She wasn't impetuous or inclined to indulge her passions.

But she was intuitive and she knew what was right.

This guy and his kiss were right.

In fact, this was the first thing that had been right in a long, long time.

His kiss awakened parts of her that had been slumbering and fueled them with new heat. Liz felt languid and sexy and absolutely certain of what was right. Just the way he'd looked at her made her feel sexy. The way he smiled was mischievous, seductive, and had tempted her to taste him. The way he walked and moved, his powerful grace, made her want to jump his bones.

His kiss was all that and more.

She just wanted more.

Liz's breasts were crushed against the rock-solid muscle of his chest, and his arms were wrapped around her tightly. Her lei was pressed between them, the perfume released by the flowers almost making her dizzy with its sweet scent. His touch was the perfect combination of gentleness and demand. She felt immersed in the true blue of his aura, and her conviction that he was exactly the kind of man she'd guessed him to be. One thing about auras: they had no ability to deceive.

His mouth was locked on hers, coaxing her and claiming her. His lips were both firm and soft, cajoling and demanding. His kiss was simultaneously passionate and sweet, so persuasive and enticing that Liz was sure she'd never get enough.

She twined her fingers into his hair, loving that it felt as silky and curly as she'd guessed it would. She ran her hands over his shoulders, liking that he was broad and tall—taller even than her—and strong. His skin was warm and his embrace seemed protective. She loved that he was all muscle but that he was gentle with her. He pulled her to her toes and deepened his kiss, the touch of his tongue against hers making her so hot that she thought she'd explode.

As if to prove how magical this embrace was, that strange firelight danced around their bodies and between them. It seemed to light the desire within Liz. Maybe it was some kind of illusion caused by the eclipse or maybe it was a new facet of her power. Liz didn't care. As the flames danced and slid over her skin, Liz's lust simmered and burned.

Like embers coaxed to burn again, stirred from ashes and coals.

Rob had never kissed her like this.

Maybe she would have fallen for him if he had. She opened her mouth to the sexy surfer, liking the way he caught his breath when she flicked her tongue across the tip of his. He wrapped his arms more tightly around her, locking her against his strength, and she felt his erection against her stomach. Liz was thrilled that he was as excited by their kiss as she was.

"Full eclipse in an hour and a half," one of the grad students from the research lab said, sounding as if he was a thousand miles away. "Let's get back to the Institute in time to see it."

"Just a few more minutes," protested another guest.

Their voices pulled Liz back to reality. Hard. That was her life now, a life among scientists and maybe a future at the Institute. It was logical and dispassionate and she had chosen it deliberately.

Liz the marine biologist didn't make out with strangers in parking lots—regardless of how gorgeous they were or how well they kissed. What if Maureen saw her? Could it jeopardize her chance at a job here?

Liz ended their sizzling kiss with an effort.

She planted her hand on his chest and pushed the surfer slightly away. It was like pushing a brick wall. He let her break the kiss, but he didn't move very far away and his arms stayed around her waist. The night was velvety dark but lit with an odd luminosity. Those flames danced around the surfer's body, silhouetting him in a halo of golden light.

How did her gift illuminate him?

Or did he have powers of his own? It was an intriguing idea, one that tempted her to linger in his embrace.

"I don't even know your name," she said quietly, as if that was the problem.

He smiled crookedly, looking both devilish and sexy. He leaned down to murmur in her ear, the feel of his warm breath against her earlobe making her shiver. "I don't know yours, so fair's fair." His lips touched her throat, a sweet kiss that made her knees weaken. "Brandon," he whispered against her skin, then pulled her closer.

Brandon. He had an accent, but hadn't said enough that she could identify it. It made him seem even more exotic and alluring. She found her hands sliding over his shoulders again, moving of their own volition, stroking as if she'd memorize the feel of him.

He pulled back and smiled that sexy smile at her, indulgent. There wasn't nearly enough air in the universe for her to take a breath. That golden glow filled the space between them, radiating and flickering, heating her body at every point of contact.

Brandon arched a brow, inviting her to confess her name.

"I'm Liz," she admitted.

He repeated her name, as if trying it out, and she liked the rumble of his voice in his chest. She could feel it against her breasts, which made it impossible to ignore her desire for him.

And just one more kiss.

The Firedaughter in her welcomed the flame he kindled.

Liz smiled at Brandon, leaning against him, and saw his eyes gleam with anticipation. She stretched to kiss him again, but there was an interruption.

"Hey, Brandon!" a guy shouted. Liz turned, still in Brandon's embrace, and saw his friends standing beside a Jeep. Something flashed in the hand of the dark-haired guy, maybe a small container. "What *is* this stuff?"

She felt Brandon's alarm like an electric shock. "Don't touch that!" he called out, stepping away from her with purpose. "Don't open it!"

What was it?

The guy who had tried to buy her a drink laughed. "It must be pretty special." He opened the container with an effort.

"Hey! Leave that!" Brandon shouted.

But his friend ripped open the container and flung its contents into the sky. Something glittered in the air, as if the vial had been filled with stardust.

Liz took a step back, instinctively distrusting that sparkle.

It reminded her too much of magic.

"No!" Brandon roared.

Liz felt the collision of something falling over her body, like ash touching her skin. Everywhere it landed, it sparked for a second.

Stardust.

No. It was magic, and not white magic.

Liz recoiled in horror. She tried to brush the dust off her, her revulsion strong. It made her body burn with a hunger that couldn't be natural. It was similar to the golden light that sparked between her and Brandon, but hotter, darker, and more primal. Violent.

This was old magic and it was strong. No matter how much of her gift she gave away, she'd recognize the power of this.

Why did Brandon have this stuff?

What was he?

She looked up only to find him staring at her. He was glittering, that same ash lighting his body with golden pricks of light. A pale blue shimmer of light danced around his body, outlining his figure against the darkness. She felt an electrical charge in the air, as if a storm was mustering. It was different from his aura, more powerful, and she sensed that it was unpredictable.

And his eye—his eye had turned brilliant red. The pupil had become a vertical slit. She caught only a glimpse of it; then he pivoted to race toward his laughing friend. His silhouette looked to Liz as if it were tinged with red fire.

Like the simmering lip of a volcano.

Hear no evil, her mother whispered in her thoughts.

After the auras came the spirits. Liz remembered the sequence well—even though it hadn't proceeded this quickly when she had been a kid.

"Come on, Liz!" Maureen shouted, and Liz turned toward the cars.

With distance, the golden glow between her and Brandon dimmed so much that she might have imagined it. The blue shimmer around his figure disappeared. Everything looked normal.

But Liz was shaken. What was going on?

Brandon and his friends were bickering around their Jeep. Brandon was obviously trying to get that shiny container back from his buddy. Liz couldn't help noticing that the argument didn't seem so amiable after all.

It also seemed like he'd forgotten her already.

She touched her hand to her forehead, thinking about the flames, that kiss, Brandon's eye changing, and the blue shimmer of light. Liz was still itching with desire, wanting to do more than kiss Brandon. She wanted to run after him and leap into the back of their Jeep, go with him wherever he went, and satisfy all her sexual fantasies in one night.

But he had a strange power, one that should make her run.

Maybe it was better that he'd turned away.

Maybe he was saving her from herself. Maybe he was on logical Liz's side.

Brandon and his pals drove out of the lot, still arguing. Liz could feel Brandon looking toward her, her skin prickling with awareness, but she deliberately didn't look at him. She'd never see him again, which was probably a good thing.

Even if her lips still burned from his powerful kiss.

Erik Sorensson, leader of the *Pyr*, stood on the roof of his loft in Chicago, watching the sky. The clouds overhead obscured any portion of the eclipse he might have seen, but Erik could still feel its power.

He felt the spark of the firestorm and knew its location. It was hot and bright, unusually so, and Erik wondered why. What was different about this firestorm? Was darkfire modifying it? Or something else?

Erik followed the conduit of ley lines that led his thoughts to every living *Pyr* and understood which dragon was feeling the firestorm's burn.

It was the mate. She was different, although Erik couldn't discern how. Perhaps the darkfire had beckoned to her or maybe it fed her powers, whatever they were, but she was the reason the flame burned so brilliantly.

Was that bad? Good? Erik wasn't sure.

He used the overcast sky as a scrying glass, trying to see the future and best navigate the threat to his kind. Instead of a dark mirror, the future could have been a dark opal touched with shimmering blue and green light. Erik recognized the effect of the darkfire but still could not guess what would result from its influence. Its light swirled in a vortex, looking both unpredictable and dangerous.

Erik stood and he pondered and, finally, he chose.

He sent two messages. The first, in old-speak, the language of the *Pyr,* was to Sloane in California, the Apothecary. Not only was Sloane closest to Hawai'i, but Erik sensed his skill would be needed.

"Go" was all Erik said to Sloane, knowing his command would be followed.

The second, a text message, was to Brandt in Australia. "Stay away," he instructed the distant *Pyr*, having no expectation that this particular dragon would do as commanded. Brandt was passionate, volatile, and unpredictable.

Like darkfire.

And the *Pyr* experiencing the firestorm was Brandt's only son.

That the pair was estranged gave Erik the conviction that Brandt's presence wouldn't help. He hoped Brandt listened to him, but he wouldn't count on that.

Erik scanned the sky one last time, still sensing that a great deal was hidden from him. There was uncertainty in the air. He—and all the *Pyr*—would have to be vigilant.

No. They would have to be prepared. Erik was going to assume that his presence was needed. He'd go with Quinn, the Smith of the *Pyr.*

Assuming he could persuade Quinn to accompany him.

"Stay away."

Brandt Merrick ordered another double. He couldn't stop himself from pulling up the message on his cell phone to stare at it. He knew why Erik had given that instruction, and he knew that Erik was right. Brandt had messed up every part of his relationship with his son, and he trusted Erik to help Brandon get his firestorm right.

Anyone had to do better than Brandt had done.

But still. He felt the burn of his son's firestorm. He experienced that surge of optimism again, as bright as it had been twenty-seven years before for him.

Him and Kay.

The firestorm's heat made Brandt burn for a second chance and yearn to reclaim everything he had lost.

He was looking at the message again when the bartender put his drink in front of him. He could smell the familiar tang of the rum straight up, but for the first time in a long time, he had no taste for it.

He had to see Kay. He had to know for sure that she wanted no part of him.

Even if she told him so all over again.

Brandt paid for the drink, left it on the bar, and strode to his truck. He had a long drive ahead of him, one that probably would be a futile journey.

But he had to know for sure.

*　　*　　*

Brandon was raging. He'd never felt anything like the violence that filled his body. It was terrifying in its power. His dragon was screaming, demanding blood. He fought the shift with all his might, perspiration on his brow as he just barely kept his human form.

How could the dragon command the shift?

How could the dragon be in charge?

The transformation should be a voluntary one, a choice that he made. But this urge came from the depths of his guts and it was almost impossible to fight back. He ignored Matt's bragging and Dylan's erratic driving as he huddled in the back of the Jeep and fought to remain in human form.

He wasn't sure what would happen if he let himself shift shape, but he was pretty sure it wouldn't be good. Would he be able to change back? Or would the monster inside own him forever?

It was going to ruin everything!

What had changed? Was it the eclipse? The firestorm? The exposed spots on his skin, where he had removed scales to compensate Chen, burned as if they were on fire.

What had happened to him? Why was his dragon so strong?

Matt had flung the Dragon Bone Powder into the wind, making trouble in response to Brandon's winning of Liz's attention. He could be childish like that, but this time Matt hadn't had any clue what he was doing. Brandon's body had responded with unexpected vehemence to Matt's actions. It had taken everything he had to keep from shifting on the spot. He knew he hadn't been able to stop his eye from changing.

It was horrifying for his dragon to suddenly become so powerful and challenge him for control. He'd wanted to rip Matt's head off for being so stupid. He'd wanted to slam his buddy hard against the Jeep and hurt him, maybe rip open his throat. He'd wanted to breathe fire, make the Jeep explode, and ensure that everyone fled the scene.

Then he wanted to seize Liz and make love to her all night long.

Independent of what she thought of the matter.

That wasn't like Brandon. It was completely at odds with his own character and he didn't like the change one bit. His base desires had the upper hand. Brandon was glad he'd only had the one beer or he wouldn't have had a chance at controlling himself. He already knew that alcohol or drugs only diminished his ability to keep the dragon contained.

But if it remained this powerful, it was only a matter of time before he lost the battle—and the war. Even now, even as they drove away from Kaneʻohe, his grip on his human form was tenuous. He was angry, angrier than he'd been in a long while, but he knew the focus of his anger wasn't really Matt.

It was the burden of being a dragon shape shifter.

It was the knowledge that he was a monster and that there wasn't a thing he could do about it.

It was the legacy of his father, and he hated his father even more than usual as they drove back to the north shore of the island. The guys probably thought he was drunk as he writhed in the backseat. Brandon was content to let them think what they wanted. It was more important that he assert his control.

But even as he fought, he resented this change. It wasn't right. It wasn't fair! He would have his chance this week to make his name in the surfing world. He didn't need any distractions.

The only distraction he'd accept was the firestorm. There had been a few moments with Liz when he'd thought there might be something good about this dragon-shifter shit. There had been that electric kiss, the caress of the firestorm, the sense of optimism and hope. He'd had that sense of union with her, the kind of connection he'd always dreamed of having.

But it had all been trashed by his dragon's base urges.

Brandon couldn't escape what he was. He couldn't change what he was. And he wasn't sure he could live with what he was. That old familiar shadow engulfed him, almost burying him beneath an oppressive weight of despair. Once he'd been almost paralyzed by his hatred of his own truth, but Chen had helped him to manage his dragon. He'd almost forgotten how awful it could be.

Or maybe the dragon had been gathering strength while he focused on other things.

Brandon knew for sure that it was worse to taste

hope, then have it snatched away, than it was to never have had hope at all.

At least he had retrieved the silver vial from Matt. He rolled it between his fingers, his hands jammed into his pockets, as he struggled for control. Maybe it would help.

Although it didn't seem to.

It seemed like hours had passed before his dragon finally retreated with a snarl to the deep shadows of his mind. It couldn't have been that long, because they weren't in Hale'iwa yet. Brandon closed his eyes, exhausted. There was no telling how long it would stay there or when it would resume the battle.

For the moment, Brandon would take the reprieve. He rolled to his back and stared at the starlit sky. His muscles were taut, his gut was churning, and his shirt was damp. He ached all over. His hands were clenched into fists.

He was angry, wanting to carve the dragon out of him and roast it slowly to death over a blazing fire.

But that was the violence of the dragon.

Brandon deliberately thought about Liz. He thought about her smile. He thought about her being his destined mate and his mouth went dry. It was strange to have anything in common with his father, but he knew that his dad must have felt this once for his mom. And that gave him a revelation.

After the divorce, his father had stepped away from the dragon side of his nature. He'd been living as a normal human man and working as a firefighter. The time that Brandt had inadvertently revealed himself to Kay had been one of the last times that Brandon knew of his dad shifting shape.

Brandon blinked. The very fact that his dad had that much control over his dragon implied that the firestorm sparked a change.

Or the consummation of the firestorm had led to the change.

What if being *Pyr* was about satisfying the firestorm?

What if the firestorm could change everything?

What if consummating the firestorm meant that Brandon's dragon-shifter nature could be shed forever—or, at least, better controlled? This could be the opportunity that Chen had told him about! Chen had insisted that Brandon could weaken his dragon by the removal of the scales and that this could create the chance to banish his dragon forever. The old guy had been vague about the details, maybe because there was no way to predict when the firestorm would happen. The idea made perfect sense to Brandon.

What if his dragon had roared because it knew its days were numbered?

The idea was exciting. Even thinking about Liz had driven the dragon further into the shadows. This could be his chance to ditch it forever. Brandon had to find out the truth.

They were almost at Hale'iwa, so he pretended to wake up. He let the guys razz him and accepted Matt's apology for taking the vial, his thoughts churning all the while.

There *was* one good thing about his dragon nature. Courtesy of his keen senses, he could find Liz anywhere, even without knowing her last name or where she was staying. Having inhaled her scent, he could follow it wherever she went. That made his quest simpler.

It also reinforced his theory that being *Pyr* was about the firestorm.

Even better than that, Brandon could shift shape once everyone was asleep, fly back to Kane'ohe, and track Liz to wherever she'd gone. He knew that the heat of the firestorm would light his path. He could find her before morning. He could have his answer soon and maybe evict the dragon for good.

He guessed that consummating the firestorm would do it.

Because now Brandon wanted more than just sex. And the firestorm had made "someday soon" become "right now." Could the firestorm deliver? Could satisfying the firestorm limit his dragon's powers? That would make it possible for him to have a normal relationship with Liz and to be a man she might want to be with.

To have the future he desired.

That was a stronger incentive than anything else in the world.

When Brandon went back to Kane'ohe tonight, he'd have to be careful. His dragon might feel threatened by his choice and want to rumble one last time. He'd have to be ready for a fight with his own dark side.

But it was easy to walk into a fight knowing that he might win.

And that the prize could be everything he'd always wanted.

Liz was restless.

She told herself that events of the evening had rattled her, but she knew that wasn't it. She was all a-tingle, her skin dancing with awareness. She felt the rhythm of the ocean, the pulse of the earth, the caress of the air. And that was nothing compared to her feeling attuned to the throb of lava in the volcano on the island.

Liz had believed for years that her gift was gone, that she had given it away. She saw now that was an illusion. Moving to the concrete jungle had dulled her connection to the planet over the past years, making it possible for her to ignore her legacy.

To imagine that it was out of her life forever.

But there was still something about Hawai'i that had awakened her.

Her Firedaughter powers were asserting themselves, and that made Liz uneasy. Things were never easy when her powers were present and accounted for.

Beyond that, having her powers back meant that she could be tested, as her mother had been.

She could fail, as her mother had.

Liz shivered and paced. Outside the window, the eclipse proceeded with steady grace, the sky darkening with every passing moment. Liz prowled her hotel room for far too long before finally going to bed. Once there, she tossed and turned in the darkness, afraid to sleep despite her exhaustion.

She was never going to sleep.

Liz got out of bed again and opened the sliding glass door. She stepped outside in her nightgown, noting that the eclipse was almost complete. The moon was turning red, casting a bloody glow over the world. It looked unreal.

So did the dragon flying in the night, his form silhouetted against the rusty red orb of the moon.

Liz took a breath. Her gift *was* back, then. She might as well make her peace with the change. She heard her mother's instruction in her thoughts again as she watched the dragon's progress.

There are beings who share this earth with us. They hide themselves from casual view. Mortals cannot see them. Only we, the daughters of Hecate, can lift the scales from our own eyes. We can see the dead. We can see the immortals. We can see the beings that are myths come to life and those descended from other realms. This is our sacred trust, to witness and say nothing. Leave these creatures be. But if they come to you for aid, give it willingly.

Liz stared at the dragon, aching with longing for her mother.

The dragon passed the moon, his silhouette becom-

ing hard to discern against the night sky. Liz sighed
and wished for more of her mother's wisdom. She
wished she had paid more attention. She wished—but
wishing accomplished nothing.

How would she survive if she were tested?

Liz closed her eyes and wished.

Then she relived every second of Brandon's marvelous kiss. Again.

Hours later, Liz was still wide-awake. She felt as if all
of her senses were on overdrive. The perfume of the
slightly crushed lei was almost overpoweringly sweet,
even though it was over on the dresser. The warm
breeze wafting through her open window carried the
scent of salt and beach. It tempted her to go into
the velvety night and explore the paradise that surrounded her. The sheets were so smooth that they
were like silk beneath her skin.

But, worst of all, she still felt that simmering heat
of unsatisfied desire. It wasn't like her to lie awake,
yearning for sex, and it certainly wasn't like her to
fantasize about a guy she barely knew, but Liz was
consumed with thoughts of Brandon.

She couldn't stop replaying the memory of his
scorching kiss. It was the one good thing that had happened to her and she couldn't leave the memory
alone. If Liz had tried to imagine a perfect kiss, that
would have been it. It had been romantic and sweet,
passionate and demanding, too. She wanted another
one, with all her heart and soul.

There was more to the connection between them than simple physical attraction. He had a mystery about him. She sensed that he had some powers, as well.

The soft crunch of approaching footsteps made her eyes fly open, and she sat up in bed. Liz crept to the sliding door to her room, the one she had left open to the ocean breeze. She saw the silhouette of a man on the path that wound through the bushes beyond the patio outside her room.

Liz might have been alarmed, but an orange glow lit her fingertips, surrounding her hand. It was just like the light she'd thought she'd seen when Brandon approached her on the beach. It sparked and burned, brightening with every passing moment, in defiance of every scientific law she'd ever learned.

Liz smiled, knowing who had come to find her.

And honest enough with herself to be glad.

Who said wishes didn't come true?

When she looked up from the radiance, Brandon had stopped in the path, as if waiting for an invitation or an acknowledgment. The moonlight and the sparks between them made anything seem possible.

Even a happy future with her returned powers.

Brandon raised a hand and saluted her, a spark flying from his fingertips to collide with her own.

"Want to go for a walk?" he asked, his tone soft and teasing. He did have an accent, and she was sure it was Australian.

Liz smiled at him. His appearance when she'd been

thinking of him, the steady indigo radiance of his aura, and her own reaction to him made it easy to forget the glimpse she'd had of him in that dust. It made it easy to dismiss her earlier trepidation.

He was just a man, a gorgeous man who wanted her.

This was the chance she'd wanted to have.

And she wasn't going to let it slip away.

She opened the door wider and walked toward him, giving him a moment to look. The lace top of this nightgown left very little to the imagination, and she was glad she'd chosen to wear it. She felt powerful and sexy, glittering with allure. She felt beautiful. The sparks between them burned more brightly, turning from orange to yellow, then sparking off Brandon. The light in his eyes told her that he liked what he saw.

She was amazed when the glow between them lit to paler yellow. It would be a white-hot fire soon, and she wouldn't be able to stand it. Already her knees and her resistance to him were dissolving. Her skin was tingling, and her body was pulsing with desire. She was warm despite the breeze, and wide-awake.

"No, I want another kiss instead." Her voice sounded huskier than usual, and he smiled. Liz stopped in front of him, watching that golden radiance grow so bright that it pushed aside the light of the moon. She frowned at it, unfamiliar with the specific magic that would cause such an effect. Was this a new manifestation of her own powers? Or had Brandon caused it? "What is this? Do you know?"

Brandon grinned and reached for her hand. His touch was warm, the feel of his skin against hers making Liz's mouth go dry. He laced their fingers together, holding their palms an inch apart. A golden light shone there, shining so vividly that Liz could hardly look at it. "Destiny," he said with complete conviction. "A sign that we were meant to be together."

Liz smiled despite herself. "Tonight?"

Brandon was completely serious, his gaze intent. "Longer than that. For good. It's a sign that we were meant for each other, that this was meant to be."

Liz had to indulge her scientific skepticism. "Maureen could have chosen another restaurant. Then what?"

"Then my friends would have, too. It was fate that we'd meet tonight, Liz." He was so certain of it that Liz wanted to believe it, too. "And that's bigger and stronger than either of us."

"You can't believe that," Liz protested, even though she loved the romance of the idea and wished it could be true. Once upon a time, she'd believed in destiny and karma and the overwhelming power of good.

"I do." His conviction tempted Liz to take another step closer.

"But we can't know already that there's anything permanent in this," she protested, the conviction fading from her words. "We don't even know each other."

Brandon tightened his grip on her hand, looking so determined that it sent a shiver through her. "No, we can't know that, not by ourselves. That's why we have to trust the flame of the firestorm." His smile was confident, his gaze so unswerving that Liz chose to believe. "The firestorm knows, and I believe."

The firestorm. It was the perfect name for this sizzling lust that had filled her body at the sight of him, the perfect term for the overwhelming tide of desire that distracted her from everything other than Brandon.

Maybe it was Hawai'ian magic. It was certainly Brandon's magic. Liz could dig up the details later. She didn't want to lose the mood of the moment, not when those flames were licking and dancing and driving her crazy, not when they were lighting Brandon's face so he looked golden and powerful.

"Is the firestorm always right?" she asked. She put her other hand on his chest, smiling at the flurry of sparks that exploded from the point of contact.

"Every time," he vowed, his other arm sliding around her waist to pull her closer. "A force of nature can't lie."

Liz smiled at that truth. They stood staring at each other for a long moment, the light dancing between them, the heat building to a crescendo; then she stretched up and touched her lips to his.

That was all it took.

Chapter 3

Perfect! Brandon couldn't have asked for more than this. He'd wondered how he'd awaken Liz without frightening her, but she'd been waiting for him. Plus she wanted exactly what he wanted. Maybe she had felt the magnetic pull between them. Maybe her intuition had told her that he had no choice but to come to her.

That had to be a good sign.

Brandon's sense of the powerful influence of destiny increased, making it seem inevitable that everything would work out perfectly between them. His resolve seemed to make the firestorm burn even brighter.

Liz was wearing a pink slip of a nightgown, and he was sure he'd never seen anything so sexy in his life. The top was made of stretchy lace that hugged her breasts tightly; then the solid skirt skimmed over her waist and hips, ending at her thighs. There were narrow straps that went over her shoulders. When she'd walked toward him, the firestorm's golden light had gilded her skin, making her look precious.

She was both delicate and feminine, and, yet again, he knew she would be incredibly striking once she got a tan. Her dark hair hung loose over her shoulders and had started to curl. But he was glad to see she had purpose, too. She was serious in a way that the beach girls weren't and he guessed that she was smart. That she looked at him this way was icing on the cake.

When she smiled at him, he couldn't believe his luck.

When she kissed him, he was convinced that nothing would ever go wrong in his life again.

Liz wound her arms around his neck and kissed him with all the passion she'd shown earlier. She smelled sweet and spicy, the scent of soap mingling with the heat of her own arousal. That she was excited by him made him even harder. His arms were full of her softness and heat, the flames of the firestorm dancing between them and over them, lighting everything with its golden glow.

He wanted this magical moment to last forever.

He kissed her less gently this time, kissed her deeply, and loved how she responded to his touch. Her fingers were knotted in his hair, and he felt her rise to her toes. This time she did rub her pelvis against him, and Brandon nearly lost it.

The heat of the firestorm raged through his body, firing his blood and inciting his passion. She opened her mouth to his kiss, demanding more of him as she hadn't earlier, and Brandon would give her all he had. Their passion sparked, heating the air around them. Brandon felt their hearts pound as one again and reveled in the sensation. This was kismet, up close and personal. Liz was everything he wanted and he was going to ensure that she felt the same way about him by the time they were done.

He caught her up in his arms and headed for the doorway, assuming this was her apartment. The bed was unmade, probably because she'd just gotten up, but the sheets smelled of clean laundry and Liz's skin. There was no better aphrodisiac for Brandon. He sat on the edge of the bed, cradling her in his arms, loving the feel of her buttocks against his thighs. She kissed him hungrily, spearing her fingers through his hair and holding him closer.

Brandon kissed her neck, her ear, her throat, wanting to taste her from head to toe. He put his hands on her shoulders and pushed down the straps of her slip. Her breasts were freed of their lace prison and he filled his hands with them, bending to take one nipple in his mouth.

Liz moaned in pleasure. She arched her back, displaying herself to him in a way that drove him crazy. He pushed the slip down to her waist and feasted on her breasts, teasing each nipple to erection and making her writhe in pleasure. He loved how responsive she was, the fact that he could please her so much making him yearn to give her more. He was harder and thicker than he'd ever been, but he was determined to wait.

Even if it killed him.

There would only be one first time for them, and no matter how many more times they were together, the memory of this night had to be perfect.

He bracketed her waist in his hands and eased her back on to the bed, kissing her belly as he did so. Liz grabbed the slip and tugged it over her own head, tossing it aside, and Brandon paused to look at her. He ran his hands over the length of her, admiring that she was both sleek and feminine.

"You're gorgeous," he murmured, watching how the light of the firestorm danced between his palms and her body, turning her skin to gold as if she did have that tan already. "Perfect," he added, then slid down the length of her. He cupped her buttocks in his hands and bent to taste her sweetness.

Her moan of pleasure nearly drove him out of his mind.

But he'd drive her crazy first.

Liz was lost in a realm of pleasure and didn't want to ever find her way out of it. Brandon touched her with the mix of tenderness and surety that she was already associating with him, the combination making her want more and more. He caressed her, he stroked her, he teased her nipples so that they were aching and hard. He kissed her as she'd never been kissed before.

And when he went down on her, she thought she would explode. She'd never gotten naked so fast and felt passion rise so quickly, but the power of this moment was overwhelming. Liz had denied her instincts for so long that she had no intention of stopping the tide now.

Brandon's tongue flicked against her, his breath driving her crazy. She felt his teeth graze her and writhed on the bed as she'd never writhed before. She had her hands locked in his hair, her hips were bucking of their own accord, and all her muscles were taut in anticipation. She was gasping and her heart was pounding, a trickle of perspiration sliding down the middle of her back.

It was that light, those strange flames that licked her body and fed her passion. The entire room was radiant gold, even though there were no lights on, the darkness illuminated by the sparks that burned between her and Brandon.

This was a love spell that totally delivered.

And so did Brandon. Liz hadn't had a partner before who was so determined to give as to receive. He urged her higher with every flick of his tongue. Liz struggled beneath his grip, not really wanting to break free. Her every nerve was singing and her blood was filled with an incendiary heat. She was sure she couldn't stand it any longer.

Then he flicked his tongue against her clitoris, and Liz came with a cry. The explosion roared through her body and she saw the sparks fly off her fingertips.

She saw the wonder in Brandon's expression and knew exactly how she was going to reciprocate. She reached for him, urging him to roll to his back. She was breathing heavily, the taste of salt on her lip. He leaned forward and kissed it away, his eyes twinkling with irresistible humor.

"Behave," she said, pretending to be stern. "It's your turn."

He lay back, displaying himself to her, smiling as she looked. Liz peeled off his shirt, then ran her hands over his muscled chest in admiration. He had more than one tattoo, the dark ink striking against the amber of his tan.

She slid her hands over that perfect six-pack, then slipped her fingers inside his shorts and eased them over his hips. He was hard and ready, and she stroked him as he kicked off his shorts. He looked like a god in the bed beside her, so perfectly formed and tanned that maybe he was an illusion.

Liz wasn't going to let him get away just yet. She folded her hand around him, then bent and took him in her mouth.

She liked the way he moaned. His fingers slid into her hair, but he didn't stop her or hurry her. Liz took her time. She caressed him and kissed him until he was even harder and thicker, liking the evidence of her power to please him. He whispered her name and stroked his fingertips over her shoulder.

When he said her name with more urgency and reached for her, Liz's heart skipped. He wanted her, not just pleasure in general. Her heart sang in recognition of a kindred spirit.

She'd reconcile herself to the reappearance of magic in her life later. For now there was only Brandon and the promise of his touch. When he moaned her name, his voice hoarse with yearning, she moved to sit astride him. Brandon smiled at her and locked his hands around her waist.

"I could have finished you off," she teased.

"No." He shook his head. "I want us to come together."

He slid his hands over her, cupping her breasts, then sliding one finger down to her wet heat. He touched her until she was shivering again, and Liz stretched higher to give him access. When her clitoris was hard again and her heart was pounding, Liz lowered her hips and took his strength inside her.

Brandon closed his eyes and moaned. He faltered for a second; then he gripped her hips in his hands. Their gazes met and locked, the intensity of their desire crackling. Those flames danced and cavorted, making it look like there was a bonfire between them.

Liz had never been so excited in her life. She could see Brandon's pulse at his throat, couldn't believe the brilliant glitter of his eyes. She felt as if they'd stepped into the middle of the sun, and tasted perspiration on her own lip.

Then Brandon moved, slowly burying himself deep within her. Liz gasped. He held her hips in his hands, his thumbs stroking her skin and his gaze locked with hers. "Okay?" he asked. and she heard the strain in his voice.

She nodded. "You're huge."

He grinned. "Or you're tight."

Liz smiled. "Or maybe that's part of the firestorm's power."

Brandon chuckled and laced his fingers with hers. "It's supposed to be epic," he said, and kissed her hand. The glow in his eyes told her that he was as excited as she was. "Let's make it last."

Unable to resist, she leaned over him and framed his face in her hands, bracing her elbows against the bed. She kissed him hungrily and he groaned, locking his arms around her as he returned her kiss. Her breasts were crushed against his chest, her mouth locked on his. His tongue drove her wild all over again

His slow movement heightened sensation, imbuing every gesture with passion and power. Liz thought she would explode. Brandon dragged himself against her clitoris with every stroke, ensuring that each one lasted half of forever. She tasted the tension in him and felt the perspiration at his temples. Her own heart was pounding and she felt more keenly alive than ever before. The firestorm's flames slid over them and between them, like an inferno coaxed to greater heat.

Liz was on fire. She was melting. She was burning. She was trapped by the passion Brandon built between them, and there was nowhere else she wanted to be. When he buried himself inside her again and groaned, she knew she couldn't stand it much longer.

"Now," she commanded.

Brandon moved more quickly then, rolling her to her back. Liz locked her legs around his waist and kissed him as if she'd never get enough. He reached between them and touched her with his fingertips, coaxing her orgasm even as he built to his own.

The tide rose high and hot within her, her heart thundering and her skin simmering. He was braced over her, and she hung on to his shoulders, pulling him deep inside her. He moved faster and harder, filling her in a way she loved. She dug her nails into his shoulders and hauled him closer, wanting to feel him everywhere. He kissed her ear, his breath driving her over the edge. Liz cried out as her orgasm cascaded into a shower of sparks.

Brandon drove deep then and she felt his heat spill inside her. She smiled at his long, low moan of pleasure. She held him tightly against her as he shuddered with his release, wanting his heat and his strength for as long as possible.

He sighed with satisfaction, then braced his elbow on the bed beside her. He kissed her just below the ear, his breath tickling. "Perfect," he murmured, and she turned to find his eyes gleaming. He slid one hand over her, his smile so warm that she wanted him all over again.

"Perfect," she agreed with a smile, running her fingers through his hair.

"Best ever," he added, and Liz nodded agreement. He ran his fingertips down her cheek and her chin, then traced the curve of her collarbone. When he met her gaze this time, his expression was mischievous. "Still, we could try to improve on it. Just to see whether it can be done."

Liz felt her smile broaden. She liked that he wasn't in a hurry to leave or intent on falling asleep. "I'm a big fan of gathering data with experimentation," she said, pretending to be serious.

Brandon looked at her. "Really?"

"Well, I'm a scientist. That's what we do. That's why I'm here."

"You work here? I thought you just arrived."

"I did. I came for a symposium."

"Are you going to stay a while?" Liz saw the concern in Brandon's eyes, a concern that convinced her that she had made the right choice.

"How long are you thinking?"

He smiled and interlaced their fingers again. "Long enough for me to convince you that the firestorm is right."

She nodded. "I'm hoping to get a more permanent post here."

Brandon's grin flashed. "Good," he said, and bent to claim her lips again.

After his kiss, Liz was breathless. "What about you?" she asked. "Are you just visiting? You're not from here. You sound like you're Australian."

Brandon nodded. "But I'm here now. I came for the waves, but I'll stay for you." Liz's heart skipped at that. He bent and kissed her slowly. His eyes were twinkling when he finally lifted his head. "So, what do you think of showers, scientifically speaking?"

"I hypothesize that they show definite promise for intimate activities," Liz said, feigning a serious manner. "Especially this one, because it's big." Liz smiled at him. "Of course, only experimentation will prove whether my hypothesis is true."

"Now I remember why I liked the scientific method so much," Brandon said. He got out of the bed, scooped her up, and headed for the bathroom with purpose. Liz kicked her legs happily, content to worry about tomorrow, implications, and repercussions when they turned up.

She was living in the moment and liking it just fine.

It was only when Liz was back in bed much later, so sated that she was finally drowsy, that she realized those sparks had disappeared. She braced herself on her elbow and looked down at Brandon, who had already fallen asleep, his arm curled around her waist.

She touched his chest, just as she had on the beach, but there were no sparks. Brandon mumbled in his sleep and caught her hand in his, trapping it against his chest. She felt his heartbeat beneath her palm.

But no sparks.

No blue shimmer.

No red light.

Just the steady radiance of that indigo aura. She might have dismissed her idea that her powers were back otherwise. His aura was less active as he slept, but the light was unmistakable.

She didn't mind the auras. She could accept their return.

She just hoped her gift didn't bring other, less happy consequences. Maybe it had just responded to Brandon. Liz smiled, reviewing his comments about destiny. Her mother would have liked him. She fell asleep smiling, with Brandon warm beside her and his arm thrown around her waist.

Her last thought was that she had indeed arrived in paradise.

Brandon awakened suddenly, his senses on full alert. He felt threatened, but he couldn't name why. He was aware of the dragon stirring within him, restless and agitated.

Had his plan failed? Or did it take more time to completely shed the dragon?

Brandon was still in Liz's bed and she was snuggled beside him, breathing deeply. They were spooned together, her sweet butt against his groin and his arm around her waist. She was soft and warm, the scent of her perfume surrounding him like a cocoon, the dark silk of her hair across his arms. It was just after dawn, and the room was still filled with pale light.

There was no golden spark of the firestorm, so it was satisfied.

But Brandon's adrenaline was pumping and he could see the shimmer of pale blue around his own body. The dragon roared, bellowing for release, and he had to clamp down hard on his impulse to shift.

Had he heard an intruder? He strained his ears but there was nothing, nothing but the soft rhythm of Liz's breathing and the waves breaking on the beach.

He'd heard *something*, though.

He was hovering on the cusp of change, just barely managing to stay there. The dragon sensed trouble. Was it just trying to take control? To reassert itself while it still could?

It sure didn't feel as if its power had weakened with the satisfaction of the firestorm, which was frightening.

Brandon couldn't stay in bed, not with his pulse racing like this, not when he was uncertain of the dragon's intent. He eased away from Liz, not wanting to awaken her. He had to solve this himself, face his dragon and kick its butt.

For good.

First, he'd check that there was no real threat. Brandon tugged on his shorts and opened the sliding glass door that led to the patio. He couldn't see anything unusual—but it was strangely silent, as if all the birds had suddenly abandoned the island. He caught his breath.

Brandon knew what that meant.

There was an ominous rumble from deep within the earth, one that Brandon felt more than he heard. Earthquake! A lifetime spent on the Pacific Rim meant that he knew the drill. He grabbed the ID that was stashed in his flip-flops beside the bed, but he never got his sandals on.

The earth's rumble became a roar and the floor began to tremble.

He saw the blue shimmer brighten around his body. He heard the dragon bellow deep inside. He had time to swear; then the change ripped through his body with lightning speed. He had no chance to stop it.

His dragon kicked *his* butt this time.

That furious anger raged through him with terrifying power, making him want to rip and shred and breathe fire. The building was vibrating so hard that he was afraid it would collapse. The prospect of destruction made his dragon laugh, which terrified Brandon. He summoned the last vestige of his control, determined to achieve something good with his dragon's power.

All he wanted to do was snatch Liz and get her out of there.

Liz awakened to find the bed shaking. Before she could figure out what was happening, the bed danced across the floor, trembling all the way. Chunks of plaster were falling from the ceiling. Sirens were going off and a fire alarm was clanging.

Worse, Brandon was gone.

The sheets were still warm where he had been sleeping. He couldn't be far.

Was this an earthquake? She'd never been in one before but this certainly fit her expectations.

There was a bellow and a shooting tongue of fire; then a dragon appeared out of nowhere and lunged at the bed. He was enormous, his scales as dark as night but edged with orange. Liz screamed as he snatched her up.

The ceiling cracked wide-open overhead, and the dragon's claws locked around her.

He felt real and solid. Liz understood that this was no nightmare.

She fought the dragon's grip instinctively as she thought, Where had he come from? Why was he here? What had he done to Brandon? What was he going to do to her? Liz struggled, but her strength was too puny to make any difference. His scales were hard, like armor, and she wasn't sure he even noticed her blows. The dragon strode across the vibrating room, like Godzilla crossing a ruined city.

"Brandon?" she shouted as the building shook harder. Half of the ceiling ripped loose and fell onto the bed, launching a huge cloud of dust. The plaster crashed down right where Liz had been sleeping, the weight of it making the bed collapse.

If she'd still been there, she would have died.

She wasn't feeling inclined to thank the dragon.

The walls were cracking and something was fizzling behind them. Gas? Water? Liz wasn't sure she wanted to know. She kicked the dragon hard in the gut and her toe collided with a soft spot.

He groaned and stumbled.

Liz saw that he was missing a scale there and the skin was exposed. She kicked him harder in the same spot, digging in her toe. He dropped her with a growl and she ran to the bathroom, hoping Brandon had taken refuge there.

He hadn't.

The bathroom was empty, water gushing through the tiles from a broken pipe in the wall. Liz heard windows breaking as the building shuddered. The floor jumped more vigorously and she was nearly thrown off her feet.

The dragon roared behind her and she slammed the bathroom door, choosing what appeared to be the safer option. She locked the door, then grabbed the robe hanging on the hook on the back. Flames shot through the cracks around the perimeter of the door, and she could smell the paint burning.

Would anyone even hear her if she screamed?

Where could she run?

The light fixture swung in the bathroom, cracked, and fell to the floor. It splashed in the growing puddle of water, the glass flying in all directions. Liz covered her face, then heard the sparks. They were leaping out of the damaged electrical outlet and falling to the floor. She had a heartbeat to recognize what would happen; then the dragon kicked down the door. He seized her from behind and leapt for the sliding glass door as she screamed in terror.

He had her purse and her clothes, which astonished her.

Was this dragon trying to save her?

Why?

She heard the crackle of the sparks hitting the water behind them and hung on. If nothing else, the dragon was taking her where she needed to go.

The building stopped its shaking just as he erupted onto the patio. He didn't stop, and carried her all the way down to the coral beach and dropped her on her feet. Liz looked back and the residence building seemed to be wavering unsteadily, like it was drunk. The earth was still again.

It was just after dawn, the sky a rosy hue. The air was still, too still.

And Liz was standing on a beach with a dragon.

He was black from head to toe, his scales as dark as midnight. Each one, though, was edged in brilliant orange, as if it was made from a coal that glowed in the darkness. The scales on his chest were a thousand shades of orange and gold, and his wings could have been made of black leather. His tail was long and powerful, and it lashed against the sand restlessly. His talons were golden, like they'd been made of precious gold. A tendril of smoke rose from his nostrils, and she had the definite sense that he was angry.

His eyes were red, his pupils vertical slits.

Reptile eyes.

Eyes that looked exactly the way Brandon's had the night before.

Liz shied away from an instinctive—crazy!—conclusion, and told herself to focus on ensuring Brandon's survival. She put out her hand, requesting her belongings, uncertain what to expect.

The dragon dropped her clothes and her purse between them. He then turned away, breathing a plume of fire at the beach as if he couldn't help himself.

Liz fell on her clothes, tugging them on more quickly than she would have believed possible. The earthquake was over. She knew what she had to do.

"I have to find Brandon," she said, and turned to head back into the residence.

The dragon roared behind her.

Liz ran, as much from the dragon as to find Brandon.

The earthquake began again, or maybe it was an aftershock. Either way, Liz had a hard time running in a straight line. She had to be sure Brandon was safe. Had he gone out into the corridor outside her unit? He had to be somewhere on the island. She couldn't just forget about him. What if he needed help?

What if he was right behind her?

The dragon bellowed, much closer than Liz would have preferred.

She heard the leathery beat of his wings even as she ran faster. He flew over her and breathed fire, his crackling stream of flame barring Liz from her goal. She made to leap over the flames, but he snatched her up easily and soared into the sky.

"No!" Liz cried. "Brandon!"

The dragon gained altitude with dizzying speed. Liz struggled against his grip, but there was no escaping him. She kicked him in that same spot again, but he only snarled. He passed her to his back claw and she couldn't reach his belly anymore. No matter how she bit or punched him, her efforts made no difference to her plight.

"Put me down!" she shouted. "I have to find Brandon!"

The dragon ignored her, heading straight up into the sky.

Liz fumed. She looked down and knew that if he dropped her from this height, she'd be in serious trouble. She looked up, unable to help admiring his grace and power.

The odd thing was that he was missing three scales; there were three places where his skin was exposed. Liz wondered whether they were shed as a natural process of renewal or whether he'd been injured. The exposed skin was both angry and red, as if it had been burned. She tapped one of the scales that she could reach, noting how hard it was and how precisely it fit with its neighbors. Would his scales grow back?

Then she shook her head, amazed that she could even be thinking about the details of dragon physiology, given her current situation. Liz looked down, astonished by how quickly the island was falling away beneath them. She could see the reef around the island, but the turquoise water was cloudy from the earthquake.

What had happened to Brandon?

Her crazy suspicion couldn't possibly be right.

Could it?

Liz looked up and watched the dragon's massive

black wings beating against the morning sky. She looked down and the residence where her room had been wavered in a cloud of dust, like a mirage in the desert. It then cracked down its length and collapsed. It fell in slow motion, emitting another puff of dust.

"Brandon!" Liz whispered, uncertain how he could have survived if he had remained in the building. She bit her lip, devastated to think that he was lost.

On the other hand, what if he'd survived because he could become a dragon? Liz looked up, still fighting the idea. She would much, much rather that Brandon just be a man.

The earth shook vehemently one more time, dust rising in Kane'ohe itself as buildings collapsed. The dragon flew directly toward the town, and she felt urgency in his increased speed. She saw a fissure open in the highway, creating a crack in the side of the ancient volcano. The gap opened from the sea, spread across the road, then rose along the side of the mountain with ridiculous ease.

There was a rumbling sound, the most ominous sound Liz had ever heard. She gasped as the crack spread and spawned a second far to the right. A large chunk of the mountainside trembled, then sheared off. It was dark, the black rock of cooled lava tearing aside vegetation as the cascade of rocks shot toward the ocean.

Liz realized with horror that it would crash on the road, then continue into the ocean.

There was one house standing in the path of the

avalanche. A woman was on the porch, staring upward, her expression horrified. The torrent of rock roared toward her, and she picked up her child. She turned to run, but Liz could see that it was too late. The avalanche was moving too fast.

Except that the dragon descended with dizzying speed. He soared down toward the woman and child. He snatched them up, racing into the sky. The woman swore softly, her eyes wide.

He'd grabbed them in the nick of time. The avalanche smashed into the house, not thirty feet below them, pushing everything into the sea. Liz watched in amazement as the avalanche continued deep into the bay before it stopped.

The child began to hiccup and cry. The woman was panting and pale. She looked at Liz, at the dragon, and then fainted.

The dragon spiraled down to the earth, which had stilled. He set the pair down on the road, on the side of their home that was closest to the town of Kaneʻohe. He looked at the child and inclined his head, then carried Liz into the air again.

Liz was thinking furiously. She remembered a story that had been in the news a few years ago, the one about dragons that she'd known her mother would have loved. She'd ignored it because fantastical beings were part of the life she'd left behind. Liz eyed the dragon and acknowledged that her past had caught up with her. She tugged her cell phone out of her purse, but the local network was down.

But if the dragon had saved her, and that woman and child, why hadn't he saved Brandon? There was one obvious conclusion, but Liz would explore every other possibility before she accepted it.

Where could Brandon have gone? Was he safe already?

Wait. That article had been about dragon shape shifters.

Liz thought of the dragon she'd seen the night before, silhouetted against the moon. She wondered suddenly how Brandon had even gotten to Coconut Island in the middle of the night. The ferry had a schedule and only did night runs by arrangement— the kid had joked with Maureen that she was making him work extra to bring their party back. There hadn't been another ferry after they'd come back, and none before that she knew of. Did Brandon have a friend with a boat?

And where had this dragon been, between her sighting of him and now?

Far too many facts were pointing to the conclusion Liz wanted to avoid. What about Brandon's eye? It had looked just like this dragon's eye. What if that had been the beginning of a transformation? She had sensed that there was something unusual about him, something that made her feel a kinship with him.

What if Brandon had a bigger secret than she did?

To Liz's relief, the dragon descended toward the ocean side of Coconut Island. The earthquake had stopped, the whole island seeming to hum in the aftermath. Fire alarms were ringing and a siren blared. Smoke rose from the one residence that had collapsed, and there were people shouting.

The dragon landed with graceful ease, setting Liz down with care. He backed away from her, their gazes locked. She wanted to ask him who he was, but he was large and powerful. Offending a dragon could be a foolish act.

Or a final one.

"Liz?" Maureen shouted in the distance, sounding panicky. "Liz, where are you?"

"Here!" Liz called back. "I'm okay."

She looked at the dragon and he nodded once, just as he had to the child. It was a regal gesture, and she had to admit that he was a beautiful creature. His gaze was simmering, indicative of his fearsome power and wrath. Then he took flight.

Watching him made her idea of dragon shape shifters seem whimsical. This primal creature couldn't be Brandon.

But then, where *was* Brandon?

Liz had to find out. She pivoted and ran down the beach toward her friend's voice.

Before she stepped off the beach, Liz looked back. That black dragon sailed high in the sky, the steady beat of his wings taking him north with tremendous speed. There was no one else on the beach to see him. He had disappeared from view by the time she found Maureen.

But he had been magnificent.

And he had saved her. Liz knew that she owed this dragon a debt, whoever he was.

Brandon had failed.

Not only hadn't he been able to control his dragon when it really mattered, but his dragon's presence had ruined everything. His firestorm, which he'd been given because of his nature, had been trashed by his dragon's appearance. His dragon hadn't been tamed or destroyed or banished; it was stronger and more violent than ever.

At least he'd been able to use the dragon's power to help Liz. He'd hoped to use his strength for good in saving that woman and child, but his triumph had been short-lived. His dragon had been all for destroying the woman and child, burning them or injuring them. Brandon hadn't wanted to leave them there on the road, but he'd had to get his dragon away from anyone who looked like lunch.

Similarly, he hadn't trusted himself to linger with Liz.

He might have shifted shape and gone back to her to explain, but he couldn't find that shimmery impulse within himself. He couldn't shift back. His dragon was raging and potent, Brandon's control so thin that it might have been a veneer. He didn't trust his dragon and the violence of that creature's urges.

He'd had to leave Liz ASAP.

There was no future with Liz, not with his dragon out of control. He'd never hurt her, which meant he had to stay away from her. He couldn't be in her presence without being sure the dragon would heed his command. If she learned his truth, she'd be horrified, just as his mom had been by his dad's true nature.

Liz would be furious when she learned that he had hidden it from her, just like his mom. The flames of the firestorm had been extinguished, so it had been satisfied, which meant that Liz would have his son. When she realized she was pregnant and that he'd known in advance that she would conceive, she'd feel betrayed, because he hadn't told her the truth ahead of time.

Their relationship was doomed even before it started, and all because of his dragon.

Somehow his dragon had gotten stronger instead of being defeated.

And it was bloodthirsty.

Brandon blamed himself for everything that had gone wrong. He should have talked to Liz beforehand, but the power of the firestorm had swept everything from its path. There'd been only Liz and the firestorm and its pulsing desire.

Brandon had been cheated by his secret nature and that made him mad. His dragon loved his anger and coaxed the flames to burn higher. In this form, vengeance made the most sense to him. The evil side of him had destroyed his dream forever—which only made him want to tear and slash and destroy everything around him. It made him want to hunt down his father and demand a toll for the legacy inflicted on him. It made him want to hunt down all the *Pyr* in the world, to slaughter them individually and ensure they paid a painful price for his loss.

That a dragon solution made the most sense to him wasn't exactly reassuring.

The timing was also terrible. Any day now could be a competition day—it would depend on the waves. To surf the Pipe without getting killed or maimed would require all of Brandon's concentration. This was his chance to claim some of the prize money and establish his career.

He needed his dragon to disappear.

Brandon still couldn't feel the shimmer that heralded the shift between forms. The dragon was too strong and had no intention of being easily put aside. Brandon had to tame his dragon somehow, reclaim his life and focus.

That he could seek out Liz when he succeeded was all the incentive he needed.

Chapter 4

As Brandon flew and couldn't find any vestige of the blue shimmer inside himself, he tried to think of a logical solution. How could he push back his dragon and restore the usual balance of power between them?

The secret might be in the waves. The reason Brandon had taken to surfing was that it was an activity that made him feel in tune with the earth and the ocean, and it tuned out his dragon. He was completely fixed on his human form and its powers when he surfed a challenging break, and that concentration seemed to keep his dragon at bay.

So he studied the breaking waves as he flew along the coast. He focused on the pattern and the rhythm. The waves were high and erratic, because of either the eclipse or the earthquake. There'd be no competition today—the surf was too wild to be safe.

That was lucky.

The better news was that the road wasn't clogged with spectators now that the competition was postponed. Brandon could shift without being witnessed.

Assuming he could shift.

His dragon was simmering still, but not so ascendant in his thoughts. His sense was that it had retreated to a cave—although it was still annoyed and watchful. He felt that he could summon the shift now that he wasn't as riled up. He did some breathing exercises as he flew a bit farther, concentrating on what he had to do.

Brandon landed to one side of the road on a quiet section at the north end of the island. He tried to shift shape on impact, but the blue shimmer didn't dance over his skin as it usually did.

He refused to freak out.

He ignored the way his dragon laughed, a throaty chuckle that reminded him of the promise of vengeance.

No. Brandon wasn't going there. He didn't care if there were other *Pyr* in the world. He didn't want to know them or find them, much less maim and kill them. His dragon could keep those ideas.

He had a surfing contest to win.

Brandon tried again to shift, again without success. His heart began to beat more quickly in fear. He'd never thought much about shifting shape. It was something he could do instinctively, and had been able to do simply by thinking about it since he'd been a teenager.

He'd never been unable to shift back to human form.

Brandon fought to school his response, knowing that his anxiety wouldn't help anything. He felt like his dragon was laughing at him, mocking him with its ascendancy. He roared and spread his wings, stretching high, then closed his eyes and focused on shifting.

It didn't happen as quickly as it should have.

He had time to panic.

Then the shimmer slid over his scales like a cool tide of water crashing over him. It was like the blue crush of a wave, driving him down into sensation and almost drowning him in its intensity. The familiar power surged through his body, asserting the change.

Brandon could have wept with relief.

Even better, a car came around the curve just when he'd assumed his human form again. He'd narrowly missed being seen in dragon form—which made him think about the woman and her child in Kane'ohe. He hoped they were okay.

The rusted Toyota pickup slowed down beside him and the driver peered at him. "Where you going? You want a ride?"

"Hale'iwa."

"Close enough. Hop in."

"Thanks!" Brandon grimaced when he sat down in the truck. He touched the bruise rising on his gut where he was missing a scale. Liz had one heck of a powerful kick, that was for sure. He did respect that she'd tried to defend herself, though. He liked her spark and her determination.

"Won't be many cars on this road today," the driver said, drawing Brandon back to the moment. "Given the avalanche at Kaneʻohe."

Brandon looked at the other man. "Bad?"

"Road's closed. Nobody killed, despite the odds. You hear about Honolulu?"

"No." Brandon wondered then at the epicenter of the earthquake. "Did the earthquake do a lot of damage?"

"It's crazy." The driver rolled his eyes and turned on the radio. Brandon listened with dismay at the reports of extensive damage in Honolulu and Waikiki, so extensive that that side of the island had been declared a national disaster.

"We got lucky over here," the driver said. There were some skewed buildings and some cracks in the pavement, but clearly the epicenter had been farther south. Brandon's gaze strayed repeatedly to the rolling surf, wherever he could catch a glimpse of it from the road. He hoped the waves would stay high and unpredictable for a couple of days. He'd need every minute he could get to build his focus and his strength.

He was glad that Liz intended to stay. He was going to need a bit of time to get himself together enough to go back and explain himself to her.

He had no doubt that she was the woman for him. If the firestorm wasn't a lie and he wasn't a moron, he'd make it work.

"You surf," the driver said with a smile, no question in his tone.

"Yeah, how'd you know?"

"All you care about is the ocean. It's going to be mean for a couple of days, even though they don't think we're getting a tsunami."

Brandon nodded. "That's good. I was wondering about tsunamis."

And that wasn't the only thing on his mind. All the way back to Hale'iwa, Brandon tried to figure out a way to fix his mistake. He really wanted to have a chance with Liz but couldn't risk screwing up again. It had been too close with his dragon. He couldn't think of how to ensure that his dragon listened to him, which meant he'd have to ask someone who knew more.

His pal Chen. Chen knew more about dragons than anyone else and had helped him to manage his dragon in the past. Chen might have some advice for him. If Chen gave him an answer, one he could work with, then he could focus on his performance in the competition.

The next time he saw Liz, he wanted to have secured his financial future. That depended on a lot of things—keeping his dragon contained, nailing the Pipe, and generally keeping his shit together. Brandon exhaled and told himself he could do it.

He had to believe that he could do anything for Liz.

And Chen would help.

The earthquake had a devastating effect on the Institute.

The sensors in the labs had gone wild before they'd either broken or shut down. The power was off, since the backup generators had been damaged in the earthquake. Liz told Maureen that she'd been walking on the beach when it happened, blaming jet lag for her inner clock being out of whack.

Maureen had believed her, but probably only because there was so much to do. They worked all morning, tugging the injured out of the collapsed building, and Liz thought they were lucky that no one had been killed. Most of the scientists and guests knew what to do when they felt an earthquake. Some had run outside during the first tremor, and those who had taken refuge from the first shake-up had gone outside immediately afterward.

No one else had seen the dragon. This would have amazed Liz, until she realized that her end of the building had been mostly vacant—they'd been intending to put up this day's arrivals for the symposium in that wing. It also gave credence to her mother's assertion that most mortals couldn't see the magical beings that shared our world.

But the woman he'd saved had seen him. Could he reveal himself to humans by choice?

Had the dragon known that she was the only one at risk? Was that why he'd saved her? Liz resolved to find out about the casualties in Kaneʻohe.

There'd been two more aftershocks but they'd been comparatively minor. That one residence building was a write-off, so they'd had to pair up for accommodation. Liz would be sharing with Maureen for the duration of her stay. Maureen was worried about having to delay or cancel the symposium, but so far, they were trying to keep to schedule. There were broken arms to bandage and cuts to dress, all basic first aid that was within the capabilities of everyone on the island.

There was no sign of Brandon. It was as if he had never been on the island the night before. But the sheets had been warm when Liz had been awakened by the earthquake. There had been no time for him to get off the island, no time for him to run very far.

The more Liz thought about it, the more convinced she was that Brandon had to be the dragon.

The research lab got its Internet connection up before cell phone service was back. That building had sustained only minor damage, whether by luck or construction techniques. Liz felt guilty claiming a laptop and searching for that dragon story she vaguely recalled, but she had to know. She found the article and sat down to read.

It was about dragon shape shifters.

The *Pyr*.

They were an ancient race sworn to defend the earth's treasures, which included the human race. The shifter shown in the YouTube video, while a different color, had definite similarities to the dragon that had saved her.

Same species.

Which led to the obvious question of what the black and orange dragon looked like in his human form.

Liz bit her lip, because she was pretty sure she knew.

Even the scientific part of her mind had to admit that there were lots of things in the world they didn't know yet, lots of species yet to be documented. Plus she couldn't think of how else Brandon could have gotten onto the island or off of it.

She'd have to ask him herself. That was how she'd know for sure. His deep blue aura told her that he was trustworthy and not someone who could deceive. He might not offer the truth of his nature to everyone, but Liz believed that if she asked him, Brandon would tell her the truth.

She checked on Kaneʻohe and discovered that there had been no deaths there, either. There was already an online story about a woman whose house had been damaged by the avalanche. Liz recognized her as the woman the dragon had swept out of harm's way.

So she and her child had been the only ones in peril in Kaneʻohe. Because of the dragon, three people had survived. That certainly fit with the idea of the *Pyr* protecting humans.

It also meshed with her mother's ideas of harming none.

The reporter in Kaneʻohe didn't give much credit to the woman's story of the dragon, but provided a string of links to news articles about the *Pyr*. It was titled *Do You Believe in Dragons?* Liz scrolled through the list. She downloaded and watched a television special, stopping it when the reporter, Melissa Smith, mentioned a firestorm.

Brandon had used that same word.

Liz replayed the story, listening carefully at the explanation of the firestorm. It was vague and obviously details were being withheld, but the firestorm was the mark of a *Pyr* meeting his destined mate.

She drummed her fingers on the desk, hearing Brandon's romantic assertion again.

She had to find him, wherever he was, and learn the truth. Liz terminated the connection and emptied the cache so no one would know what she'd been researching, then turned off the laptop. She went to find Maureen so she could borrow her car and catch a ferry ride to Kane'ohe.

The *Slayer* Jorge prided himself on being where the action was.

After numerous insults from the *Pyr*—including a long captivity, essentially buried alive on Bardsey Island in Wales—Jorge was ready to even the score. He wouldn't be happy with a single *Pyr* living out his life in freedom and peace.

They would all die, preferably all at Jorge's claw. He would hunt them individually, if necessary, and ensure that their deaths were slow and painful.

He'd been disgusted to discover how few *Slayers* were left, never mind that the *Pyr* had been seen and documented by humans. The *Pyr* were so stupid that they deserved to lose the battle for domination of the world. The darkfire was loosed by some idiot's miscalculation, which just added to the unpredictability of it all.

Jorge wasn't stupid. He knew he needed at least one ally. Magnus was gone, but so was the Dragon's Blood Elixir and the Elixir's source. That had been a terrific tool for enslaving young *Slayers*, but it was destroyed. Jorge needed more than an ally; he needed a tool.

And he wouldn't mind an additional supply of the Elixir.

He chose Chen for all three. He'd underestimated the ancient *Slayer* more than once, but it wouldn't happen again. Chen was powerful. Chen had secrets. Chen had old magic on his side, and he'd had that brand to enslave dragons, no matter what color their blood. Plus Chen had drunk of the Elixir, which meant that there was residue of it in his body.

Chen was the dragon to see.

Jorge would make an alliance, steal Chen's sorcery, then eliminate his only real competition.

He would win. Easily. Chen was wily, but Jorge was vengeful.

Jorge had followed the sound of Chen's chants, perceived the fault lines in the earth's crust that the old *Slayer* had made, and had followed the trail to Oʻahu. He hadn't rushed. He hadn't attracted attention. He had changed names and passports, disguised his dragon scent—a feat he could do, thanks to the Elixir still coursing in his own veins—and made his way steadily closer.

That Chen also could also disguise his scent made the hunt more interesting.

Jorge suspected that it was the Elixir alone that let him sense Chen's location. Otherwise, Erik Sorensson would have been hunting Chen, and he apparently wasn't. The brilliant quicksilver thread that drew Jorge ever closer to Chen had to be visible to him because of their shared connection to the Elixir.

He refused to worry about the glisten of blue-green that occasionally touched that thread. This wasn't about darkfire.

Jorge had reached O'ahu two days before the eclipse. Like Chen, he'd sensed the firestorm in the wind. On the morning after the eclipse, he'd enjoyed the destruction caused by the earthquake.

Then he'd followed Chen's trail to Hale'iwa. He'd driven past one old Chinese man walking alone on the highway, leaning heavily on his cane, and had been tempted to run over the elderly idiot just for being both persistent and stupid.

But he had no time for frivolous games.

And savagery could draw attention.

In Hale'iwa, Jorge stood outside Chen's lair and felt the frosty tingle of Chen's protective dragonsmoke barrier. He'd smiled, knowing that he was the only dragon who could cross this line. He and Chen were the sole survivors of those who had drunk the Elixir.

Which meant they were the only two who could take the salamander form and, more important, the only two dragons who could spontaneously manifest elsewhere. He wondered whether Chen remembered him. He doubted that Chen forgot much. Jorge manifested inside the lair and deliberately chose to unmask his scent.

That would give the *Slayer* a fright.

The lair was austerely decorated. Jorge was reminded of a Japanese shrine. The walls were empty. The windows were shuttered. There was no furniture, just a cushion on the floor against one wall. He could hear the surf on the beach and the wind crossing the roof overhead. He closed his eyes and felt the rhythm of the earth far beneath the lair, and understood why Chen had chosen such minimalist decor.

He could focus on the elements, and, almost certainly, on controlling them.

Jorge headed for the large central room and paused in shock at the threshold. The floor was covered by a layer of sand. The sand had been worked into a great spiral, one that filled the room, with whorls that turned in on themselves. The hills had to be six inches high, the troughs not more than a scattering of sand across the wood floor.

What was it for? Jorge's scalp prickled and he sensed that he was in the presence of potent magic.

This was what he had come for.

He saw something gleaming at the center of the whorl.

Jorge walked across the sand sculpture, not caring that he disturbed it. In fact, he liked the disregard of his footprints in the sand.

In the middle were three black dragon scales. Their arrangement—like three points of a compass—convinced Jorge that Chen had need of one more to complete whatever spell he was making.

Whose scales were these? Chen was red in dragon form. The only other black dragon Jorge knew was Erik, but Erik was more of a pewter color.

He wondered whether this dragon was the one who was having a firestorm. This black dragon must be close, since Chen was hunting his scales and apparently anticipated getting another one soon. The victim must be a weakened *Pyr*, one that Chen meant to enslave. *Slayers* had no firestorms, after all.

Jorge crouched in the middle of the spiral, yearning to seize the power that he sensed in it. He had nothing to offer Chen, nothing with which to negotiate an alliance.

He decided to change that.

Jorge bent and took one scale. It looked like obsidian in the light, a thin line of brilliant orange around its rim. Actually, it looked like a coal, one that was still glowing with the embers of a faded fire.

He put it in his pocket.

Jorge smiled in anticipation of his next meeting with Chen, then manifested outside the lair. He walked through the town, enjoying that people thought he was just another tourist, and took care to disguise his scent again. There was just a tendril of it, enough to taunt Chen, enough to show that he was in Hale'iwa.

Jorge would talk to Chen on his own terms, and not one minute sooner.

In the meantime, he wondered what would happen if he broke the scale. A person didn't have to fully understand magic to mess it up. He'd wait a while, long enough for Chen to realize he'd been robbed, then find out.

Jorge was pretty sure it would hurt somebody, and that made him smile.

Sara Keegan, partner of Quinn the Smith and herself Seer of the *Pyr*, was ready to drop even though it was just after lunch on a routine Saturday. She sat down at the kitchen table and sipped a cup of tea. She could hear Quinn talking to their older son, Garrett, as they headed back to Quinn's workshop together. Ewan, the second of their sons, was sleeping blissfully in his crib.

Sara sipped her tea. Too bad Ewan hadn't been inclined to sleep the night before. Sara had gotten up to nurse him at eleven, an hour early, fed up with his fussing and restlessness, but he hadn't gone back to sleep after his feeding.

She couldn't figure out what had troubled Ewan the night before, but he had refused to sleep a wink. That would have been one thing, but he had also screamed himself into a fury and wouldn't be soothed. That had put her nerves on edge. Quinn had been restless, too. At the time, she'd thought the baby was keeping both of them awake, but now she wondered whether Ewan's mood had something to do with the *Pyr*.

There had been a lunar eclipse the night before. She guessed from Quinn's gruff manner this morning that a firestorm had been sparked somewhere. He would have felt it and might be wondering whether they would be expected to join the *Pyr* there.

But Ewan shouldn't be able to sense any of that dragon stuff yet. The *Pyr* came into their powers at puberty, and that was mercifully far in the future. Sara sipped her hot tea and yearned for a nap.

An hour wouldn't hurt anything and she'd feel much better. The problem was that Sara wasn't positive she'd wake up in an hour. She might sleep four, and that would put everything off.

She was just stifling a yawn when there came a crack like lightning.

A brilliant light flashed outside and Sara was wide-awake. She raced to the window in time to see sparks radiating from the lightning rod on the roof of the studio. She ran to the studio, fearing that Quinn was hurt, only to find him striding for the house as soon as she got outside. He had Garrett in his arms and looked intent.

The sky was perfectly clear and blue. The snow all around their country home was pristine and the woods were quiet. A last strand of dark smoke wound upward from the lightning rod, and Sara could smell ash.

Something was terribly wrong.

"What's burning?" she asked.

"I thought you knew," Quinn said. "Where's Ewan?"

"He's asleep." Even as she spoke, Sara hurried back into the house.

To her relief, their baby was sleeping quietly, his fist in his mouth. Sara picked him up all the same, needing to feel his warmth against her. She turned to face Quinn, who had paused in the bedroom doorway behind her, and saw the flames in the mirror over the dresser.

There were letters there, like handwriting wrought of flames, burning on the glass. It made absolutely no sense, but Sara knew better than to ignore it.

She also knew better than to expect it to last. Portents tended to fade.

She handed Ewan to Quinn, grabbed a pen and paper, and wrote down the verse written in burning letters on the mirror.

"What are you doing?" Quinn asked, standing behind her with the boys.

"Can't you see the words?" Sara asked, not pausing in her transcription.

"What words?"

"There's a verse, written in fire, on the mirror."

"One ring to rule them all," Quinn suggested, humor in his tone.

"Not quite," Sara said, scribbling to get it all down as she saw the letters start to fade. The mirror glimmered, flashing once before all the text disappeared.

It looked perfectly normal again.

"Gone," Sara said, putting down her pen.

"Not gone," Quinn corrected, nodding at the pad of paper as he juggled the weight of their sons. "Read it to me."

"Dragon lost and dragon found;
Dragon denied and dragon bound.
Down to embers, his fire chills,
In thrall to one whose intent is ill.
Firedaughter's spark can ignite the flame,
Give him strength to fight again.
Or will both be lost on ocean's tide
Surrendered as a failed test's price?"

Sara glanced up at Quinn, only to find his expression thoughtful. "What's a Firedaughter?"

"My father spoke of them. They're witches who can assume the form of fire."

"They can become fire? Literally?"

Quinn nodded. "I think there's more than that, as well." He frowned. "My father always spoke of them with awe, maybe a bit of fear. He preferred to not talk about them."

Sara got her keys and her purse, newly invigorated. "I'm going down to the bookstore. I'll find out what I can."

"But you're closed today."

Sara paused on the threshold and glanced back at him with a smile. "I've known you long enough, Quinn

Tyrrell, to recognize the influence of a firestorm. This may be the only chance I have to do any research."

Quinn's lips tightened and he averted his gaze.

"Won't you go?" Sara asked, then continued when he didn't immediately reply. "You used to go to firestorms, to heal the armor of the *Pyr* in question. Who is it this time?"

"No one I know," Quinn said flatly. He shook his head. "It doesn't feel right to me."

"What does it feel like?"

He winced. "Darkfire."

Sara swallowed. He referred to the force that had been set loose before Rafferty's firestorm. Darkfire seemed to turn everything upside down. She knew that Quinn distrusted its power and that's why they hadn't gone to the last firestorm.

"You can't stay away forever," she said, tugging on her coat. "It's your responsibility."

Quinn looked grim. "I have a responsibility to you, as well."

Sara kissed him, pausing when her lips were still close to his cheek. "I have a feeling this *Pyr* needs us, Quinn. Not just you, but me, too. I think that's why I got the prophecy."

Quinn frowned and exhaled, looking down at the boys. Ewan was still sleeping, but Garrett was clearly listening. There were times when Sara thought he understood far more than he should for a boy who was not quite three years old.

"I'll take Ewan with me to the shop. I'm sure he'll

keep sleeping after last night. Why don't you go into your studio?" Sara smiled. "The forge always helps you think."

Quinn nodded and gave Garrett a bounce. "I have a piece of reclaimed wrought iron that's been tempting me. Garrett can help me."

Garrett grinned, then lifted his hands the way dragons lifted their claws in challenge before they fought. He bared his teeth and pretended to breathe fire.

Was he just playing dragon?

Or did he sense a coming battle?

Sara gathered her things and tucked Ewan into a carrier. She was heading out to the car when Quinn called to her. "Come into the studio instead," he said, his expression grim. "Erik's coming."

So the *Pyr* did need them. Sara wondered what Erik knew.

Quinn Tyrrell wasn't surprised to see a pewter and ebony dragon land in the snowy field beyond his studio. He wasn't surprised when that dragon shimmered blue and a tall man with dark hair took the dragon's place. He certainly wasn't surprised when Erik Sorensson strode determinedly toward him and his workshop.

That Erik came in person to make his request for Quinn's help indicated how important the leader of the *Pyr* perceived Quinn's participation to be. Or maybe it was because Quinn had refused to go to the last firestorm.

Sara rocked Ewan and watched by the window, not saying anything.

The forge was roaring, the flames hungry and powerful. The firestorm, however distant, could also give something to his work. Quinn found that the iron worked more readily on the days surrounding the spark of a firestorm—it seemed that there was a perfect link between his vision for the piece and the reality of the shape it assumed.

Garrett played in the corner of the workshop. Quinn knew that his eldest son would make a good Smith, perhaps even a better one than Quinn was himself. Garrett was drawn to the forge and to the flame, and he was invariably close when Quinn was working. Going to school was difficult for him, as Garrett seemed to believe that he was missing the more important lessons while he was at nursery school.

In a way, he was right.

Erik rapped once on the door before he entered the studio, and on the threshold he shook the snowflakes out of his hair. He looked Quinn in the eye. "You know why I've come." He nodded to Sara, and Quinn guessed that Erik spoke aloud—instead of using old-speak—in deference to her.

Quinn nodded agreement and shoved a rod of wrought iron into the forge. Garrett gave a cry of delight and came running to his "uncle," who crouched down to speak to him.

Quinn watched the flames lick the wrought iron

and saw it heat to orange and then to yellow. He liked wrought iron, and he salvaged it wherever he could. It worked well and it carried power. Quinn knew the history of this piece as soon as the flame touched it, then understood what it would be.

Perhaps what it had always wanted to be.

"You know I have concerns," Quinn said to Erik. He pulled the metal from the fire and hammered it on his anvil, finding satisfaction in how readily it took the shape in his mind. After half a dozen blows, he returned it to the fire to heat again.

"As do I," Erik admitted.

"I had a prophecy this morning," Sara said, then showed the piece of paper to Erik.

"You dreamed it?" he asked, but she shook her head.

"I saw it. Written on a mirror, in letters of flames."

Erik glanced in surprise at Quinn, who shook his head. "I couldn't see it."

"A Firedaughter," Erik mused as he read, then looked again at Quinn. "Do you know anything of such a creature?"

"My father mentioned them. He seemed wary of witches who could become flames."

"Who is the *Pyr*?" Sara asked.

"It's Brandon." Erik paused. "Brandt's son."

Quinn pulled the iron from the fire again and hammered it with force. "I thought Brandt didn't want anything to do with us."

Erik smiled. "For a long time, you didn't want anything to do with us. Surely you can understand a change of heart?"

"So, it's Brandt asking for us to help?" Quinn shoved the iron back into the fire.

Erik exhaled. "No. He and his son are still estranged. I already sent Sloane."

The Apothecary was a good *Pyr*, and Quinn didn't want to leave him exposed to any threat. Brandt would have been easier to decline.

Still, he was concerned. "Can you see the future?" Quinn asked, referring to Erik's gift of foresight.

"Not enough of it for my taste," Erik admitted, then frowned. "It's the darkfire. It muddles everything. I think, perhaps, it introduces more possibilities and instability."

Quinn pulled the metal from the fire again and returned to his anvil. Another half a dozen blows, and he had flattened it to a circle like a platter. Erik and Sara watched with interest as he returned it to the fire. When it was heated again, Quinn worked the perimeter, creating what looked like the bronze mirror of an ancient princess.

Erik nodded in approval and admiration. "Your prowess grows daily."

"It's not done yet," Quinn said, shoving it back into the fire again. "But it should be done enough to serve your purpose."

Erik caught his breath in sudden understanding. "You want me to scry with it."

"I need to know about the safety of Sara and the boys if I come." Quinn looked Erik in the eye. "There can be no doubt."

Quinn knew that Erik's integrity was beyond question and that he could believe whatever Erik told him. He hauled the metal from the fire and pivoted so that he held it before Erik. Sara stepped forward, holding Ewan close.

Erik straightened, keeping his hand on Garrett's dark head. There was no need to hold the boy back; the next Smith understood the power of fire. Garrett's eyes were round as he watched the pair of them.

Erik leaned closer and his gaze danced over the cooling surface. Quinn saw the marvel light his eyes and knew he'd been right about this piece.

He'd give it to Erik when it was done.

"The mates and children are not at risk," Erik said with finality.

"Mates?" Sara echoed, and Erik looked up at Quinn.

"I would not ask you to undertake this quest alone."

So Erik thought Quinn's presence was so critical that he was prepared to take Eileen and Zoë, his own partner and only child, to the site of the firestorm. That reassured Quinn a great deal.

"What about you and me?"

Erik's lips tightened, his gaze locking with Quinn's. "There is always danger for those who respond to the touch of darkfire."

He was right. Being *Pyr* was not without risk. There were no guarantees.

"Brandon and his mate?" Sara asked.

"I don't know. I fear the tinge of this darkfire, though." Erik shuddered. "It feels portentous."

Quinn knew exactly what Erik meant, although he might have preferred otherwise. "I didn't think Fire-daughters existed anymore."

Erik smiled. "Like dragons, maybe?"

Quinn was always curious to learn more about the element of fire.

But at what price?

He watched Erik's fingers in Garrett's dark hair and knew that the leader of the *Pyr* understood the burden of choosing between responsibilities. He nodded once, his decision made, and extinguished the flame.

Sara watched him closely, and he knew she understood his choice. He also felt that she approved of it.

He left the unfinished metal disk to cool, took off his gloves, and hung up his apron. He scooped up Garrett as he did his final check of the workshop, well aware that Erik was waiting.

Quinn paused beside Erik and looked the leader of the *Pyr* in the eye. "Then we go."

Erik liked to appear impassive but he was unable to completely hide his pleasure in this. "I took the liberty of checking commercial flights," he said. "There's a flight to Chicago out of the Traverse City airport in two hours. If you can make that, we can be on the same nonstop to Honolulu in nine hours. We'll be there in the morning, and well rested."

"We'll be on it." Sara and Quinn said in unison.

Liz went straight to the restaurant where she'd met Brandon.

The restoration of cell phone service meant that her phone had been ringing nonstop. She'd managed to reassure people back on the East Coast that everyone was fine. Most of the damage had apparently been on the other side of the island, in Honolulu. Liz couldn't even look at the images online of flattened hotels and crushed cars.

She felt very lucky and could only hope that Brandon had been just as lucky.

To her relief, the same waitress was working as had been last night.

To her dismay, the waitress's aura was so bright that it was impossible to ignore. It was vivid yellow with a tinge of orange, a warm and welcoming aura indicative of a positive spirit.

The auras, Liz had to concede, were back. She figured she might as well use the data since she had it.

The waitress was a sunny, trustworthy person, inclined to help. That was good.

The waitress glanced at Liz's new flip-flops and smiled. "You've had quite the intro to island life, haven't you?"

"That earthquake was a first for me."

"Me, too. At least here." The waitress made a face.

"I'm good with volcanoes. They do their business slowly and there's time to run. Earthquakes, though, are why I left California."

Liz was surprised. "You don't get a lot of them here?"

The waitress shook her head. "Not like that one." She shrugged. "I understand that it usually happens under the ocean. Never mind that avalanche outside of town. But then all the weather in the world is going to hell. What can I get you?"

"Just a bit of information. You know those guys who were here last night?"

The waitress's eyes started to twinkle. "The hot surfer guys? The ones a girl would have to be dead not to notice?"

Liz blushed. "Yes, them. Who are they?"

"I don't know their names. Surfers don't come here often." She smiled and started to turn away. "I just enjoy the view when they do."

"Any idea where I'd find them?"

The waitress looked Liz up and down. "Forgive me for saying so, but you don't look the type."

"What type?"

"Mainland girl on vacation, looking to get lucky. Or surfer-boy fan girl. Either way, you don't fit. Especially if you're at the Institute."

"I'm a marine biologist." Liz was sure she couldn't have blushed any more. "I was talking to one of them about the reefs," she improvised. "He mentioned a fish I've never seen before."

"Uh-huh. So, the day after we get slammed with an earthquake, you've got to find him. Because of some little fish."

"Okay. I want to check that he's okay, too."

The waitress smiled, glanced away, then met Liz's gaze. "You want surfers, you need to go up to Hale'iwa. They're all up there in December."

"Why in December?"

"It's the waves. They're best at this time of year on the north shore. And there are the competitions, as well. It's about the only time they can make money doing what they do." The waitress grinned. "Unless they can get a gig as a boy toy. Does marine biology pay well?"

Liz ignored that.

Hale'iwa. She pulled out her cell phone and Binged the town. From the map of the island, it looked as if she could drive there in a couple of hours.

The waitress laughed. "Oh, honey, you've got it bad."

Liz knew there was nothing she could say to change the other woman's perspective. Besides, it was nearly noon. If she wanted to drive to Hale'iwa, find Brandon, and get back by the last ferry to Coconut Island, she'd have to hurry.

"That main road?" she said. "It looks like I just follow it around the island."

"That would have worked yesterday." Her words reminded Liz of the debris from the landslide, which would have barricaded the road. "You're going to have to go back through the tunnel to Honolulu, then take the road up the middle of the island to the north shore."

Liz found the road on her map, then looked up at the waitress. "Any way to do that without taking a tunnel through the mountain?"

"Well, you could go all around Diamond Head, then through Honolulu, but it would take you hours. Especially today. On the other hand, I wouldn't be driving through those tunnels when there are aftershocks. It all depends how badly you want to check on him." She grinned. "Or find that little fish."

Liz studied the map. She measured the distance. She thought about the dragon saving her and the woman with the child.

She had to know.

She didn't have time to take the scenic route. If she was going to Brandon, she had to go through the tunnels. There'd be no auras, because she'd be alone. She could ignore the whispers, if there were any.

Because her desire to talk to Brandon was strong enough to justify this risk.

Even if the waitress shook her head when Liz turned to leave.

Chapter 5

The person Brandon found first wasn't Chen.
It was Kira.

She shouted at him as soon as he got out of the truck in Hale'iwa, and he could tell by the sparkle in her eyes that she was excited about something. Kira was of mixed descent, her skin tanned to a rich gold and her hair almost black. She looked Hawaiian from a distance, but her eyes were an unexpectedly clear green. She was petite and curvy, always wearing a bright bikini and floral-print sarong of her own design. She could rip a wave like no woman Brandon had ever seen surf. Her shop in Sunset Beach was always busy, but never so busy that she wouldn't close up and hit the beach for a couple of hours.

She'd been one of the first locals here to befriend him, and just seeing her easy smile made him feel less jangled and confused. Kira was part of his human life.

Maybe if he focused on that side of his life and ignored the dragon, it would leave him alone.

He heard it laugh deep in his mind at the very idea.

"What's up?" Brandon asked. "You look happy."

"I had an idea. Remember that wet suit you tried out a month back?"

Brandon nodded. Kira had wanted to get into the business of outfitting surfers for a while. It made sense, as they were the majority of her customers, and their gear would be more profitable for her to sell than just the casual clothes she currently designed.

"The one that was a bit tight in the shoulders?" It had been a great wet suit and he could have used a new one, but that one had restricted his shoulders too much. He wouldn't be able to paddle properly in it, and that was too high a price to pay, even for a deal on a wet suit.

"Right. Well, I marked up that one and had the supplier make a modified version." She flicked a quick glance at him. "Custom, just for you."

Brandon stopped and stared at her. "No way. You shouldn't have spent the money, Kira."

"It's an investment." Kira's eyes were dancing at Brandon's confusion. "Want to try it on?"

Brandon held up his hands. "But, Kira, you can't do this for me because I can't pay you for it. It wouldn't be right."

"Oh yes, you can pay me back. That's my idea!"

Brandon spread his hands, inviting her explanation.

"You're going to surf the Pipe, aren't you? You scored that wild-card slot?"

Brandon nodded. "I did, by some miracle."

"Not a miracle. You're natural and one of the best, too. Everybody knows it, and it's about time someone gave you a break." Kira kept talking, the words spilling from her lips so fast that Brandon wondered why she was worried. "It's the wet suit you liked—short legs, short sleeves. Yellow with black." She stopped and grinned. "And I just happened to have my new logo silk-screened onto the front of the wet suit in red."

Brandon laughed, understanding. "So when I compete, you get advertising."

"If you win anything, it will be amazing." She leaned closer. "Nail the Pipe and you can have *anything* from me." The warmth in her eyes made Brandon uncomfortable. He had a feeling she wasn't just talking about wet suits.

"One deal at a time, Kira." He eyed the surf. "The waves are so rough, they might have to cancel."

"No," she said with such conviction that he glanced at her in surprise. "Look, I was practically born on the beach, and I know the Banzai Pipeline better than I know myself. I *feel* that break right in my blood. I know what it's going to do when."

"Kira, that doesn't make any sense."

Kira was referring to the specific wave break where the last contest in the Triple Crown would be held. The Banzai Pipeline was known all over the world for being magnificent and fierce. On this section of coast, the shape of the coral reef compelled the surf to not just break by curling over itself, but to create a hollow tube. In addition, the tube was unusually large, enough that a good surfer could surf inside the tube, a feat called barreling.

Of course, if the surfer made a mistake, he or she would be pummeled into the coral reef. Broken boards and broken limbs were common on the Pipe, and, on average, one surfer a year died trying to ride that wave.

In his time on Oʻahu, Brandon had heard his share of superstitions and convictions about that break. He'd never expected such whimsy from Kira.

"Sure it does," she insisted, marching toward her yellow Volkswagen bug with determination. It was one of the old ones and a convertible, too. "Didn't you know that my mom was one of the first women to surf the Pipe?" Brandon shook his head, but Kira nodded. "She only ever barreled it once, and she said it changed her life."

"I can believe it," Brandon said. "It changed mine." There was something magical about riding inside the curl of that wave, surrounded by blue and green water and buffeted by the sound of roaring water. No matter how many times Brandon did it, he felt euphoric afterward. It was the ultimate natural high.

"Probably not in the same way," Kira said with a wink. "She said it was amazing, that it either lasted ten seconds or ten hours."

Brandon smiled. The sense of being out of time had been strong for him, too.

"And she said that everything came together in a kind of perfect sense."

Brandon nodded agreement. The Pipe was particularly special to him because inside that wave was the one place his dragon shut right up.

"And she knew she was pregnant, right then."

He stared at Kira. "Whoa."

Kira nodded as she unlocked her car. "She came right out of the ocean and went for her test. It was so early that they had to do it twice to make sure." She pulled out something yellow, looked at Brandon, then shook out the wet suit. "She always called me the Banzai Baby."

The logo on the wet suit bore the words BANZAI BABY with a lightning bolt underscoring them. It blazed right across the chest and looked awesome.

"Great logo," Brandon said, admiring the wet suit. Kira went through the modifications to the design with him, showing how she'd added to it where he had found it restrictive and trimmed it where he'd thought it gaped. "It looks fantastic."

"So, will you?" She looked up at him with shining eyes, her expression making Brandon think that maybe she wanted more than this favor from him.

But then, he'd thought that before.

He didn't want to let her down, though. He'd wear her logo only if he thought he was going to kick ass, and that depended on when the competition would be held. "They're not competing today, are they? The beach is too quiet."

"No, it'll be the day after tomorrow."

"You can't know that." The competitions were

scheduled for twelve-day periods, with the actual surfing on three days. The hope was that there would be three days of good curls out of the twelve, and the decision was made by seven in the morning each day.

"I tell you, I know the Pipe. Tomorrow the other breaks will be good, and the Pipe will be better than today. It won't be optimal until Tuesday, though. Trust me."

Brandon looked at Kira and realized he did trust her instincts. She'd been calling good waves for as long as he'd known her. In fact, he'd teased her more than once that she must have a crystal ball to determine in advance which days her shop should be closed.

So he had three days to get it together. He pursed his lips, thinking.

Kira leaned closer, looking expectant. "Try it on."

Brandon glanced up and down the road, his own excitement rising. He had a sponsor. He had a wild-card slot. He had his chance. It was time for the dragon to get slammed back into the cave and locked in there for a good. He'd have to do a parking-lot change, but he was used to that. "You got a towel?"

Kira rolled her eyes. "You think I'm a grom or something?"

Brandon laughed at the idea of anyone considering her a beginner. He knotted her towel around his waist and slipped out of his shorts, pulling up the wet suit. It fit like it was made for him. He supposed that was because it had been. He peeled off the towel and tugged the wet suit over his shoulders, reaching back to pull up the zipper.

"Perfect," he said, flexing and stretching. He bent and turned, feeling no restriction at all. It was like a second skin; he was amazed at how well it fit. Two women hung out the windows of a passing car and wolf-whistled at him.

Kira sighed with an admiration that wasn't completely a joke. "Oh yeah."

"Thanks, Kira. I'll try to do you proud." Brandon changed back out of the suit, then gave her a quick hug. "Have you seen Matt and Dylan?"

Kira pointed down the road. "They headed for 'Ehukai Beach. You want a ride?"

The temptation was too much. "Will you stop at my place so I can grab a board from my quiver?" There was always a chance that the surf might become better and he could train.

"Optimist!" she accused, and he grinned.

"Gotta be sure I win in my new suit."

But the truth was that Brandon needed every possible moment to get control over his dragon again. After all, everything was at stake.

Liz wasn't exactly calm as she drove through the tunnel toward Honolulu.

She didn't want to hear any whispers or see any auras, and she was worried about what might happen after that. Her knuckles were white on the steering wheel as the shadow of the tunnel entry fell over the car.

She felt swallowed in darkness.

It took only a moment for her awareness of the power surrounding her to become sharper and clearer. She sensed the rhythm of the earth, the slow erosion of rock, the creeping movement of tectonic plates beneath the island. The shadows were filled with possibilities, but Liz kept her gaze locked on the road ahead. The molten core of the Earth was close here, which must be at least part of the reason her powers had been reawakened.

She was not going to think about consequences.

Liz stared at the bright light that indicated the exit from the tunnel, wishing for the moments to hurry. She was almost there. She could ignore the prickling of her skin, the feeling of electricity all around her, and the vibration of the Earth's forces.

The brilliant flash of blue-green light within the car made her gasp.

It was gone as quickly as it had appeared, making her hope that she had imagined it.

But she wasn't imagining the burning sensation on her right arm.

Liz glanced down and stared in horror. There was a mark on the back of her right forearm. It was a symbol, an ancient symbol, emblazoned on her skin like a brand. It glowed briefly with that faint blue-green light, then became as mundane as a black-ink tattoo.

Liz shuddered and swallowed, her panic rising. She

knew it wouldn't scrub off or disappear. The symbol was a warning to prepare herself, that her time of trial was coming soon.

One more time, Liz wished she'd learned more from her mother while she'd had the chance. It wasn't very reassuring that her mother had known so much more than Liz and she had still failed the test.

Liz took a deep breath and gripped the steering wheel, reminding herself that she'd been acing exams for years.

Even if the stakes hadn't been quite so high.

Chen crawled through a deadened fissure of lava in his salamander form, too tired to hurry toward the surface. He acknowledged that there were successes and failures thus far in his plan. He'd really made his mark on Oʻahu with the earthquake he'd summoned. He felt a measure of pride in the havoc that he'd wreaked on the pitiful human population.

They had no idea how much worse it would be.

He'd been deep in the earth, singing songs of power to awaken the old volcano Koʻolau. She was stirring, responding to his chants, awakening. The earthquake had been a bonus, an extra reaction to his chant while Koʻolau seethed.

Even in triumph, though, Chen was exhausted. He had to take a break to restore himself; then he would continue to coax Koʻolau's anger. He smiled, anticipating the terror that a massive eruption of this volcano would create, since most assumed it to be extinct.

He also liked that it was unclear even to him where the eruption would be. The Koʻolau range ran down the northeastern edge of the island, the original crater long since destroyed by erosion. There were tens of thousands of ancient cracks and fissures, all closed over on the surface. When the molten lava rose hot and fast within the volcano, the weakest barriers would collapse first. The eruption could occur anywhere from Haleʻiwa to Diamond Head, and, with any luck, it would be simultaneous at several locations. Chen enjoyed the element of surprise in his plan, and hoped for the worst.

On a more personal level, he also was encouraged by the way that the earthquake had compelled Brandon to shift shape. He'd felt the young *Pyr*'s involuntary transformation as surely as if the boy had been standing beside him, the abrupt change giving Chen a little surge of power even on the other side of the island.

The young *Pyr* was nearly in his thrall. The promise of completely claiming the dragon shifter delighted him with its possibilities. Not only would he claim Brandon's power and affinities, but he'd be able to command him like a slave for as long as he survived.

One more scale would do it. The number four was potent in Chen's dragon magic. Four elements. Four cardinal directions. Four scales.

It would be ideal if Brandon's capitulation was what made Koʻolau's eruption inevitable; Brandon's affinity was with the earth, after all. What if Chen could command him to participate in the song to rile Koʻolau? Chen loved that idea as soon as he'd had it. As a coup de grâce, he'd be able to ensure the young *Pyr*'s complete loss of spirit if Brandon believed himself and his dragon responsible for destroying Oʻahu—the island he loved—forever.

If the *Pyr* killed himself out of remorse or died of anguish, Chen would be able to replenish his supply of Dragon Bone Powder.

It was win-win.

Chen didn't trust the darkfire, however. That strange blue-green flame had flickered in Chen's thoughts when Brandon's firestorm sparked, almost as if it was a trick of the light caused by the eclipse. Chen knew better. The darkfire was going to mess with Chen's plans. He expected that Erik Sorensson and the other *Pyr* would try to mess with his plans, on top of it all.

He doubted, after all, that he was the only one to have felt Brandon's firestorm and involuntary shift. No. Erik Sorensson would meddle.

Chen would have to be vigilant to succeed.

Victory was so very close.

It was early afternoon by the time Chen shifted shape deep in the central valley of Oʻahu. Unfortunately, the fissure he'd chosen had led him to the surface farther away from Haleʻiwa than he'd hoped. He blamed his exhaustion for his mistake. Once again he took the form of an elderly Chinese man, but he was tired enough that he didn't have to pretend to lean heavily on his cane. He began to walk down the road to Hale'iwa, where he was sure he would find Brandon again.

When the old turquoise Mercedes pulled over and the young woman at the wheel offered him a ride, Chen's heart leapt with delight. It hadn't been his exhaustion that had led him to this place.

It had been destiny.

Because this woman was none other than Brandon's human mate.

Chen was so delighted that he even let her help him into the front passenger's seat.

That was when he realized that she was no ordinary mortal. As soon as she touched his arm, he felt the power of her sorcery. A Firedaughter! He had not met one in centuries. This was the curse of the darkfire; this was the challenge it had cast his way.

But did she understand her gifts? Was she in command of them? She had not cloaked herself in a web of protective spells, which gave Chen hope. He settled into the car and closed his eyes, the better to assess her powers.

The fact was that if he seized a *Pyr* and a Firedaughter, claiming the powers of both, he would be invincible.

On one hand, Liz was glad that she'd stopped for the old Chinese man. She wasn't sure how he would have made it anywhere, since he appeared to be so frail. He was visibly relieved once she got him into the car. It wouldn't hurt to have some human company, not with her thoughts racing.

And that mark on her arm.

On the other hand, there was something about the old man that gave her the creeps. He didn't have an aura, which should have reassured her, but instead it troubled her. She had a strange sense that he wasn't what he seemed, except she couldn't figure out what else he could be other than a frail elderly man.

So she wasn't very disappointed when he dozed off as soon as he got into the car. Liz focused on reality and the beautiful scenery. The road was pretty much empty, mountains rising on the right. She'd passed the Dole pineapple plantation and could still see fields of pineapples on either side of the road. The Mercedes didn't have air-conditioning, but they didn't need it. Liz just rolled down all the windows, letting the wind blow through the car.

She drove and listened to the old man snoring gently. She felt the tension ease out of her. Maybe she'd take the long way back to Kaneʻohe. Maybe everything would be just fine.

Her companion stirred after a few minutes and rolled up his window. She turned to find him smiling at her.

"Better?"

"Much better." He bowed his head formally. "I thank you."

Liz couldn't understand why he'd been walking in

a comparatively remote area. Where had he come from? "Do you live here? Or in Hale'iwa?"

"I visit Hale'iwa," he said, speaking carefully as if English wasn't his first language. "I come from my home."

"Around here?"

He shook his head. "Far away. Asia."

"So you don't live on the island." Liz smiled. Nice, polite chitchat suited her perfectly. "I don't, either."

"Ah." His eyes lit. "Do you come for the dragon, too?"

Liz was so surprised that the car swerved. "Dragon?"

The old man nodded. "I come for the dragon." He spoke with such conviction that Liz felt a shudder run down her spine. There was a darkness underlying his words.

A threat. As if he hunted the dragon.

This old man? Liz forced herself to be practical. "You've seen a dragon here?" she asked lightly. "You mean like an iguana? A dragon lizard?"

He cast her a sly glance, one that chilled her blood. "A real dragon. He lives here, makes fire and smoke." He nodded. "In my country, dragons make rain. They make earthquakes. They respond in anger when we do not make offerings." He tapped on his knee. "I think it is the same here."

Liz couldn't deny her sense that he was lying to her—and maybe even toying with her. But why? Who was he, really?

"Have you actually seen a dragon here?"

He grinned, then held up a crooked finger. "There

is just one. Black, black as night, with eyes of red. Like lava." He nodded. "Very powerful dragon."

Liz's bad feeling multiplied a hundred times. This old man had no good plans for the dragon—and if the dragon was the good guy, this must be the bad guy. Her instincts were screaming at her to run away from this old man, which logically made no sense. She could beat him in a fight, easily.

Even without using her powers.

She kept her tone light. "Where do you see this dragon?"

"I see him when he chooses to let me see him." The old man turned to face her, his expression intent. "You understand that this is a magical beast. He is sometimes a dragon, sometimes a man."

He sounded so much like her mother that Liz was surprised. "A *Pyr*," she whispered, without meaning to do so.

The old man shrugged, apparently not recognizing the word. "The people here, they call him a *kupua*. Son of a goddess, so he can become something other than a man. As a man, he is handsome and strong, young. As a dragon, he breathes the fire of his mother and has her temper."

Liz's heart leapt to her throat. "What goddess?"

The old man smiled. "Pele," he said, gesturing to the hills. "She who made these lands."

Pele, Liz knew, was the goddess of the volcanoes, a deity responsible for lava and eruptions, who had a temper to match the volatility of her creations.

The old man's eyes glittered as he looked at her, and Liz felt exposed. "Pele has dragon sons and Fire-daughters." As Liz stared at him in shock, he laughed.

He couldn't really know what she was, could he?

Liz pretended not to understand and talked about the dragon. "Do you know where to find this *kupua* dragon?"

"I have seen him in Hale'iwa, so I wait there. I come to pay homage to him, to make offerings, as people here do not." He shook his head. "But this time, I came too late. The dragon is angry."

Liz fixed her gaze on the road ahead. "You think this dragon caused the earthquake."

"It is what dragons do. They have power and they use it." He leaned toward Liz, his gaze bright. "They teach us with their lessons." He hissed the last word with unexpected force.

Lessons like earthquakes?

"That's a pretty hard lesson."

The old man shrugged. "And yet people never change. So there will be more lessons. The dragon does not relent in his teaching, whether we listen or not. This one, he could call to his mother, who could do more than make the earth shake."

Volcanic eruptions? Liz glanced at the mountains. She was sure she'd read that the volcanoes on O'ahu were extinct.

Liz frowned, unable to accept that even if Brandon was a dragon shape shifter, he'd been responsible for the damage of this morning. It wasn't in his character—or in his aura—to willfully hurt anyone.

Liz slanted a glance at her companion and trusted her instinct to not tell him that she'd seen a dragon, too. There was something that made her wary, maybe his apparent conviction that people deserved to experience the earthquake. He seemed oddly satisfied with the dragon's act of retaliation.

Still, he might know more that was useful.

"So, what are the offerings a dragon wants?" she asked, as if indulging him.

"You must offer to the dragon whatever is most precious to you. He will know if you lie. Dragons know all." He tapped his chest. "They see to the heart. This is what makes them powerful—and dangerous."

Had Brandon seen to her heart? Liz had a feeling that he had.

Maybe he had recognized that they both had secrets and burdens to bear.

She concentrated on her driving for a few minutes. As they got closer to the coast, there was more traffic, as well as more cars parked on the shoulder. She followed the old man's directions into the town of Hale'iwa and was charmed by its easy atmosphere.

"I stay there," the old man said, indicating where she could let him out. There were a number of houses clustered behind the clothing stores and galleries. Liz noticed a grocery store and made note of a gas station down the way. She might need to fill up before she headed back. There were also a lot of cars parallel parked along the road.

Most of the cars had roof racks with surfboards, and there were surfboards leaning against railings on porches. There was no parking available near the spot the old man wanted to stop, so Liz simply stopped and put on her hazard lights. He didn't look as if he could walk much farther. She had to hope that the town was quiet enough that she wouldn't get rear-ended. She got out and went around the car to help the older man. She was her mother's daughter, as much as she might have liked to change that.

"Where do you find the dragon?" she asked again when he was on his feet, and he smiled up at her. Again she felt conflicted by her reaction. He appeared to be so benign, but she wanted to run away from him as quickly as possible.

Where was his aura?

Was he a ghost? One of the spirits from other realms? According to locals, Hawai'i was rumored to be filled with ghosts.

"You do not." He touched his chest. "You wish to see him. You make him offerings. And if you are lucky, the dragon will hear the secret of your heart and find you." He smiled, then bowed formally before her, bracing himself on his cane. "I thank you."

"You're welcome. Are you okay from here?"

"I am strong," he said, then leaned on his cane so heavily that he undermined his own assertion. Liz watched him go a little way, not at all sure that he could manage on his own. She felt both protective of this older man and deeply suspicious of him. Which impulse was the right one?

He pivoted and glanced back at her just then, his expression so mischievous that Liz halfway imagined he'd heard her thoughts. Was he laughing at her? "But today, if I wished to find the dragon, I would look on 'Ehukai Beach."

"'Ehukai Beach," Liz echoed.

The old man nodded and turned his back on her. Liz watched him hobble away, humming quietly. He seemed oddly satisfied with himself, although she couldn't imagine why. Maybe he was just glad to be close to his accommodation.

Okay, 'Ehukai Beach. She got back into the car and pulled up her map. It was only a couple of miles away. When she glanced at the street, there was no sign of the older man.

Funny that he had disappeared just the way the dragon had.

Maybe he *was* stronger than he'd looked.

Brandon wasn't as reassured by watching the ocean waves as he'd expected to be.

Usually the sight of the ocean's power soothed his dragon, just as riding the waves kept him focused on his human side. It was as if the rhythm of the rolling waves lulled his dragon to sleep.

Today was exactly the opposite. The waves were wild, rising high and crashing hard on the coral reef.

To Brandon's dismay, his dragon seemed to feed on that energy. He felt an exhilaration, a gleeful joy in the violence of the sea, and that jubilation wasn't a part of his human nature.

What was different? Was it because the turmoil in the sea had been caused by the earthquake? Or was this just a sign that his dragon was less under his control?

Was his dragon more tempestuous because it knew that Brandon would soon be rid of it? It was easy to believe that it might fight harder at the end.

Brandon knew only that he had to conquer his dragon to have a chance with Liz. He watched the waves, studying their pattern. His dragon dared him, tempted him, nudged him toward the challenge of this surf without taking the time to prepare. When Brandon went, it would be by his choice.

Some of the guys were on the beach, watching the water. Although they'd brought their boards, the boards remained on their roof racks. They were joking around and they'd greeted Brandon, but no one was in the water.

The risk was too high.

But Brandon knew this break. If anyone could ride it today, it would be him. He knew its hazards and quirks well, probably even better than Kira. As he watched the surf and noted the familiarity of the break, he became convinced that he could do it.

Maybe Brandon could finish the dragon today with a bold move. If he was right, he could put the torment of his shifter nature behind him, for good.

He could return to Liz immediately.

At that realization, Brandon's decision was made. He got his board out of the back of Kira's Volkswagen. Liz's company was all the incentive he needed to borrow Kira's towel again and change into the new wet suit.

"You're joking," Kira said, her shock clear as she watched him.

"No." Brandon cast her a smile. "I'm not joking."

He didn't wait for her to argue with him. He walked onto the beach, heading directly for the waves crashing on the shore.

Kira ran behind him. "But you can't! It's not safe."

Living with a dragon he couldn't control wasn't safe.

Brandon kept walking.

"Brandon, this is crazy!" Kira shouted. "You'll die."

He looked back to see her more agitated than he'd ever seen her. The guys on the beach had turned to watch, their curiosity clear.

She shook a finger at him. "It'll be crap PR for me if you die in that wet suit!"

"Then I won't die," Brandon said easily, turning back to the ocean.

"Hey," Dylan said, striding to his side. "Don't go out there."

"I'm going."

"Look at those waves!" Dylan gestured to the sea, his concern clear. "You wipe out and you'll be history. It's merciless out there today."

Brandon watched the waves. The break was easing slightly to the right. Good. He liked it better there.

"You've got your big chance this week," Kira said from his other side. "Don't go out there just to do something macho and stupid, and wreck it all."

"If you break only a board, you'll be lucky," Dylan added.

"I thought you said I was the best at this break," Brandon said to Kira. She nodded reluctantly, her gaze sliding to the pounding surf and back to him. "I can do it."

"You shouldn't go out there alone," Dylan began.

Matt interrupted from behind them. "I'll go out with you. Let me get my board."

Kira shoved a hand through her hair and bit her lip. "So you're both either stupid or crazy."

Brandon touched her shoulder. "You know it's all about what you believe," he reminded her. "I know I can do this, and so I'm going to."

Kira swore and wrapped her arms around herself. She seemed to realize that she couldn't change his mind. Matt came back then, having changed into his wet suit, carrying his shortboard. He and Brandon bumped fists, then charged into the surf.

The other guys on the beach cheered and whistled, crowding closer to the water to watch. By the time Brandon put his board in the water and started to paddle, he couldn't hear them anymore.

There was just the pounding of the sea.

The dragon made only a low growl.

Brandon grinned. He paddled with all his might, lunging through the wave to the outside. Matt was right with him, his eyes filled with excitement. The ocean was dark and roiling on the outside, awesome in its power.

He pointed to the left, indicating the break to Matt. Brandon was on the inside, so he'd take the first wave. He gave Matt a thumbs-up as the next wave reared high against the horizon, then turned and started to paddle toward the beach as fast as he could.

"Go, go, go!" Matt shouted behind him.

The wave swelled under Brandon, lifting him high as it surged toward the beach. He'd caught a massive one and, as always, this moment made his heart thunder with excitement. He was on his feet, balancing on his board, filled with the sense that he could touch the sky. He rode just below the crest on the green wave, the white wave breaking beside him exactly as he'd anticipated, racing toward the beach.

Everything was perfect. His dragon was silent. He was completely in control, in his human form.

This would be it.

There was more parking at 'Ehukai Beach, but then, that was probably because the waves were crashing on the shore so forcefully that the surfers had stayed home. Liz parked the Mercedes and got out, surprised to find anyone there.

A group of about a dozen surfers stood close to the water, transfixed by something out at sea. The water was roiling and the surf was high. She could feel the fury of the ocean and wished her powers allowed her to pacify it. That was the task of Waterdaughters, but Liz wasn't sure that even they could calm the waters on this day.

To Liz's shock, there were two guys on surfboards out in the angry waves. One was paddling toward the shore, apparently targeting the incoming wave.

"Go, go, go!" shouted one of the guys on the beach, although Liz couldn't imagine that the surfer could hear him. The wave rolled beneath the surfer, lifting him and his board high on its great, dark swell.

He had a steady aura of indigo.

Liz hurried to the beach, knowing who it had to be.

"Get up, Brandon!" one of the guys shouted. "Get *up!*"

There was one woman among the group of guys at the beach. She glanced at Liz, then back at the surfer. She looked worried.

Brandon was on his feet, balancing perfectly. The wave crested beside him and he rode the dark curve of the wave. He wasn't that far from the beach and she could see him grin in triumph.

That cockiness made Liz mad.

What the hell was he doing? It had to be suicide to surf when the ocean was this wild. She had come all this way to check that he was okay, only to discover that he was trying to kill himself. Liz's temper flared, as hot and potent as it had once been.

The reaction of the other surfers certainly indicated that Brandon's choice was dangerous. Liz had the sense that they couldn't bear to watch but couldn't turn away.

The woman folded her arms across her chest and watched fixedly, her lips tight. She made a sound of disgust, then pivoted to walk away.

"Excuse me," Liz said, hearing the anger in her own tone. "Is that Brandon?"

"Yes," she said hotly. "Stupid moron."

Liz had to agree. "It must be dangerous to surf when the sea is like this."

The woman's eyes flashed. "This break kills at least one surfer a year. Today's the kind of day that statistic could come true." She nodded at the guys. "They all think he has balls, but I think he has shit for brains."

With that, she marched away. She got into a yellow Volkswagen bug, started it, and squealed the tires as she drove away.

Liz didn't blame her for being angry. She was probably one of Brandon's friends.

She stared back at him, both fascinated by his skill and terrified for him. As she might have expected, he was a graceful athlete, making something that had to be hard look effortless. The wave curled beside him, a froth of white spilling down to one side. The curl seemed to have an opening, like the end of a massive tube. She saw the flash of Brandon's smile as he was almost surrounded by the wave.

One of the guys on the beach gave a whistle.

Brandon crouched lower. He stayed right at the

front of the curl, and she knew he must be somehow doing it on purpose. One hand trailed in the wave behind him, his fingers buried in the water; the other was outstretched for balance. She could appreciate that it was exciting to be so close to such power, but it was treacherous, too.

The wave propelled him toward the beach with incredible speed. The water churned right behind him, no more than an arm's length away, smashing down into the reef with incredible force.

He was a step away from disaster.

On purpose.

Liz fumed. She'd driven through a tunnel in the mountain when there were still aftershocks from the earthquake. She'd abandoned her colleagues and her friend Maureen because she was so worried about Brandon.

And here he was, risking his life for fun.

Liz could have spit sparks. She was so mad that she was tempted to just turn her back and walked away from him forever. But no. She'd spent hours getting here—she'd have the pleasure of telling him off before she drove back.

She strode down the beach toward the surf, livid. The other surfers stepped back to make way for her and she heard them whisper as she marched to the lip of the water. She intended to meet Brandon when he rode to shore, but he must have sensed her presence.

He glanced up from the wave and he was close enough that she could see his surprise.

That didn't improve her mood. So he hadn't thought he'd see her again. All that talk of kismet and destiny and true love had been garbage, just garbage he'd spewed to get into bed with her. He was no different from his predatory friend. Liz's anger boiled and she had even more to say.

But Brandon miscalculated in that moment.

She saw him lose that balance point.

He disappeared under the curl of the wave and his friends swore. The wave smashed over Brandon, driving him down into the reef. His surfboard leapt for the sky, was submerged, then bounced up again. The wave rushed in to the beach and the surfboard bobbed on the surface in the wake of the wave.

There was no sign of Brandon.

"Shit," one of the guys whispered.

Liz couldn't believe it. The sight of her had shocked him so much that he'd made a mistake. It couldn't be her fault that he died in this crazy surf. She wouldn't be responsible for two deaths! Her anger faded with record speed, only to be replaced by fear.

Brandon didn't come up. Another wave crashed over the place where he'd gone down and she held her breath. His friends clustered closer, their agitation clear. A third wave reared up, breaking on the lip of coral like a shadow of doom.

"No one lasts three waves," one guy murmured.

"Come on, Brandon," urged another. "Come *on*!"

There was a roar of anger, not very different from the earthquake that morning. A brilliant shimmer of pale blue light lit the water like a flash of lightning, but one that came from the reef below.

Liz was the least surprised of the entire group when a massive black dragon erupted from the surf. It leapt out of the ocean, raging and thrashing as the water ran off its wings and tail. It shook off the water and spread its wings wide, breathing a plume of fire at the waves that had nearly crushed it.

Then it dove back into the ocean's waves again.

"What the . . ." murmured the guy beside her.

"It can't be," said another.

"What happened to Brandon?" asked a third. "Did the dragon take him down?"

Liz knew where he was.

Brandon was a dragon shape shifter.

One of the *Pyr*.

She had her irrefutable proof.

Chapter 6

Suddenly one of the guys shouted and pointed out to sea. "It's Matt!" he cried.

They turned as one and Liz couldn't help but look, too. A second surfer had turned toward the shore and was paddling for a wave. This one seemed darker and faster. Angrier. Liz could feel its fury, which was saying something. She had only a slightly greater-than-normal connection to the element of water. The surfer had a green aura, a spiky one, and she guessed that it was the friend of Brandon's who had tried to buy her a drink.

"Fuck," murmured one of the guys.

"Leave it!" shouted one of the others. Matt kept paddling. She doubted that he had seen the dragon, given the intensity of his concentration. He would have been looking out to the horizon, watching the incoming waves swell.

It was odd how much angrier the ocean had become.

Even in front of the wave, where the dragon had disappeared into the water again, the sea was churning and dark. It could have been boiling. There was more agitation in the water than there had been—and it looked even more dangerous. Liz had the strange sense that the waves were responding to the dragon's mood.

Could the dragon control the sea?

She remembered what the old Chinese man had said. Was the dragon demanding a toll from people who didn't do as he desired? Would the dragon stir up the sea to injure people?

The dragon was Brandon. Liz was sure Brandon wouldn't deliberately hurt anyone.

But this Matt was the friend who had opened that silver vial against Brandon's express command.

Was Brandon vengeful?

Liz had a hard time believing it. Why didn't he shift back to human form? Why didn't he come out of the water? She caught a glimpse of the end of his tail and the occasional talon flicking out of the water.

What was he waiting for?

The wave surged beneath Matt, just as it had beneath Brandon, all jade power.

"Leave it," murmured another of the guys. "It's too fucking big."

But Matt didn't leave it. He sprang to his feet on his board, but even Liz could tell that he wasn't as in control as Brandon had been. The wave broke and curled, precisely as its predecessors had when striking the same spot on the reef. It spilled white foam down right beside Matt—he'd chosen his spot well. The wave was enormous, taller and more powerful than the last had been, and seemed to keep swelling bigger. She thought she could see the fear on Matt's face, and that couldn't be good.

He wobbled on his board and she almost closed her eyes, dreading what would happen next.

She was glad she didn't. The dragon bellowed and leapt into the air, flying high over the waves. He swooped low over Matt, and Liz guessed that he was going to save the surfer. Matt was obviously less certain of his intent. He took one look at the dragon, closing fast with talons extended, and lost his balance.

It was possible that he jumped.

Either way, he fell into the raging dark wave, which frothed right over him. His board sprang into the air. Then both were churned down into the reef by the breaking wave. Matt's board came to the surface in two parts. One half was washed toward the beach but the other bobbed like a buoy, staying in place.

"It's the leash," one guy said.

"What leash?" Liz asked.

The guy glanced at her.

"I know Brandon."

His gaze flicked over her, then he looked back at the bobbing board. His expression was grim. "You wear a leash from your ankle to your board so you don't have to chase it all over the place. The board's not moving because the leash is caught on the reef. It doesn't happen often, but when it does, it sucks."

Because Matt was attached to the other end of the leash. Liz understood their fear. He must not be able to reach the surface.

"He's not coming up," another guy said. "We can't lose both of them in one day."

Liz realized that they thought Brandon had died.

"Shit, look at the next wave!"

"They're getting bigger. It's turning bad."

"They shouldn't have gone out there."

The dragon dove into the surf, apparently targeting Matt.

The looming wave crashed over the spot where the dragon had disappeared. The roar of the wave's power was deafening and Liz couldn't imagine how anyone could survive its impact. She folded her arms across herself, knowing the force of the water would drive anyone down into the coral reef and smash them hard against it. She'd been caught once or twice on research trips by rogue waves and she'd never forget the pummeling they'd given her.

And she never went onto a reef with surf like this. The waves had to be thirty feet high.

Lab work was infinitely safer.

The trough of the wave passed over the spot, and the broken yellow board came to the surface again.

There was no sign of Brandon or the dragon. The water seethed, boiling like black ink. Another wave was rising high against the horizon.

"It's not easy to free the leash with the water pounding all around you," the guy beside her explained. "It's hard to even tell which way is up when you get slammed like that. It's all dark until the wave passes."

"No one survives three waves," Liz repeated, swallowing her fear.

The guy winced and nodded. "And that's if you don't hit your head."

The next wave slammed down hard, turning the area to froth. When the wave had passed, they all took steps closer to the water, straining to spot either surfer. There was no sign of them or the dragon, just that broken yellow board tugging at its tether.

The third wave crashed over the spot with ferocious strength. Liz felt the skepticism and uncertainty in the group, though none of them said anything more. The water seemed to agitate longer over the spot; then the part of the board that had been caught washed toward the beach. Had the leash broken?

A dark head appeared so abruptly that the surfer might have been flung from the bottom of the sea.

Liz had a pretty good idea what or who had tossed him to freedom.

The dragon appeared next, leaping into the sky and snatching up Matt on the way. His enormous black wings beat loudly, water falling from him like a shower of jewels, and he carried a struggling Matt to the beach. He set down the surfer without landing, then soared into the sky.

There was no sign of the cockiness Matt had shown the night before. He was shaking. There was blood on his temple, and his skin was pale beneath his tan.

The guys ran to help him. Matt's chest heaved, and suddenly he spewed forth a stream of ocean water. Then he sat down heavily in the last couple of inches of water and put his head in his hands. Liz could see that he was trembling from his ordeal.

The dragon was high in the sky, flying west.

The guy who had been talking to her went and picked up Brandon's board. He stared out at the water, his expression stricken, then rejoined the others. Two of the guys watched the dragon flying away.

Liz went one better.

She ran to her car and followed him.

Brandon had nearly killed his friend.

Matt had been so shocked by the sight of Brandon in dragon form that he had wiped out. He could easily have drowned.

Of course, he'd only seen Brandon in dragon form because the dragon was calling the shots. Brandon couldn't control his transformation. The dragon had decided to claim him and he hadn't been able to stop the change. He couldn't shift shape back to human form when he wanted to, like right now. He feared that he had only succeeded when he did because the dragon had let him do it.

And that wasn't good.

In fact, it was steadily getting worse.

His dragon wasn't just powerful; it was commanding him.

Brandon had been shocked to see Liz, both amazed

and awed that she had followed him. He'd been astounded to see the sparks flying from the ends of her hair and her eyes flashing just as they had the night before.

Hadn't the firestorm been satisfied? He'd certainly felt just as strong of a surge of desire when he'd seen her this time.

But the dragon had claimed that rush of power and used it against Brandon. The dragon had roared and Brandon had lost it, and the dragon claimed his body as he fell. It had fed off the anger of the sea, ocean and dragon urging each other to greater violence. The dragon had wanted vengeance on Matt for his scheme to target Liz, and, worse, had demanded that Brandon take a penance out of his friend's hide. He'd managed to resist the powerful urge to rip and shred, but only barely.

Probably only because Matt had wiped out.

No matter how he looked at it, Brandon was responsible for Matt's injury and it was only raw luck that his friend hadn't died. There was no way he was going to approach Liz when his dragon was running wild like this.

In fact, he knew he shouldn't be close to anybody in this state. He wasn't sure how to fix the situation, either. Had this change happened because of the firestorm? Was it both blessing and curse? He had to talk to Chen, but he couldn't risk being among people in Hale'iwa. Who knew what would set off his dragon? Of course, that was assuming that eventually the dragon let him shift back to human form.

Brandon was cursed.

Just like his dad.

His nature was evil.

Just as his mom had insisted.

He flew west, hating what he was and what he had inherited from his father. Their inner dragons weren't just primal beasts; they were wicked. How could any part of him want to see Matt dead?

The peninsula of Ka'ena Point stretched beneath him in the distance, a jagged point of ancient lava that ended in the sea. Legend insisted that this was where souls met eternity.

Brandon remembered the story and was tempted. He was ready for his soul to meet eternity. If he couldn't have a normal life, if he couldn't even be among people, he couldn't see the point in living. His affliction was only getting worse.

He was ready to jump off the point and let his dragon be smashed into the relentless surf of the sea. He was ready to see his dragon destroyed, even if he had to be destroyed with it. There was no hope for him or the future with his dragon out of control. The promise of the firestorm was a lie, just as it had been for his father.

It was when he glanced back at everything he'd leave behind that he saw the turquoise Mercedes barreling along the highway beneath him.

Liz.

Relief and trepidation rolled through Brandon in equal parts. He wanted to see her again, with all his heart. He wanted to talk to her. But he was afraid that his dragon might injure her.

All the same, just seeing her approach soothed his anger. He felt the fury of the dragon fade at the sight of her car, and just being close to her made his situation less terrifying. He could feel the blue shimmer that heralded his transformation and knew that he could do it.

Because Liz was close.

Brandon suddenly understood that Liz could help him. The gift of the firestorm was that her presence gave him more control over his dragon. She could be his salvation. Together they could defeat the dragon's terrifying force.

That candle in his darkness flickered to light again, and he dared once more to hope.

Did she know that he was a dragon shape shifter? Was that why she was following him? Brandon didn't believe it. If she'd guessed the truth, she would have been driving in the opposite direction, putting as much distance between them as possible. She'd do what his mom had done and banish him from her life.

He didn't want to deceive her, but he couldn't risk losing her.

He had to tell her the truth.

Right now.

The road pretty much ended where the state park began, and there was a gate to keep vehicles out. If Brandon went all the way to the point, Liz would have to walk in. The trail was rough and it could take her hours. If she'd followed the dragon this far, whatever her reason, Brandon guessed that she wouldn't give up and turn back.

He changed his course, aiming to land where the road disintegrated to rubble and potholes. He landed and shifted shape, just out of sight of where she'd have to park the car. He was so relieved to be back in human form that he could have wept. He heard the crunch of tires on gravel. He heard the engine shut off, then heard the door slam.

He had to risk losing Liz and trust in the future. He had to confess to her. The prospect terrified him, even though he knew it was the right thing to do.

And, really, if Liz turned away, his dragon would win. Everything was on the line.

As Liz walked closer, he felt his sense of control return and grow stronger. Brandon thought he had to stay away from Liz to ensure her safety, but, actually, he had to stay close to her to keep his dragon in check.

All he had to do was convince Liz to keep him in her life. She came around the corner, her eyes flashing with the anger that made her look incandescent, and he wasn't entirely sure he'd have a chance to do that.

Liz saw the dragon land, just past the barrier that blocked the rough road. She parked at the end of the highway, where there was a notice that the area beyond the gate was a state park. How far into the park was he? How far would she have to hike? What would she find when she reached him? She had no gear, much less any supplies, and spent a moment considering the wisdom of entering the park to meet a dragon alone.

But the dragon was Brandon.

And she knew he'd never hurt her.

Even if she felt like hurting him, or at least yelling at him, given that he'd gone out into that dangerous surf. What had he been thinking? And why had he shifted shape in front of his friends like that?

He'd saved people this morning, though. Had he anticipated that Matt would wipe out and nearly drown? Did dragons have foresight?

Liz had a thousand questions. She'd come this far and she wasn't going back without some answers.

Whatever they might be.

She rolled up the windows and locked the car, regretted her flip-flops, then slung her purse over her shoulder and headed onto the trail.

The path clung to the rocky coast and was breathtakingly beautiful. There was almost a straight drop to the sea on one side, and Liz could see those furious waves slamming against the coast below her. They were beautiful from this safe distance, the way they cast spray into the air like diamonds and swirled in magnificent shades of blue.

The ocean stretched off, seemingly forever, and the wind was warm. The hill rose high and rocky on the other side of the path. The land was arid, the vegetation here sparse and tough. She should have had water and boots, and hoped that Brandon was close.

Liz rounded a kink in the path and stopped cold.

Brandon was on the trail just ahead of her. He looked exhausted and wary, his wet suit and hair were still wet, and he didn't even have flip-flops.

He studied her in silence. She sensed that he was uncertain of what she would say or do, but the intensity of his gaze hinted that his feelings hadn't changed. That put a lump in her throat.

She'd been right to follow him.

And her relief that he was—mostly—okay weakened her knees.

"What were you even doing in that surf?" she said when he didn't say anything, and heard her voice rise. "I don't know whether to kiss you or chew you out."

Brandon almost smiled. "I vote for option number one." He still didn't come closer, as if he thought she was unpredictable. "And it's a long story. I'll tell it to you if you'll hear me out."

But Liz already knew part of the story. "You're a dragon shape shifter," she said. "One of the *Pyr*."

Relief lit his eyes. "You know!"

"I guessed."

"But you're here." This seemed to astonish him.

"Why wouldn't I be?"

Brandon gave a hoot of joy and flung his fists into the air. He laughed as he scooped her up and swung her around in triumph. Liz couldn't help but smile at the exuberance of his reaction. "You're here! You're not afraid of me."

So that was it.

He kissed her, quickly but thoroughly, leaving Liz

flustered and flushed. The man could have invented kissing, he did it so well, and her body responded to his touch as surely as it had that first time.

She still couldn't resist him. She locked her arms around his neck and kissed him back, letting him taste her relief and gratitude.

Several moments later, he lifted his head and smiled down at her. "I can't believe it. How'd you figure it out?"

"I never saw both of you at the same time. That made no sense." She slid her hands over his shoulders, unable to stop touching him. He felt so warm and solid and strong. "The sheets were warm this morning, you were gone, but the dragon was in my room. There was no ferry to the island after ours, but I saw a dragon in flight. Then you turned up." She met his gaze. "Plus there was that bit at the beach just now."

"So you knew even before you came after me?"

"I wasn't positive."

He laughed and kissed her again. His eyes sparkled like sunlight on the waves, and Liz couldn't help but be infected by his mood.

"I don't know why you're so surprised," she said. "I came after you to check that you were okay. You were gone, and even though the most logical conclusion was that you were the dragon, I needed to know for sure. The building collapsed, but they didn't find any bodies." She exhaled, remembering her fear, and tightened her grip on his shoulders. "I had to know that you were okay."

Brandon's expression filled with wonder. "You're amazing," he whispered, then framed her face in his hands and kissed her again.

Liz didn't understand why he thought as much, but there were better things to do than talk. Brandon deepened his kiss and Liz opened her mouth to him, pulling him closer. She wanted to feel his body against hers. She wanted to touch him all over. His hands slid under her shirt and he unfastened her bra to caress her breasts. His palms were warm and his touch was mesmerizing. Liz arched her back and moaned when he broke his kiss.

"It's happening again," he said, looking dazed.

"What is?"

"My heartbeat—it synchronizes with yours." He lifted her hand and flattened her palm against his chest, trapping her hand under his own. He smiled down at her as she felt their hearts beating in unison. "It makes me dizzy," he said with a grin that made her mouth go dry. "Like you're a drug and I can't get enough."

Liz knew exactly what he meant. "Is the firestorm supposed to create an addiction?" she teased, and he laughed.

"Maybe."

She stretched up and kissed him, leaving her hand under his. She felt his heart skip a beat and hers do the same; then he caught her closer with a groan.

"Maybe we should find somewhere more private," he murmured against her throat. Liz pulled back so that she could look up at his face. His eyes were glinting, lit with a wickedness that made her heart beat faster.

"First you owe me an explanation," she said sternly. "You never told me what you were doing out there. Surfing when the waves are that high is crazy."

Brandon shook his head. "It wasn't crazy. This morning, my dragon was responding to the surf. It was raging and violent and wanting to destroy everything it could." He frowned. "In the past, physical exertion—like surfing—has been a way to keep my dragon in his place. I thought I could beat it back if I surfed. I thought that if I could tame it again, I could come back to see you. I thought we could have a chance of a future."

Liz was relieved by his concern. He wanted to be in charge of his unpredictable dragon.

His eyes glinted and she saw his competitiveness and his confidence. "I wanted to dominate it once and for all."

"But you didn't."

His eyes darkened with concern and he held her a little tighter. "It's getting stronger and that frightens me, Liz. I couldn't shift back this morning after the earthquake. That's why I had to leave you. It shouldn't be that way, but I wasn't in control." He nodded toward the ocean. "I wasn't in control out there, either. It took charge and compelled me to shift."

Liz swallowed, seeing how much that troubled him. "But you've shifted back now. What changed?"

He smiled at her so warmly that her heart skipped a beat. "You. You changed everything. I thought this morning that I had to get away from you, to keep you safe, but, actually, I have more control over the dragon when you're close." He bent and brushed his lips across hers so gently that Liz yearned for more. "Maybe staying with you can keep the dragon from ruining everything."

"I don't understand."

"That's what happened to my parents." Brandon frowned, but didn't release her from his embrace. "Being *Pyr* runs in families. My dad is a dragon shifter, too. My mom told him he was a monster and that his powers were evil. They split up." His smile was cautious and his gaze searching. "You can imagine what she said when I came into my powers at fifteen."

"You're not a monster," Liz insisted.

"You sound sure."

"I am." She reached up and kissed his cheek. She heard him catch his breath and looked into his eyes.

"I can't believe you're here," he murmured. His gaze was so filled with admiration that Liz had to kiss him again. Moments later, they parted, and Liz knew she wasn't the only one who wanted more.

Brandon nuzzled the side of her neck and kissed her earlobe, his touch making Liz dizzy. "Is there a blanket in that car?" he whispered in her ear.

"Why?" Liz sounded breathless even to herself.

"I want to make sure my dragon stays put." Brandon had that mischievous glint in his eyes again and looked even more sexy with his hair so tousled from

Liz's fingers. His hands were setting her skin on fire, distracting her so much that Liz had problems thinking straight.

"How is a blanket going to help you surf?"

"When I surf, I'm so focused on the physical challenge that my dragon is silenced. That's why I surf a lot." His smile broadened as he held her gaze. "I'm thinking of another physical challenge that might push the dragon even farther back into his cave." He arched a brow, looking so unpredictable and sexy that Liz couldn't resist him. "Interested in doing a little experiment?"

Liz laughed. Brandon ducked his head beneath the hem of her shirt, cupped her breast, and took her nipple in his mouth. He touched her as if he had to persuade her to agree with his plan, but Liz was too busy enjoying his caress to set him straight. She gasped as Brandon grazed her nipple with his teeth. She ran her hands through his hair and held him closer, wanting more. He unfastened her jeans and slid one hand beneath her panties, his fingers caressing her wet heat.

"Who needs a blanket?" she managed to whisper, and Brandon chuckled against her skin. He scooped her up and tossed her over his shoulder, heading off the path and up the hill. "Hey! I can walk."

"Think of it as a favor to me," he teased. "Physical exertion. You're helping me with my dragon one more time."

Liz laughed despite herself. "So this is for the greater good?"

"I can't think of a better reason. Can you?" He stopped at the crest of the hill and turned around to face the sea. There was more wind here and a greater sense of solitude.

Brandon caught her around the waist and lowered her to her feet, letting her slide down the length of him. Liz felt muscles and solid heat every inch of the way and was smiling by the time they were nose to nose. She let her flip-flops fall off when he held her there. She was crushed against Brandon's chest and his eyes were glowing. She thought that things couldn't get more perfect.

He leaned toward her, his expression sultry, and she was more than ready for another simmering kiss.

But Brandon screamed and convulsed in pain.

The transformation happened faster than ever before, and this time, it attacked Brandon without any warning. The shimmer was firing through his body before he had any inkling that it was coming. He felt a stabbing pain in his chest as he flung Liz away from himself.

He had to ensure that he didn't hurt her, even inadvertently.

He roared in fury as the change claimed him and the dragon seized the upper hand. This was wrong! He should be in control! How could the dragon be calling the shots?

Brandon was livid that the curse of his blood should betray him—and attempt to ruin everything. Pain seared the spot where he was missing a scale, and he raged dragonfire at the sky in frustration. What was wrong?

How could everything be screwed up now, when everything he wanted was within reach with Liz? How could the dragon fuck with him like this?

Brandon wasn't supposed to let humans see him shift shape. He knew that, but his dragon had apparently forgotten.

And he really hadn't wanted Liz to see the change. Even if she was good with the concept or with his having both forms, even if she believed that he wasn't a monster, the sight of his physical transformation might have changed her mind.

It had changed his mom's mind.

Brandon turned to face her warily, uncertain what to expect. She had fallen backward and had her hands braced against the ground behind her. Her hair was disheveled, but her gaze was locked steadily upon him. She looked surprised but not freaked.

Curious.

The dragon's fury dimmed to a simmer.

When Liz smiled tentatively, Brandon couldn't believe his luck. The firestorm had brought him a gift beyond all expectation.

"Done?" Liz asked, and he nodded. He was amazed that she could take this in stride. Even though he'd known that Liz wasn't like other women, this was more than he'd ever expected.

He didn't answer her aloud, though. He didn't want to spook her by speaking while in dragon form.

Although Liz didn't appear to be frightened at all. She got up and brushed off her jeans. "That was something," she said. Then her eyes narrowed. "You didn't choose to change, did you?"

Brandon shook his head.

She nodded, then her gaze turned assessing as she surveyed him. "You're bleeding," she said, and pointed to his chest. "Is that normal?"

Brandon looked down and saw the blood running from a fresh wound. It looked as if he had been cut— or as if one missing scale had just been pulled out of his hide, taking a chunk of flesh with it. The blood flowed red and warm over his scales.

He shook his head again. How could he be wounded? Was it pain that had prompted the shift? But what had injured him?

Liz approached him and he felt the comforting presence of the blue shimmer. With every step she took, he was more confident that he could change back to his human form. He didn't want to startle her, though.

Liz touched his skin beside the wound, and Brandon flinched involuntarily. To his relief, his dragon's snarl was a more relaxed growl, the beast responding favorably to Liz's presence and touch.

She was the key to his salvation.

"Can you shift back?" she asked. "I want to see whether you have this injury in both forms, maybe treat it." She winced. "It looks serious."

Brandon nodded agreement. He put out one claw

and she put her hand in his claw, understanding him so well that he knew she was perfect for him. She fingered his talon, checking it out, then smiled at him. The contrast between her slender fingers and his sharp claw said everything that needed to be said about her trust in him.

"Right beside you," she said with such resolve that he knew he'd be able to change. She gripped his talon tightly.

Brandon closed his eyes and the blue shimmer was as accessible as it had been once upon a time. He summoned it, and it followed his bidding. The change rocked through him, stretching his muscles and sinews, firing his blood, and leaving him shaken with its power.

He opened his eyes, glad to find Liz's hand still in his own. "You're not afraid." He was still amazed by her.

She shook her head and smiled. "You've never hurt me. You saved me this morning, in fact."

"But the dragon is violent. . . ."

"Not toward me. And not toward that woman and her child, or even Matt. The *Pyr* are supposed to be the custodians of the earth and the defenders of mankind, you know. Maybe your dragon means well but can't express it."

Brandon shook his head. "No. It's violent and vicious. I've got to ditch it."

She studied him for a moment and he sensed she had something to say. Then her gaze fell to his chest and he saw the blood that was soaking through the wet suit. Kira was going to kill him! "How do you get out of this thing?"

Brandon reached back and unfastened the zipper that ran down his spine. He peeled the wet suit off his shoulders and wiped off the blood with his fingers. His gut was bruised in several places, and Liz winced at the sight.

"From the surf?"

"From someone kicking me," Brandon said, grinning at her surprise. "Hard."

"I did that to you?" When he nodded, she smiled back. "Sorry. I don't usually find myself in a dragon's clutches."

"Get used to it," he teased impulsively.

She blushed as she rummaged in her purse. She came up with a first aid kid and set to work, staunching the bleeding. The woman was full of surprises.

"You always travel with a first aid kit?"

"Yes, actually, I do. Maybe that's going to be useful when I'm with you." She touched his bruises with a careful fingertip. "So, injuries remain with you when you change forms? And these three spots are where you're missing scales?"

Brandon nodded.

"What about your clothes?"

"We fold them away. Fast. It's a secret."

Liz gave him a considering glance. "Why?"

Brandon shrugged. "There's an old story that if someone seizes the clothes of a dragon when he shifts, that person can keep the dragon from shifting back. I'm not sure if it's true, but my dad was always insistent that it had to be done fast." He grimaced. "It was pretty much the only thing he taught me about being *Pyr*."

"That sounds like selkies and their seal skins," Liz mused nodding. "What happened to these scales? Do you just lose them as part of your body's routine?"

Brandon shook his head. "When new ones grow, they form under the old ones. The old ones are shed only when the new ones are completely grown."

Liz nodded. "So there are never any gaps in your armor. Okay, that makes sense. But these?"

"I traded them."

Liz looked up with astonishment. "*Traded* them? You mean, you pulled them out on purpose and gave them away?"

He nodded, sensing her displeasure but not understanding its reason.

She stepped back and put her hands on her hips. Her eyes were doing that sparky thing again. "Even knowing that story?"

"It's a myth!"

"You don't know that! Your dad taught you only one thing, so it must be important!"

It did make sense when she put it that way.

"He wasn't exactly a good example to me. Maybe he was just making demands. Rules. He loves rules."

Liz's lips tightened. "What did you trade them for? What could possibly be worth mutilating yourself?"

"It wasn't like that! I thought they would grow back," Brandon said. "They always did before."

She glared at him, arching a brow.

"The powder," he admitted. "There's this powder that this friend of mine uses. He thinks it's a restorative, like multivitamins, but it has helped me to control my dragon. Pulling scales seemed to weaken the dragon, too. I traded for the powder."

"Holy shit," Liz said and turned to walk away, her disgust clear.

"I thought they would grow back!" he shouted, but she dropped her forehead to her hand. "What's going on? I thought it was no big deal." His voice rose. "I thought it was creating possibilities for me and making things happen!"

When Liz spun to face him, Brandon knew he was wrong.

She was scared.

Why?

Chapter 7

A binding spell.

Liz felt sick. Someone had cast a binding spell over Brandon. He couldn't control his dragon because somebody else was in charge of that side of his nature. And the spellcaster had succeeded because he or she had a physical part of Brandon to anchor the spell. Nail clippings, blood, hair, or scales; a physical souvenir from the victim was critical to a successful binding spell.

The sorcerer had chosen scales because the real target was the dragon.

She had sensed dark magic, evil magic. She hadn't expected to be engulfed in the world of her childhood again, or to need all those lessons she'd been taught. She didn't want to revisit the past or reopen those old memories.

But she wanted to help Brandon.

Liz was pretty sure that Brandon was bleeding because that scale had been destroyed. It all made a kind of sense that had once been so familiar to her as to be second nature.

The mark on her arm made Liz reluctant to embrace the realm of magic again. It reminded her that there could be a price to pay—and soon. Even so, there had to be a way to break the spell that had snared Brandon—if they could get the scales, maybe, or if she could find the scientific basis for whatever was happening to him.

The other *Pyr* might be able to help him. They might recognize this situation and be able to deal with it themselves.

Liz turned to find Brandon watching her in obvious confusion, waiting for her to explain. How could he not know more about his own nature? How could his father have not taught him more?

"So, you traded three scales, thinking they'd grow back. Have they grown back at all?" she asked, already knowing the answer. A binding spell sapped the power of the victim, and a lack of routine regenerative growth on the body was the first sign of the spell's power.

Brandon shook his head.

"When did you last get a haircut?" she asked, her mouth dry.

"What?"

"When?"

"I don't know. It's been a while, actually."

"When did you trim your nails last?"

His grin flashed. "What is this—a personal-hygiene test?"

"When?" Liz barked.

"Whoa! You're all flashy again."

"What do you mean?"

His gaze roved over her and he looked awestruck. "There are sparks coming from the ends of your hair. It looks like you're filled with fire! Or maybe becoming a flame."

Liz averted her gaze, shocked that her true nature was so visible to him. "I'm just angry because it's important," she said, not wanting to talk about her challenges just yet.

Brandon wasn't the only one who wasn't fully in control of his powers, which wasn't the most reassuring realization possible.

Brandon looked at his fingernails. "Come to think of it, I haven't had to bother with them. I thought they were growing more slowly because it was winter."

There *was* a binding spell on Brandon. Who had cast it? What was the spellcaster's plan?

She'd given away her own powers, but they'd returned. Were they strong enough that she could save Brandon? Would that make her stronger or weaker before her own test?

Maybe she could help him with plain old logic and human intervention.

Liz had to try that first.

"Okay. Let's go back to the beginning. Tell me everything. You came out here today because you couldn't shift back by choice, right?"

"Right. And I left you this morning for the same

reason." He shuddered. "It's awful, Liz. The dragon wants to destroy everything. I can barely keep it from doing so."

That was the will of the spellcaster. He or she wanted Brandon to be destructive. "No," Liz said firmly. "The dragon is a part of you, and your giving nature will follow you between forms."

"No," Brandon argued. "The dragon is evil. Mine is stronger than I am now, and it's violent." His gaze was tormented. "I don't want to hurt anybody, but the dragon isn't giving me a lot of choice."

Liz's heart skipped a beat, but then she frowned. "Remember that you saved me this morning in the earthquake. And you saved that woman and her child." She gestured back along the shore. "And just now, you saved Matt. Your dragon has done good things today, no matter what you think of it."

"But not by choice." Brandon's lips tightened. "Matt would never have wiped out if he hadn't been surprised by the sight of my dragon. He saw the dragon only because the dragon wanted to rip his throat out. And he would never have been out surfing today if I hadn't tried to force down my dragon by surfing myself."

"Your dragon is being controlled by someone else," Liz insisted. "It's acting on that person's malice."

Brandon stared at her. "What?"

"It's a binding spell. You've been enchanted, and the scales anchored the spell." She gestured to his wound. "I'll bet that one of them was just destroyed."

"Like a voodoo doll?"

"Similar. Who did you give the scales to?"

Brandon lifted his hands. "Wait a minute. He's a friend of mine! You're saying he's some kind of warlock or something. That's crazy!"

Liz looked pointedly at the wound.

"Maybe someone stole them from him." Brandon frowned when Liz said nothing. "How do you know about binding spells, anyway? Are you some kind of a witch?"

Liz changed the subject with force, her anger simmering. "You don't believe me? Then let's walk through the evidence."

"Easy, Liz. Don't smite me for being skeptical."

Liz took a deep breath. "When was the first time you couldn't control the dragon?"

Brandon thought for a moment. "Last night," he said. "I thought it was the firestorm."

"Or the eclipse," Liz suggested.

Brandon shook his head. "No. I've seen a bunch of those. I've surfed under the eclipse before, which is awesome. This never happened before."

"But the firestorm is supposed to be a good thing."

He nodded. "A gift. Plus I can only be in control when you're around."

That was when Liz remembered something from the night before. "Matt had something of yours outside the restaurant."

Brandon's eyes lit. "That was the powder!"

"That you swapped your scales for?" At his nod,

Liz had a very bad feeling. "What exactly does the powder do?"

"Like I said, it's helped to keep my dragon contained in the past and brings me luck."

"What kind of luck?"

Brandon's grin flashed and he looked roguish. "Women. For some reason, it attracts them."

Liz couldn't imagine how Brandon thought he needed help to attract women. And she didn't appreciate the possibility of his having used magical powders to seduce her.

A firestorm that heralded a future together was fine. Coercion or potions to make her easy were not. Liz glared at him.

He must have seen a change in Liz's expression because he raised his hands in surrender. "No smiting! I was determined to not use it last night, not once I saw you. I knew, Liz, that you were special. And you are."

Liz was relieved. "But Matt spread it in the air, anyway."

Brandon winced. "The thing is that I wanted to give it back to my friend. I thought he needed it more than me. He wasn't doing so well when I saw him yesterday, so I'd intended to give it back to him today." His expression turned rueful. "Provided I could think of a way to do that without insulting him. But now it's scattered to the winds."

Liz remembered the sight of Brandon when the powder had taken flight, the way he had shimmered and his eye had changed. The powder had triggered the spellcaster's control over Brandon's dragon. His friend and source of the powder had to somehow be involved with the spellcaster, maybe against his own awareness.

Or maybe this so-called friend was the spellcaster.

What was that powder?

She forced herself to think about biology and physical responses to substances. Anything was better than thinking about magic—and magic could have a base in biology. If she knew exactly what the powder was, maybe she could break the binding spell. Maybe there was an antidote.

"Was that the first time that you nearly shifted involuntarily? After Matt released the powder?"

Brandon frowned, then met her gaze again. "Yes. I had to fight the dragon all the way back to Hale'iwa."

Liz tried to think of it in biological terms, even though she guessed this was the dark magic she'd sensed. "There are many, many substances that act in a beneficial way in small quantities but are toxic in large quantities. That's true for all species. What if this powder is a substance that unleashes your dragon?"

"Like a drug it reacts to." His eyes lit at the thought. "So, it'll wear off, like it always does. It just might take longer because there was more of it."

"Where do you get it? Can you get more?"

"I don't want more!"

"For testing purposes. We have to have some to figure out what it is." Liz nodded. "Then we can ensure that you avoid it." She intuitively knew it wasn't the whole answer, but she would try every possibility before she welcomed magic back into her life.

"I could ask Chen for more," Brandon said. "But he said it was the last of it."

"Maybe he's holding out on you. Maybe he kept a bit back." Liz shrugged. "If not, maybe there's enough residue in the vial for testing."

Brandon nodded. "I left it at my place when I went back to get a board."

"Good. Then you need to talk to some of the other *Pyr*," Liz said, certain this was the most obvious choice.

Brandon took affront at this suggestion, much to her surprise. "What for?"

"To ask about their firestorms."

He shook his head. "I don't talk to other *Pyr*."

"Well, maybe you should. They might be able to give you some advice."

"Never!"

Liz was surprised by his vehemence. "That makes no sense...."

"It makes perfect sense! I'm not going to let those people into my life. Into *our* lives. Forget it."

This was the last thing she'd expected him to be stubborn about.

"How else are you going to learn to understand your nature?" Liz demanded, propping her hands on her hips to confront him. "You can find out about their experiences and learn from that. Just because you and your dad don't get along doesn't mean that all dragons are bad. Maybe what you're going through is typical...."

His eyes flashed with unexpected heat. "Liz, you don't understand. This thing is evil. It's nasty and it's bloodthirsty, and if you think I'm going to hang out with a bunch of dragons who are just the same, even in the interest of understanding my nature better, you can think again. I'm not going to put you at risk, not now that I've found you."

"Then what's your plan?"

His lips set. "I want to be rid of it forever. I just have to figure out how."

"Nobody can change what they are," Liz argued. "Your physiology isn't going to change just because you want it to."

"Then I'll make it change!"

"It's a binding spell. We'll break the spell...."

"I don't believe in magic, Liz. I believe in what I'm feeling. This thing is inside me and it's baying for blood. I'm not going to play." Brandon jabbed his finger at his own chest. "This is a contest and only one of us can win. That means the other loses. But if the dragon is going to win, I'll take us both out instead. That's how much this matters."

He stalked toward her car, leaving Liz with the urge to shake him. He wouldn't be able to change his nature. He had to regain control of his dragon and destroy the binding spell, and the best chance of that, in her opinion, was to talk to others. If there was dragon magic at work, they were the most likely to know the answers.

She was tempted to quote her mother, which just made her more angry.

"How are you going to make it change?" she demanded, hearing her frustration.

"I'll figure it out!"

"Or commit suicide instead," she yelled back at him. "Good plan!"

Brandon pivoted to face her, his gaze simmering. She saw surprise light his features, but she didn't care. She stormed toward him, shaking her finger at him.

"You said that my presence makes it easier for you to control the dragon," she said. "Maybe walking away from me right now isn't the smartest choice you could make."

His gaze danced over her, and she saw his anger fade. "You're literally spitting sparks," he said with awe, lifting a hand toward her as if warming it before a fire. "I thought the firestorm was satisfied."

"What are you talking about?"

"Look at you. You're on fire again! Your eyes are flashing and there are sparks flying in every direction. This is different from the firestorm. This is what I saw when you turned up on the beach and just a few minutes ago, too." He looked into her eyes, his own bright with curiosity, and she had the sense he could see right into her soul. "So, come on, Liz. Tell me. What *are* you?"

Liz panicked. She'd been a freak in high school and she knew how that story had ended. The mark on her arm seemed to itch. Her mother had died because of her.

She wouldn't put Brandon at risk.

*   *   *

Liz took a step back from Brandon, and he could see that she was frightened. She spoke curtly, and the light that had illuminated her was gone—as if she'd banished it on purpose. "I'm a marine biologist; that's all. I'm just mad because you're not being sensible."

"No." That wasn't the truth and Brandon knew it. "No, this is more than anger. There's something special about you." He smiled because she looked so freaked out. He was hoping to reassure her. "More special than I already thought. It's how you know about spells. You must be some kind of witch. Tell me."

"No!" Liz cried and headed for driver's-side door. "There is *nothing* special or unusual about me. You're seeing things!" She hauled open the door with a savage gesture, as if she couldn't put distance between them fast enough.

What was going on?

"You feel pretty strongly about that." Brandon said softly.

"I do." She gave him a hot look, one that showed him her fear. Her voice rose in challenge. "Do you want a ride back to Haleʻiwa or not?"

Brandon leaned on the hood of the car with both fists, his gaze unswerving. "You know my big secret," he said quietly. "Maybe you should tell me yours. Maybe it would make you feel better about it." He smiled just a little, already guessing that it wouldn't reassure her. "Maybe trust is the foundation of the firestorm."

"I don't have a secret," Liz insisted, and got into the car. She slammed the car door. "I do, though, have an appointment in Kaneʻohe. Ride or not?"

When she started the engine, Brandon got into the car. He had no doubt that she would leave him behind when she was this upset, but he wanted to know why. She backed out and turned around, never glancing his way, and he noticed the nervousness in her gestures.

He also saw the symbol on her upper right arm. He was sure it hadn't been there the night before—he'd caressed every inch of her. It wasn't a tattoo. It looked like a brand. But it was fully healed.

Did it have something to do with her being so scared?

He let her drive for a moment, then spoke in measured tones, returning to their earlier topic of discussion. "Okay, you're right. Being with you does help me control my dragon. So the firestorm can't be what affected the dragon's power. The firestorm—and you—are challenging the dragon." He turned to her, noticing how she deliberately stared straight ahead. "You can help me because you're special—and maybe I can help you in exchange. But only if you talk to me."

Her lips tightened, and he knew her answer before she even spoke. "Let's find your friend. I think we should get your scales back and learn more about this powder."

"Sounds like the subject is closed."

"It is."

"Is that because of this?" Brandon touched the

new mark on her arm with a gentle fingertip, and she flinched. "Does it hurt?"

"I don't want to talk about it. The less you know, the better."

Brandon didn't agree, although he guessed he wasn't going to get anywhere in this argument right now. "You're going to have to tell somebody, Liz. And if you're going to tell anybody, I think I'm your best choice."

She flicked a frightened glance his way.

"Think about it. I know what it's like to have a nasty secret, one that could maybe ruin everything if people knew. We already have this connection, and your power is somehow feeding mine. That tells me that we need to work through this together."

If anything, his words seemed to scare her even more. Her knuckles were white on the steering wheel and he could feel the agitation in her pulse.

What was she afraid of?

"I'll wait, though," he added calmly.

"Don't hold your breath," Liz murmured.

Brandon looked out the window, watching the surf and drumming his fingers on the car door. "Okay, we have to figure out what to tell everyone who was at the beach."

"They'll be looking for a corpse," Liz agreed, and he had the sense that she was glad to be talking about something else.

"So, maybe you found me," Brandon suggested. "There's a riptide on that beach. You could have found me all bashed up and washed down the coast."

"What about the dragon?"

"What *about* the dragon?" He granted her an intent look, not appreciating that she wanted to share his secret with the world when she wouldn't share hers with him. Liz held his gaze for a moment, then turned back to the road. Brandon felt his lips tighten but he again spoke calmly. "Let's pretend we know even less than they do."

"It's not much of a strategy."

"The alternative is telling them the truth about me, and I am not going there." He gave her a hot look. "You, of all people, should understand that."

Liz blushed. "You don't understand what's at stake."

"Because you won't tell me."

There was silence between them then, and Brandon wondered if her hesitation was due to doubts about his intentions.

He cleared his throat, determined to straighten that out immediately. "Listen, Liz, I believe everything I said about forever and kismet and the firestorm." He spoke softly but with conviction. "But that can only happen if I'm whole. I'm not going to risk the dragon taking a toll from you, ever."

Liz kept driving, but he saw her swallow.

"We can do it together, Liz," he said. "The firestorm is the only good thing about this dragon stuff, and it's the key to solving everything. We have to work together, which means you need to believe in the future, as well."

She said nothing and he knew she was really frightened.

"My dad said that a firestorm brings a *Pyr* the woman he needs to make him more than he already is."

"I thought your parents split up."

"They did." Brandon turned to look out the window, and he felt Liz steal a glance at him. "But he told me he would never love anyone else, no matter how long he lived." He glanced back at her suddenly and caught her gaze. Her eyes widened as she stared at him, and he knew he must look intent and determined.

He felt her pulse flutter.

She wasn't immune to him. She believed in the firestorm, too—but she was afraid that whatever she feared was stronger than both of them.

That just meant that Brandon had to figure out the truth and show her that she was wrong. He stole another glance at that symbol, ensuring that he would remember it.

There had to be a way to look it up. Maybe its meaning would tell him what he needed to know.

When Liz parked in front of the beach bar where Brandon's buddies always hung out, Brandon made a show of getting out of the back of Liz's car, just as they had agreed. He acted as if he was more beat up than he was, but the sight of him even pretending to be injured was troubling to Liz.

As he'd predicted, he was spotted instantly and was immediately surrounded by his concerned friends.

Liz rubbed the mark on her arm and hung back, worried. Was she doomed to lose every single person in her life she cared about? As soon as she'd had the thought, Liz couldn't shake it. It couldn't be a coincidence that the first time she'd allowed herself to care for someone, the mark of her impending test had appeared.

Could she help Brandon defeat his dragon, only to lose him?

The mark on her skin felt like it was burning.

No. She had to face her test alone and pass it. She had to leave Brandon to ensure that he wasn't at risk. That was the only way to keep him safe and to guarantee that they even had a chance at a future.

Liz became aware of someone watching her and looked around. There was a dark-haired guy across the street, sitting on the steps of a porch. He had his elbows braced on his knees and his fingers steepled together as he watched.

Without blinking.

There was a knowing smile on his lips.

He could have been a statue, he was so still.

Liz turned her back on him and tried to ignore the weight of his gaze. Curious strangers weren't her problem right now.

"Brandon! We thought you were a goner!" one of Brandon's friends said with obvious relief. "You okay?"

"What about the dragon?" the blond friend who'd

been with Brandon the night before asked. "Did he kick your ass?"

Brandon shook his head. "I don't know about a dragon. I don't remember much. Just water."

Despite her dismay, Liz almost smiled. He was as terrible a liar as she'd expected. He was genuine, right to the heart. She ached a bit with the certainty that she had to walk away from him, even for a short period of time. Her mother's test had occurred within three days of the mark's appearance. Would Liz's come that soon? In a way, she hoped so. In another, she was terrified of failure.

Maybe she could help Brandon before she left him.

Brandon shuddered as his friends looked on. "Lots of water." He straightened and ran a hand through his hair. He couldn't look any of them in the eye as he told his false story. "Then I got hauled underwater. Thank goodness Liz found me." He gestured to her, and his friends nodded acknowledgment of her.

"Liz, this is Dylan," he indicated the blond friend. "And Matt." This was the dark-haired guy who'd tried to buy her a drink. "Rick." This was the guy with dreadlocks who had talked to Liz at the beach. "And Kira." The petite woman was striking, with silky dark hair that hung to her hips and bright green eyes. They were all stunningly attractive people, toned and tanned. Liz felt pale and out of shape.

"You were at the beach," Dylan said.

Liz nodded. "Looking for Brandon." She smiled at him but knew her smile didn't reach her eyes. "I didn't think he'd be trying to drown." He watched her, his intensity reminding her of the truth of his nature. There were moments when his dragon nature seemed so obvious.

"It must have been the dragon that pulled you underwater," Matt said with conviction.

"Or a riptide," Kira interjected, her skepticism clear. "You better not have damaged that wet suit."

"It's got some blood on it, but I think I can wash it out." Brandon straightened and turned, letting Kira check it out. "Kira had the wet suit made for me, to advertise her new line of gear," he told Liz, then he grinned at Kira. "I thought I just had to keep from dying in it," he teased her.

"You could have been killed out there today!" Kira punctuated her words with a punch on his shoulder. "What a dumb-ass thing to do." Matt started to say something, but Kira turned on him. "And you're no better. You're both stupid, maybe too stupid to live." She turned and walked away, anger in every line of her body.

Matt fluttered his hand against his chest. "I can tell you love me, Kira!"

"Dream on!" she shouted at him, her lips curling in a reluctant smile.

"Oh, I do, Banzai Baby. I do!" Matt shouted, and Kira blushed. She made a dismissive wave and got into her car, then drove away.

Brandon took Liz's hand in his and gave her a smile. She fought her instinctive urge to respond to him. Maybe it would be easier for him to let her go if he thought she didn't care. He had a persistence about him that meant he wouldn't take no for an answer.

And Liz loved that.

"You should have been a goner," Dylan said. "I mean, you never came up for air."

"Like I said, it was a blue crush," Brandon insisted. "I managed to get the leash off, then was pulled under by the water." Liz had a feeling that his explanation wasn't going to fly.

"Or the dragon," Rick said.

Brandon's expression changed slightly, and Liz sensed his fear that his story wouldn't hold together. She couldn't think of what to say. Sadly, they were both lousy liars.

To Liz's surprise, it was Matt who gave credence to the story.

"Brandon can always hold his breath the longest," Matt reminded them. "Don't you remember the last time we swam underwater with rocks? He went three times farther than any of us."

"You're right," Rick said. "It's eerie how long you can hold your breath. I'd forgotten that you were superhuman." They laughed together and teased Brandon a bit.

"Like Kira said, it must have been a riptide," Liz said, trying to encourage this acceptance. "Aren't there a lot of them around here?" The guys nodded agreement and their skepticism visibly faded. "I found him down the coast, washed up on the beach like old seaweed."

The guys laughed at that and nudged Brandon.

"Puking salt water, probably," Matt teased with a grin.

"Always a good opener," Dylan said, flicking Liz a significant glance.

Brandon grinned back at Matt. "You have words with a rock or something?" he asked, indicating the gash on Matt's temple.

"An argument with the reef. I lost." Matt shrugged. "My leash was snagged on the reef and I couldn't get to the surface. I couldn't reach my ankle to unfasten it, either. If it hadn't been for that dragon, I would have been a goner."

"Did you really see a dragon?" Brandon asked, feigning skepticism. "Because I never did." The assertion rang with such insincerity that Liz winced.

And the tone of the conversation changed again.

"How could you not remember the dragon?" Rick demanded. "He was right there, and huge." He lifted his hands, mocking a dragon's pose. "Didn't you feel him pull you under?"

"It was the wave that took me under." Brandon scoffed. "What have you guys been smoking? You're seeing *dragons*?"

Dylan, meanwhile, roared back at Rick. "He could fly, too. Freaking awesome." He turned to Liz. "You're the one who followed the dragon. You saw him."

They all turned to face Liz, and she knew she'd

never be able to lie her way out of this corner. "I did," she admitted quietly, feeling Brandon's disapproval.

"Where'd he go?" Dylan asked.

"I don't know," she lied. "As soon as I saw Brandon, I pulled over. I lost sight of him then." She gestured vaguely. "He was headed toward that point."

To her dismay, they locked on to that detail.

"Ka'ena Point," Rick said. "It'd be a good place to hide out for a dragon. It's not very popular, and it's a bit wild."

"We should head out there," Dylan suggested, his eyes alight with the idea. "See if we can find him, get a closer look."

"I don't think that's a good plan," Brandon said. "You don't even know if there is a dragon."

"I do." Matt gave him a look.

"Be serious," Rick said. "We saw him. Just because you were too busy trying to die doesn't mean he wasn't there."

"But . . ." Brandon protested.

"I'm in," Matt said. "I want to see the dragon that saved my butt."

"Excellent!" Dylan said. "Let's go."

"But you took the Jeep in for repairs today," Matt said, and Dylan winced.

"Hey, can we use your car?" Rick asked Liz.

She shook her head. "No, sorry. It's not mine. I've got to get it back, actually." She glanced at her watch, thinking that would be the end of it. They wouldn't walk to the point.

"But we've got to find that dragon while we can," Matt insisted. "He might not stay there long."

"I don't think that's a good idea," Brandon said again. "I mean, if there is a dragon, he might breathe fire on you or something."

The guys laughed at this and ignored him. "You think he has treasure?" Rick asked. "Dragons are supposed to."

"Hey, you should ask that old guy you're always talking to," Dylan said to Brandon. "He goes on and on about dragons. He might know something more."

"He might give us some clues," Matt said. "Wasn't he here today?"

"Hey, hey!" Brandon interjected, his tone taking on a tinge of desperation. "Leave it alone. Let's focus on the competition, get a beer, celebrate our survival."

The guys looked at each other, then shook their heads as one. "I say we find a dragon instead," Dylan said, and the other two nodded vigorously. "Come on. We'll go borrow Kira's car."

Brandon flung Liz a panicked look. "They'll never give it up," he muttered, and she recognized that the competitive spirit that drove these surfers would manifest in other parts of their lives, too.

"You won't find a dragon at Ka'ena Point," a guy with a deep voice said, speaking with authority. Liz glanced up to find a muscled guy with dark hair and dark eyes leaning against the doorway to the bar. He was a bit shorter than Brandon, and older, too. She looked, but the guy who had been watching from the other side of the road had disappeared. This was a different guy.

Brandon bristled visibly, and when Liz glanced his way in confusion, she saw that his eye had changed to a red reptile eye. There was a shimmer of pale blue light silhouetting his body, competing with the indigo of his aura.

What was wrong?

Liz looked at the new arrival and guessed. He, too, was shimmering pale blue around his perimeter, on the cusp of change.

This guy was another *Pyr*.

Liz had wanted to find another dragon shape shifter so Brandon could ask for advice, but it looked like the dragon shape shifters had found Brandon.

She could only be glad of that. Maybe he'd get the help he needed.

But Brandon looked both livid and unwilling to accept help from this *Pyr*.

Brandon was startled by the new arrival's words. What made him think the dragon was his business? Or that he could interfere in their conversation?

When had he turned up? And why hadn't Brandon heard him coming or noticed him sooner? His dragon senses were sharper than human senses and he wasn't used to being surprised.

His dragon exhaled, a long, slow hiss of irritation, and Brandon guessed the truth.

He was *Pyr*.

He took a deep breath and smelled the truth of this *Pyr*'s nature, now that he was paying attention. What did he want? Nothing good, Brandon was sure. His dragon snarled, ready to rumble.

"What do you mean?" Dylan asked the new arrival. "Do you know where he went?"

"There was no dragon," the guy said, his voice low and melodic. There was something compelling about the way he spoke, and Brandon noticed that there were flames dancing in the pupils of his eyes.

Liz swore softly under her breath and turned her back on him.

Brandon looked between the two of them in confusion. What did those flames mean?

"What's with your eyes?" Dylan asked, stepping closer to the guy.

As if he were fascinated.

Or hypnotized.

The guy looked deeply into Dylan's eyes. He seemed to open his eyes even wider and he didn't blink, giving Dylan a clear view of those weird flames. "There was no dragon. You saw no dragon because there was no dragon."

Dylan shuddered. He swallowed, then touched his own forehead. He kept staring into the guy's eyes. "No dragon," he said softly, but his words lacked conviction.

"There's no such thing as a dragon," the guy insisted, that deep voice winding into Brandon's ears with persuasive power. He noticed that all three guys were staring at this new arrival, seeming to hang on his words. The flames in the guy's eyes grew brighter. They leaned closer to stare.

"No dragon," the new guy said.

"No dragon," the guys murmured in unison.

"No reason to go to Ka'ena Point," the new arrival said.

"No reason to go to Ka'ena Point," the guys agreed in a quiet chorus.

"Brandon was caught by a riptide," the guy said, and Brandon's friends repeated the statement. They sounded like zombies. In fact, they looked like zombies, staring at this new guy with such intensity. It was like he was hypnotizing them or something.

Liz was looking determinedly across the street. The line of her shoulders was stiff, though, and she was drumming her fingers on her elbow.

"Matt got lucky," the guy said, still speaking with deliberation. The guys repeated that, as well, heaving a collective sigh of relief. "Might as well have a beer," this new dragon suggested, and Brandon's friends agreed with that. The guy gestured to the bar and said the magic words that would get them moving. "I'll buy the first round."

Matt, Dylan, and Rick lunged into the bar like they hadn't had a beer in weeks. The dark-haired dragon nodded to the bartender, then turned back to Brandon.

"You're *Pyr*," Brandon accused.

He didn't answer, just stepped closer with delibera-tion. "You're supposed to beguile anyone who sees you shift," the guy said. His voice was soft, but there was power in it. He might not have been yelling, but Brandon knew he was getting shit.

"I don't know how to beguile," Brandon insisted.

"That's stupid. We all know how to do it. . . ."

"I don't want to know how to do it! Convincing people to believe things they don't want to believe is just wrong."

"Spellcasting," Liz said flatly. The guy flicked a look at her, and Brandon knew he saw the radiance in her eyes, too. He considered her for a moment, then looked back at Brandon.

"Not exactly," he said. "More like hypnosis. It works best if the person already wants to believe your suggestion."

Liz sniffed. "You're right. That's different."

It wasn't different enough, as far as Brandon was concerned.

The guy nodded and turned back to Brandon. "We have to talk."

"No. We don't have to talk. I don't want to hear anything you have to say."

"I was sent by the leader of the *Pyr* to help you. . . ."

"I don't want or need any help. Thanks."

"But your father . . ."

Brandon jabbed a finger through the air at the guy, interrupting him. "That you know my dad says nothing good about you, as far as I'm concerned. Leave me alone."

The guy's mouth tightened into a firm line. "The *Pyr* can help you."

"I don't want the kind of help you can give me. I'll solve this myself. Come on, Liz."

Liz held her ground, even when Brandon reached for her hand.

The guy studied Brandon for a long moment, so motionless that he couldn't have been anyone other than a dragon shifter. His eyes were very dark brown, almost fathomless. His expression was carefully neutral, and Brandon wondered whether this dragon shifter didn't know what to expect from him.

"Sloane Forbes," he said softly, but he offered his hand to Liz. "You must be the mate, if you'll forgive our archaic language."

She smiled tightly at Sloane, much to Brandon's dismay. "I'd expect the *Pyr* to have an old language." She indicated Brandon. "I'm glad you've come. We have a lot of questions."

"Hey, we do not," Brandon protested. "We can handle this ourselves."

"This is an opportunity," Liz said. When Brandon didn't reply, she kept talking to Sloane. "We had a firestorm last night."

Sloane nodded, eyeing the space between them. "And it's satisfied. Good." Brandon realized he'd been looking for the firestorm's sparks. "That's one fewer group of questions we'll need to answer."

"Why exactly are you here?" Brandon asked, recognizing that his tone sounded rude—or at least unwelcoming—and not really minding that.

Sloane didn't seem to mind, either. Or maybe he wasn't surprised. He smiled. "I'm the Apothecary of our kind. Our leader, Erik, believes you need to be healed, so he sent me to your firestorm."

"You can't heal what's wrong with me," Brandon said in a heated rush. "Unless you're going to cut my dragon out of my guts for good."

"Impossible," Sloane said, shaking his head. He studied Brandon again, and the younger *Pyr* wondered how much he could see.

Brandon gave Liz's hand an insistent tug. "Look, nice of you to drop by, and thanks for your help with the guys, but I don't need a dragon to fix what's wrong with me. I need to ditch the dragon, and I already know that you're not going to help me do that."

Brandon glanced across the bar and saw exactly the man he wanted to question. Chen! "Excuse me. I've got to meet a friend."

He almost hauled Liz into the bar. Halfway to Chen's table, she stopped and he looked at her in confusion.

"I'll catch up to you in a minute," she said, and leaned closer to whisper. "Ladies' room!"

Why did he sense that she was lying to him?

Why would she lie about that?

Brandon nodded and forced a smile for her, gesturing to the washrooms. She hurried away. He checked, but that Sloane guy handed some cash to the bartender, then left without a backward glance.

Good riddance.

Brandon inhaled deeply, paying attention, but his keen sense of smell told him that there were no other *Pyr* in his vicinity. Good. He headed for Chen, more than ready for some answers about that powder.

Chapter 8

Liz hated when she needed to be two places at once. She saw Brandon make a beeline for a table in the far corner of the bar and guessed that the man sitting there with his back to her was the friend who had traded him the powder. She really wanted to hear all that the guy had to say.

But she also didn't want to lose the chance to talk to the *Pyr* who had shown up. That the leader of the *Pyr* had sent Sloane to heal Brandon convinced her that the *Pyr* were good to each other. Brandon was wrong—but she had to learn more while she could, before Sloane left. She had to ensure that Brandon was in good hands—or claws—before she had to step away from him and deal with her own history.

Make that three places she was supposed to be. It was after noon and the symposium was scheduled to begin with a cocktail party at seven. Given that Liz was a guest of the Institute and one invited at Maureen's behest, she couldn't afford to not be there.

Four places. She hadn't lied about needing the facilities.

Liz chose to pursue Sloane first.

To her relief, Sloane hadn't gone far. He was outside, on the street side of the bar. He was standing out of sight of the people in the bar—Brandon and his friends, probably—and leaning against the back fender of Maureen's car.

As if he'd expected her.

He nodded at the sight of her but looked grim. "How'd you know this was my car?"

Sloane touched the side of his nose. "We have sharper senses than humans. Does he know you're here?"

Liz shook her head. "I have to be quick. Are you really the Apothecary of the *Pyr*?"

Sloane nodded. "Who is he talking to? I couldn't see his face."

"He said there was an old guy, a friend who swapped him some powder for his scales."

Sloane inhaled sharply in disapproval, and Liz realized he'd guessed who Brandon's elderly friend was.

"There's something about that powder, isn't there? It doesn't just make him lucky, like he thinks. He says the old guy uses it as a restorative."

Sloane snorted. "I'll bet." He studied her for a moment. "How much do you want to know?"

"Everything. I need to help Brandon."

Sloane smiled a little. He leaned closer and dropped his voice, nodding toward the bar. His words fell quickly. "Brandon's not with any old guy and certainly not with a friend. That has to be Chen, an ancient *Slayer* who has been trying to gain control of the *Pyr* for years. He's the only one who has that powder and the only one who would trade it for scales." He arched a brow. "He's also one of the few who can disguise his scent. That's why I didn't know he was here."

"What's a *Slayer*?"

"*Pyr* gone bad. Choosing selfishness and personal gain instead of service to the earth and defense of humanity. Their blood turns black, and the story is that the darkness of their blood is a sign of the darkness in their hearts." Sloane's gaze was bright. "How much do you know about us and Brandon?"

"Not enough. Brandon says the dragon is ascendant, that he can't control it. He says that's new and he originally thought it was because of the firestorm. I think it's because of the powder Chen gave him." She quickly told Sloane her theory about the binding spell, and he nodded.

If anything, he looked grimmer.

"I told him that he should talk to other *Pyr*, find out more, but he doesn't want anything to do with the *Pyr*. He's convinced that the dragon is evil. He wants to kill it."

"He can't, not without killing himself."

Liz nodded. "That's his solution." She sighed. "He's afraid of it and its growing power. He says it's violent and wants to injure everyone." She considered Sloane. "Am I right? Is the powder part of it?"

He nodded. "It must be Dragon Bone Powder. I'd need to smell it to be sure."

"That sounds gross. What is it?"

"It's exactly what you think it is. It's made from incinerated *Pyr*, and the smell of it has an effect on us. It does strengthen the dragon, but not usually as much as what Brandon is experiencing." He eyed her again. "What are you? Why do you know about binding spells?"

Liz stepped back and averted her gaze. "Maybe I read about them somewhere."

Sloane shook his head. "No. You have powers yourself." His gaze was intense and he seemed to take a deep whiff of the air. "There's something different about you."

"No, there isn't."

Sloane looked Liz in the eye. "Don't imagine that you'll be able to avoid your nature any more than Brandon can avoid his."

"I don't know what you're talking about."

"Yes, you do, but you don't have to tell me more. You already know that I'm right." He straightened and moved away from the car. "See if you can get some of the powder. Then I'll know for sure what it is."

Liz could deal with that request. She thought it was a small thing to ask, and with Sloane's help, she'd be relatively sure that Brandon would be okay. Brandon had the vial and there might be enough in it to confirm Sloane's theory. "I'll try. How will I find you when I do get it?"

"You won't," Sloane said, then smiled. "But don't worry; I can find you. You'd better go to him before he realizes we're talking." When she would have turned away, he caught her shoulders in his hands and looked into her eyes. There were no flames dancing there. "I think you already understand that what's happening to him isn't his nature. There's something else at work, and I am here to heal him." Liz nodded, and Sloane smiled at her. "Rafferty, one of our kind, insists that the firestorm brings us the perfect mate, the one who can complete us and make us more than we are alone."

"Brandon says he can shift back when he feels my presence."

Sloane nodded. "So, you *can* heal him, whatever your powers are."

"I don't . . ."

Sloane shook his head. "I'll bet that you will need to do more than just be in his presence to solve this."

Liz looked away, but told Sloane only part of the truth. "You don't understand. I gave my powers away. I sacrificed them. They're gone."

"Looks to me like they're back, and Brandon needs you to embrace them." Sloane smiled at her, looking more confident than Liz felt. "You'll both be healed by the firestorm, which is more than right." Liz might have argued with Sloane, but he continued, and his words stopped her cold. "Anything less wouldn't be fair to your son."

"My son?" Liz stared at Sloane in confusion. "What son?"

Sloane dropped his hands and backed away, his expression turning guilty. "I thought he'd told you everything about the firestorm."

She stared at the other *Pyr*, aghast. "*His* son," she murmured.

"That's why the sparks disappear," Sloane said softly. "I'm sorry. I thought you knew."

Love. Destiny. Forever.

And a baby on the way!

How could Brandon have done to that her? How could she have forgotten about precautions herself? Was it just because of the overwhelming power of the firestorm? She wasn't on birth control, either. If Brandon hadn't been *Pyr*, she wouldn't have believed that conception could be a done deal, but she knew that she was working with a species with special powers.

And the sparks *had* died.

As much as she might have wished otherwise, she believed Sloane.

Liz spun around, more furious than she'd been in a long time. She didn't want to have a child of either gender. She didn't want to pass along her genetic ability and its burden to anybody.

How could Brandon have neglected to tell her?

And what was she going to do about it?

Liz marched into the bar, heading straight for the corner table where Brandon was engaged in earnest conversation with an elderly man. He glanced up as she approached the table, and his smile began to fade. Liz didn't slow down.

Until she was standing right at the table. "How could you not tell me?" she demanded.

Brandon looked confused. "Tell you what?"

Brandon's companion chuckled and she glanced at him for the first time.

It was the same elderly Chinese man to whom Liz had given a ride.

Who was the *Slayer* targeting Brandon.

Befriending him, lying to him, and weakening him.

Driving him closer to suicide.

And it was working because Brandon believed the best of people.

This was the spellcaster.

One more time, she couldn't decide whether to deck Brandon or haul him back to her room for another passionate night. She seized his hand. "I have to talk to you," she said curtly. "Right now and not here!" She tugged him to his feet.

Only when he was following her did she stride back to her car, simmering with anger. How could Brandon not see the danger? How could he have forgotten to mention that she'd get pregnant? Everything was happening so fast, and Liz didn't want to make choices she'd regret.

There was no sign of Sloane on the street. She pulled the keys from her purse and realized that her hands were shaking. She was tempted to return to the real and sheltered nature of her academic and scientific life without further delay.

Liz waited by the car, though, checking her watch.

A baby!

Something was wrong. Brandon wondered what had happened. Liz had just gone to the washroom, but now she was upset.

He'd thought she wanted to meet Chen and find out more about the powder.

He left Chen, excusing himself for a moment, and went after Liz. He found her standing beside her borrowed car, her forehead in her hand. "What's wrong?"

"What's wrong?" she demanded, her eyes flashing with fire. Once again, the sparks were flying from the tips of her hair, her presence just about crackling with energy. She spoke in a low hiss, which was the only mercy. "You knock me up, forget to mention it, and you wonder what's wrong when I learn the truth?"

Brandon took a step back, uncertain how to defend himself.

Liz wasn't experiencing any similar lack of coherence. She was furious. "I'll guess that the son that results from the firestorm being satisfied will be another *Pyr*. Don't you think you could have mentioned that I'm going to have a dragon baby in nine months?"

"I told you that it was the firestorm. . . ."

"But not what that meant!" She looked like she would breathe fire. "I didn't exactly have time to stop and check for a citation."

"I thought it didn't matter," Brandon started, but quickly saw that his choice of words was all wrong.

"Didn't matter?" Liz flung out her hands. "How could it not matter?"

"Well, because we'll be together," Brandon insisted, hoping that making his intentions clear to her would reassure her. "We could get married—or not, if you don't want to. . . . But we'll be together for the duration. I want you to understand that I'll do better than my father. I thought the timing of a baby was less important than that we've found each other."

"Unless you decide to kill yourself in order to dominate the dragon."

He shoved a hand through his hair and spoke with agitation. "I hadn't thought that would be necessary, not at the time. And even now that's a last-ditch choice." He caught at her hand. "Liz, I want to be with you. I'm okay with us having kids. Aren't you?"

She stared at him, then avoided his question. "You really believe in the firestorm's promise, don't you?"

"Yes."

"Why? What about your parents? Did they have a firestorm? I thought you said they split up."

"But it wasn't because of the firestorm. It wasn't even that they weren't right for each other."

"I don't understand. You said that your mom didn't like his truth."

Brandon folded his arms across his chest and tried to explain. "I think they were good together. I think that if he had told her sooner, maybe they could have worked through it." He fixed Liz with a look. "I think the main reason they split up was that my dad lied to my mom for so long about his nature. She felt betrayed."

Liz arched a brow and gave him a hard look. "Explain the difference here to me."

"I didn't lie to you!"

"A lie of omission can be just as important."

"No," Brandon argued. "No. This isn't fair. Okay, I made a mistake, but I was going to talk to you. I had every intention of doing the right thing. I intended to *try*, which my dad never did. He just bailed. But there was an earthquake this morning, let's remember, and then my dragon took charge. I had to leave to keep you safe. I think I should be able to argue for some slack because of all that!"

"How much slack?"

"A day! *One* day! I wanted to tell you today!" Brandon spread his hands. "I would have talked to you this morning when you woke up. I never meant to lie to you and I never meant to deceive you."

"And after you left?"

"I was going to nail that bastard dragon, get him back where he belonged, then come to you again." He fixed her with a hard look. "I wasn't leaving you, Liz. You have to believe that."

He held her gaze and knew she wanted to believe him. He took her hand again. "Last night was just so magical, Liz, like it was meant to be. I wanted to just be in the moment and talk later. I wanted it to be perfect. Didn't you?"

Liz exhaled and looked across the street. Brandon felt the fight go out of her. He thought she was blinking away tears, but then she looked right at him. "Yes. I did," she said quietly. "It was special. And this is also my fault because I didn't insist on any protection, either."

"It was the firestorm!" Brandon said. "It's supposed to be wonderful, Liz. It's once in a lifetime. It's supposed to be a great memory that you share forever."

Liz seemed to be fighting a smile. "Were you always such a romantic?"

"I didn't think so." Brandon fought his own smile and lost. "Maybe you changed that, too." He interlaced his fingers with hers, once again feeling his heart match its pace to hers.

She sobered and looked at their hands. "How is your lie different from your dad's?"

"It was years before he told her," Brandon said. "And I don't think he would have told her at all if she hadn't caught him in his dragon form. I have no idea what he told her about the firestorm when it happened. But when she saw him in dragon form, she freaked out, and they fought." He swallowed and looked down. "My dad's not much of a diplomat. And he's a quitter. He just left and never tried to change her mind. So he was wrong."

When he met Liz's gaze, her expression was intense. "So were you," she said softly, pulling her fingers from his. "This is huge. I don't want to have kids. Ever."

Brandon was shocked. "Why not?"

"Because I know what any kid would inherit from me, and I'm never going to pass that on." She spoke with so much force that he was startled. She would have turned away, but Brandon wasn't going to let her go.

He caught her shoulders in his hands, compelling her to look at him. "Just tell me what you are. Just tell me, Liz, and we'll solve it together."

She shook her head. "My legacy is a curse, and it can kill. I'm not going to let the victim be you." And she turned away from him, moving to get into the car. "I really hope it isn't the baby, either."

"You can't leave!"

"I have to," she said and got into the car. "I have to pass this test myself before I promise anything to anyone."

"But you'll come back."

"Not necessarily," she said, her strained expression making him think they both still wanted the same thing. "I have to go."

Brandon was dismayed by her attitude. What challenge was before her? "But if you pass the test? What then?"

Liz shook her head. "I'm not sure I can."

He saw her doubt and it terrified him. "Tell me more! Let me help!"

Liz shook her head. "No. Good-bye, Brandon." She turned the key in the ignition.

No! This wasn't how a firestorm was supposed to be!

*   *   *

"Liz! Give me a chance! Give *us* a chance." Brandon had his hands on the door and leaned in to appeal to her.

Liz's resolve melted a little. He was irresistible—not just because he was gorgeous. It was his determination to do the right thing, his sense of honor, and his conviction that romantic stories really could come true.

Maybe they could, if he'd had a firestorm with someone who hadn't been living without her powers for fourteen years and was now faced with the ultimate test.

"Just let me go, Brandon."

"I won't. Let me come with you to Kaneʻohe," he urged. "My dragon is easier to control in your presence, and we can talk about everything. Let me come to the symposium with you." He smiled. "Like a date."

"No. It won't work."

"Sure it will! The good guys always win in the end."

"No, Brandon. You don't know what you're up against here. Just give that vial to Sloane. You have to trust him."

"I don't have to trust anybody," Brandon said. "You don't have to think badly of Chen. I just left him at the table there—"

Liz interrupted him, her tone hard. "He's old enough to survive without you."

Brandon looked at her with astonishment. "That's cold for someone you've never even met. He's frail and he's been my friend."

Liz pursed her lips, not wanting to reveal how much

Sloane had told her. On the other hand, she had to warn Brandon that Chen was a *Slayer*. "Are you sure about that?"

Brandon frowned. "Yes! He's the one person who understands the challenge of my dragon."

"He took your scales."

"To help me. To weaken the dragon so that I could dominate it."

"Doesn't seem to be working now."

Her skepticism clearly annoyed him. "How can you dislike someone you don't even know? You're not being fair. Let's at least go over there and talk to him. Let's find out if you're right or not before we condemn him." He shrugged. "Maybe he knows something more or has an explanation."

"Are you sure he's your friend?" She leaned out the window and whispered. "What if he's a *Slayer*? What if he's the one who cast the binding spell? He is the one who demanded the scales in exchange for the powder."

Brandon took a step back, his horror clear. "You had a good talk with that Sloane guy, didn't you? He's told you stuff that isn't true." His voice rose in anger. "You *lied* to me, and went to talk to him instead. Yet you're calling me on a lie of omission!"

"I did what had to be done," Liz insisted. "You need to learn from the other *Pyr*. It only makes sense to gather information...."

"Sloane's turning you against me and against my friend, and filling your thoughts with lies. What did he demand that you do for him?" Brandon's eyes lit in sudden understanding. "He's the one who told you about the baby!"

Liz looked down. "You didn't," she reminded him.

"But I was going to. I would have talked to you about it this morning, if there hadn't been an earth-quake." Brandon flung out his hands. "He's making me look like an asshole, Liz. How can you imagine that he's on our side?"

"Your so-called friend is the problem, not Sloane. I have to get back to Kaneʻohe."

"Wait for me, Liz!"

"No. I can't." Liz had to put distance between them before her test began.

"Will you just tell me what you have to do?"

Liz frowned. She couldn't see how it was relevant, and Brandon had enough on his plate. "It's just part of what I am. I'm the only one who can solve it."

Brandon shook his head. "That's not good enough."

"You don't need to know more. It's my responsibility."

"No. We should solve it together." Brandon leaned in the window to make another appeal, and only her fear that he might pay a price for being in her life made it possible to deny him. "Come and meet Chen; then you'll see that he's not some evil magician."

"Don't you see, Brandon? He's cast a spell. Until it's broken, you're not going to be able to assess how honest he's being with you."

"But you could."

"No. You need to get the vial and give it to Sloane. I need to deal with this debt and get back to the symposium."

"We need to work through all of this together. Wait twenty minutes and I'll come with you."

"No. I can't risk it." Liz looked away, but Brandon caught her chin in his hand. His hand was warm, his grip firm but gentle.

"Talk to me," he urged.

Liz shook her head and put the car into gear. She felt sick with foreboding but she wouldn't make promises without being sure she could keep them. "Goodbye," she said, then drove away, blinking back her tears.

"Liz!" Brandon roared, but she didn't look back.

She was doing her best and, once more, she feared it wouldn't be enough.

Why wouldn't Liz tell him what was going on?

She couldn't possibly believe that anything could get worse for him. Brandon hated that she'd left him behind. He could already feel his dragon stirring, becoming more powerful even before the taillights of her car had disappeared. He stormed back to his rental, which was just around the corner, and grabbed the vial. He jammed it into his pocket as he returned to the bar, unable to avoid the sense that his firestorm wasn't proceeding much better than his father's had.

And that knowledge burned.

It was odd how bright Liz got when she was angry

with him, light dancing off her fingertips and the ends of her hair. She had some kind of power—he just knew it. Her abilities were probably why his dragon responded to her presence. He didn't believe all that stuff about the binding spell, and he was annoyed that the *Pyr* were trying to meddle in his life.

But Liz—Liz was everything he wanted in a woman. She was smart and strong. She wasn't afraid of him in either form. She trusted him and she had good instincts. She didn't give up when the solution wasn't obvious.

Then why had she left?

What was she afraid of?

One thing was for sure—Brandon was going to find out, and he was going to find out today. He'd talk to Chen, then go to Kane'ohe and meet Liz there. He'd find out, once and for all, whether her suspicions were right about Chen.

He'd borrow Dylan's Jeep or Kira's bug. If he couldn't borrow either, he'd fly there in dragon form, confident that he'd be able to shift back to human form in her presence. When there was time and quiet, he'd convince her to confide in him.

He smiled in anticipation of Liz's surprise when she found him at her door—and smiled even more in anticipation of how he'd remind her that they were meant to be together. She was angry with him about the baby, and rightly so. He would have told her already if there hadn't been so much else going on.

He'd tell her everything.

And she'd listen, because she'd calm down on her drive across the island. She'd feel better once she was back at the Institute and was sure she wasn't letting anyone down. Brandon respected her sense of responsibility and her loyalty to her friends.

He'd do the one thing she'd asked of him before he went after her. But he'd take the vial to her, not to Sloane. She could test the powder for him.

Brandon strode across the bar toward Chen.

With any luck, he'd be on his way to Kane'ohe in fifteen minutes.

Chen was still seething.

Someone had invaded his lair this morning.

Worse, someone had invaded his lair and stolen one of the scales he had collected from Brandon. Worse yet, the villain in question had broken one of the scales, proving that he knew their importance. Now, instead of needing a single scale to complete his spell, Chen had need of two more.

It hadn't been any ordinary intruder. It certainly hadn't been a human one. The thief had been a *Slayer*, of that Chen was certain, because there wasn't a whiff of scent outside his lair. There also had been no disruption of his dragonsmoke barrier, woven so high and thick that it would strike any dragon intruder to ice on contact.

No. The villain had gone around the dragonsmoke, not through it.

He was *Slayer*, and his feats proved that he had drunk the Dragon's Blood Elixir.

There was only one *Slayer* other than Chen who had drunk the Elixir and survived.

Jorge had come for vengeance.

And the last of the Elixir.

In a way, it would be interesting to see who won this feud. Would Chen replenish his Dragon Bone Powder with Jorge's corpse, or would Jorge suck the last vestiges of Elixir from Chen's own marrow?

Chen gripped his glass more tightly than was necessary and knew which *Slayer* he would bet on. He was quite sure that he had a better plan than Jorge. He also knew he was smarter. He had deceived Jorge more than once in the past.

Jorge was angry and passionate. That could lead a dragon to make mistakes of the most fateful kind. Jorge was also proud—another fatal flaw. Chen sipped his juice and resolved to work with these weaknesses.

Just as he would work with the meddling of the Apothecary. It was laughable that the *Pyr* had sent only one of their kind to face Chen. Of course, they probably thought they were merely supporting Brandon's firestorm. They must not have realized that Chen was here.

Which gave him time to spring the trap. He'd be gone before they arrived.

Or he would have been, if it hadn't been for Jorge.

His anger simmered, and Brandon chose that moment to reappear.

"You okay?" the young *Pyr* asked as he slid back into his seat. "You look a bit pale, Chen."

Chen coughed weakly. "It is the sun," he said. "I have become unaccustomed to it. I walked here without my cane."

Brandon looked worried. "Look, I'm sorry, but I don't have any more of that powder you gave me."

"It was a gift, my friend." Chen coughed.

"I know it makes you feel better, but my friend wasted it when he was joking around." Brandon grimaced. "I was going to give it back to you, but it's gone."

Chen swallowed a smile. Little did this foolish *Pyr* know that the Dragon Bone Powder was never wasted. "It was a gift between friends. You owe me no apology."

Brandon looked around, then leaned over the table. "Look, Chen, I can't stay long, but I wanted to ask your advice. Do you remember what you used to tell me about the dragon? About control?"

Chen nodded wearily. "Yes, yes. All power must remain in its place."

"Exactly. But I have a problem."

Chen coughed again, apparently disinterested. "We know this, my friend, but you have worked hard . . ."

"No, Chen, it got stronger. A lot stronger. It had something to do with the eclipse, maybe, or —" Brandon fell silent.

"Or?" Chen prompted.

"I had my firestorm," the young *Pyr* whispered.

"I do not know this term," Chen lied. "Should I understand?"

Brandon grimaced. "I met a girl and sparks flew, and my dad told me once that this was the mark of the firestorm. I thought it would make everything better and put the dragon in its place."

"But?" Chen pretended to be confused. What a moron this *Pyr* was! Of course his dragon had been empowered by the firestorm! But it had been the powder that had pushed that power beyond Brandon's control.

And the scales in Chen's possession had shifted that control to Chen. He nearly snarled aloud at Jorge's audacity.

"You okay?" Brandon asked. He'd leaned back and his expression was wary.

"I am sorry," Chen said. "I am tired today. Please tell me of your fire, fire . . ."

"Firestorm. It must have made the dragon stronger. I changed shape without meaning to do it, and it was really hard to change back."

Chen nodded thoughtfully. He frowned, letting Brandon worry about this a bit longer. "You must strike at the dragon's heart," he said finally. "You must weaken it so that it surrenders to your will."

"Well, how do I do that?"

Chen smiled. "You know. We have done this before." He sipped his juice, holding Brandon's gaze.

The young *Pyr*'s horror was clear. "Another scale? You want me to rip another scale free?"

Chen's eyes narrowed. This reaction was new and unwelcome. His resistance was the mate's fault. "Perhaps two would be better," he suggested, keeping his tone level with an effort.

"No way!"

Chen stifled his irritation. *No?* Brandon dared to deny Chen's will? It was outrageous that he should now become defiant.

It was the Firedaughter. She was the one turning Brandon against him. Chen could afford to play this game no longer. He had to seize what he wanted and complete his scheme immediately.

While the mate was gone.

He forced himself to keep a philosophical tone. "It will weaken your adversary."

"I'm not sure that's a good idea. I think I should keep the rest. Liz thinks it's wrong that I gave them up, and I agree with her."

Chen snarled at the acknowledgment of the mate's influence.

"After all, they're not growing back the way I'd expected them to."

Chen wanted to breathe fire.

"Perhaps your Liz knows less of dragons than I do," he said, keeping his tone mild.

Brandon drummed his fingers on the table, discontented. "What do you do with them, anyway?"

"I admire them. All of nature is beautiful, even that which is dangerous." Chen gestured to the beach. "Think of the waves you ride, which look so beautiful but maim and kill. They are not unlike your dragon. They must be respected. They must be controlled."

"No," Brandon said with finality. "That plan's not working. I need to find another way." He leaned closer. "Liz thinks it might be a binding spell. Have you ever heard of that?"

Chen was livid. This was the darkfire's influence. First Jorge stole from him; then the mate bolstered Brandon's defiance. Did they not understand that he was destined to rule all? Did they not understand that resistance was futile?

Brandon's eyes narrowed as he watched Chen. At his expression, Chen looked down at his hands and glimpsed the pale blue shimmer of the light that flashed before the shift to dragon form. There was just the barest flicker of it showing, enough that a person might doubt his own eyes. He quenched it immediately, extinguishing the light that could reveal him for what he truly was.

And he created a distraction. He turned his thoughts to the lightbulb in the fixture hanging over the next table. He murmured to its electric flame and coaxed it to burn too brightly. Using his affinity with fire and his ability to turn that element to his will, he urged the current to a surge of power.

The bulb shattered with a pop, creating both a flash of light and a shower of broken glass. The people seated there leapt up in dismay, the bartender called out, and someone came to sweep up the mess. The bar erupted in noisy chatter.

Brandon looked at the light, then back at Chen's hands, then inhaled deeply.

Chen almost smiled. The young dragon would detect no scent from Chen, for he had his scent completely disguised. That ability was the gift of the Elixir. Brandon was still suspicious, though, and Chen knew he was trying to reconcile that glimpse of blue shimmer with Chen having no *Pyr* or *Slayer* scent.

He'd have to work quickly to secure this prize, before the mate cheated him of it.

Chen sighed. "As you say, we must find another way. I am too tired right now, my old friend. Let me think about this." He started to push himself to his feet, leaning heavily on the table as if he were too feeble to stand. "You said you must go."

Brandon immediately reached over and grabbed his elbow. "Let me help you first."

"No, no. I am just a feeble old man. Your girlfriend will be looking for you."

Indecision warred in the young dragon's eyes; then duty won him over. "It'll just take a minute."

Chen nearly chortled in delight. The young *Pyr* was such a fool.

Reckless of the danger before him, Brandon held Chen's elbow as the *Slayer* pretended to waver on his feet. "Maybe you should go back to your place and crash for a while. Get some sleep."

Chen nodded. "Yes, yes. This is very wise advice." He took a step and deliberately let his knee buckle.

Brandon caught him, and the *Slayer* smothered his delight with an effort. So gullible! It would almost be too easy to take this one down.

And, really, he deserved no less for daring to refuse Chen's request.

"Here. I'll help you. Lean on my arm. It can't be that far to your place."

"You know where I stay?"

"Not exactly, but I know it's in town," Brandon said with a smile. "You always walk. You can make it back if I help you."

Chen passed a hand over his forehead. "Ah yes. I forget so much now. You are kind." He leaned heavily on Brandon and let the young *Pyr* lead him out to the street.

"You don't have any more of that powder, do you, Chen?" Brandon asked. "Just a little?"

Chen smiled, feigning ignorance. "You wish to charm your girlfriend?"

"No, um, not really." The young *Pyr* smiled. "But maybe it wouldn't hurt."

Chen patted Brandon's arm. "I have a little, not much, but I will share it with you. It is in my room."

"Excellent. Thanks, Chen. I knew you were a good friend."

Chen nearly chortled to himself in anticipation. He had been content to stalk his prey before, and had enjoyed persuading Brandon to cooperate in his own destruction. But Chen couldn't afford to wait any longer.

Especially if his prey was going to become willful.

The house Chen had bought was set back from the others in town, approached by a winding path that was very private. Chen now saw its usefulness as he had never before. The restaurants and shops were busy, and people who were home were inside, preparing for their evening meals. There would be no witnesses when he shifted, attacked, and dragged his victim into his lair. The dragonsmoke barrier was thick and deep, and it would burn like fiery ice if the young *Pyr* tried to escape, weakening him even more.

Chen would enslave Brandon before dark and double his power besides. Jorge would get a surprise when he returned.

For Chen had no doubt that the *Slayer* intended to try to bargain with him.

Chen chuckled to himself, hiding his anticipation with a cough.

In New York, the *Pyr* Niall Talbot hung up the phone with a frown. He was in the office of his ecotourism company, alone on a Saturday to catch up on his filing. He'd just talked to Sloane and was intrigued by what his old friend had told him about this firestorm. Of course, he'd felt it spark earlier and had known it was far away. It had a funny feeling to it, though, one that reminded him of the tingle of darkfire.

He shared Sloane's sense that this young dragon might need the help of the *Pyr* to see his way clearly through the storm. Not everyone would go to the firestorm, as the darkfire had fed dissent within the ranks of the *Pyr*. But Niall and Sloane went way back, and Niall trusted his friend's assessment of the situation.

If Rox agreed, they would go.

Niall had already pulled up the Web site for the Billabong Pipeline Masters when his partner Rox came up the stairs from her tattoo shop. He smiled when she peeked around the corner of his door.

"Am I interrupting serious work?"

"No. Check this out." Niall clicked through to the brief résumé of one of the wild-card contestants, Brandon Merrick. One glance at the young *Pyr* and he knew his mate would be up for the trip.

"Nice tribals," Rox said, peering at the screen. Niall wasn't surprised that she was most interested in the surfer's tattoos. Tribal tattoos were more graphic in design than Rox's own designs and usually rendered in black only. Rox worked with a veritable rainbow of colors. "That one's unusual," she said, pointing to the design on his arm.

"Is it? I thought they were just different designs."

"No, no." Rox was looking intently at the shot. She pushed Niall's hand aside and took control of the laptop, zooming in on the tattoo of choice. It was a spiral. "They're symbolic, deeply so. In a lot of South Pacific cultures a tattoo artist is a kind of shaman. He chooses the tattoo design for the customer on the basis of his understanding of that person's needs."

She focused on one of the other tattoos. "This one is a protection symbol, usually used for someone who tends to be targeted by others. This one is for a warrior, someone who fights, usually someone idealistic and driven by principle." Rox returned to the spiral tattoo that had initially intrigued her. "This spiral, though, is shamanistic in itself."

"For a shaman?"

"Or a seer. Someone who ventures into uncharted turf. Physical or psychic."

"Like a Dreamwalker," Niall suggested. "You could give me one."

Rox smiled at him and shook her head. "No. It's more than copyright or intellectual property. It's not my area of expertise and I'm not going to trespass. This is the work of a shaman, chosen by him for this guy, and it's powerful stuff."

"Powerful enough to protect him from *Slayers*?"

Rox looked at Niall in astonishment. "He's *Pyr*? This surfer is a *Pyr*?"

"He had his firestorm this weekend."

Rox looked back at the screen. "That's not the only reason you're looking at this, is it? You think he's in trouble."

"I have a bad feeling. Sloane, too."

"So do I." Rox shook her head. "Someone gave him these designs for a reason, and knowing how you guys are, his big fight is going to be now, during his firestorm."

"Because he has something to lose." Niall took Rox's hand in his and squeezed her fingers.

He watched her swallow; then she nodded. "My sister will take the boys, if you want to go."

Niall got to his feet. "I want to go, but we'll all go. I can feel the darkfire, and I don't trust it. I want us all together." He smiled for Rox. "Erik and Quinn are going tonight. If we hurry, we can get to Chicago and be on the same flight."

Rox rolled her eyes and grinned. "No dragon flights? That's the best part of travelling with you!"

"Not all the way to Hawaiʻi, when we're not sure what we'll find when we get there."

"Hawaiʻi!" Rox cried in delight. She looked back at the Web site displayed on the laptop, then slapped her forehead. "Of course. I'm packing my tattoo guns, then I'll be ready to go. We can buy sunscreen and bathing suits on the beach."

Niall caught her close and gave her a searing kiss. "I love how decisive you are."

"That's not all you love about me," Rox teased, her eyes dancing. "But we'll review that later. Let's go!"

Chapter 9

There was something weird going on.

Brandon felt as if his senses were on full alert, the way they had been when he'd sensed the earthquake that morning well before it had started. He felt edgy and on the cusp of violence, as if his dragon was going to break free once again.

It must be because Liz had left. She would be halfway down the island by now, and sheer distance from her was giving his dragon more power.

He was disconcerted by the shimmer of blue that he thought he had seen around Chen. Had he imagined it? Because even he, with his rudimentary dragon powers, could smell a *Pyr* when he paid attention, and Chen smelled completely human. Were his eyes playing tricks on him? Was that part of the dragon gaining the upper hand?

One thing Brandon knew was that he had to solve this and get to Liz.

All he had to do was get a bit of that powder at Chen's. Maybe there was some residue trapped in the container he had, enough that Liz could test it. He wasn't going to open the container and risk losing whatever remained inside. Liz could do it.

The man leaning on his arm was almost a ghost of what Chen had been when Brandon had first met him. He really must be dying. He certainly didn't have a lot of strength. Brandon was practically carrying him. He felt sorry for his old friend, just fading away without any family or friends beside him.

Well, except Brandon.

How could Sloane suggest that Chen was a *Slayer*? It was the same as his father making pronouncements about his human friends, wanting control of Brandon's life. And Sloane was acting like Brandon's dad, too—just popping up unexpectedly with ideas and demands and plans. Brandon resented that Sloane had tried to influence Liz, and he could have done without Sloane telling her about the baby.

Brandon had wanted to do that himself.

He didn't blame Liz for believing Sloane's suspicions. She didn't know Chen. She didn't know anything much about the *Pyr*. And she was understandably angry with him for not telling her the whole truth.

Brandon wished he had. At least she knew some of it, and it had been only a day. He was doing better than his own father.

And he was going to do even better than he had so far.

He slanted a glance at the frail man hanging on to his arm. He must have imagined the blue shimmer that had seemed to dance around the perimeter of Chen's body. Brandon had caught only the barest glimpse of it, so little that he didn't trust his eyes. Chen couldn't be a *Slayer*, not without smelling like a dragon shifter. That shimmer must have had something to do with that lightbulb exploding. Like the light in it had gone crazy or something.

Still, Brandon couldn't dismiss his uneasiness.

What was Liz refusing to tell him? Why did she get all sparky when she was angry with him? What was she afraid of?

It took a thousand years for them to get across the street, a thousand anxious years as cars swerved around them and Brandon thought about the time passing. Chen seemed to move more and more slowly, as if he were going to run out of steam in the middle of the road. Brandon again felt uneasy at the idea of leaving him alone.

"Chen, do you have any family or close friends I should call for you? It seems like maybe you should have some company tonight."

Chen coughed. "No family. All dead. No friends." He gave Brandon a weak smile. "Just one good friend. It is enough."

Brandon felt a twinge of guilt. Should he stay with Chen tonight? It would be awful to leave him to die alone, but Brandon really had to pursue Liz.

"You know that powder, Chen?"

"I know it well."

"What is it, really?"

Chen gave him a surprisingly sly smile. "Ancient Chinese secret," he said, and Brandon was startled by his sense that Chen was messing with him. His manner had suddenly changed so much. Chen never made jokes, and he'd spoken both quickly and clearly.

Without an accent.

The look in his eyes had almost been predatory.

And his eyes had shone as they never did.

Brandon's dragon snarled with new vigor.

"I beg your pardon?" Brandon asked. They stepped onto a path that twisted away from the main road and headed toward the mountains. It wound from one side to the other, making a course that reminded Brandon of a snake.

His dragon disliked that their destination was hidden by foliage.

In fact, the vegetation grew surprisingly dense on either side of the path, blocking the views of the surrounding houses. The hair prickled on the back of his neck, and he found himself agreeing with his dragon's distrust of the situation.

He felt threatened. That's what was the same as earlier that morning. His dragon had responded exactly like this right before the earthquake—right before the ceiling had fallen and could have killed Liz.

There was a risk or a danger lurking on this path. Did someone intend to mug Chen because he was a weak old man? Were they going to get jumped by some kid? Brandon scanned the shadows on either side, looking for trouble.

Chen shuffled his feet as they walked, nodding. "It is an old secret remedy," he said, sounding more like his usual self. "The grandfather of my grandfather made it first and he taught me."

"Your grandfather's grandfather?" Brandon asked, thinking that Chen was getting confused. No human could live that long. "But what's in it?"

Chen chuckled, and it was a surprisingly dark sound. "It is secret."

"Can't you tell me? One friend to another?" Brandon smiled when Chen glanced up, trying to look friendly and trustworthy.

"Dragon bones," a guy contributed.

Brandon looked up with surprise. There had been no one on the path, but now there was a big, buff guy with a blond buzz cut who was blocking their way.

He had appeared without Brandon hearing him approach.

"Isn't that right, Chen? You make it out of incinerated dragon shape shifters?" The guy winked at Brandon, and it wasn't a friendly expression. "I'll guess that you're going to be the source of the new supply."

"Fool!" Chen roared. There was no disputing the fact that he was shimmering blue now. He straightened and was nearly as tall as Brandon. Chen's entire body was surrounded by a halo of bright, flickering blue light.

Brandon's mouth fell open.

Chen was *Pyr*!

In the blink of an eye, Chen became a red dragon with gold scales and gold horns. Brandon was shocked. Chen reared back and breathed fire at the guy in the path. The plume of flame was long and vivid, and the fire licked the wooden porch of the house that had been behind the guy.

It missed the guy because he'd become a dragon of vivid yellow and taken flight.

Brandon thought the pair would fight each other, but the yellow dragon laughed. He thrashed his tail through the air and took a long, deep breath as he hovered overhead. "Mmm. I smell fresh mate," he snarled, then disappeared as if he had never been.

He was going to target Liz!

"No!" Brandon had to fly to the defense of his mate. His dragon roared, compelling him to shift shape faster than he ever had before.

It didn't matter, though. The red dragon that was Chen turned on him with a snarl and moved quicker than lightning.

By the time Brandon had shifted shape, Chen's claws were already locked tightly around his neck. The other dragon squeezed, and his delight in the pain he caused was clear. Even in dragon form, Brandon couldn't fight the other dragon's deathly grip.

He tried.

He slashed at his opponent, still astonished that his friend would attack him. His talons dug into Chen's shoulder and the blood ran black over his scales.

Chen was *Slayer*.

Brandon should have listened to Liz.

He struggled with new vigor, knowing his chances of ever listening to Liz again were fading fast. Chen was murmuring something, something that made Brandon's dragon sleepy and ineffective. The spots where his scales were missing burned, as if touched by fire, sapping the strength from his body.

She was right about the binding spell, too.

Brandon felt like an idiot. He got in one good punch, landing a claw to Chen's gut, and the *Slayer*'s grip loosened slightly.

Chen bared his teeth then, and Brandon heard the hiss of dragonsmoke.

He struggled, but the dragonsmoke snaked toward his gut. He screamed when it plunged into the wound like a knife and he roared as he felt it sucking his strength. Chen chuckled darkly and his claws tightened even more around Brandon's throat. He squeezed the life out of Brandon as his spell—because it couldn't be anything else—was commanding Brandon's dragon to surrender. All Brandon could see were those eyes, eyes as malicious as Chen's had been only once.

Chen had been lying to him.

And it was too late for Brandon to do anything about it. Only now he realized why Chen knew so much about dragons. He'd been manipulated. He'd distrusted his observations, he'd failed to listen to Liz, and he'd been surprised.

And now he would die for it.

Brandon saw the colors of the vegetation dim even as he thrashed against his opponent's ferocious grip. Chen was not as feeble in dragon form as he was in human form—his ability to fight hard made Brandon wonder whether he was feeble at all.

The taunt in old-speak floated to Brandon's ears, piercing the veil of pain. He recognized the yellow dragon's voice. *"If I have the mate and you have the Pyr, which one of us will he surrender to, Chen? Let's find out."*

Chen roared with fury at the challenge, so he had heard it, too.

The yellow dragon would kill Liz; Brandon knew it.

He had to stop them both.

Terror gave him new strength and he whipped his tail against Chen, struggling with all his might. Chen snarled and his grip loosened slightly, giving Brandon time to hope.

Suddenly there was a dizzying flash. He had the sense of being lifted and of moving through a fog. He felt nauseated, then cold. Chen's grip loosened and Brandon fell onto a hard floor.

For a moment he thought he was alone, but his dragon wasn't convinced. Brandon looked again and saw a red lizard running across the floor. It slipped through the crack under the door. Brandon rose to his knees and saw an Asian woman in a tight dress marching down the path. She disappeared from sight.

Then he *was* alone.

Was she Chen, too?

Brandon lunged for the door and collided with a burning wall of ice. He fell back with a shout of pain and narrowed his eyes, only then discerning the dragon-smoke barrier.

He was a prisoner.

Chen's prisoner.

And they were going to kill Liz.

Brandon closed his eyes, hating that his mistakes had led him to this place. He hadn't wanted to have any involvement with the *Pyr*, but now he was in serious trouble, with no idea how to solve it. He had to start to make amends, and fast.

Liz's life depended on it.

Brandon shouted in old-speak as clearly as he could. *"Help me! Help my mate!"*

There was no reply.

But then, it wasn't as if he'd practiced his dragon skills. No, he'd spent time in the surf, honing those skills, determined to make himself a future that way.

Now neither he nor Liz had a future.

And there was nothing he could do about it.

Liz's anger with Brandon lasted all the way down the middle of the island, until she got close to Honolulu. It was when the entry to the tunnel loomed before her that frustration abandoned her.

Because fear took its place.

Her grip tightened on the steering wheel as the entry to the tunnel came steadily closer. There hadn't been any aftershocks for a while, she told herself.

She'd driven through the mountain once already since the earthquake and everything had been (mostly) fine. It wasn't that long of a tunnel, and she couldn't think of anything worse happening than the mark appearing on her arm. The drive wouldn't take long; then she could just stay in Kane'ohe.

All her rationalizations sounded like exactly what they were.

She glanced at her watch and knew she didn't have time to follow the coast around Diamond Head. She couldn't be late. She owed it to Maureen to be there. She could do this.

She had to do this.

The entry to the tunnel loomed closer. Liz swallowed, told herself to remain calm, and drove into the tunnel as if everything was just fine.

The darkness closed around the car like a shroud. Her heart was pounding and her palms were damp. She refused to think about just how much mountain was over top of her. She refused to look at the passenger's seat or acknowledge the prickling of that brand. She kept her gaze locked on the road and closed her ears.

Hear no evil.

But Liz didn't hear the spirits. She smelled something burning instead.

Oh no. Not her test. Not here and now!

Light—orange light that crackled into flames— sparked on the passenger's seat. Liz could smell the vinyl burning and hear the snap of the flames. Her right arm was getting singed, and from the corner of her eye, she could see brilliant, hot lava pooling on the floor.

Holy shit. Liz glanced right and the car swerved.

From the passenger's seat, a woman of flame and smoke, a woman whose fiery garments made that lava pool on the floor, smiled back at her. She was all black and orange, all heat and shadow, and her eyes were dark with mystery.

Pele. Liz gripped the steering wheel in terror. She was being visited by a deity.

In a way, it was a relief to confront a goddess instead of the test of her powers.

She really had to make sure she didn't tick Pele off.

"You are surprised," Pele murmured, her voice dark and sensuous.

"And honored, my lady."

The goddess chuckled. She arranged her robes, and sparks flicked toward the dashboard. "My presence reveals the importance of your role."

"You honor me too much, my lady," Liz said, keeping her manner deferential. "My skill is nothing compared to yours."

"You are wrong," Pele said sternly. "You are stronger than you know. Your gift is potent and it is needed to break the spell that awakens the earth."

Liz swallowed. She didn't dare to look directly at Pele, but she knew the goddess was speaking of the dark magic she had already sensed. "I gave my gift away, my lady."

"You are no different from him," Pele said. "You

cannot change what you are or cast it away. You gave of your power, but it is still with you. It has slumbered like embers of the fire, awaiting the moment of need."

Liz glanced at the goddess in her surprise.

Pele smiled, the raw power in her expression making Liz look back to the road. She could see a pinprick of light ahead and fixed her gaze on that. Pele's words were low and hot, insistent and inescapable. "You have only to feed the fire to bring it to a blaze again. Make no mistake—this burden is yours, Firedaughter. You have been chosen. You can triumph or you can fail."

"But my test—"

"Comes to you in this place, where only you can make the difference." Pele flicked her robes again, sending an array of sparks into the darkness. "There is a certain elegance to it that reveals the hand of the greatest goddess of all. You must embrace the fire that is yours to command."

"Fire kills," Liz insisted, her nostrils as filled with the scent of the ashes that had been her mother as if she still stood on that hill. "Fire burns and destroys."

Especially when she tried to command it.

"Fire purifies," Pele insisted. "Fire is your weapon of choice. Fire sears and fire heals. You know this, Firedaughter. It is your legacy."

"You don't understand. My mother died because of me! I could die! My child could die!"

"So you would let the dragon die instead? This would make the life of your child better?"

Liz gasped in horror. "I left him. He should be safe...."

Pele shook her head. "Only you can break the spell that binds him."

Brandon was going to die without her help? But how could she count on her powers again? And how could she be sure that using her powers at all wouldn't increase the danger?

Pele chuckled under her breath. "Perhaps only he can ensure that you pass your test."

What? How could that be?

With a thousand questions, Liz turned to the goddess, but Pele was gone as quickly as if she had never been there. The passenger's seat was pristine, to Liz's relief, and there was only a faint whiff of an extinguished flame in the car.

Not wanting more company, Liz accelerated, racing toward light and sanity and Kaneʻohe.

Her eyes widened when a rumble echoed beneath the car. She had time to hope it was an illusion before the road shook hard.

The car swerved into the next lane without Liz meaning to do so. Fortunately, there was no other car near her. The road cracked in a great fissure right ahead of her and she floored the accelerator, hoping to cross the chasm before it yawned too wide. She saw a tendril of steam rise out of the crack and feared the worst.

The car seemed to welcome the opportunity to show off. It accelerated like a racing car, leaping easily over the yawning crevasse in the road. Liz shot out of the other side of the tunnel just as the shaking became much worse.

In the rearview mirror, she could see burning orange light erupting from that crack in the road. Lava. A stream of brilliant sparks shot into the air, cars honked, and she heard collisions behind her. She raced down the side of the mountain, wanting only to get back to the Institute—and as far away from the erupting volcano as possible.

She heard the rumble of sliding rock and didn't have to look to know what was happening. The dark magic had awakened the volcano. That's what Pele had been warning her about.

But how was Liz going to stop it?

She drove down toward the parking lot like a wild woman, going even faster when she heard the avalanche slam into the road behind her. People were screaming. Houses were collapsing. Rock was rolling down to the sea. The avalanche was descending through the residential neighborhood with savage force. Liz rocketed down the winding road like a race-car driver, managing miraculously to stay just ahead of the tumbling tide of stone.

Liz got to the parking lot and squealed the tires as she parked in Maureen's spot. The car was at a bit of an angle, but Liz didn't care about precision parking. She saw the rising dust of the avalanche and wanted to get as far away as possible, as quickly as possible.

Far back up the mountain, she could see lava spewing high, like a fireworks display of brilliant orange and red. There was a river of lava already moving down the side of the mountain, so hot that it moved comparatively quickly. She grabbed her purse, locked Maureen's car, and pivoted to run to the dock.

Only to find a blond man with a chilly smile blocking her way. He took a deep, appreciative breath, as if he liked her perfume, and she couldn't imagine how he could smell her from so far away.

"So," he said softly, his voice filled with threat. "You're the mate."

The term he used told Liz that he must be another of the dragon shifters. His hungry expression gave her a clue that he wasn't one of the good guys. Sirens were blaring and chaos had erupted behind her. No one was even going to notice if she screamed, or come to her help if she called.

The man smiled, as if enjoying that she'd realized the desperation of her situation. She had the sense that he'd been waiting, letting her fear build to its maximum point. She was reminded of a cat playing with a mouse, ensuring that the victim understood its plight before the inevitable end.

Liz wasn't feeling like her demise was inevitable.

The man shimmered blue around his perimeter, flung his hands into the sky, and shifted shape. He became an enormous dragon the color of a yellow topaz, proving her suspicions true. It looked like his talons were made of gold, and his scales seemed to be edged in gold. He had an awful lot of very sharp teeth.

He took flight and breathed fire at Liz, his eyes shining with fury. For the first time, Liz's legacy seemed like a gift. She could fight fire with fire.

Maybe only a Firedaughter could face down this *Slayer* and win.

Her son was going to survive and so would she.

With that thought, Liz felt the old power rise within her. The heat of her gift surged through her veins, responding to her need and her command, just as Pele had said it would.

When the dragon lunged toward her, claws extended, Liz didn't bother to scream.

This *Slayer* was going to get more than he expected.

Liz raced toward the *Slayer* instead of away from him, making for the end of the dock. As she ran, she flung her purse strap over her shoulder so it hung across her body and left her hands free. She ducked beneath the airborne dragon and closed her eyes against his blast of flames. She was sure she felt his talons slide through her hair.

Only surprise had made him miss.

Liz knew that trick wouldn't work again. She had to fight fire with fire. She recited the ancient words in her thoughts once, ensuring that she had the order and pronunciation right. It had been a long time, and there would be no second chances, but she remembered them perfectly.

She would speak no evil.

At the end of the dock, Liz pivoted and flung up

her left hand. The dragon was closing fast, his eyes shining in anticipation of a nice, light snack.

She called to the power that was hers by right and flung up a wall of burning flame between herself and the dragon. The spell worked with such vigor and speed that Liz was astonished.

She was stronger than ever.

But there was no time to marvel at her feat.

She spun to dive into the bay. She heard the dragon roar in frustration, probably because he couldn't stop in time to avoid the fire. When she broke the surface, she smelled something burning and hoped it was him.

Liz glanced back in time to see him circling the end of the dock. His scales were singed and smoldering, a thread of smoke rising from his burned hide. With obvious frustration, he slashed at the wooden hut on the end of the dock, then set it on fire by breathing a plume of flames at it. There must have been a tank of fuel stashed there, because the shack exploded, sending a tower of flame into the sky.

Then he turned to glare at her.

Liz swam for the island with all her might. He couldn't burn her while she was in the water, but she murmured a protection spell all the same. She was a strong swimmer and the water was much warmer than it was in New England.

Coconut Island wasn't far away.

She knew she could make it.

The ocean welled around her, its deep songs melding with her thoughts. She felt the power of the ele-

ment of water and was dizzied by its influence on her.
There was no buffer here—no concrete, no boat hull,
no wet suit. She was surrounded by the lullaby of the
water and caressed by it on every side. How had her
mother dealt with so much energy? If she was going
to survive, Liz had to focus and ignore her intuitive
connection with the earth's elements.

She swam hard, her body straining. She felt something brush against her leg and nearly panicked. It
was a bad time to remember that Kane'ohe Bay was
a breeding ground for hammerhead sharks.

Only in the winter.

Which would include December.

Funny how knowing that the young sharks were
harmless to humans didn't slow her heartbeat much.
Liz opened her eyes under the water and saw dozens
of them, their dark shadows sliding around and beneath her.

They were juveniles, she told herself sternly. No
more than two feet long.

And even adult hammerheads had very little taste
for humans. She was safe.

Well, from the sharks.

Liz swam faster. The sharks brushed against her
repeatedly, as if they needed to touch her, as if they
recognized that she was a woman in connection with
the planet. Liz could have done without the affection.

The dragon swooped low over her and breathed a
long, slow stream of fire. It fried through the protection spell, and Liz knew she'd need more spell power

to protect herself from this one's evil intent. The flame scorched Liz's back before she dove underwater. It was as if he were searing her on one side before roasting her thoroughly.

She was halfway to the island. She kept moving forward with powerful strokes, even underwater. The school of juvenile hammerheads swirled around her, dark shadows with gleaming eyes. She could hear them murmuring to each other.

Overhead, the shadow of the dragon disappeared. She lunged for the surface and gulped a deep breath, amazed at how much he had already increased the temperature of the water. He was turning in the sky over the island and coming back around for another attack. Liz swam with all her might, eyeing his position. She could see the lust in his eyes and the ferocious shine of his teeth. She saw him open his mouth to breathe fire again and swoop low. He moved fast.

Liz dove deep and kicked hard. The dark shadow of the dragon passed overhead, his fire making the water boil above her. The hammerhead sharks dove deeper into the bay, surrounding her in a dark gray swirl. Were they protecting her? Or isolating her? Liz knew what her mother would have said, but those teeth made her wonder.

Could dragons swim? Would he dive in after her next time and snatch her out of the ocean?

Liz kept swimming. She wasn't at all sure how she'd evade the dragon once she got to the island.

Never mind how she'd get out of the ocean. It was

too easy to imagine him compelling her to spend too long underwater, but she refused to panic at the prospect. She had to outsmart him, and that meant keeping calm. She should have looked to see if he was missing any scales.

That was when she realized she hadn't seen his shadow pass overhead again. Where had he gone? Liz cautiously broke the surface and took a breath, daring to look around. She stayed low, wondering why the dragon would have abandoned his attack.

She quickly saw that he hadn't had a choice. The yellow dragon was locked in combat with another dragon above and behind Liz, closer to the parking lot. The second dragon was a deep red, the red of Chinese lacquer. Each scale again looked as if it was edged in gold, his talons were gold, and he had golden horns. The two of them looked like jeweled treasures.

But they were pounding the crap out of each other, which worked for Liz in a big way.

The dragons locked claws and tumbled end over end through the sky. Their tails twined together and Liz understood that they were trying to overpower each other. Their teeth flashed as each snapped at the other, and their talons ripped into each other's flesh. Liz saw more than one explosion of orange fire and a lot of blood flowing.

It was all black and it sizzled when it dropped into the ocean, emitting a plume of steam.

She remembered what Sloane had said and knew they were both *Slayers*.

They must be fighting over her. It was not good news to be on the Must Have list for two different *Slayers*. It had to be because of the firestorm.

Because of the baby. Liz's hand curved over her belly protectively.

No matter what his intentions were, the new *Slayer* was giving her a chance to escape, and Liz was going to use it.

Liz swam the last distance to the island and pulled herself onto the dock. There was no one around, presumably because they were all still making repairs to the damaged equipment. She raised her hands and turned around in place, surrounding herself with a spiral of her mother's favorite protection spell. It was resonant and powerful, a good spell to use in an emergency. It was also one that left the spellcaster exhausted.

Liz would take dead tired over plain old dead any day.

She finished the last flourish of the spell and felt its cocoon close around her. It would move with her, although it would fade in time. For the moment, she was as safe as she could be.

She took one last look at the fighting pair and saw the red one get slammed hard by the new arrival. He grabbed the yellow one by the neck and shoved his face into the ocean, as if he'd forcibly hold him underwater.

The yellow dragon thrashed, his powerful tail thumping his opponent. His wings beat. His claws tore. The red dragon held fast and breathed a stream of fire at his captive for good measure. The ocean boiled, the water turning black around the fighting pair.

Liz heard a roar of outrage.

And then the yellow dragon disappeared.

The red one hovered over the surface of the water, his dark wings beating with slow power. He flew back and forth, examining the water, then turned gracefully to look at her.

With that one look, Liz understood that he hadn't been saving her—he'd been saving her for himself. He flew toward her with power and fury, his eyes shining with hatred and his talons extended.

It was a little bit hard to believe in the efficacy of an invisible spell when a dragon had her in his sights.

Liz spun around to run, not at all sure she could run fast enough.

"You ready to listen yet?"

The old-speak slid into Brandon's thoughts, startling him as it always did. He stood up and looked out the windows of his prison, only to see Sloane standing in the path, almost exactly where Brandon had been attacked. The other *Pyr* had his arms folded across his chest and his expression was guarded.

Brandon knew he was lucky that the other *Pyr* had come to him at all.

"I'm sorry," he replied in kind. *"I've made a huge mistake."*

The Apothecary nodded and scanned the front of the building. *"Serious dragonsmoke barrier here. I'll guess that permissions are set against you."*

"Burns like acid."

Sloane nodded. *"From this side, too."* He flicked a look at Brandon. *"Find anything interesting in the lair?"*

Brandon gestured to the larger main room. *"A spiral in sand, with two of my scales in the middle."* He frowned. *"But I've given him three. I can't find the last one."*

Sloane wasn't listening anymore. He was walking back and forth, his expression intent. *"Who else was here?"*

"Some yellow Slayer. Blond guy. Blue eyes."

Sloane exhaled. *"I thought I'd caught a whiff of Jorge in town, but it was so fleeting."* He scanned the area, nodding in thought, then looked at the sky.

"I think they were going after Liz."

Sloane gave Brandon a stern glance. *"Bad plan to leave your mate undefended."*

Brandon exhaled with impatience. *"Look, okay, I've messed up,"* he said, his temper simmering. *"But it would be better to help me than to lecture me. I know I was wrong. I need to fix it. I need to defend Liz!"*

"You need the Pyr, and you need your own dragon nature, and until you admit that, there's nothing I can do to help you," Sloane said flatly.

To Brandon's dismay, the Apothecary turned to walk away.

"All right!" Brandon shouted out loud. He pounded on the window to get Sloane's attention and was relieved when the other *Pyr* turned to glance over his shoulder.

"Choose," Sloane said softly, so softly that only Brandon could hear him.

He stared at the floor. He feared he was lost himself. But he had to believe in the promise of the firestorm, and he had to believe in the future. He looked back at Sloane and met the other *Pyr*'s gaze steadily. He answered in old-speak and used the formal form of address, knowing he was asking for a lot in dragon terms. *"Please defend Liz and my son."*

Sloane surveyed him for a moment, then nodded. *"I will do my best,"* he replied in kind, then flung his hands into the air. There was a brilliant shimmer of blue as Sloane transformed to a sleek dragon. His scales were all the hues of tourmalines, shading from green to purple and back again over his length. His claws were gold and his scales were tipped in gold. He could have been a jeweled ornament, but he flew with grace and breathed fire. He gave Brandon one last look—as if to emphasize that his best might not be good enough—then took flight over the trees and disappeared.

Brandon looked around his prison, his frustration rising. He had to get free. He had to help Liz. He couldn't get through the dragonsmoke barrier alone, but Chen had moved him through it.

Brandon looked at the elaborately worked spiral of

sand on the floor and had an idea. He deliberately walked across the spiral, dragging his feet and cutting a path through the carefully stacked sand furrows. He felt electricity around his feet and looked down to see red sparks flying from the sand each place he disturbed it.

He started to kick it, making it fly into the air on every side. He didn't understand the spell or its working, but he'd trash this spiral.

If nothing else, it would annoy Chen and maybe prompt his return.

That might give Brandon a chance.

Chapter 10

Liz took two steps before there was a flash of blue-green light.

The light was strange, like colored lightning. It made all the hairs on her body stand up, and Liz shivered involuntarily at its sudden energy. It reminded Liz of the light in the car that had presaged the appearance of the mark on her arm, and she wasn't very glad to see it again.

When the light faded, there was a dark-haired guy standing where the dock attached to the shore. He looked Italian and was also gorgeous, but wasn't Sloane. It was the guy who had been watching her and Brandon in Hale'iwa from the porch on the other side of the road.

Liz held her ground, hoping he was *Pyr*.

He smiled with a serenity Liz didn't share.

He lifted his hand and she saw that he held a large quartz crystal. It was like one of her mom's crystals, the ones she'd used for divining. He pointed it at the attacking dragon and a bolt of blue-green light fired from the end of the stone, like a laser.

Liz blinked in surprise and turned to look.

The red dragon was hit in the chest by the ray of light.

He screamed in pain, as if he had been struck by lightning. He arched his back and bared his teeth. He lost the rhythm of flight, his wings apparently useless, and plummeted toward the ocean.

Just when he should have splashed into the turquoise waters of the bay, he disappeared.

Liz's knees were shaking and she thought her heart was going to explode from beating so hard. She turned with some uncertainty to the dark-haired guy, who was considering his crystal with satisfaction. That smile still played over his lips and widened slightly when he looked at her.

"I am Marco, although they call me the Sleeper," he said, his voice deep. He spoke as if he had all the time in the world, the absolute opposite of what Liz was feeling.

"You're *Pyr*, too," she guessed, hoping it was true.

He nodded, his gaze sliding to the area where the other two dragons had recently been.

"And they're *Slayers*," she guessed, remembering what Sloane had told her.

He nodded again. "A particularly treacherous kind of *Slayer*. Those two are the only ones who can spontaneously manifest elsewhere."

"That's how they disappeared, then." Liz pushed her wet hair back from her face and realized she was chilled. "Where'd they go?"

"Who can say?" Marco shrugged as if it didn't matter. "They also can disguise their scents."

There was great news. Liz didn't share his indifference. "They were targeting me. Why? Because of Brandon?"

"Only the true *Pyr* have firestorms. Only true *Pyr* father more *Pyr*." Marco met her gaze steadily. "Many *Slayers* believe that the weakest link in the process is the human mate."

That wasn't the most reassuring thing Liz had heard.

She heaved a sigh. "You were in Hale'iwa. How did you get here?"

Marco held out the crystal. "See the spark within it?"

Liz peered into the stone. There was a blue-green light flickering in its core, like a glint of lightning held captive. She nodded, wondering what it was.

"Darkfire," Marco said, turning the stone in his hand as he watched the darkfire burn. "Trapped in this crystal. Obedient to me."

"Why?"

"Because I am the heir of the Cantor. Darkfire is my realm and responsibility."

"What does it do?"

"It introduces unpredictability, challenges expectations, turns possibilities into reality." Marco considered her. He didn't blink, and his perusal was so steady that she had the feeling he could read her thoughts. "Like you, your presence here, your powers, and your being part of the firestorm. There is a better reason for the *Slayers* to target you. You are more than human, aren't you?"

Liz felt herself blush. "I'm not sure what you mean," she lied.

Marco nodded toward the burning dock by the parking lot. "I saw the wall of fire you created. Few humans can cast such spells."

"I don't really want to talk about it."

Marco smiled. "We do not need to talk about it. You know what you will have to do." He gave her an intent look, one that reminded Liz of her grandmother's glare, then once again turned his attention to his crystal.

Liz wasn't feeling quite so calm. Her spells had worked only in the very short term against the dragon. That two *Slayers* who could spontaneously manifest were somewhere in the world, looking to eliminate her and the child she hadn't even believed she was carrying, was far from ideal. Her test was pending, and she'd had all the warning she would get. Never mind that the one *Pyr* who could defend her was in Hale'iwa, talking to the old guy he called his friend, the guy Sloane had said was a *Slayer*.

"He is snared," Marco said softly, without glancing up.

"Who?" Liz asked, even though she knew the answer.

"Brandon. You know this. You recognized the binding spell. It was cast by the red *Slayer*."

Liz's heart sank. "Chen?"

Marco nodded.

"Then where's Brandon? He went to talk to him."

Marco lifted one brow. "You also know that you are the only one who can aid him."

"Me? I don't understand how I should help him. What about all of you *Pyr*? Don't dragons deal with dragon spells?"

"Not usually. In these times, we rely more on force and negotiation." He smiled again with such tranquillity that Liz wanted to deck him. "Our dragon magic is mostly forgotten."

"Who would forget their own magic?"

"Surely you cannot blame anyone for trying to forget when you have done the same?" Marco's voice was silky.

He knew. Liz glared at him, knowing that she must look fierce. He didn't know the whole story. He didn't understand what she'd seen. Some stranger wasn't going to tell her what to do and what choices to make.

If she listened to anyone, it would be Pele.

She knew that a Firedaughter had the power to heal.

She didn't know how much of her powers she retained, despite Pele's assurances. She could try to help Brandon and choke in the last minute, only getting them into more trouble.

Marco smiled, as if he had heard her thoughts.

"How apt he would find a Firedaughter," he murmured. Before Liz could respond to that, he came to her side and offered the crystal to her. "Take this."

Liz recoiled. "I can't use a crystal like that. They're for divining and healing. They're not *weapons*."

Marco was—predictably—untroubled by her reaction. "Darkfire is a kind of fire, thus it is in your realm, too."

"No. I don't believe it. . . ."

"Then keep it in trust for me until your son is born."

"Why don't you just keep it yourself?"

"Because it wants to be with you." He lifted it to his ear, as if listening, then nodded. "Yes. It does."

Liz opened her mouth to protest, then saw the conviction in his dark eyes. And she recognized this logic, this kind of certainty in what had to be done, who had to do it, and how it had to be facilitated. Her mother had talked to her crystals, too, and listened to them. Liz considered the large crystal and knew that Marco was right—because the blue-green flame flickered with greater intensity when he offered her the stone.

She should have it.

She would need it.

She put out her hand, and Marco smiled.

No sooner had Liz accepted the weight of the crystal in her hand than Marco flung his hands into the sky. He leapt up and shifted shape with such grace that Liz's breath was taken away. He became a dragon, too, a large and sleek one.

He was who he said he was. Liz was reassured.

His flight across Kane'ohe Bay was filled with the same leisurely grace as his smile, and Liz felt a new conviction settle over her as she watched him go. The dragons were beautiful creatures—when they weren't trying to kill her. Liz watched Marco soar high over the mountains, and accepted the truth.

She had to embrace her powers, then use them to free Brandon. She had to believe once again. She had to move beyond the past. Her biggest obstacle was probably her fear of failure, but she'd conquered fear before. She would face a challenge similar to the one that had killed her mother, but she would need to win. It was the only way that the firestorm would fulfill its promise—to both of them.

Marco disappeared from sight, and she had to hope that he was going to Brandon.

Liz turned the crystal in her hand but saw no secrets lurking in its depths. Yet. She lifted it to her ear and listened but heard nothing.

She put it in her purse.

Liz guessed she'd be seeing Marco again, when her son was born—if not before.

Her son. Her son would be a *Pyr*. She was going to be living at the intersection between the world of the *Pyr* and the world of humans for the foreseeable future.

She'd better get used to it.

"Well, there you are!" Maureen exclaimed from behind her. "You're soaking wet."

"There wasn't a shuttle . . ."

"You should have just called." Maureen put an arm around Liz and urged her toward the residence. "You weren't caught in that eruption, were you?"

"It was right behind me. The mountain fell just as I came out of the tunnel." Liz smiled at her friend. "Your car's okay."

"I'm more worried about you than the car! You must be shaken up." Maureen gave her shoulders a squeeze. "I was so concerned for you today, but look at you."

"I just took a swim. . . ."

"But your eyes are shining like diamonds." Maureen nodded with satisfaction but held up a hand. "You don't have to tell me a thing. I'm just glad that Hawai'i is agreeing with you so well." She rolled her eyes. "Despite all that's going on. I'm glad you're here. I forgot to give you a key to my room this morning. They managed to dig out your luggage—it doesn't look as if you'd unpacked much—and that's all been moved."

"That's great. Thank you."

"We have some last-minute changes, so I hope you don't mind me abandoning you again." Maureen's brow furrowed.

"No, that's fine. I really appreciate everything, Maureen, and don't want to be a pain . . ."

"Never!" Maureen gave Liz a quick hug, then waved at two students carrying a folding table. "No, no. We need that in the other hall. I'll show you." With a cheerful wave, she was gone, doing what she did best.

Liz headed for the room, knowing what she had to do.

Brandon had disrupted the entire spiral, and the floor of the room looked like a beach. The sand wasn't making any electrical charge when he kicked through it anymore, so he believed he had dissipated its power. He did feel more in control of his dragon. That had to be a good sign.

Especially if Chen came back.

Brandon's two scales were still perched in the sand in the middle of the room. They glowed faintly, as if they were hooked to an alarm system. He wouldn't have put that past Chen.

Since the *Slayer* wasn't answering his summons so far, Brandon would trip the alarm.

He strode across the room and bent to pick up his scales. His fingertips had just brushed the closest one when there was a brilliant flash of light.

The blond guy was right in front of him, crouched on the other side of the scales, grinning like a maniac. Jorge. The other *Slayer*. Before Brandon could make sense of the way he had abruptly appeared, Jorge decked him. Brandon fell backward, and Jorge seized a scale.

"I'll just take these," Jorge said. "Seeing as you don't need them anymore."

Brandon tasted blood and roared in pain. He was

sprawled on his ass, blood running down his chin, but he rolled to his feet. "No chance! They're mine!"

"Dead dragons don't need armor," Jorge sneered. His eyes glinted with malice as he turned the scale in the light. "But why don't you just come and get it?" He deliberately lifted the scale, as if displaying it to Brandon, then snapped it in half.

Brandon felt as if he'd been knifed in the gut. He bent over, the pain excruciating. He was bleeding again, and he was sure the wound would correspond to a spot where he was missing a scale.

Jorge chuckled and pocketed the broken pieces. He obviously enjoyed Brandon's anguish. He reached for the last scale in the sand. "Guess you'll have to decide who to answer to soon," he said, looking so smug that Brandon wanted to rip his throat out.

For once, Brandon's dragon had the right idea.

"Maybe there won't be much left of you for Chen to claim." Jorge glanced down at the final scale, his expression malicious, and Brandon guessed what he was going to do.

Brandon's dragon roared, and he let the beast loose.

He shifted shape quickly and bounded forward. He seized Jorge by the throat, then breathed a plume of brilliant orange dragonfire, aiming it at the man caught in his grasp. Jorge's hair burned and his skin reddened.

Jorge snarled in fury, then shifted in Brandon's grip. He became a topaz yellow dragon that was as slippery as a snake. His scales were already singed, which made no sense, but Brandon would worry about that later. He breathed fire and turned more of them black.

Jorge twisted and snapped at Brandon. His sharp teeth caught at Brandon's shoulder. Jorge bit deep and tore Brandon's flesh, ripping out a chunk and spitting blood on the floor.

Brandon caught the *Slayer* by the throat and slammed his head into the wall so hard that the building shook. It was satisfying to see the black blood flow from Jorge's temple, so satisfying that he did it again.

Jorge snarled and thrashed within Brandon's grip.

"Give me that broken scale."

"Get it yourself." Jorge drove his tail upward, slamming it into Brandon's genitals. The blow was enough for Brandon to loosen his grip a bit. He saw stars for a moment and fought his nausea.

Jorge slithered away.

The *Slayer* dove for the last scale, but Brandon jumped on to his back. He bit at one wing, tearing it loose from the joint, and Jorge screamed as he fell to the floor. Hard. He still reached for that second scale, but Brandon breathed fire at his outstretched claw. The scales blackened and smoked, crackling as they burned, until Jorge withdrew his claw.

He reared back then, slamming Brandon into the ceiling. Brandon wound his tail beneath the *Slayer* quickly, getting even for that blow to the genitals. Jorge roared in pain, and that was before Brandon bit down and ripped his right wing free of his body. Black blood flowed from the wound, dripping into the sand on the floor and hissing on contact.

Jorge spun in Brandon's grasp and jabbed his talon straight into the third undefended spot on his belly. All the breath went out of Brandon at the strike, and he faltered just long enough for Jorge to slash across his face with his claws.

Brandon fell backward from the blow, and braced himself for Jorge to land on top of him.

But the *Slayer* stood before him, one wing stretched high, his tail coiled across the floor.

He exhaled slowly, his eyes glittering like cut glass.

Brandon felt the temperature of the room drop; then a barb pierced the wound that had bled first. The pain was excruciating and it burned like acid.

Dragonsmoke.

Jorge was breathing dragonsmoke. Brandon narrowed his eyes and looked more closely, only then seeing the tendril of frosty white dragonsmoke that stretched like a cord between himself and Jorge. He started to get up, intending to attack his opponent, only to realize that his strength was sapped.

Jorge chuckled, never breaking the thread of dragonsmoke.

Somehow it was stealing energy from Brandon. He watched as the *Slayer* smiled more broadly. He looked larger and brighter. He was feeding on Brandon, like a kind of vampire, stealing Brandon's power and making it his own.

Fury gave Brandon new strength. He bellowed and

breathed a stream of fire at the offending tendril of dragonsmoke. The dragonsmoke was unaffected. He tore at it with his talons, but each time his claw passed through it, the smoke burned. Then he leapt at Jorge, who was enjoying his pain far too much.

But Jorge lifted that broken scale high and crushed the two pieces to cinders in his claw right before Brandon's eyes. The pain was overwhelming, so excruciating that Brandon thought he would pass out. He felt as if a chunk of his gut was being ripped out of him and shredded before his eyes.

Brandon fell to the floor and shifted back to his human form. He panted and tasted his own sweat as well as his blood. He was exhausted and terrified that this would be the end of him. The pain was more than anything he'd ever borne before. He was more battered than he had ever been before. He shifted back to his dragon form as soon as he could, not at all ready to surrender the fight.

Somehow he had to protect Liz.

Somehow he had to keep Jorge from finishing him off.

He had to trick the *Slayer* into underestimating him.

"Rotating between forms," Jorge muttered with satisfaction. "A classic sign of a *Pyr* near death. Maybe Chen will come home to find a corpse."

Brandon knew he could work with that assumption.

He could fake out Jorge. Because he not only knew

that Jorge would collect the second scale and leave Chen's lair, but that Jorge would leave the same way he'd arrived. He'd spontaneously manifest elsewhere.

Jorge was Brandon's ticket out of captivity.

Brandon repeatedly changed to his human form and back to dragon again, keeping his eyes nearly closed. He wanted to look as if he were out cold, but he kept one eye open the barest bit so he could keep track of Jorge. It made him dizzy to shift so quickly and frequently, but he had to have the element of surprise on his side again.

The *Slayer* chuckled, then shifted back to human form. He went back to pick up that second scale. He turned his back on Brandon, and Brandon coiled his power to move. Jorge bent over, his fingers touched the scale, and he started to shimmer.

Brandon leapt and seized his ankle. Jorge roared and tried to shake him off, but Brandon held fast. He locked both hands around Jorge's ankle, determined to not let go. Jorge punched Brandon, obviously trying to leave him behind, but Brandon knew salvation when he'd found it. Jorge kicked him in the face and probably loosened a tooth, but Brandon had more to lose than his teeth.

He held on.

Because his life depended on it.

Just as he'd anticipated, Jorge had been in the act of spontaneously manifesting elsewhere. Just as he'd hoped, Jorge couldn't stop his disappearing act once it had begun. Brandon was soon surrounded by that

strange silvery fog again and felt nauseated. He held
tightly to the *Slayer*'s ankle, not at all sure where he'd
end up if he let go.

In fact, he wasn't sure where he'd end up, anyway.

But wherever it was, he'd have to kick Jorge's butt
to get free. He needed energy for that.

Maybe it was time he learned to breathe a dragonsmoke conduit himself.

Liz opened her suitcase on the cot that had been set
up in Maureen's room and rummaged in it a bit, to
make it look as if she had been unpacking. Then she
emptied her wet purse on the bathroom floor. Her
phone was dead after its dip in the bay, but that was
to be expected. The purse was not in very good shape,
but she would sponge as much water as possible out
of it later. She could also lay out her ID and cash to
dry.

First, she had to do something more important. She
opened the zippered pocket in the purse lining and
took out a small black velvet bag. It was wet, as well,
the silk velvet dripping and smelling of the sea.

But then, her mother had always loved the ocean.
Liz smiled sadly to herself as she undid the drawstring
and tipped out the contents into her hand. The pendant was sterling silver, about the size of a dollar coin,
and it hung from a silver chain. A lump rose in Liz's
throat at the sight of it.

She would never forget that night.

Maybe that had been the point.

She turned the pendant over in her hand, her tears rising at the sight of the incomplete pentacle etched on the back side. A Wiccan pentacle has five points, one for each element and the one pointing skyward for the element of spirit that presided over fire, water, air, and earth. This pentacle had only three points drawn. One of the lower ones—for fire—was missing, as was the point for spirit.

Her mother had died in a test of fire and spirit.

Liz didn't want to think about that night. Still her chest was tight, as if her body would remember what her mind preferred not to recall.

It had been her fault.

She knew that she'd been ducking that night's memory and understood that her period of grace was over. She had to accept the truth before her own challenge began.

Liz held the pendant, pressing it between her palms and folding her hands together as if to pray. She dropped to her knees and touched her forehead to her index fingers.

And for the first time in fourteen years, Liz let herself remember.

She was weeping when she heard her mother's voice in her thoughts. That was when she realized she had been giving Brandon the advice she'd been hearing all her life. She spread her hands and looked at the pendant. One tear fell and shone on the silver—one tear for the anguish of seeing her mother killed.

"You have a gift," her mother whispered in Liz's

thoughts, her words filled with familiar conviction. *"You were born the third daughter of the third daughter, the one who can pierce the veil between the worlds. Like us, you can see the dead and the gods. Like us, you can see the fantastical beings whose worlds intersect our own. But only you can move between magic, death, and life to heal. That is the power of the Firedaughter.*

"Three by three, your gift is strong. You are strong, my Elizabeth. Your gift will frighten you with its power. But like all ghosts with purpose, it will not be denied. It will summon you, and if you do not reply, it will fetch you. If you fight it, it may abandon you in one of those other realms and seize your innate ability to pierce the veil. If you turn your back upon it, you can never be what you were born to be. If you mean to survive, if you mean to fulfill your destiny, you must learn to use your gift. Embrace it, for it is the only thing that can ensure you survive the test."

After her mother's death, Liz had lived in denial. Until coming to Hawai'i, she'd thought she was winning against the powers that had once shaped her life. City concrete had kept the voices of the elements at bay. Working in solitude had diminished her connection to others and dulled her sensitivity. A rigid focus on science and intellect, at the expense of magic and emotion, had made her feel that she was in control.

But her gift had only been slumbering. Embers glowing in the ashes, awaiting only a breath of wind to be kindled again.

Or maybe a firestorm.

Now she would face her own test, when she had so much to lose.

Liz had no more time to weep. She pulled the chain over her head and her mother's pendant settled between her breasts. The weight of it was reassuring. She looked at herself in the mirror and saw the diamonds Maureen had mentioned dancing in her eyes.

If the prize was a future with Brandon, Liz was ready to take the test. If her son's life hung in the balance, Liz was prepared to fight any force that came against her.

First, she had to ensure that she had sanctuary. There wasn't time to protect the entire island. She'd focus on this room so that she and Maureen would have a haven. She needed salt to mark the perimeter and secure the openings, and Liz was pretty sure she could find some in the kitchen.

There wasn't much time before the party.

She had better get to work.

Jorge manifested on a deserted cliff, then flung Brandon into the dirt. Brandon had time to recognize Ka'ena Point; then the *Slayer* shifted shape and fell on him with claws extended.

Jorge wasn't missing any scales.

Brandon shifted shape to his dragon form to defend himself, figuring he had a better chance against a dragon even though he was missing scales.

Jorge wasn't taking any chances this time that Brandon might survive. The *Slayer* tore at Brandon's chest, ripping open his flesh so that the blood flowed. Brandon bit deeply into the *Slayer* and tore off his other wing, spitting it into the dirt. The black blood flowed copiously, burning Brandon's hide wherever it touched. Jorge snarled and bared his teeth to breathe either fire or smoke, when Brandon had an idea.

Jorge's wings were destroyed.

He decked the *Slayer*, then snatched him up, racing out over the ocean. He flew fast and hard, ensuring that the island was left far behind them. If he left Jorge with no choice, maybe the *Slayer* would disappear.

If he left Jorge with no strength, maybe the *Slayer* would have no ability to disappear.

Brandon hovered in the air with Jorge in his clutches and deliberately breathed a long, slow stream of dragonsmoke. He had never put much effort into mastering this particular skill, but he found it came fairly easily to him. He coaxed the dragonsmoke to unfurl and wind its way toward Jorge. He drove it into one of the injuries he'd given the *Slayer* and immediately felt a surge of power move through the conduit of smoke.

Jorge must have felt it, too.

"No!" he screamed, struggling with new vigor.

Brandon breathed slowly and evenly, the power he was gaining from Jorge helping him to remain easily at the same altitude. Jorge struggled and bit. He slashed at Brandon's belly in a frenzy. Brandon soared high into the sky, carrying Jorge to the clouds.

Then he dropped him. He descended after the *Slayer*, keeping pace with his fall and ensuring that the ribbon of dragonsmoke remained intact.

Jorge thrashed in the air, obviously trying to fly. His instincts were stronger than his knowledge of his situation. He flailed, his black blood spraying in every direction. He swore. He tried to fling a tendril of dragonsmoke toward Brandon, but evidently the stress of plummeting toward the ocean ruined his concentration. His dragonsmoke was like a string of hyphens, a line broken at regular intervals.

Brandon could feel the *Slayer* weakening, just as he could feel his own strength growing. Jorge looked like he was trying to summon that power to move through space and time, but only a faint flicker passed over his silhouette.

"Save me!" Jorge cried when the choppy surface of the sea was close.

Brandon laughed. "Save yourself," he retorted.

Jorge screamed as he splashed into the ocean, dozens of miles from the coast of Oʻahu. Brandon dove into the water after his opponent and watched the *Slayer* sink toward the ocean floor. Jorge rotated between forms, transforming from a man to a dragon and back again repeatedly, but he kept sinking.

When the darkness of the ocean's depths obscured the sight of him, Brandon returned to the surface in triumph. He soared out of the sea, glad of his dragon's power, and turned his course toward Kaneʻohe.

And Liz.

*   *   *

By the time Liz was dressed for the cocktail party, she had reviewed every spell and charm she had ever learned. She'd forced herself to recall the wording of the incantations and the tone of voice, the mood, and the gestures. She wasn't entirely sure what powers she'd need, but she wanted her entire arsenal at hand.

No wonder she was also buzzing with adrenaline. Trouble could strike at any time. As soon as she stepped outside of this protective circle, she could be attacked. There was no word from Brandon, which made her fear that he was in danger. She should never have left him in Hale'iwa with Chen. Pele was right: it was Liz's task to heal Brandon.

She'd brought a sleeveless black dress that always made her feel confident. It was fitted through the waist and flared around her knees. She slipped on a pair of black sandals and wound up her hair. She wore a pair of jet and silver earrings that had been her grandmother's, and put her mother's pendant inside the dress. Only the chain was visible. A stroke of lipstick across her lips, Marco's crystal in her evening bag, and she was ready to go.

She eyed her reflection in the mirror. Here went nothing.

Maureen came into the room and must have misinterpreted Liz's expression, because she laughed. "It won't be so bad," she chided, then produced a vivid pink hibiscus bloom. "For you," she said with a smile, and tucked it behind Liz's ear. "Left side means you're single," she whispered. "Now go on and have fun."

"You probably think I should have a drink right away."

"Can't hurt," Maureen said, heading for the bathroom. "I'll be there in ten, and your wineglass had better be half-empty." She shook a finger at Liz from the threshold to the bathroom. "If I find you in a corner, I'll introduce you to the most boring man in the room and you'll be stuck with him for hours."

Liz laughed, knowing Maureen would be good to her word. "There's a threat."

"Negative enforcement," Maureen said cheerfully, and shut the bathroom door. "Works every time."

Liz tugged the lanyard with her name tag over her head and headed out, as ready for war as she could be.

The party was exactly as Liz had expected. This was her world and she should have found comfort in it.

Instead, she was jittery.

Several of the visiting scientists had apparently miscalculated the effect of alcohol on their jet-lagged constitutions. This was providing entertainment. The sober ones wanted to talk about work, and Liz wondered which one of them was the boring man Maureen had threatened to introduce her to. There seemed to be a number of candidates.

She could see the auras of everyone in the room, which was less disconcerting than it had been the night before. She was getting used to seeing them again and using the information they provided. The auras were all mellow hums of blue and green with the occasional shimmer of gold or pink.

Except for the one woman in the corner. She was Asian and dressed in a tight-fitting red Chinese dress. Her heels had to be five inches tall and they were as shiny and red as a candy apple. Her lipstick matched her shoes perfectly. She looked completely incongruous, and although people glanced surreptitiously at her, no one spoke to her. She didn't initiate any conversations herself, either, just stood against the wall and sipped what looked like a glass of juice.

She had no aura.

And she was watching Liz as hungrily as a hawk.

She had to be some kind of supernatural being. Was she a *Pyr*? Weren't the *Pyr* all men? Liz wasn't sure. Maybe some other kind of being had been attracted to her firestorm—or her powers. She kept her distance from the woman, resolved to letting her make the first move.

There was a lot of conversation about the earthquake that morning and an exchange of stories from those who had experienced it and those who had arrived after it was over. Everyone had a story of disrupted plans to tell, but no one had been injured. There was also excitement over the volcanic eruption in the Ko'olau range earlier that day. A prominent scientist had been interviewed on the news and had speculated about a rogue vent being opened by the earthquake. This theory was hotly discussed.

No one, interestingly, blamed dragons, dragon shape shifters, or an infuriated goddess named Pele. Certainly no one talked about Firedaughters. Liz knew she should have been relieved by that. Instead, she felt as if the other scientists were missing the point.

"Dr. Barrett!" a plump woman exclaimed as she evidently read Liz's name tag. She offered her hand. "What a pleasure to meet you. I'm Hazel Wentworth."

Liz shook Dr. Wentworth's hand with enthusiasm, knowing her by reputation. "Yes, of course. You're at UC, aren't you?" This could be the opportunity she sought. She was sure that Dr. Wentworth was on the advisory panel that reviewed applications to do research at the Papahānaumokuākea Marine National Monument.

Hazel nodded. "Yes, and we're very excited about your findings with regards to coral disease and the emergence of tumors on certain species."

"I was intrigued by the research I saw linking specific algae species with the emergence of coral disease," Liz said, mentioning the name of the marine biologist responsible for that research.

"Yes, he's done excellent work," Hazel agreed with enthusiasm. "But your tentative link between pollution and the susceptibility of certain species to genetic mutation as a result of exposure opens an exciting new realm of possibilities in ensuring the welfare of the reef."

They entered an enthusiastic and technical discussion, exactly the chat Liz had hoped to have. She could only halfway attend the conversation, though, because her sense of being watched was so very strong. Each time she glanced over her shoulder, that Chinese woman's gaze was locked upon her.

And her smile was unfriendly.

The only person Liz knew without an aura was Chen, and that was because he wasn't a person—he was a *Slayer* and a dragon shifter. Could this be Chen? The hair was practically standing up on the back of Liz's neck with her awareness of the woman's steady gaze. When Maureen arrived and nodded approval at her nearly empty glass, Liz decided she couldn't stand it anymore.

She had to know.

If it was Chen, the *Slayer* was targeting her.

If there was going to be a fight, Liz wanted to get it over with. She wasn't going to be stalked, threatened, and distracted. She wanted to save Brandon and get back to the business of being in love.

She exchanged cards with Hazel and promised to send her several of her as-yet-published papers. Hazel expressed her pleasure in their conversation, suggesting that they would have to have a longer chat before the symposium ended.

"Perhaps you might like to visit the reserve," Hazel said. "Even if there isn't time for you to make a trip yourself, I could have samples collected and sent to you."

"That would be wonderful!" Liz thanked the other biologist, not even trying to hide her pleasure.

Then she excused herself.

The room where the party was being held had sliding doors along one exterior wall, and they were open to the velvety perfection of the night. It was hard to believe that there had been an earthquake and even a small volcanic eruption when the ocean looked so tranquil and the breeze was filled with the scents of flowers.

Liz put down her empty wineglass and stepped out into the night.

The Chinese woman followed her, her heels clicking on the patio stones.

Liz reasoned that she might as well get out of sight of the party. None of these people could help her. They could only get injured if the woman was Chen—and she knew that Chen wouldn't care if they were hurt. Her professional reputation wouldn't be enhanced by whatever she had to do, either. She kicked off her shoes and headed for the beach. On the way, she tugged out Marco's crystal and discarded her purse.

Liz hoped like hell she could use this thing, because the woman was right behind her. She was going to need all the help she could get.

Brandon flew as quickly as he could across the island. He didn't like being so visible, but he didn't have a choice. His main concern was getting to Liz before either of the *Slayers* did.

That they could travel instantly through space and manifest elsewhere didn't put time on his side.

Brandon was descending toward Kane'ohe Bay when he saw the vivid flash of orange light on Coconut Island's far side.

Dragonfire!

He feared the worst and landed quickly. He shifted to human form and raced toward the flames, hoping to keep the element of surprise on his side. He came around the ocean side of the island and stayed in the shadows. A building had been flattened during the earthquake and there was no sign of anyone around the debris at night. The light flashed again and Brandon ran forward, not knowing what he'd find.

He heard Liz call out. She shouted a string of words that sounded like an incantation, and suddenly it seemed that the shadows all around him were filled with life. They appeared to have become an army of dark shapes instead of simply shadows. Were those eyes he glimpsed in the darkness? Brandon didn't have time to look closely.

He rounded the last bit of shrubbery and saw Chen in flight in his dragon form. His scales were almost luminous against the night, so red and shiny that they could have been made of lacquer. The gold on his scales and horns flashed as his claws slashed through the night toward the woman standing with one hand outstretched.

His Liz looked very small before the furious airborne dragon, and when Chen breathed fire, she was silhouetted against the orange flames. She didn't flinch, though, and she didn't back away. She also wasn't burned.

She shouted again, and the shadows surged around and past Brandon. He was in the midst of a tumult, surrounded by a thousand voices and brushed by even more shadowy figures. They clustered around Liz, and Brandon recognized that she had summoned them.

This must be her power.

A heartbeat later, he saw that it was only part of what she could do. Her figure was suddenly illuminated, outlined by brilliant orange flames. No, she became a flame. She was in the middle of the fire, part of it, feeding it and commanding it.

She looked like a fire goddess come to life. Brandon was amazed. He could still see her silhouetted inside the column of fire, but her figure was all black and orange. Firelight and shadow. Sparks flew into the night from her.

Chen lunged at her, talons extended. Brandon recovered from his shock and leapt forward, shifting shape on the way.

Liz flung up her hand and the flame that surrounded her extended into the sky in a flurry of sparks. It coalesced into a rope of fire. It was like a blazing lasso that she cast toward the attacking Chen. Chen screamed as the circle of flame closed around him, and Brandon heard the hiss of his scales being scorched. The *Slayer* roared in pain and slashed at the fiery rope without success.

It was a spell, a powerful one.

This was how she knew about binding spells. She could cast them.

The shadows, meanwhile, encircled Chen, smothering him, blinding him. Chen raged and thrashed, but that burning rope wound around him over and over again, until he was trussed tightly with a cord of fire. Brandon thought he deserved everything he was getting.

Chen tipped back his head and raged dragonfire. Brandon was just as shocked as the *Slayer* when his flames joined with the column of fire from Liz, defecting to the other side and giving her more power.

Brandon was awed by his mate all over again.

The *Slayer* screamed in anguish, thrashing within his burning prison. He turned his radiant gaze upon Liz, his anger tangible. "How dare you?" he demanded.

"I could ask you the same thing." Liz held up a crystal in her left hand, pointing it as the enraged *Slayer*. "Release Brandon from your spell," she commanded.

"Never!" Chen roared.

A bolt of blue-green light shot from the end of the crystal, searing Chen in the chest. What was that thing? Brandon had never seen a crystal used like a laser before.

Meanwhile, the *Slayer* arched his back in pain, emitting a low hiss of fury. Then his tail thrashed and his eyes shone with anger. Brandon heard music and conversation from the other side of the island and had to assume that a party was keeping anyone from coming to investigate.

A bolt of lightning fired from the sky, and Brandon feared it had somehow been summoned by Chen. When it illuminated a protective cocoon that surrounded Liz, then sliced through it with white heat, he knew he was right. Liz screamed in pain and fell to her knees when the lightning bolt struck her. Brandon smelled charring flesh and cinders. The burning rope shone like embers from a bonfire.

He raced toward Liz, fearing the worst.

But when the light faded, both Chen and Liz were gone.

So were the moving shadows.

He glanced around the empty beach, knowing his eyes hadn't deceived him. Chen must have spontaneously manifested elsewhere, dragging Liz with him. Either the binding spell had provided enough of a link or Chen had snatched her during that bright flash of light. Brandon guessed that Chen would surely retaliate for her entrapment of him.

But how?

And where?

Brandon saw lightning flash on the horizon, far out to sea, and guessed. There was a storm gathering, one that hadn't been there before. It wasn't natural and it hadn't developed over time. No, the weather pattern was being manipulated, and he guessed it was being affected by Chen.

Brandon feared then that Chen would extinguish Liz's fire spells by drowning her.

He had to get to her in time.

Chapter 11

Liz nearly fainted when the lightning struck her. She felt her mother's pendant take the hit, and the melting silver burned against her skin. She fell backward from the *Slayer*'s assault, and her hold over her fire spell wavered for just an instant.

The fire rope slipped.

It was all the opportunity Chen needed.

He wriggled free and seized her, his claw tightening around her. Liz had time to see the evil gleaming in his reptile eye and to glance down his dark gullet when he laughed. Then there was a flash of light and the beach of Coconut Island disappeared.

She was surrounded by a gray fog, one that made her feel nauseated. Chen's tight grip around her abdomen didn't help. She guessed that nothing good was going to happen to her, and knew she needed to keep hold of the crystal.

Suddenly she was just above the surface of the sea.

It was raining hard, and lightning flashed from the clouds overhead. Liz had time to notice that there was darkness and water on all sides before she was plunged into the dark water.

Chen dove deep, dragging her down toward the bottom of the ocean. Liz knew she was doomed if he released her there.

If he released her at all.

She instinctively held her breath. Chen was swimming deeper with alarming speed. Liz summoned a strength she hadn't known she possessed and jammed the point of the crystal into Chen's eye.

He roared, the sound swallowed by the sea, and flung her aside.

She saw the flash of his malicious smile and knew he thought that she'd never make it to the surface. Chen shifted shape in a brilliant shimmer of blue light, becoming a red salamander that almost glowed against the darkness of the ocean. He swam away, diving down to the ocean floor, his form swallowed by the darkness.

Liz didn't have the time or the ability to chase Chen. Instead, she fixed her gaze skyward and began to move to the surface with powerful, steady strokes. She was a strong swimmer and as long as she didn't panic, she was sure she could make it. She exhaled gradually and slowly, determined to survive.

Brandon flew right into the storm. He circled the surface of the water, searching for some clue to where

Liz might be. He flew low over the choppy surface, breathing deeply, seeking her scent.

When he caught a whiff of her, he nearly hooted in delight.

Instead he took a deep breath and dove into the dark water. Once again, his dragon powers felt good. He was stronger in dragon form. He could hold his breath longer and swim farther. And his keen dragon vision allowed him to spy Liz in a black dress in the inky, dark water just beneath him.

He swam toward her and snatched her up. She took one look at him, and then her eyes closed. A feeble trail of bubbles came from her nostrils. He'd reached her just in time. Brandon surged for the surface with her in his grasp. When he emerged from the water with a gasping breath, he shifted shape. He had learned years before how to tread water and give mouth-to-mouth resuscitation, and he was glad of it now.

The storm was already passing, as sure a sign as could be that it was unnatural. It took only a few breaths from him for Liz to begin choking. He held her as she coughed up the seawater, her body ensuring its own survival even when she wasn't fully conscious. The sea calmed around him, and he felt his exhaustion.

Never mind the salt water in his wounds.

Relief left him numb. He felt his exhaustion from the trials of the day and knew he needed a moment's respite before he headed for dry land. Brandon caught

Liz against his chest and rolled to his back, floating on the surface of the sea. It was a long way back to the island.

He just needed to restore his strength. Liz had passed out but she was breathing, her hand curled on his chest. At least they were out of the storm. The dark clouds were blowing away to the east, taking the lightning with them. The sky was dark overhead and filled with stars, the ocean a dark murmur around them. Brandon watched the moon rise and assessed the distance to the island.

It was really far.

Liz was cold. He had to get her out of the water so she was warm and safe. He summoned every vestige of strength left in him and shifted shape. He took flight, carrying his precious burden, and made steady progress toward the shore.

Brandon thought he was hallucinating when he saw a tourmaline dragon descending out of the sky toward him. He had never been so glad to see a dragon in his life. The scent told him the new arrival's identity.

Just when they needed an Apothecary.

"Is she all right?" Sloane asked, his concern clear.

"No, but she's alive." Brandon held Liz closely, trying to warm her with his body. *"She was struck by lightning,"* he added. *"Chen's lightning."*

"There's something unusual about your mate."

"I know." Brandon had to tell him the rest aloud because he needed practice with his old-speak. Now he felt motivated to do it. "She trapped Chen with a

rope of fire. It was some kind of spell. I think she weakened him with it. And he was angry enough to summon the lightning."

Sloane looked at Liz with amazement.

"Not only that," Brandon said. "She used this crystal as a weapon. It shot out a blue-green light, like a laser." He realized that Sloane was helping him, too. By encouraging him to talk, the Apothecary helped Brandon forget his own exhaustion. To his relief, the island was growing steadily closer.

"Darkfire," Sloane breathed. "I didn't know anyone but Marco could do that." He gave Liz an assessing glance.

Brandon didn't know what that meant, but he was relieved that his heart was matching its beat to hers again. The sensation made him dizzy, and he hoped that the strength of his pulse would feed her own. "She's the one who can break Chen's spell over me. She's the one who understands it. That's the gift of the firestorm."

He heard the smile in Sloane's voice when that dragon replied, "You sound like Rafferty."

"Who's that?"

"One of the *Pyr* who believes very strongly in the firestorm."

Brandon looked down at Liz and acknowledged that there was a lot he didn't know about his own nature. Liz had been right that he needed to find out more—and she was probably right that he couldn't just make his dragon go away. "I'd like to meet him,"

Brandon said quietly, knowing that Sloane would hear him.

"You will eventually, I'm sure. I've asked for help from Erik and the others. Some of the *Pyr* will arrive soon."

It was new to feel such relief in the promise of dragons arriving, but Brandon already understood that these *Pyr* could help him. "Not my dad?"

"Not your dad."

That was a relief. He wasn't ready for fireworks just yet.

"You don't look so good yourself," Sloane commented. "But I can't believe you got free of that dragonsmoke barrier without being incinerated. How did you do it?"

Brandon quickly updated Sloane on his battle with Jorge. "I've got that vial, too. Maybe there's some residue of the powder in it."

The other *Pyr* nodded with approval once he'd heard it all. "Good. We'll have a day, maybe more. Let's get a hotel room, a suite with two bedrooms. Somewhere private and expensive. You spend the time with Liz—do some healing—and I'll defend the perimeter. My treat."

Before Brandon could thank Sloane, the other dragon descended in a slow spiral over Oʻahu. Brandon recognized the north shore and directed him to the beach for the best resort in the area.

They both shifted shape in the shallows on the beach, but Liz didn't stir. Brandon carried her in his arms, he and Sloane striding out of the surf and toward the hotel. They must have made quite a sight, but Brandon didn't care.

Liz was okay, and he wasn't going to leave her again.

Liz's nostrils were filled with the smell of ash. She could taste cinders on her tongue and she was sure she could feel her skin sizzling as it was touched by fire. She cried out, fearing that she had been claimed.

Instead she was nude in a luxurious king-sized bed. The crystal that Marco had given her was on the nightstand. She looked around herself in astonishment, wondering how she had managed to move from the ocean's depths to a hotel suite.

The room was large and beautifully decorated, and an entire wall of sliding glass was opened to the warm breeze. She could see the sea and the faint tinge of dawn at the horizon. The balcony had planters along the railing, and they were filled with lush growth. Liz took a deep breath and tried to release some tension.

She was safe.

And relatively unscathed.

Back in paradise again.

That was when she realized she wasn't alone. Brandon, also nude, was stretched out beside her. He was watching her with a mixture of amusement and concern, his gaze warm upon her. "Always a surprise to survive a dragon attack, isn't it?" he asked, and Liz couldn't help but smile in return.

"Yes." She took another deep breath, not quite ready to change the mood in the room. She was glad to be safe and glad to see that he was okay, although the bandages on his abdomen and shoulder hinted that he had also survived a dragon attack.

There was fresh blood seeping through the two bandages on his abdomen, and she guessed that this was where his scales were missing from his dragon form.

"I'm sorry," he said, taking her hand in his. He was warm and his touch was gentle. "I was totally wrong about Chen."

"He tricked you," Liz said.

Brandon nodded. "And he did it again. I wanted to ask if he had some more of that powder, but he got very weak. I offered to help him get home." He winced. "Then I saw what he really was."

"He attacked you?"

"And trapped me. I'm only here because I got lucky. He pursued Jorge when Jorge went after you." He kissed her fingertips, his gaze meeting hers in a silent query.

It was time for Liz to tell him the truth. She nodded and swallowed.

Brandon lifted the sheet and with a gesture invited her to curl against him. He tucked the sheet over them, and Liz found it very reassuring to lean against his heat. It made it easier to confide in him. He kept his hand locked around hers and his other arm around her shoulders.

"Jorge appeared in Kane'ohe and attacked me." She squeezed his hand. "I'm sorry, too. I had to use my powers to survive, and I did." She looked up at him. "I should have told you about my family legacy, but I really didn't want to be a part of it."

"I guess we have that much in common." Brandon kissed her temple, and Liz tingled at his touch.

"Except I thought my powers were gone. I gave them away fourteen years ago. I didn't think I had them anymore, so I didn't think it was important that I remembered any of it." Liz shrugged, then touched her lips to Brandon's chest. "I didn't think I could do anything about it."

"What were your powers?" Sloane asked quietly from the doorway.

Both Brandon and Liz started, but Sloane smiled. He was wearing a T-shirt and jeans, and his feet were bare. Liz realized that the room must be part of a suite.

"I can hear you from the other room," he said. "But it seemed rude to eavesdrop. I've breathed a thick dragonsmoke barrier and everything is quiet. I think both Chen and Jorge have been weakened. They've both drunk the Dragon's Blood Elixir, so they will heal, but we have a bit of time to compare notes and figure out what to do."

Liz was relieved to have another *Pyr* in the vicinity, especially since he had said he was the Apothecary. To her surprise, Brandon didn't seem to have a distrust of Sloane anymore.

"Give us a minute," Brandon said, and Sloane turned away. Brandon went to the bathroom and returned with two plush white bathrobes. When he and Liz had put them on, he summoned Sloane back to the room.

Brandon sat on the bed again and leaned against the headboard. Liz perched on the mattress near him, and Sloane stayed in the doorway. Brandon's next words revealed the change that had occurred in his thinking, much to Liz's pleasure. "How about the others?"

"Erik Sorensson is on his way." Sloane smiled at Liz. "He's the leader of the *Pyr* and lives in Chicago. He'll arrive tomorrow morning with his partner and their daughter. I asked him to talk to Quinn, the Smith who repairs our scales. I'm not sure whether Quinn will leave Sara undefended or if he will bring her and their two sons. He might decline to come."

Liz hugged her knees. "Then who will fix Brandon's armor?"

"Let's take it one issue at a time. If Quinn comes, we won't have to worry about an alternate solution." Sloane held Liz's gaze. "The darkfire has changed many things."

Liz didn't understand that, but Brandon snapped his fingers. He went into the bathroom again and returned with a familiar silver vial. He tossed it to Sloane. The Apothecary caught it, then opened it and grimaced. He capped it again quickly and tossed it back to Brandon. "Just what we thought. Dragon

Bone Powder." He shuddered, then turned to Liz with a smile. "I'd really like to know more about your powers."

"Like I said, I thought they were gone."

"You did really well against Chen," Brandon said. "I've never seen anything like that lasso of fire."

Liz took a deep breath. "I'm a Firedaughter. I have a connection to the element of fire. I can command it and summon it, control flames—stuff like that. I can become flame for short intervals, by choice." She frowned at her fingers. "I come from a long line of witches. The women in my family have always had special powers, and as soon as a daughter shows some ability, her mother teaches her how to manage and use her powers. I learned to cast spells when I was five, after my mother caught me playing with the flames in the fireplace."

"So the control of elements comes naturally?" Sloane asked.

"Yes and no," Liz admitted. "It's a natural development in our family, a sign of how well we are attuned to the elements and the unseen. The women in our family are watched closely in case a connection does appear. Some are Firedaughters, like me. Others are Airdaughters, Waterdaughters, Earthdaughters. Some are just witches."

Sloane came into the room and sat down. "But you didn't want to be a Firedaughter?"

Liz frowned. "There is a test that comes to each of us. It's announced by the appearance of a mark on our skin." She smiled. "Some people call it a witch's mark."

"How soon?" Brandon asked.

"Usually within three days." Liz looked down.

"What happened to make you turn away from your powers?" Brandon asked, clearly guessing that the story wouldn't be easy for Liz to tell. She glanced up at him, and he smiled crookedly. "Remember the heartbeat thing," he said. "I'm feeling your anxiety as if it were my own."

Liz nodded understanding, liking the unfamiliar sense of not being alone. It had been a long time since she had had an ally. "My mother's mark appeared when I was eighteen. She was an Airdaughter." She reached for her mother's pendant, only to realize that it was gone. Only the silver chain hung around her neck and there was a circular burn on her skin below her collarbone.

"That's where Chen's lightning struck you," Brandon said. "I was afraid it would kill you."

"Fight fire with fire," Liz said with a wry smile. "That's what I was taught. Fire cauterizes," she said, remembering Pele's words. "Fire purifies and fire heals."

"Your mother tried to prepare you for the worst," Sloane suggested.

"So, what happened?" Brandon asked. "What was the test?"

Liz couldn't look directly at him. She had condemned herself for so long and was afraid he would condemn her, too. "It was the sabbat, and my mother was casting a circle with her coven. Most of them were family—aunts and cousins. None of them would ever be as powerful as my mother was. The wind was up that night and the gusts made me uneasy. The circle was still being cast when we realized something was wrong."

"Her test," Brandon said softly.

Liz nodded. "All of the candles were immediately extinguished and the air became as cold as the grave. A cold flame lit, all by itself, in the middle of the circle. It burned like a tall pillar, taller than me, but threw no heat. The rest of the coven scattered in terror. There was just my mother, the flame, and me.

"My mother showed her powers to prove that she could pass her test. She calmed the winds first, because her primary connection was with air; then she roused them to even greater fury." Liz swallowed. "I remember the four winds tearing through the circle, creating whirlwinds and pressure changes that popped my ears. I remember my mother dismissing them abruptly, showing a control that awed me. I remember rain slashing down on us, changing from a hot shower to pelting ice to a gentle mist. She was completely in charge of all she summoned and radiant with her power. I remember the earth rumbling below our feet in discontent, stirring and shifting, then sprouting flowers in every direction. It was magical."

"Wow." Sloane spoke softly.

"And I remember that column of flame burning

vividly through the entire display. It gradually filled almost the whole of the marked circle and seemed to reach the stars. I recognized that this would be my mother's greatest test, her command over the element of fire. That's why it was last. It was the element that she knew the least." Liz swallowed. "I remember her hesitation when she faced it. I saw her swallow. I knew she believed that she might fail."

Liz pleated the sheet between her fingers, her voice becoming soft. "I wanted to help her." She swallowed and looked across the room, devastated again by the impact of her choice.

"I don't understand. What did you do?" Sloane asked. "What could you do?"

Liz appreciated the question. It gave her the chance to focus on the technicalities instead of her emotions. "I gave her my power. When I direct fire, I cast my will toward it. It's similar to spellcasting but feels different. Hotter for me. Essentially, I toss part of my fire power in the direction of the result that I want. I'd done that before. My aunt, who was also a Firedaughter, taught me to do it once my gift was evident." Liz smiled. "She'd line up burning candles on the mantle in her kitchen and tell me which one to make burn faster. Then she'd made me light and extinguish them. Eventually she'd command me to light the fire in the fireplace."

Sloane nodded understanding. "It's great to have someone to teach you about your powers," he said, and Liz felt Brandon stiffen a little beside her. Sloane glanced at Brandon, then nodded at Liz. "Let's hear the rest of Liz's story."

"So, I gathered up every scrap of will I could find in myself," Liz said. "I was terrified that my mother might not pass her test."

"What happens then?" Brandon asked.

"It's like a final exam. If you fail, you lose it all. If you pass, you gain the fifth element, that of spirit."

Sloane nodded understanding, obviously familiar with this concept. "The fifth point on the pentacle."

"The top one," Liz agreed with a small smile. She sighed and squared her shoulders." So I gathered my gift and I cast it to my mother. She sensed my choice. She turned to embrace it, but it was far too much for her. I can see the fireball that I flung through the air to her. I can see the look on her face when she realized she couldn't harness it. I can still feel my own horror and helplessness—I knew too late what would happen and I couldn't stop it. She was so strong. I thought she could do anything." Liz's tears fell and her voice caught. "I can smell her incineration."

"It killed her?" Sloane asked.

"*I* killed her," Liz corrected, her voice hard.

"What about the pillar of fire?" Brandon asked.

"It disappeared." Liz snapped her fingers. "Just like that. Everything was suddenly still and dark. The winds were gone, like doldrums. There were no stars or moon, and the candles had long been gutted. Water was glistening on everything and it was cold, so cold that it chilled me to the bone. I was alone. All that was left of my mother was her pendant." Liz touched the chain around her neck. "And now I've even lost that."

"What about your powers?" Sloane asked.

"Gone, as surely as if they had never been. I couldn't even light a match afterward." Liz sighed. "It suited me to not be a Firedaughter anymore. I left home after my mother's funeral, and I've never been back. I don't keep in touch with my family at all, and I'm not interested in magic. I figured that exchange cost me my gift and my mother." She turned to Brandon. "You can see why I've been determined ever since to never bear a child. No one should have to face that."

"I'm sorry," Brandon said. "I should have told you."

She covered his hand with hers. "You're such a romantic," she said softly. "I like that the firestorm was everything you wanted it to be. It was magical for me, too. If you'd told me the truth, I'm not sure anything would have been different, anyway."

"Why not?"

Liz smiled. "Conception from one night? At the wrong time of my cycle? I'm a scientist. I wouldn't have believed you."

"Even given your forebears' experience?" Sloane asked.

Liz shrugged. "When I got to Hawai'i, I was still convinced that magic couldn't be part of my life. The marine biologist in me would have declared the odds too long—or maybe insisted on a condom, which, given your story, likely would have failed. I certainly wouldn't have shared this story that first night." She glanced up and met Brandon's gaze. "I'm not sure I could have resisted you, either." She smiled and saw his answering smile. "I don't regret anything. I was just surprised."

"I'm sorry," he said again, and bent to kiss her.

Sloane cleared his throat. "Not to interrupt, but maybe we could clear up a couple of things."

"Maybe they could wait," Brandon said, his tone so unwelcoming that Liz smiled.

Sloane smiled, too, but he still asked, "Why are your powers back?"

It was a good question. "I don't know. I felt their return right after landing. When we drove through the tunnel, I saw Maureen's aura. That's how it started when I was a kid. First, seeing auras. Then hearing spirits. Then speaking spells."

"See no evil. Hear no evil. Speak no evil," Sloane murmured.

"That was my mother's mantra." Liz made a suggestion. "I wonder whether it's because the fire in the earth is so close to the surface here. It might be proximity that reawakened my gifts. Every time I drove that tunnel through the volcano, something else came back."

"Maybe the firestorm sparked your gift again," Brandon suggested.

Liz frowned. "Or maybe it was Pele." The two guys clearly didn't understand. "The goddess of the volcanoes. She appeared to me, again when I was in the tunnel, driving back to Kaneʻohe today, and spoke to me about my gift. She said it just needed time to regenerate, that I could never really give it away, that a connection to the elements is, well, elemental."

"Like I can't ditch my dragon," Brandon said, holding her tightly against his side. She looked up to find him smiling. "Now, who was the wise woman who told me that?"

Sloane cleared his throat. "We *Pyr* each have an affinity to two elements. Usually, fire is one. The affinity often manifests in more intellectual or emotional ways, though. My own affinity to water, for example, appears as empathy. That helps with my ability to heal, because I can diagnose more effectively."

"So, you can't create rain, then?" Liz asked. "Or be a waterfall?"

Sloane seemed startled by the idea. "I don't know. I've never tried."

"I can summon waves," Brandon said, and both Liz and Sloane looked at him in surprise. "Sure. There are days, you know, when the surf is low and there are no good breaks to be found. If I really want to surf, I sit on the beach and I think about the ocean. I feel its rhythm. I watch the waves and I visualize how they could break better. I think of them becoming higher and more regular, and they do. It takes time, but it works."

"Have you ever made it rain?" Liz asked him with excitement. His affinity with water was more similar to what the Waterdaughters in her family could do.

"Never tried," he admitted with a smile. "You can't surf in the rain." His eyes twinkled and his fingers slid into her hair in a slow caress. "But I do have a thing for a marine biologist," he murmured, his voice so low that Liz felt all tingly. "Does that count?"

"Definitely," Liz said, and reached up for his kiss.

"I think I'll find something else to do," Sloane said, but Liz wasn't very interested in his plans. Brandon's mouth closed over hers and he pulled her close, his kiss as sweet and potent as she remembered. She heard the door shut to the bedroom, then a low rumble of what might have been thunder.

She pulled away to look at him with surprise. "Are you making it rain?"

Brandon laughed. "No, that's old-speak. The way dragons talk to each other. It's low, so humans hear it as thunder or passing trains."

"What did you say?"

"I told Sloane to go away for a while, that we need some privacy." Brandon bent to brush his lips across hers again. "I promise to try to make it rain later."

"First things first?" Liz teased, and he grinned.

"Absolutely. Let's make love first."

Liz touched her fingertips to one of his bandages. "Won't it hurt you?"

Brandon grinned. "If it does, it'll be totally worth it just to be with you again."

Liz had no argument with that.

Brandon rolled her to her back, bracing himself over her. He cast back the sheet and ran his hand over her, starting at her shoulder. His fingertips teased and tickled, his touch warm and exciting. His eyes were glinting with mischief and Liz found herself smiling back at him without understanding his intent. "Did you know that when the *Pyr* survive a fight, their first impulse is to celebrate?"

"Celebrate victory?"

"Celebrate that they're alive." Brandon bent and kissed her neck, his breath fanning across her ear and making her shiver. He flattened his hand and ran his palm over her belly with a possessive ease that made her yearn for more. "We indulge in physical pleasure and lose ourselves in sensation." His fingers slipped through the hair at the top of her thighs and Liz spread her legs wider.

"Really? You eat a big meal?"

"Well, feasting can be part of it. So can drinking." His fingertips caressed her so surely that Liz gasped. "Some probably run marathons."

"Surf," Liz said breathlessly.

"I've done that. But making love with you is definitely my favorite way to celebrate." He kissed her then, deeply and lingeringly. "It's almost worth fighting Jorge again," he murmured, his eyes so dark that Liz couldn't think of a thing to say. Brandon smiled, then his mouth locked over hers one more time, his fingers so busy that she thought the celebration might not last very long at all.

Of course, she wasn't counting on his ability to feel her reactions as keenly as his own.

*   *   *

Brandon had told Liz the truth. He was so relieved to have survived that he wanted to celebrate—that he was alive and with Liz, nude and in a huge bed, made the particular choice of celebration inevitable. He loved that his sense of connection with her had been exactly right, that they had so much in common and that they were making some progress in conquering their respective histories.

He ran his hand over her sleek strength, liking the smooth softness of her skin. She was so fair that she looked delicate, but he already knew she was tougher than she appeared. The curve of her breast filled his hand perfectly, as if they'd been made to fit together, and Brandon knew that other parts of them fit well, too.

There was no doubt about it: Liz was the woman for him and his perfect mate.

He bent and captured her lips with his, deepening his kiss when she slipped her fingers into his hair and drew him closer. He liked the honesty of her kiss. He liked that her passion was clear and true. He touched her soft heat and swallowed her moan of pleasure.

This time, it would be even better than the last time.

Every time, it would be better than the last time. He'd make sure of it.

He broke his kiss, smiling at how drowsy she looked. Her cheeks were a bit flushed and her eyes were sparkling. He touched his lips gently to the burn

mark below her collarbone, appreciating that she'd
defended herself when he hadn't been able to defend
her. She gasped at his touch and he kissed her breast,
flicking his tongue across the nipple until it tightened
to a peak. His fingers moved against her all the while,
and he felt her become wetter and warmer beneath
his caress.

He trailed kisses down the length of her and pushed
her thighs wider apart. Just a touch of his fingers and
Liz opened herself to him. When his mouth closed
over her, she made a little cry of pleasure, one that
made him smile. He held her feet in his hands, caressing her insteps with his thumbs as his tongue teased
her. She moaned and twisted, and Brandon took her
to the cusp of pleasure.

He paused deliberately, and she growled in frustra-
tion. "Tease!" she accused, and threw a pillow at him.
Brandon laughed; then Liz launched herself at him.
The bed was big enough to give them room to play.

Brandon caught her and rolled to his back, holding
her against his chest. Her laughter faded as she touched
the wound on his shoulder with cautious fingertips.
That gash was healing quickly, thanks to Sloane's unguent, and it had already scabbed over. It was tender,
but not nearly as sore as the wounds on his abdomen.

He knew that Sloane didn't like the look of them.

Liz met his gaze as her fingertips hovered near the
bandage. "Chen?"

"Jorge."

She removed the bandage, then bent and touched

her lips to the healing wound, a kiss as light as the caress of a butterfly. Then she did the same to the spots on his abdomen, without removing the bandages, her soft touch sending warmth through Brandon's body. She slid down the length of him, and he was sure he wouldn't be able to stand it if she took him in her mouth. He felt himself get harder and thicker just at the prospect.

But Liz looked up at him with bright eyes. "Let me see you in dragon form," she whispered.

Brandon recoiled in horror from the idea. "No!"

"It's part of you," Liz insisted. "It's part of who you are. I want to know all of you."

Brandon swallowed and averted his gaze, his mood changing with her suggestion. "It's evil."

"Only because someone evil has been driving it. When you're in charge, your dragon saves lives and works for good. Let me see him." Liz smiled. "Let me *see* you."

Brandon slipped from beneath her and rolled to the side of the bed. He had to think about this, and he couldn't think about anything other than Liz when she was sprawled on top of him, naked.

Maybe his dragon wasn't such a bad legacy. Being *Pyr* had brought him the firestorm, which had revealed his connection to Liz. He'd noticed her immediately, but the firestorm had made their quick union possible. And he'd been able to save her from the earthquake, partly because he'd sensed it early and partly because he'd been able to fly above the island to keep her safe. Now Sloane had arrived, because they were both *Pyr*, which had both helped Brandon to save Liz and started his own healing.

"Think of it as a scientific exploration," Liz said, and Brandon couldn't help smiling.

"Studying a new species?" he teased.

Liz smiled. "I want to know all about you, and not just for the sake of science." She then pointed at his injuries. "Wounds follow you between forms, right? I want to see those injuries, have a look at why two are still bleeding and the others aren't."

"You know why. Those are where my scales are missing."

Liz arched a brow, bouncing a bit on the side of the bed. "And the others are just where *Slayers* tried to rip your guts out? Seems to me that they should all be pretty serious."

"You want to see how strong his magic is."

She shrugged and smiled.

Her suggestion did make sense. If she could see the difference in the wounds, because of her powers, maybe she could help him to heal.

Brandon considered the generous dimensions of the room and wondered whether Sloane had chosen this suite because the ceilings were so high. "Okay," he said, and gave her fingers a squeeze. He stood up and moved to the middle of the room. He tugged off the bandages, and Liz came to look at the wounds. The two on his belly were already weeping blood, and they looked puffier than the others.

Sloane's unguent wasn't making a difference to them.

Liz met his gaze steadily. Her concern was clear, and it spooked him a bit. After all, she knew more about magic and its effects than he did.

Then she took a step back, giving him space to change forms.

Brandon reminded himself that she'd witnessed his transformation before. He winked, pretending to feel more confident than he was. "This one's for you," he said, then summoned the shift.

Chapter 12

The blue shimmer surrounded Brandon instantly. It was biddable and under his command, and Brandon knew that was because of Liz's presence. He felt the tingle of energy pass over his flesh and surge through his body, and this time he tried to feel the good in it. It was powerful and primal to change like this, and when he welcomed the change—instead of fighting it—it roared through him like a tsunami. He tipped back his head and bellowed, taking pleasure in the raw strength of the transformation.

He felt the sharpening of his senses as he changed. They were keen, anyway, but he was even more observant in dragon form. His eyesight was sharper—he could focus on any item and magnify his vision of it without moving any closer. He could smell nuances and distant scents.

He could hear Sloane breathing dragonsmoke in the next room in a slow hiss, the elevators in the hotel, and the gossip of the staff already arriving in the kitchens far below the room. He could hear the call of the sea, the ebb and flow of the tide, and feel the frisson of energy in life on the reef.

He turned to Liz to find her smiling at him. Not afraid. Relief flooded through him and he offered her a claw. She stepped closer and now he could see the faint shimmer of firelight that surrounded her body. It was like an aura or the light that emanated from the hidden moon when it was eclipsed by the Earth.

She took his claw, and the pleasure that surged through Brandon astonished him. Her touch felt right and good, as if she alone could be the anchor of his universe. It wasn't just that his senses that were amplified; his emotional reaction to Liz was more powerful, too.

Liz flattened her other hand and ran her palm over his scales. Her caress was warm and soothing as well as arousing. Brandon felt hot with desire, his every nerve tingling with awareness of her touch. He looked down and he saw the sparkle of light between her hand and his own scaled hide.

It was like the firestorm, dimmed but still bright.

Burning hot and fueling his ardor for his mate.

Because she was a Firedaughter. He thought of the sparks that flew from her when she was angry and knew it was part of the same suite of powers.

Liz flicked a glance at him and smiled, and he was sure that she was feeling exactly the same thing as he. She studied his wounds, her brow furrowed. "I'm no doctor, but these two don't look like they're going to heal."

"I think Sloane has the same feeling."

Liz nodded and lifted her left hand away from him. "Let me try." There was resolve in her tone, a confidence that gave Brandon faith. She blew on her palm, murmured something he didn't understand, then pressed the flat of her hand hard against one open wound.

Pain fired through Brandon from that point and he threw back his head to roar. He felt as if his skin was being seared, like she had put a hot iron against his belly.

"Fire cauterizes," Liz said, keeping her hand flat against him. "Fire cleanses and purifies." He looked at her and saw that she was once again illuminated with that inner fire. Sparks flew from the ends of her hair, and her eyes were aglow with confidence. She was radiant and beautiful, looking like a deity herself.

No. She was a Firedaughter.

Brandon knew she was right about the purification. He could feel the difference in this heat. It wasn't digging deep to injure him or to destroy him. It wasn't trying to control him or kill him. It was cauterizing his skin, like the sting of Sloane's unguent but a hundred times fiercer.

"Fire heals," he said, gasping when she lifted her hand away.

There were tears in his eyes and his heart was pounding from the pain. Brandon looked down and saw that the bit of exposed skin was bright red. The wound was closed and the blood around it had dried. It wasn't angry and blistered anymore, and it didn't look like it would fester. In fact, his skin was so smooth that it looked as if he'd received the injury a week or more before.

Brandon wondered whether the spot would be impermeable to dragonsmoke.

He shifted to human form, and the healing was consistent. He cast Liz a grin.

"Okay?" Liz asked softly.

Brandon drew her into his arms and kissed her. He didn't doubt that she could feel his skin trembling after her touch. "More than okay," he said. "Better."

She smiled at him and let her fingertips slide over the spot again. Her touch soothed the skin, making it tingle and cool. "So, I haven't forgotten everything," she said.

"Will you do the other one?"

"Do you think you can bear it now? We could wait."

"No." Brandon shook his head. "We don't know when they're coming back. I need to be as strong as possible in order to defend you." He lifted his hands. "Which form?"

"It's bigger in your dragon form and I think it's easier to see."

"Okay, once more, with feeling," he said, summoning the shimmer from deep in his thoughts. "Then we'll really have something to celebrate."

Liz laughed just as the change rocked through him. Brandon was already thinking of a thousand ways to show his gratitude for her help.

He was definitely going to make it worth her while to be with him.

Liz was awed by Brandon's trust. She appreciated that it hadn't been easy for him to choose to shift shape at all, let alone to do it in front of her. She hadn't planned to try to heal him, but as soon as she saw the angry heat of those areas of exposed skin, she'd remembered Pele's words.

And she'd known why she was his partner. She'd seen the hand of destiny and the role she could play in his life. She'd acted on instinct, and it had worked beautifully. She was as amazed as Brandon by her ability to heal him.

She knew it must have hurt, so she was glad when he'd asked her to do the other spot. Where his third scale was missing, the skin was smooth and unbroken — there was just a gap in his armor. She wanted Brandon to be strong, not just so that he could defend her but so that he was healed. Plus she was pretty sure that Chen and Jorge would be back.

She healed the second spot the same way as the first, seeing that he was in pain but enduring it for the greater good. She was so proud of him and couldn't blame him when he roared with satisfaction when she was done. He blew a plume of dragonfire across the room, bellowed with joy, then snatched her up in his claws. Liz laughed at his delight; then he began to shine with that strange blue light again.

A heartbeat later, she was in Brandon's arms and he was kissing her as if he'd never get enough of her. She ran her hands over him, feeling that the damaged skin was smoother even though it was still warm. He'd endured so much and now it was time to give the man some pleasure to balance the pain.

Liz locked her hands around his hips, then bent and took his strength in her mouth. Brandon moaned and his fingers slid into her hair. He braced his legs against the floor, welcoming her touch, and Liz ensured that she made it last. He was so strong, so confident, and she never wanted to be without him. She suckled him and slid her tongue over him, caressing him so that he got harder and thicker.

When she was sure he was about to explode, she stopped and looked up at him.

"Tease!" he breathed, then grinned. He caught her in his arms and dove onto the bed. Liz was stretched out beside him, pressed against his strength. He kissed her deeply, rolling her beneath him. He was inside her in one smooth stroke, filling her with his heat. Liz moaned with pleasure and rolled her hips.

And when he moved slowly, deliberately feeding her desire again, she thought she might explode.

She also knew that this was just the beginning.

Chen was livid.

He dove deep into the earth, chanting to the

magma that seethed below the surface. He swam as far down the crevasse of the ocean vent as he dared, inciting fury in the volcano and urging action.

He had been burned.

He had had the darkfire crystal poked into his eye!

He had been cheated.

He wanted vengeance.

Chen manifested in his lair, dripping wet and steaming with anger. He could scarcely see out of his damaged eye and his black blood was flowing from that wound with vigor. The sand spiral on the floor that was part of his charm was destroyed, and one deep breath told him who was responsible. That same breath revealed how his prey had escaped this perfect prison.

Jorge.

Brandon's scales were all gone, and Chen could guess where they were. He would have to start the spell all over again to ensure success in claiming Brandon, and he didn't have time. He could feel the *Pyr* gathering and triumph slipping from his grasp.

Again.

Brandon was supposed to be an easy victory, but things on the island had turned complicated. Chen wanted a prize. He wanted it now. And he wanted a prize that would both dishearten and weaken the *Pyr*. He'd waited long enough for Viv Jason—who'd vowed that she was Chen's ally—to bring him the *Pyr* Thorolf as a sacrifice.

She must have lied.

Chen would collect his due himself.

When he slaughtered Thorolf, he would claim that *Pyr*'s affinity for air. That would strengthen Chen's own powers, giving him a greater ability to spellcast. And then Brandon would once more be in his grasp.

He loved the idea as soon as he had it.

Bangkok was his destination of choice.

Brandon awakened when the first fingers of sunlight reached into the room. He could hear the birds stirring outside and the rumble of old-speak from the main room. He stayed in bed, wrapped around Liz as she slept, and listened. There were three other *Pyr* from the sounds of it, and Sloane was bringing them up to date. Brandon smiled that the Apothecary knew what Liz had done to his skin the night before.

He didn't recognize the voices of the other three dragons, but he assumed two must be Erik and Quinn. He felt Liz's warmth against him and acknowledged the change she'd already made in his life. Just days ago, he'd been determined to shake his *Pyr* legacy. Since his firestorm, he was coming to terms with the truth of his nature and he was reassured to have the other *Pyr* at his back. Liz had been right about that.

He was, though, still glad that his dad hadn't arrived.

Maybe his dad's own nature had been the problem, not his dragon-shifter abilities.

Maybe the other *Pyr* knew that, too.

Maybe his mom had been calling his dad a monster

because of the way he acted, not because of what he could become.

It was a startling idea. Brandon rolled to his back and stared at the ceiling, thinking about this. Could she have just been reacting to the fact that his dad had deceived her?

But no. If that were the case, she wouldn't have called Brandon a monster, too. His mom knew he wasn't evil—she'd raised him. He could still hear her furious accusation and it still stung.

"You awake?" Sloane asked in old-speak, the volume of the question in Brandon's thoughts revealing that it had been directed at him.

"You already know it," Brandon replied, and Liz stirred.

"Your breathing changed," Sloane said. *"Come meet the team."*

Liz braced herself on her elbow, looking between the window and Brandon. "It's not thunder, is it?" she asked.

"There are more *Pyr* here," Brandon told her. "They want to make a plan."

Liz surveyed herself. "Do I have time for a shower?"

"A quick one," Sloane said, obviously overhearing her question. *"No celebrating in there."*

Brandon laughed, and Liz watched him without comprehension. "They said we can't celebrate in the shower."

Liz got out of bed with purpose. There was a defiant glint in her eye, one that made Brandon's thoughts turn in a predictable direction. "If we do, they'll have to wait," she said, then smiled at him.

"I'm not sure they will." Brandon rolled out of bed and caught her hand, spinning her around for a quick kiss. When they were both breathless and his heart was racing along with hers, he tugged her toward the bathroom.

He turned on the shower, adjusting the temperature, and admired the size of the stall. Liz was looking for toothbrushes in the basket of toiletries offered by the hotel. Brandon turned back to make a teasing comment and saw the change in her skin.

He stared, incredulous, as the bathroom filled with steam. Liz laid out toiletries on the counter, obviously unaware of the transformation.

"Look at your burn," he said softly.

Liz's hand rose to her collarbone as she glanced at him; then she looked at her reflection in the mirror. The angry red burn below her collarbone had faded during the night and her skin was again as pale as porcelain there. But now there was a design etched on her flesh, almost like a tattoo.

It was a five-pointed star, but with two points missing.

"My mother's pentacle," Liz whispered, tracing the outline of the star with one fingertip. "This is what was on her pendant."

Brandon adjusted the silver chain she still wore, pulling it down in front with his fingertip as if a pendant hung on it. The tattoo was exactly where the pendant must have been. "Looks like you got the permanent version," he said, then saw that Liz's eyes were filled with tears. He pulled her into his arms. "Tell me."

"It was the only thing I had of hers, other than the memory of that night," she confessed against his skin. "I was upset that it was lost."

"Not lost," Brandon said. "Her pendant took the hit for you so that you could survive." Liz looked up at him. "Like your mom was looking out for you."

She smiled tremulously. "I like that." She reached up and kissed him again. "Thank you."

Brandon kissed her back, catching her against him.

He was thinking that there might be a small celebration in the shower and the *Pyr* would have to wait. But when Liz pulled back, he saw that the mark on her forearm had darkened, like a tattoo that had been shaded. She saw it, too, and her lips tightened as she looked down at it.

Then she met his gaze, her own filled with concern. "The test," she whispered. "What if I fail?"

"You won't," Brandon said, hoping he was right as he urged her into the shower. "No time to celebrate, after all," he said, then made a face.

As he'd hoped, Liz laughed. "We'll just have to make up for it later."

Fifteen minutes after she woke up, Liz was in her little black dress again. It had been hung up in the bathroom overnight to dry, along with her underwear, and it looked better than she'd expected was possible after that dunk in the ocean. Maybe someone had rinsed the salt water out of it. She had no shoes and her hair was clean but wet. She felt less than at her best when Brandon led her into the main room to meet the other *Pyr*.

They looked like normal men, just as Brandon did in his human form, except they were all particularly muscled and handsome—just as Brandon was. They also had a kind of intensity about them, and when they all turned to meet Liz, she felt as if she was being targeted by lasers. Their auras were universally radiant, lit by an inner fire.

They were passionate, then. Maybe quicker to anger. She would be careful with her words until she knew them better.

There were three women in the living room, as well, two sitting on the long couch and one pacing in front of the window. Their auras were in cool shades of blue and green and purple, making them good balances for their dragon partners. There were also a lot of toddlers and babies, which made Liz think about the promise of the firestorm.

What would be the fate of her child? That mark on her arm taunted her with unwelcome possibilities.

Sloane came to her with a smile. "We don't mean to overwhelm you," he said, and she noticed the ripple of purple in the golden glow of his aura. He was the healer and the Apothecary, and she could see his empathy in the aura that surrounded him. Her instinct from the beginning had been to trust him.

"I think it's great that you've come to help," Liz said. "I know that Brandon hasn't been close to all of you."

"The firestorm demands our support," a tall man said. He had a softened British accent, perhaps from time spent outside of England. His hair was touched with silver at his temples and he was direct. His aura glowed red around him when he offered his hand. A radiant and reliable fire. Liz had the sense that he was protective and honorable. "Erik Sorensson," he said.

"Leader of the *Pyr*," Sloane added softly.

Liz noticed that Erik shook both her hand and Brandon's, so she assumed Brandon had never met him before. His grip was resolute and his hand warm.

"My partner, Eileen, and our daughter, Zoë," Erik continued, gesturing to the woman on the couch who was rocking a dark-haired toddler. Eileen smiled and waved her fingertips in greeting. She touched her finger to her lips then, glancing down at the sleeping child.

Liz smiled. She'd bet the little girl hadn't been sleeping for long.

"Niall Talbot," said the blond man. He was shorter than the others, built more like a wrestler—and he was rocking a blond baby. "And my partner, Rox."

That woman crossed the room with purpose. Her aura snapped with golden lights and the baby in her arms looked just like the one Niall was rocking. Twins, then. "Glad to meet you," Rox said, then looked Brandon in the eye. "When this is over, I'd like to talk to you about the artist who did your tribals."

"Okay." Brandon appeared to be surprised by this, and Sloane smiled.

"Rox is a tattoo artist." He pulled up his sleeve, displaying a large tattoo on his upper arm of a caduceus with two entangled dragons. Brandon's eyes rounded in admiration. "This is nothing compared to the back piece she gave Niall."

Niall smiled, but Rox's gaze had fallen to the mark on Liz's arm. She met Liz's gaze with concern. "Does that mean something to you?"

Liz swallowed. "That my powers will be tested. Soon."

A ripple of concern passed though the room. Erik's eyes narrowed as he stared at her. "What are the stakes?" Erik asked.

"Liz's mother died in her test," Brandon said, and Liz saw that the *Pyr* didn't like this news. It was a bad time to tell them that she was out of practice.

Maybe they were concerned because they knew it already.

"Quinn Tyrrell," said a dark-haired man with eyes of striking blue. He was more muscled than the others and had a quiet intensity about him. Liz felt the strength in his grip and didn't hide her relief that he had come.

"The Smith," Sloane contributed. "And his mate, Sara."

The petite woman stood up, leaving the couch to come to Liz's side.

"Sara is the Seer," Sloane explained. "She often has visions of prophecies or hidden realities that help us."

"Works better when I'm pregnant," Sara said ruefully, gesturing to the two dark-haired boys sleeping near her. The youngest boy started to fuss, and she went back to the couch to pick him up. Then she pulled a shawl over her shoulder and settled back to nurse the baby. Liz could see her aura dim as she focused on nourishing her son.

Quinn watched her, his love clear.

"You're the one who fixes the scales of the *Pyr*," Liz said, and Quinn met her gaze.

"Yes. That's why I've come." He flicked a glance at Brandon. "I'd like to see where those scales are missing."

"Liz just healed the skin," Brandon said with pride and lifted his shirt. Both the Apothecary and the Smith considered the unbound wounds. Liz could see that they were impressed.

"Here's the thing," Brandon continued. "My dragon has been getting stronger. Liz thinks it's a binding spell cast by Chen. But it's easier to control everything when she's around. That has to be from the firestorm."

"You mentioned the binding spell before," Sloane said.

"But I broke the spell," Brandon said. "When I was trapped by Chen, I trashed the spiral of sand."

"No." Liz shook her head. "You ruined the physical tool that Chen was using to build his spell, but the spell is still there."

"I don't understand," Niall said. The others shook their heads and looked at Liz.

Erik smiled slightly, as if in apology. "There is magic in our kind, but much of the wisdom has been lost. We were nearly hunted to extinction and the price in lore has been high."

Liz nodded in understanding of that. "Okay. Simply put, spellcasting doesn't work like it does in the movies. I can't say some magic words and wave my hand and make something happen. The universe doesn't work like that." The women didn't seem to be surprised by this assertion.

"How does it work, then?" Sloane asked.

"The universe is filled with currents of energy. They each chart their own course and entangle with other energies and are influenced by our choices and our moods. Every option is out there somewhere, but some are stronger possibilities than others. Those have more energy associated with them, maybe because of consensus, and often their path will be the one that happens."

"A soup of possibilities," Eileen said, nodding. "And sometimes one flavor or spice is stronger than the others."

"Depending what's been mixed in and how much," Brandon agreed. "I get it."

"And choices probably affect the overall network," Sara guessed.

Liz nodded. "So, when I cast a spell, I'm trying to influence which current comes to fruition. I'm adding my energy and my will to one particular option."

"You put your weight behind it," Sloane said.

"But there's nothing saying that I'll succeed," Liz said. "I might back a loser. I might not be strong enough to influence the outcome or to swing the tide. There are also the choices of others affecting the shape of what's to come."

"Real-time voting," Rox murmured.

"Continuous real-time voting," Eileen agreed.

"My point is that by casting my energy into the network of spells, I create a connection to the vortex," Liz continued. "One manifestation of that occurs if my target is a specific individual—my attempt to influence that person forges a link between us. The binding spell doesn't just tie the victim to the spellcaster's will—it makes a conduit between the spellcaster and the victim."

Brandon folded his arms across his chest. "So Chen is trying to control me. . . ."

"No," Liz corrected. "Chen is trying to steal your life force to boost his own power."

"Get out," Brandon said with obvious shock.

"That's how dragonsmoke works, too," Sloane said with excitement. "It steals energy from its victim and feeds that strength back to the attacker."

Erik nodded. "That's why it weakens you so fast when it's directed at you. It's strengthening your opponent at the same time."

Liz wasn't surprised. Dragonsmoke, then, could act as a kind of binding spell. It was easier to explain this since they already had an experience of it. "In targeting you, Chen created a connection between the two of you. Your energy is linked to his because of the spell. There's a bond there."

"And it can transmit both ways," Sloane said with a nod.

Brandon's eyes narrowed. "Does that mean the spell can turn back on him?"

Liz nodded. "In fact, that's usually a sign that it's working. There's an old Wiccan saying that whatever you send out into the world comes back on you three-fold. So, Chen targeted you with a malicious spell. My mother would say that his luck has been turning bad because that ill will is bouncing back on him."

Sloane frowned. "But that also means the spell is working."

"That's right," Liz agreed.

"Can't we create a counterspell?" Brandon demanded, his frustration clear.

"It's not that easy. Magic opens the door. It doesn't fix things. It can create opportunities, though."

"So, what's my opportunity?"

Liz swallowed, knowing they weren't going to like her suggestion. "You tug the line and pull him out of hiding, on your terms instead of his." She folded her arms across her chest. "And you do it now, when he's recovering from an injury. When he's weak."

*   *   *

The *Pyr* caught their breath collectively.

Brandon liked Liz's idea right away. "That's brilliant. Let's do it!"

Erik's eyes lit with purpose. "This has potential," he said, and started to pace the length of the room and back. "Let's walk through it. We know that Chen is weakened right now, because he was wounded in his last attack."

"He's also been singing to the earth," Quinn said. "Trying to cause destruction. Commanding an element is tiring."

"Never mind the fights," Brandon said. "Now's the time to strike!"

"Wait a minute," Erik said. "There's still a binding spell, and it's still linked to you. We need to ensure that you're protected before we start this."

Brandon was surprised by his concern. "I'll get through it. I have incentive."

Erik smiled at him, his expression paternal. "I'd like to make sure of that."

"There's still one more scale," Liz said. "Right? Didn't you give Chen three?"

"Jorge has broken two of them," Brandon said. "The third one was at Chen's lair when we left."

"One of them will have gone back for it," Quinn said. "It's too useful to them."

"They've been targeting dragonsmoke at the unprotected spots," Brandon said. "How do I get scales there again?"

Quinn frowned. "I'm afraid that this isn't normal.

I'm not sure that I can repair the scales when there's a spell like this."

"I'm pretty sure the repair won't take. Not yet, anyway," Liz said, and Brandon liked that she was trying to find the solution. "Brandon said that the scales regenerate naturally, that the *Pyr* never have gaps in their armor."

"That's not quite true," Sloane said. "When a *Pyr* falls in love, he loses a scale. That one never grows back."

"That's it!" Liz said with triumph. She was all sparkly again, lit with that inner fire. Brandon saw the others notice this and look at her in wonder. "Three scales! You gave three scales to Chen, but they haven't grown back, right?"

"Right." Brandon didn't understand.

"So you must have lost three people you loved. That's why they're not growing back, and maybe that's why you could even pull them out in the first place."

Brandon frowned. "It sounds good, but I've never had a firestorm before."

"What about other romantic relationships?" Niall asked.

"High school sweetheart?" Sloane asked.

Brandon shook his head. "Lots of women, but nothing serious. Just fun. Mostly they're just surfing fans." He squeezed Liz's fingers. "Nothing like this."

"You must have experienced some loss," Erik mused.

"What's past is past," Brandon said, uncomfortable with all these new acquaintances wanting to discuss his romantic history. "What does it matter?"

"Because if you are healed, you'll be less vulnerable to attack," Sloane said softly. "By magic or by force."

"And that means we can fight more effectively together," Niall said.

Right. They weren't just acquaintances—they were allies and they were trying to help him. Brandon still couldn't think of any time his heart had been broken, though.

"What about your parents?" Liz asked. "You're pretty bitter about your mom throwing you out, and you're hard on your dad for his choices."

Brandon bristled at the reminder. "Well, he was wrong. . . ."

"Maybe he was," Erik said, his voice low. "Maybe he wasn't able to do anything else." He held Brandon's gaze steadily. "Maybe you need to hear his view of things."

"I don't think so," Brandon protested. "There are things that can't be unsaid."

"You sound like your father," Erik muttered.

"You know him?" Brandon asked. "Because I sure don't."

"Funny you remind me of him, then," Erik mused, his eyes glittering. "Maybe some things are bred in the bone."

That wasn't a very welcome comparison to Brandon's thinking. "More than the dragon stuff? I don't think so. I'm as different from him as possible."

"How so?" Sloane asked.

"I keep my word," Brandon said hotly. "And I don't abandon anyone I care about."

Erik nodded slowly, then slanted an intent glance across the room. "I have argued with Brandt, more than once, about his choices. Brandt is volatile and irritating in the passion of his nature, but his heart is good."

"Then he should learn to keep his mouth shut," Brandon snapped. "And keep his responsibilities."

"He also has some ability to admit when he's wrong."

"That must be new," Brandon retorted. "I'm twenty-six and he's been gone more than half my life. I'm not that hard to find."

Erik's lips tightened. "He is your father."

"How would I know?" Brandon demanded. "He abandoned me before I could walk, then only came back for a short lesson on being a dragon shifter."

Erik's eyes glittered. "Maybe he didn't have a choice."

"I don't believe it," Brandon said. "He left me and he doesn't care, and if anyone is going to try to heal that relationship, it had better be him. I don't think it can be fixed."

"What about your mom?" Liz asked quietly. "Maybe she regrets her choice. Does she have any idea how to find you?"

Brandon met her gaze warily. "We don't keep in touch. She knows I'm in Hawai'i. Like I said, I'm not that hard to track, with the surfing competition and all."

"If she knows you're in Hawai'i, she'll be worried about you," Liz said, her tone filled with appeal. Brandon recalled his own doubts about his mom's condemnation of him, and Liz's plea found a resonance in him. "She'll have seen the earthquake on the news. You should call her." She grimaced. "I'd lend you my cell phone, but it didn't survive that swim across the bay."

"Then I'll do it later," Brandon said. "Let's tug on Chen now, while he's weakest. Let's get this done."

"First things first." Sloane pulled his cell phone out of his pocket and tossed it across the room.

Brandon caught it instinctively but shook his head. "Later."

"Now," Niall said.

Quinn folded his arms across his chest. "Call."

The women straightened, watching Brandon with bright eyes.

"I believe Kay will be glad to hear from you," Erik said softly.

Brandon looked down at the phone, his uncertainty clear.

"Everyone has spoken in anger once and regretted it later," Eileen said.

"If one of my sons was in an earthquake zone, it wouldn't matter how long it had been since I'd talked to him or how we'd parted," Sara said quietly. "I'd want to hear his voice."

Rox smiled. "And maybe I'd cut him a bunch of slack, just out of relief."

"A scientific experiment," Liz added. "It won't hurt. Just give her a quick call. Check in and say hello. Then we can go fight dragons."

Brandon pursed his lips, looked at the cell phone, then down at Liz. "When you put it like that, it seems stupid not to call."

Liz smiled. "I'd say stubborn," she said, and Eileen chuckled.

"None of us has any experience with that character trait, do we?" she murmured, earning a quick look from Erik. Rox and Sara exchanged a glance, and Brandon noticed the sense of camaraderie these women shared. Liz had been right. He needed this community of *Pyr*.

And Liz would need them, too.

There was no point in asking for advice, then not following it. He hated when people did that, and he wasn't going to be one of them.

Brandon took a deep breath, walked out onto the balcony to improve the reception, squared his shoulders, and called his mom.

Chapter 13

Kay Merrick welcomed the chaos of the holiday season. She was completely overbooked with orders this year, and she was even gladder of it than usual. Working twenty hours a day ensured that she had no time to think. No time to be lonely. No time to worry that she hadn't heard from her son, Brandon, since the earthquakes.

Surviving Christmas Day would be another feat altogether, but she'd get through it. She always did.

Even if this year would be the twenty-fifth anniversary of her first Christmas without Brandt.

She told herself that the only thing she regretted about her booming business was that she wouldn't be able to watch the surfing competition live from Hawai'i. She'd upgraded her cable to get the specialty station, just to see Brandon compete. She'd taped the other two competitions and watched hungrily as her son succeeded at what he did best.

She replayed it over and over again, as greedy for detail as a rabid fan girl. Her son was even stronger and more handsome than she recalled and exuded his father's confidence. The commentators had noted that the third part of the competition was likely to be his chance to shine, and Kay wanted to watch it live. No chance of that, not this holiday season. The recording would have to do.

She'd also been avidly checking the news for details of damage and deaths after the earthquake. She hoped and prayed that Brandon was okay, that he'd remained on the north shore, which had seemed to be comparatively unscathed. She hated that she didn't know for sure and had no good way to find out.

Watching the videos of her son thousands of miles away just made Kay more keenly aware of what she'd lost. She'd said hard things out of anger and fear and never had the chance to take them back.

Well, maybe Kay hadn't made the chance. Pride got in her way. And when she heard from Brandon—which wasn't often—he usually mentioned that he was sending an e-mail from a public computer. That didn't exactly open the door to apologies and exchanging confidences.

Her cell phone rang just as she was reaching to take tart shells out of the oven. Kay glanced at them, but they weren't quite ready. "Rachel!" she called to her assistant. "These are within a hair of being done. Can you keep an eye on them?"

"I'm all over it," the younger woman said with her usual cheerfulness.

Kay checked the caller ID on her phone. Sloane Forbes. She didn't know anybody by that name, and she didn't have the capacity to take on any more holiday orders. Might as well get that straight early.

"Hello, Mr. Forbes," she said briskly by way of greeting. "I do hope that you're calling with regards to something for the New Year. We're quite overwhelmed this holiday season...."

"Hey, Mom."

Kay fell silent at the sound of a voice she would recognize anywhere.

"Still working too hard?"

Kay's knees gave out beneath her and she sat down hard on a stool. "Brandon," she whispered, unable to believe it was true.

"Yeah," he said, and took a shaky breath, proof that he wasn't as confident as he sounded. "I've owed you an apology for a long time, Mom. I'm sorry."

"So am I," Kay admitted, feeling her tears start to flow.

Brandon took another deep breath. "So, Mom, I met this girl, and she told me I should give you a call. I'm thinking she's the one."

Kay smiled through her tears. "I'm glad."

"Her name is Liz," Brandon said, and Kay could hear his love for this girl in his voice. Everything was coming together for him and she was so happy to hear from him again. She could have listened to him all day long—to hell with the tarts.

When they ended the call, agreeing to keep in touch, Kay sat holding her cell phone tightly, marveling at what had just happened.

That was when she realized that her son must have had his firestorm, that this Liz was the woman who could have his son. Like Kay had been, she was probably already pregnant. She'd probably been overwhelmed by the sparks and the power and the raw charisma of a *Pyr* determined to win her heart.

Kay remembered that very well.

She was going to be a grandmother, she realized with a shock.

Kay looked around her commercial kitchen, at the scheduled bookings on the wall chart and the stacked boxes waiting to be filled with cakes and pastries, and she knew exactly where she wanted to be. None of this could compete with the chance to stand on a beach in Hawai'i and watch her son's life come together. She'd meet Liz. She'd be there when he triumphed.

And she'd start to try to make up for all the years they'd lost.

Liz watched Brandon punch in a number. The *Pyr* and their partners pretended to avert their interest, but she knew they were all listening. With their keen hearing, they'd be able to hear every word.

They were as protective of one of their own as she
had guessed dragons would be. That reminded her of
her mother's circle, and she realized how much she
had missed that sense of community. Plus the *Pyr* and
their partners were more welcoming of her than she'd
expected. Like Brandon, they believed implicitly that
the firestorm could not be wrong. That level of trust
was also familiar to Liz, and just as completely forgotten.

She caught Rox looking at the mark on her arm
again, the woman's concern clear, and covered it with
her other hand. She would be glad to join this group
if she could. Liz, though, would require more proof
that she wasn't bringing peril to this group by joining
them.

She knew that she had to use her gifts to guarantee Brandon's freedom. But how? She knew she
could summon Chen by tugging on the binding spell
from this end, but what would she or the *Pyr* do once
the *Slayer* turned up?

Sara came to Liz's side then. She was holding a
piece of paper with some writing on it. "Does this
verse mean anything to you?" Her tone revealed her
conviction that Liz would understand it perfectly.

Dragon lost and dragon found;
Dragon denied and dragon bound.
Down to embers, his fire chills,
In thrall to one whose intent is ill.
Firedaughter's spark can ignite the flame,

Give him strength to fight again.
Or will both be lost on ocean's tide
Surrendered as a failed test's price?

Liz shuddered and handed it back to Sara, not even wanting to touch it. It was one thing to think that she might fail her test, but she didn't even want to think about Brandon being caught up in the repercussions.

"How did you get the mark?" Rox asked, having come to Liz's other side. She read the verse; then the two other women exchanged a glance.

Liz explained about her family tradition of witch-craft, telling them all what she'd told Sloane and Brandon. Brandon ended his call when she was nearly done and came to her side, putting his arm around her shoulders.

"Okay?" she asked.

He grinned. "Perfect. You were right." The others exchanged pleased glances, then looked at Liz.

"You must hold the key to breaking the spell Chen cast over Brandon," Sara said. "Tell us what to do to help."

"Well, that's the thing," Liz said. "I can bring him to us—I'm pretty sure of that. I'm just not sure what to do when he gets here."

"How can you protect Brandon from being claimed?" Erik asked.

"I would use a protective circle against a demon. It might work against Chen, too."

"What about the spiral?" Brandon asked, and Liz

looked at him in surprise. "The spiral on the floor of his lair must have been part of his spell." He gestured. "It was big. It filled the whole room and was made of ridges of sand. My scales were at the middle."

"At the vortex," Sloane said.

"What did it look like?" Liz asked, her excitement rising.

"A big spiral," Brandon said.

"No. Which way did it turn?" From beside the phone, Liz grabbed a pad of paper that had the hotel logo on it. She drew two spirals, one that radiated from the center in a clockwise direction and one that radiated from the center in a counterclockwise direction.

"This way," Brandon said, touching the second one. "Does it matter?"

Liz smiled, hearing her mother's lessons all over again. She pointed at the first one. "This one is sunwise. It's an emanation of creative energy. Like the sun, it sends its power out into the universe." She tapped the other, the one that had been the same as the spell on the floor. "This one is destructive. It pulls power in, cheating it of the universe and drawing it to the center."

"Sounds like Chen," Niall said quietly, and the *Pyr* nodded.

"Okay," Liz said, glad she could solve half of the problem. Maybe if she helped Brandon to secure his freedom, he could somehow help her pass her test. She'd worry about that later. "I can see how to make this work. I need a few things, including a secluded beach."

"There's one a couple of miles away from here," Brandon said. "It doesn't have easy access from the highway or a good surfing break, so it's always quiet."

"Good. Let's be there at noon." She pointed at the *Pyr*. "You need a plan of what to do when Chen turns up. How are you going to destroy him?" Liz felt their determination and again had the sense of being part of a caring and powerful community.

"He's drunk the Elixir," Erik said. "He won't go down easily."

"We've seen that before," Sloane agreed, and the *Pyr* began to confer in old-speak.

At least Liz assumed that was what they were doing, because there was no reason for there to be thunder on such a clear day.

She turned the page on the notepad and started to make a list of supplies. The women leaned over her shoulder, watching her write, each one claiming an item on Liz's list, then departing to find it.

This could work.

At noon, they were on the beach. Brandon watched Liz direct the others, admiring her confidence and knowledge. She had sketched a large circle in the sand and conferred with Erik about its dimensions. She wanted to ensure that the *Pyr* had room to fight in dragon form, but the larger the protective circle, the weaker its barrier would be.

Then she used the compass to identify and mark the cardinal compass points. She planted a hurricane lantern at each one. There was a big candle in each lantern; the glass ensured that it couldn't blow out easily.

She considered the sky worriedly. There were a number of small clouds floating across the expanse of blue, and the wind was light. The waves on the ocean were small and regular, the surface beyond the break as smooth as glass. It should have been a perfect day, but Brandon had a feeling that something was brewing.

Was he just sensitive to Liz's magic?

She turned to the *Pyr* with resolve. "Can you change shape? I need to see you to decide where you should be."

There was a brilliant shimmer of pale blue light; then four dragons stood on the beach with them. Liz considered each of them in turn, then beckoned the massive pewter and ebony dragon that was Erik. "North for you," she said, and Erik moved into position. "You with him," Liz instructed Eileen. "Stay inside the mark where the circle will be, and once it's cast, do not step out of it."

"Got it," Eileen said. Liz handed her a matchbook. Zoë stood with her mother and watched with wide eyes.

"East for you," Liz said to Niall. Brandon wondered whether there was a rationale to her choices or whether she was working instinctively. Niall— amethyst and silver in dragon form—and Rox and their two infant sons took the eastern cardinal point, and, once again, Liz gave the mate a matchbook.

Rox kicked off her black platform shoes, leaving them outside the circle. She was wearing two baby carriers, so one child was in front and one in the back. It worked only because the babies were small, since Rox was petite herself. It wouldn't work in a few months.

They had talked about keeping the children somewhere else, somewhere safe, but there was no safer place, according to Liz, than inside the circle. Their fathers had been vehement that they wanted to personally defend their families. The children were all awake and even the infants appeared to be avidly interested. Brandon wondered whether they could sense the anticipation of the others.

"West," Liz said to Sloane, and he did as he was bidden, his tourmaline scales gleaming in the sunlight.

"And south," Liz said to Quinn. He was sapphire and steel in dragon form, more muscular than any of the other *Pyr*. He took his place, Sara beside him, one boy in a baby carrier and the other standing in front of his father with shining eyes.

Garrett. The older boy was named Garrett. He lifted his hands as if he were a dragon and clawed at the air, baring his teeth and pretending to fight. Sara tousled his hair.

"Tails coiled inside the circle," Liz instructed, and the *Pyr* slid their tails across the sand. They each had their tails unfurled to the left, which gave the circle a scaled perimeter.

She smiled approval, then beckoned to Brandon. "Stay in human form," she said. "It will make you look weaker."

"He'll probably make me change forms, anyway, to show his power."

"Maybe he can't, since his spell is weakened and so is he," Sloane said.

Liz gave Brandon a look. "You could pretend that he's making you change. Give him a false sense of power."

Brandon nodded agreement with that plan. "That puts surprise on our side. I like it." She indicated the very center of the circle, positioning him to face the north. He met the steely gaze of Erik and knew that everyone understood how high the stakes were. "Is this going to work?" he asked Liz in an undertone.

"It should work," she said. "I will summon him. He will come for the bait, which is you. The *Pyr* can surprise him, and everyone else will be safe within the circle." She bit her lip. "Recognize that I'm trying to make him appear inside the circle. He won't be able to leave it, if everything goes according to plan, but he might be able to manifest elsewhere, since that's one of his powers."

"He'd leave the same way he comes in," Brandon said.

Liz nodded. "The idea is that you will all injure him badly enough that he can't do that."

"He will have to be killed," Erik said with resolve.

"No injury will be sufficient," Sloane agreed.

"So we take him hard and fast," Quinn said, then nodded. "I'm ready."

"Use dragonsmoke," Niall said. "If we can establish a conduit, we can sap him of his energy."

"I say we build a dragonsmoke barrier as Liz casts her circle," Erik said. "It takes time to build a fortified barrier." At Liz's nod, the four older *Pyr* began to breathe slowly and steadily. Brandon knew Liz wouldn't be able to see the dragonsmoke they breathed, but she'd certainly feel how the air chilled.

"Stay inside the circle," Liz reminded the women again. "Do not break the perimeter, no matter what happens."

They nodded agreement, but Liz looked each one in the eye. Brandon understood that this was the vulnerability of the plan.

But there was no other choice. They had to try to defeat Chen while he was weak. Brandon watched Liz raise her hands to the sky and hoped this wasn't the way they parted forever.

She began to chant something in a language he didn't understand; then she picked up the bucket of salt she'd brought and began to cast the protective circle around them all.

One thing about rituals was that they were reassuring. Liz calmed down as she began to cast the circle. It was routine work, something she'd done a thousand times, and the familiar gestures and words built her confidence.

There was so much that was unpredictable about this spell. She didn't know this area well or have the familiarity with its vibrations she would have preferred. She didn't know nearly enough about dragons, either *Pyr* or *Slayer*, to be sure that she was covering the important possibilities. She wasn't sure that Chen was weakened enough that he could be defeated, and she feared that Brandon could be not just bait but also prey.

It didn't hurt to have five dragons with her, much less their own understanding of their nature. She hoped they could make decisions on the fly, and expected that Erik would be good at that.

She'd assigned each *Pyr* to a cardinal point on instinct, her choices based on the colors of their scales and any sense of conviction. She remembered Sloane saying that each *Pyr* had affinities to two elements and kept that in her mind as she chose.

Erik had been an obvious choice for the north, which was associated with both the colors black and silver. In Wiccan thinking, north was governed by earth. As leader of the *Pyr*, she guessed that Erik had a firm interest in the physical welfare of the other dragon shifters—his paternal tendency, after all, had brought him to Brandon and was manifesting in his protectiveness.

Sloane, as Apothecary of the *Pyr*, belonged in the west. She'd been uncertain of that for a moment, since west was governed by blue and Quinn was sapphire in dragon form. But Sloane had empathy and sympathy.

He'd need that to heal others, and that association with water was more important to Liz in making the assignment than the color of his scales.

Niall was an easier choice. East was associated with the element of air and the color white in Wiccan symbolism. Although Niall was amethyst and silver, there was something ethereal about him, something electric about his presence. Liz went with her gut and assumed he had a connection to the element of air.

And Quinn was in the south, the cardinal point governing fire, passion, and the color red. Although his scales were not red, he worked with fire routinely and there would be a lot of glowing red coals and iron in his life. That the Aztecs associated the southern direction with the color blue just gave more credence to Liz's choice.

The *Pyr* felt right to her in those places. She looked around at them, noting the vivid hue of their auras and the way the light crackled against the sky. The circle was already lit with flickering light.

Once the circle was cast, Liz welcomed the elements at each cardinal point of the compass. She noticed that the wind was gusting more with every passing moment. Erik was watching the sky, his dragon eyes glittering. The ocean was becoming choppier, too, the waves growing in size. She saw Brandon watching the surf, a frown on his brow. Liz could feel the power she was summoning and assumed the elements were responding to her call.

Once the perimeter was secured, she began the

beckoning chant. Brandon held the silver vial that Chen had given him days before, the one that had held the Dragon Bone Powder. At her nod, he held it in front of himself, the anchor to the spell she was casting. It had been Chen's possession, so it also had a link to the *Slayer*. Liz kept it fixed in her thoughts.

She began at the north and shuffled her feet in the sand, creating a trough that wound in a counterclockwise direction. She repeated the spell, and Eileen followed her, adding her voice to the chant and deepening the trough of the spiral. She guided Zoë to stay between the two of them.

Liz was reminded of the spiral dance she had done once at a Wiccan gathering. She reached back with her right hand and took Zoë's left hand, never breaking her chant. Eileen watched and ensured that the link was made the same way. Each of them would have their right hand back and their left hand forward.

Give with the left and receive with the right. Liz heard her mother's instruction as if that woman was directly behind her. Liz would be the terminus of the energy they built—and she might need every scrap of it. Her heart skipped with trepidation.

At the western point, Sloane bowed his head as they passed, as if paying homage to the power Liz could already feel building.

When they passed the southern point, Sara stepped into the trough behind Eileen. Liz felt the tips of her hair illuminate as Sara's power was added to the line, and she felt seared by the connection to their son Garrett. The boy was remarkably powerful, even at his young age. Quinn's eyes narrowed as if he understood what she was feeling, and Liz realized that he knew his son had an affinity to fire, too.

There were sparks dancing over Liz's skin by the time they passed the east and Rox joined their conga line. She, too, joined hands, and Liz caught her breath at the surge of energy she felt added to their line. These were powerful women, each in their own right, and Liz supposed she should have expected as much from the mates of dragon shifters.

The power was growing exponentially, making the hairs on her arms stand up. The auras of the *Pyr* were becoming brighter and radiating more broadly. The women chanted together, completing the first round of the circle, and Liz saw the approval in Erik's eyes. She turned inward, making the circle into a spiral, and raised her voice. The women became louder, too.

Black clouds were gathering overhead and the wind swirled around the outside of the circle. She was reminded of wind sprites that could dance in whirlwinds and hoped there were other spirits gathering to help them.

The women sang together with force, the *Pyr* joining the chorus. Liz felt the crackle of energy in the circle and she saw the flicker of flames around the perimeter. She felt the power continue to increase. The mark on her chest from her mother's pendant tingled. Her blood sizzled. Her skin shone. The Firedaughter flame rolled over her and illuminated her, charging her every gesture with the element of fire. The inside of the circle was filled with a golden glow, a radiant orb of fire power.

Liz reached the middle of the circle and raised her left hand. The power the women had gathered ran through her body like an electrical current. Liz finished the chorus, then shouted the command to complete the spell, even as she lifted Brandon's hand and that silver vial toward the sky.

There was a crack of lightning, its jagged light slicing through the air. The lightning touched the end of the vial. She saw the silver vial light with white fire. She gaped at the image of her mother within the flame's dancing lights; then the auras of the *Pyr* were extinguished.

And everything happened very fast.

Thorolf was in bed in a flat in Bangkok. It was late, really late, and the city beyond the window was coming as close to silence as it ever did. He rolled over, reaching for Viv's warmth.

He was exhausted.

He was a bit drunk.

He'd had more sex since meeting Viv than ever in his life—which was saying something. Thorolf loved women and he loved sex.

Yet he just couldn't get enough of Viv. She nestled against him and he was instantly ready, all over again. He had just closed his eyes and touched his lips to her nape, had just heard her sigh of satisfaction, when someone jumped him from behind.

He felt the talons lock into his shoulder.

He smelled *Slayer*, way too late.

He roared and spun, intent on defending Viv.

Gold talons dug deeply into his skin, holding him captive. Thorolf glanced back and Chen chuckled, murmuring something that disoriented Thorolf. He was breathing dragonsmoke, weaving it around Thorolf with dizzying speed and sucking him dry. He was also bleeding, his black *Slayer* blood running from a wound in one eye. It scorched the floor when it dripped onto it, but the injury didn't seem to weaken him.

Thorolf struggled. He fought. He tried to shift shape but couldn't. It just didn't work.

Chen laughed softly, unsurprised.

That was when Thorolf panicked.

It made absolutely no difference. He was completely powerless, as he had never been in his life. Chen held him down, his ferocious strength keeping Thorolf captive. He rolled Thorolf to his back and bared his teeth, closing in to eat Thorolf's guts.

Yet Viv slept, oblivious to his struggle, rubbing her feet against him like a cat. He had the biggest erection of his life, which just made the moment more surreal.

There was nothing sexy about being devoured by Chen.

It was his worst nightmare come true.

Thorolf heard himself moan as he felt Chen's breath on his belly.

He thrashed, and the dragonsmoke net burned him all over. He bellowed, hoping that this was a nightmare and he'd wake up. A tempest swirled in the room, an unnatural wind that ripped at the blinds and cast the dishes to the floor. It seemed to echo Thorolf's anguish, and he wondered whether he had created it somehow.

Niall could control the wind.

Could he?

Thorolf tried to feed the wind's frenzy, tried to make it blow harder and colder. He tried to make it disperse the dragonsmoke, and, to his delight, it worked. He wished for sand in the wind and he laughed when Chen roared in pain beneath a volley of fine gravel. That roar broke the line of dragonsmoke and was the only opportunity Thorolf needed.

He lunged through the remaining net of dragonsmoke, ignoring the way it scathed him. He pounded Chen in the face, jabbing his fist into that damaged eye. Chen roared in pain and thrashed his tail. One blow sent Thorolf sprawling into the far wall.

He still couldn't shift, and now he'd hit his head. He waited on the floor, feigning unconsciousness, waiting for his moment. Viv, incredibly, remained asleep. Chen bared his teeth and breathed dragonfire as he stalked closer.

Suddenly he pounced.

Thorolf lunged straight at his opponent and drove his head into the *Slayer*'s gut. He slammed a stool hard into the *Slayer*'s genitals. Chen choked. He staggered backward, his plume of dragonfire scorching the air. Thorolf kicked him in the face and tried again to shift shape.

No luck.

He glanced out the window and thought he saw a person dressed in black on the street below, looking up at his flat's windows. The blinds were open and the dragonfire would make the fight clear to anyone who was looking.

Thorolf saw the pale oval of the observer's face and guessed that the thief he'd once let escape was still following him.

Why?

Then Chen's plume of flames erupted behind him, turning the window into a mirror. Thorolf saw the reflection of a snake in the window glass, wide-awake and watching. There was a green viper coiled in the bed where Viv had been, its eyes sparkling like jewels. It opened its mouth and he saw its sharp fangs, the hungry flick of its tongue.

"We had a deal," the viper cried, and launched itself at Chen. Its fangs sank deeply into the *Slayer*'s hide, and Thorolf wondered what toxin was in its bite.

Because Chen wavered, like a reflection on the surface of a lake, and abruptly disappeared.

The flames vanished, as well, turning the window to an inky square of night once more.

Thorolf spun in horror, fearing for Viv, but Chen really was gone. The flames were gone. The viper was gone. And Viv was reaching for him, concern in her expression.

He was sweating.

He was naked.

He sank to the floor, trembling, feeling as though he was going to be sick.

"Bad dream, baby?" Viv murmured, pulling him into her arms and kissing him gently. "You gotta take it easy with that firewater," she teased gently, wiping the perspiration from his face. "That shit will kill you."

Thorolf looked at her, and she smiled. He exhaled shakily. It must have been a nightmare. He looked back out the window, but there was no sign of the thief.

If that person had ever even been there.

"You okay, baby?" Viv murmured. She kissed his cheek, her lips lingering against his skin. A glow lit her eyes as she smiled. "Don't worry. I know how to make the bad dreams go away," she whispered, rubbing herself against him. Thorolf grinned and caught her close.

Just a dream.

Nothing more than that.

Thorolf just wasn't as young as he used to be.

Yeah. That was it. He carried Viv back to bed, and it was a long time before either of them tried to sleep again.

Chen cursed as he was snatched from Bangkok and flung through time against his will. He was being hauled back to Hawai'i, unable to resist the spell cast by the witch who carried Brandon's child.

At least he understood why Viv Jason hadn't delivered Thorolf to him as agreed: she wanted him for herself. She was out of luck. Chen had already decided the *Pyr* would be his due.

That bite of hers meant war.

His blinded eye meant war, even if the Elixir would ultimately heal it.

He'd take out Brandon's mate and Brandon, then return for Viv and Thorolf.

They'd all learn their lesson for daring to wrest control from him.

On the beach on O'ahu, Brandon was transfixed by the sight of Liz. She was radiant with the fire within her, so filled with power that she looked like she might explode into a flurry of sparks. Her eyes were lit with an inner flame and there were sparks flying from her fingertips, as before. This time, though, her body was so bright with orange light that she could have been made of fire.

She lifted their entwined hands and burned even brighter. He felt his dragon roar with pleasure and a spark shoot through his own body, electrifying him. She was his mate and he loved her.

Then the lightning bolt hit, and his dragon bellowed.

His dragon didn't hesitate and it didn't wait for Brandon's agreement. The shift rocketed through Brandon's body, compelling him to change forms. He beat his wings against the sky and raged in frustration. He tipped his head back and breathed fire at the sky.

His dragon was in control again!

He saw immediately that Liz thought he had shifted on purpose, as discussed. She didn't realize that his dragon was ascendant again. His dragon shouldn't have been in charge of his body, not when he stood so close to Liz, but he guessed that Chen had some other means on his side.

He looked around and saw the twinkle of Dragon Bone Powder around the lip of the vial. His body was reacting to even that trace of the powder that buttressed Chen's control over him. He felt an odd sensation on his chest, like a prickling, but when he looked down, he saw a red salamander running across the spiral in the sand.

With a gold salamander fast behind him.

It was Chen who had compelled him to change!

Neither salamander had been there a moment before and Brandon knew it. He dove and snatched at the pair, seizing one in each claw, but Jorge slipped through his fingers. Chen shifted shape, becoming a young Chinese man in jeans and leather. There was a cut on his cheek, and he favored one leg. One of his eyes was a mess, too. The element of surprise was on Chen's side, and Brandon's grip faltered when he found this stranger in his grasp. The young man punched Brandon in the face, his lip curling as Chen's had. Sure of his identity, Brandon breathed fire at him.

Chen became a dragon with scales of lacquer red that were edged in gold. His eyes flashed and he leapt at Brandon, biting into his shoulder. Brandon struck him with his tail, digging his own claws into the wound on Chen's face. Black *Slayer* blood fell, burning Brandon's scales wherever it touched. Brandon grabbed the *Slayer* and shoved his head into the beach, compelling him to breathe sand.

Chen shifted shape again, becoming a beautiful Chinese woman. Brandon was sufficiently startled once more that his grip faltered—he couldn't torture a woman!—which was the only opportunity she needed to drive her spike heel into the wound on his belly. He fell back in anguish, remembering the woman who had appeared outside Chen's place, just as she pivoted to fight. She had the same gash on her cheek and the same damaged eye.

She was Chen.

Brandon punched the *Slayer* and went after him, determined to not let him out of his grasp. He pounced on Chen and held him down.

What was wrong with the others? Brandon glanced at the other *Pyr*, only to find that they were frozen in place.

"Another spell," he whispered, and Chen laughed.

He changed back to dragon form again, leaping at Brandon with talons all bared.

He latched on to Brandon, digging his claws deep into Brandon's hide.

The entire scene was suddenly illuminated in brilliant blue-green light.

Darkfire!

*   *   *

When the auras of the *Pyr* were extinguished, Liz feared the worst. Where there had been a bright play of color, suddenly there was no light at all. The circle was dark and still, like the calm before the storm.

She saw that the *Pyr* appeared to have turned to stone. Their mates were similarly snared, but the children were as active as they had been before.

When Liz saw the red salamander appear out of nothing beside Brandon, she knew exactly what kind of salamander it had to be.

Its name was Chen.

Right behind it appeared another salamander, this one in shades of gold. It popped out of the air exactly the same way. Liz guessed that this was Jorge.

Meanwhile, Brandon gave a cry and shifted shape. He snatched for the two salamanders but managed to hold on to only the red one. The gold one raced across the sand and leapt for the boundary of the circle.

Garrett moved with astonishing speed, grabbing for the gold salamander.

Liz cried out a warning, but Jorge plunged through the circle she'd created. He screamed as he punctured the barrier that kept them all safe, and Liz hoped that both the circle and the dragonsmoke had burned him badly. She saw the rent in the circle's protective veil, like a tear in a silk curtain. She saw that destroyed barrier ripple in the wind and the energy she had raised begin to leak through it.

To her horror, Garrett charged through the barrier after the golden salamander.

Liz raced after the boy, shouting at him to stop. Twenty feet outside the circle, he snatched up the salamander with a hoot. He had time to turn to face her, his expression triumphant as he held the squirming salamander high over his head.

Then Jorge shifted shape. Garrett shouted as the enormous golden dragon snatched him up in his claws and leapt for the sky. Jorge turned to fly away, carrying the struggling boy in front of him.

Liz pulled out the darkfire crystal. At least there was no risk of her hitting the child; Garrett was completely obscured by Jorge's body.

She fired the crystal at Jorge. The beam of blue-green light that emanated from the stone struck him in the spine. He screamed and fell toward the earth, his black blood dripping from the wound in a lethal river. He dropped Garrett, and Liz ran to scoop up the little boy, fearing he had been hurt.

As she pulled him into her arms, he clung to her neck. She spun around to return to the circle.

Only to be confronted with a pillar of flame she'd seen once before.

Liz swallowed.

Her test was beginning, and at the worst possible time.

Chapter 14

Brandon knew he was fighting for his life. He turned his dragon's strength to his own desire and thrashed Chen hard with his tail. The *Slayer*'s grip faltered, and it was the chance that Brandon needed to tear himself loose, then turn the tables on his opponent. Brandon snatched the *Slayer*. Chen struggled within his grip, and there was a blue shimmer around his body.

Brandon had to weaken him before he disappeared. He remembered Niall's comment about dragonsmoke. Brandon had used dragonsmoke on Jorge, working on intuition, but maybe he could use it even more effectively now that he understood it better. He held tightly to Chen and breathed dragonsmoke in a long, slow plume. He drove his dragonsmoke into the wound in Chen's eye and felt the moment it locked on to the *Slayer*'s life force.

As he had before, he felt a boost of energy and saw

his opponent flag. Brandon pushed harder, breathing a thicker conduit and driving it deeper into the wound. He focused on his dragonsmoke and commanded it in the same way he had summoned waves to a beach.

It was like he'd stuck his thumb into an electrical socket. The power was almost overwhelming in its intensity. Chen moaned, visibly weakening by the second. This was his chance! Brandon concentrated on the dragonsmoke, pushing it into Chen's wound and deliberately drawing out as much strength as he could. To Brandon's relief, the incoming power strengthened his control over his dragon and allowed him to diminish Chen's hold over him.

Brandon breathed, exhaling dragonsmoke and inhaling Chen's energy. Chen struggled, but his efforts became more feeble each time. He tried to escape, but Brandon ensured that his dragonsmoke thread was thick and robust, that it couldn't be easily broken. Each breath brought him closer to victory. Brandon would suck the *Slayer* dry and render him powerless forever.

Chen rotated between forms, becoming the woman, the old man, the young man, then the dragon again. Brandon waited, knowing what form he would ultimately take. He hoped the *Slayer* didn't have enough strength to manifest elsewhere, then concentrated on trying to make that so.

When Chen became a salamander again and slipped from Brandon's grasp, Brandon snatched him up again and squeezed tightly. He felt bones break and tissue crush. He let his talons dig deeply into Chen's soft hide. The *Slayer* screamed, but Brandon didn't release him. He didn't enjoy the suffering of any creature, but he wasn't going to let this villain off easily.

This was the dragon who had targeted Brandon, who had tried to enslave him, who would have hurt Liz. Brandon knew that if roles had been reversed, Chen would have shown him no mercy. He savored the sight of the black blood dripping from his claws. He heard Chen moan and felt the *Slayer*'s heart palpitate.

Then Chen went limp.

Just as relief surged through Brandon, he saw a sudden flash of blue-green light. He knew the darkfire had to be in Liz's vicinity and he turned to look.

To his surprise, Liz was outside of the circle she'd cast. There was a pillar of flame in front of her, and Brandon remembered her story.

This was her test! The mark on her arm was glowing red, lit by an inner fire. Garrett stood behind Liz, watching the flames with awe.

Liz visibly took a breath, then stepped forward, fearless and confident. Brandon could feel the rapid pounding of her heart, though, and knew she was afraid of failure. What could he do to help? Liz raised her arms before the column of crackling flames and recounted a spell. Brandon didn't understand her words or recognize the language, but he smiled as he felt the change in the air around him.

Air. She was proving her mastery over air first.

At Liz's command, the wind tore over the beach in silent fury, bending the trees to the ground and making the sand fly. It swirled around Liz and the column of fire, making sparks dance high into the air and Brandon's ears pop.

Liz spoke again and the wind calmed at her dictate, reverting to a gentle breeze.

Brandon was amazed by what she could do.

Air. She'd nailed air.

She swallowed, then gestured to the pillar of flame. She called another invocation. The flames grew higher and brighter, the column of fire turning to a pillar of white heat. Brandon shifted back to human form and stepped forward, wanting to be closer to her. He felt her heart skip because his did the same. She didn't look away from her task, her concentration intense. Brandon flung the crushed carcass of Chen into the flames, certain the old *Slayer* deserved no less than incineration, and went to her side.

He and Liz would both put their challenges behind themselves today, then step into their future together.

He smiled as Liz coaxed the fire to burn higher and hotter yet. It seemed to touch the sky or even become one with the sun. When the pillar of crackling flames was blinding in its heat and intensity, Liz spread her hands and spoke again. She steadily damped the flames until they were embers, glowing red in the sand.

She cast Brandon a proud smile, and he grinned at her.

Garrett clapped in approval.

Liz took a deep breath, and Brandon felt her confidence falter. He realized that she had addressed the elements that were easier for her first. He reached out and took her hand, not certain whether his touch would hamper or help her. She squeezed his fingers once, as if in gratitude, then walked around the pile of embers.

Was she choosing a cardinal point of the compass? Or just summoning her strength? Brandon wasn't certain, but he trusted Liz to know what she was doing.

The mark on her arm, after all, was half-gone. He could see that two of the points of the pentacle that had been emblazoned on her chest were flickering with golden light, too.

Those must be the elements she had proven herself able to command.

Brandon glanced back at the *Pyr*, who still stood frozen in the remnants of Liz's protective circle with their mates. He didn't like that they were snared like that, but didn't want to interfere with Liz's concentration by asking questions. Maybe only some people could witness the test of a Firedaughter.

He was glad to be one of them.

When Liz stood on the opposite side of the embers, she squared her shoulders and gestured with both hands again. Brandon liked that he could watch her make her magic and, once again, he admired the glint of fire in her eyes and sparking off her fingertips.

This time, Liz's invocation must have been to the earth, because it rumbled far beneath their feet. There was a flicker of movement in the glowing embers left from the pillar of fire; then an earthquake shook the beach with savage force.

Brandon saw Liz's surprise and knew she hadn't called for this. Was it an aftershock from the earthquake the day before? Chen had created that one—was this the result of instability he had caused, or was the *Slayer* still clinging to life?

Brandon shifted shape and plunged his talons into the embers before himself, stirring through them in search of a red salamander.

In that moment, Liz cried out in dismay. The beach trembled so hard that she fell to her knees and a great fissure opened in the sand. It bisected the circle of embers, some of them falling into the crevasse. Sand poured into the widening gap. Liz gasped as she lost her footing and slipped toward the hole. Brandon abandoned his search and lunged toward her, intent on carrying her to safety.

No sooner had Brandon caught Liz than pain stabbed suddenly in his gut. He tipped back his head and roared, breathing flames at the sky in his anguish.

"Brandon! What's wrong?"

Brandon lifted his claw away, revealing the current of red blood that flowed from a new wound. It was where the third scale he'd given to Chen had been.

"Someone has broken that last scale," Liz said. Brandon nodded agreement, feeling faint with the pain. This one hurt far more than the other two had and left him trembling.

"It's just been broken now," Liz said, looking around in fear. "That means Jorge wants to weaken you before he attacks."

There was a resonant crack and the crevasse in the beach gaped wider. Lava bubbled in the fissure, shooting upward in a shower of fiery sparks. It surged toward the surface, rising fast and hot. He heard Liz call to the fire and felt it settle back to a simmer, on the cusp of boiling but not rushing forth.

"It's not up to me," she said, panic in her voice. "I can't push it all the way back. Something else is driving it."

Or someone.

Brandon glanced back at the *Pyr* in terror, only to see that they had been freed from the spell. They roared in unison, seizing their mates and children. Brandon saw Sloane take flight, then Niall.

Had Liz failed her test? Was it over?

Would she die, like her mother? Brandon couldn't even think about it.

He pivoted, dizzy with pain, and reached for Liz.

But she was gone.

Neither of them saw Zoë race across the sand, ignoring Eileen's shout. The little girl snatched up a black scale rimmed with orange, the scale that had fallen from Brandon's hide just before he spied Chen as a red salamander. Garrett had already been running back into the circle when Zoë bolted. Sara was calling him as frantically as Eileen called to her daughter. Zoë exchanged a glance with Garrett, then put the scale into the pocket of her pink overalls.

They joined hands and ran together, only to be snatched up by their respective fathers and flown to safety.

In the moment that Brandon had looked away, Jorge had manifested beside Liz in human form. Now he stood silhouetted against the brilliant blue of the midday sky, his eyes gleaming with intent. He had snatched Liz and held her captive.

Brandon froze. Although Brandon was in dragon form, there was blood running down his chest and he was shaking from the pain of his wounds. Jorge, in human form, looked lethal and mercenary.

Brandon was injured but he had the motivation to take the *Slayer* down.

Liz kicked Jorge in the groin with vicious force, and he swore. Brandon made to leap forward as Jorge shifted shape in a brilliant shimmer of blue, becoming a golden dragon.

With a talon at Liz's throat.

Brandon didn't dare move closer. His wings, to Brandon's dismay, were already growing back. They weren't as big as they had been, but Jorge's recovery was still amazing. This was the healing power of the Elixir in action.

"The old *Slayer* did me a favor in the end," Jorge

said. "Too bad he didn't survive to see his handi-work."

"What do you mean?" Brandon asked.

"Chen. Didn't you know? He had an affinity with the Earth. He could cause earthquakes and volcanic eruptions. Like the one right behind you."

Liz began to recount a spell, but Jorge clapped a claw across her mouth, rendering her silent. She struggled against the *Slayer*, and Brandon wanted to rip Jorge apart—but he couldn't risk Liz.

"No incantations," Jorge hissed, then glared at Brandon. "I want Chen's body. I'll trade you for your mate."

Brandon wanted to destroy Jorge, but he had to choose his moment to ensure that Liz was safely away from him first. First, he'd feed Jorge's confidence. Brandon didn't think it would take much.

He would also pretend to be much more seriously injured than he was to encourage Jorge to underesti-mate him. He closed his eyes and let himself waver as if unsteady.

"You want Chen? I dropped his body right over here," Brandon said, turning as if to look and keeping his voice weak. "He was in salamander form, not very big." He fell to his knees and pretended to search through the embers, moving as if he were nearly out of strength.

Brandon wasn't going to negotiate with this villain, but he didn't mind deceiving him. He was thinking furiously about Chen's affinity to the earth giving him the power to summon earthquakes. Brandon knew he had an affinity to the sea, because he'd used it to summon waves.

He decided to call up a big one.

He just needed a bit of time.

"What do you want it for, anyway?" he asked, pushing aside rubble and rocks as if the effort was too much for him. In reality, he was focused on the sea and on beckoning that big wave. The depths of the ocean were already stirring in response to his summons.

"The Elixir," Jorge hissed. "I want more. I *need* more, but the supply is destroyed. The only source is other *Slayers* who have drunk of it."

"How's that?" Brandon asked, coaxing the surf closer. He'd never done it so quickly before and was surprised to feel the power of the ocean's response.

It would be a tsunami.

Jorge grinned. "It's always in the body somewhere. I eat Chen's corpse and I get the Elixir he consumed. It's that simple."

"I was sure he was right here," Brandon said, peering at the ground. He heard the water that had been lapping on the beach recede, a sign of a big incoming wave. It was close! Just a minute or two more. He pretended to know less than he did. "What does the Elixir do?"

"In quantity, it ensures immortality. In smaller doses, it permits faster healing and greater resiliency." Jorge smiled. The last thing Jorge needed, as far as Brandon was concerned, was more power.

He turned to the *Slayer*, though, and raised one claw to his bleeding chest. "You're kidding. It could heal me?"

Jorge grinned. "Play it right and I'll let you have a taste."

"Really?" Brandon pretended to be pleased. In reality, he'd heard this line before. He guessed that the Elixir was addictive, and that one taste ensured that a dragon was hooked forever.

"Here it is!" he exclaimed, as if he'd discovered Chen's body. The wave was surging closer. Brandon reached down, pretending to pick something up. The wave was roiling toward shore and he felt Liz's awareness of it. "Let her go," he said, turning as if he had something in his hand. He deliberately faltered then, feigning weakness from his injury and loss of blood.

"Give it to me first!" Jorge demanded as he stepped forward.

Brandon coughed.

"Give it to me!" Jorge leapt closer, impatient.

Brandon attacked fast, taking the *Slayer* by surprise. He decked the golden dragon, breathed fire, and seized Liz. He tripped Jorge, shoving him toward the crevasse filled with bubbling lava, then leapt into the air.

"Liar!" Jorge might have given chase, but he didn't have the chance.

Liz called to the fire, the words of her spell incomprehensible to Brandon but her meaning clear. The lava seethed and boiled, spilling forward with new vigor. It burst toward Jorge in a torrent of flame.

But there was more. Along with the lava erupting from the fissure in the earth was a woman made of flame. Her hair was long and dark, and the orange flower in her hair burned brightly. She was dressed in fire, made of lava and flame, and her eyes were fathomless shadows.

"Pele," Liz whispered, and bowed her head in deference. "It was not my intent to disturb you."

Brandon understood that he was seeing the goddess of the volcano.

"There are times, Firedaughter, when I do not mind disruption." Pele became larger and larger, looming behind Jorge, her expression filling with fury. She raised her hands high behind the *Slayer*, then exhaled a hot plume of laughter.

Jorge fell back in surprise, tripping over his own tail.

Pele laughed.

Then she seized him with burning hands. Jorge screamed in pain as the smell of seared flesh filled the air. He shifted shape, rotating rapidly between forms, but the goddess didn't let him go. Pele laughed and kissed him with gusto, then threw him back into the fissure.

She blew Liz and Brandon a kiss, then dove into the brilliant orange pool of lava. Jorge gave one last yell; then he was drawn down into the depths of the earth by the retreating goddess.

No sooner had she disappeared than Brandon heard the massive wave breaking on the beach and rolling toward them with incredible force. Liz pivoted and called to the sea, her spell coaxing Brandon's wave to become bigger and more powerful. She might not have been able to summon it herself, but she could shape it and guide it.

He caught Liz in his grasp and leapt into the air, beating his wings hard so that he carried them above the tsunami.

The wall of water slammed into the beach, deluging everything and running down into the fissure of the volcano. Steam rose in billows as the eruption was halted and the earth stilled at the cooling touch of the ocean. The wave charged inland.

"The people," Liz whispered as the water advanced. "No one can get hurt!"

She raised her hands in supplication and they called to the water together, each in their own way. Liz's spell calmed the sea, and Brandon was pleased to see the third point on the pentacle that marked her flesh begin to glow.

She let the ocean flood the one beach, the beach that had been occupied only by the *Pyr*, to spend its force, then urged it to recede. Brandon hovered over the glistening sand, holding his mate and letting her complete her test.

He knew that Liz was calling to the fire because the volcano's tempest slowed to a rumble, the lava drawing back into the earth.

She spread her arms again, her exhaustion clear, and called another spell. Brandon watched the earth tremble below them. It heaved and shook, then the fissure that had opened was shut. The beach stilled with a last shiver.

Both *Slayers* were gone.

The fourth point on Liz's pentacle began to shine, as if touched by sunlight. The mark on her arm sparkled once, then disappeared completely.

And to Brandon's delight, the top point of the pentacle on Liz's skin illuminated. It shone with an inner radiance that lit the whole pentacle before the light faded. Afterward, the mark looked just like a tattoo.

"You did it!" he cried in jubilation, and Liz laughed.

"I couldn't have done it without you."

They laughed together and he soared high into the sky with his mate in his grasp.

"One more thing," Liz said, and laid the flat of her hand against Brandon's newest wound. He hovered in place, knowing what she would do. He gritted his teeth as she seared the place where he had removed that third scale, the one that Jorge had just broken. He endured the pain because he knew her touch would ensure his healing.

When he opened his eyes, Liz was sparkling in his arms, and he felt a sense of well-being beyond anything he'd ever experienced. He was whole and he was healed; he'd had his firestorm and won his mate.

Forever.

Brandon saw the other *Pyr* hovering high overhead, waiting for them. They held their partners and their children, safe in the sky. Sirens were blaring and car horns were honking, but he could see from his vantage point that the coast had had only a small amount of flooding. He pivoted and flew high into the sky, intent on being alone with the woman he loved.

They had defeated the *Slayer* who had tried to destroy Brandon, and Liz had passed her test. Both were cause for celebration.

Celebration dragon style.

Brandt strolled the Australian beach where he had often met Kay, once upon a time. It was night and he was alone, just the starry sky overhead and the surf pounding on the beach. He'd stopped at a bar for some courage, but he didn't think he was really going to need it.

Kay wasn't here.

The beach had changed in twenty-five years, of course. There were more buildings clustered on the road nearby, and they were taller than they once had been. The beach, even in the evening, carried the scent of many people who had been there during the day, instead of the few who had once appreciated it. It had been an overlooked haven back in the day, and it had been a secret place for Kay and Brandt.

He remembered the heat of their early encounters. He smiled in recollection of the passion and the power of the firestorm, the sparkle of Kay's eyes and the sound of her laughter. They'd made love on this beach when they'd had it to themselves.

Even after they'd married, they'd met here when she was afraid or sad. He'd found her here the first time he'd answered a call to a burning building that had subsequently collapsed. Two firemen had died, but not him. There would have been a third lost if he hadn't been able to shift shape to save both his co-worker and himself.

Kay had heard half the news and come here, terrified. She'd been pregnant and fearful of being left alone.

He hadn't managed to prevent that.

Brandt kicked the sand as he walked. She'd come here when her mom died and he'd held her as she cried.

She'd come here after she'd seen his dragon and after they'd argued, but he hadn't had the nerve to approach her that time lest he hear more. He'd watched her, then turned away, not knowing how to begin.

They had said so many hurtful things.

Brandt wasn't sure why impulse had brought him here now. He sure didn't want to hear any of those things again, and he didn't imagine that Kay still came here. She lived up in the hills now, far from the beach and the sea. He'd waited two nights, and knew he should go back south. He should go back to work, forget the past, try to make a future.

He turned to go back to his truck and he saw her.

Kay was getting out of her car. As he watched, she kicked off her sandals and walked out onto the sand, the tension sliding out of her shoulders. She didn't look much different to him, even if there was silver in her hair along with the gold. She'd cut it short, just as she'd always threatened to do. She was still slim and graceful and the sexiest woman alive.

Her smile was sadder than he would have liked.

He froze in place, watching her, knowing that she thought she was alone. She tipped her head back and looked at the stars, just the way she always had. Her skirt fluttered around her knees and she swung her sandals in one hand.

He knew the moment she realized she wasn't the only one on the beach.

They stared at each other for an endless moment, a hundred horrible words from the past between them. He lifted one hand and she looked away, then she swallowed and walked straight toward him. Brandt braced himself for a lecture.

She stopped six feet away and inhaled sharply. "You're drunk."

As blunt as ever. He had missed that.

"No." Brandt shook his head. "I've had a drink, but I don't know why. There's not enough of it in the world to make me forget."

"You want to forget?" she asked, her tone sharp. "Forget what?"

"Forget how much I hurt you." Brandt sighed.

"Forget that I did everything wrong and lost everything that mattered."

Kay blinked and nodded, averting her gaze. She stared at the sea. "I'd like to forget sometimes that I could say such hurtful things." She looked back at him, her eyes bright. "Maybe forget that I can be too proud to make anything come right again."

Brandt was shocked by her implication. He stared at her, unable to believe that the chance he'd wanted could be his. He was sure that if he said anything, he'd say the wrong thing and destroy this opportunity before it even was fully real.

"He phoned me today," Kay said, and there was no doubt in Brandt's mind who she meant. She smiled a little. "He says he's met a girl."

"He had his firestorm," Brandt said and she looked at him. "I felt it." Now he was the one who looked out to the horizon. "I wanted to go, but Erik told me not to."

"Erik?"

"Leader of the *Pyr*. A guy I should have listened to years ago." Brandt shrugged and his throat was tight. "I thought I'd try to do things differently, maybe not screw up my son's life again."

Kay tilted her head to look at him. "You think this Erik can be a better father to your son than you? I think if you'd been around, you'd have been a great father."

Brandt shook his head. "I would have just ruined it, Kay. That's my talent. The only thing I do well is fight fires." He forced a smile, not daring to hope for more than this. "It's good to see you."

Kay put her hand on his arm and her touch electrified him, as it always had. "Is there someone else?"

"There never will be," Brandt admitted. "That's just how it is. I love you."

He couldn't hold her gaze, not when she looked so surprised. It was his fault that she was surprised by his feelings; another failure on his part.

Brandt glanced down at her hand on his arm and saw that the ring he had put on her finger was still there. He met Kay's gaze in surprise, and her smile broadened.

"I understand that well enough," she said softly, and her eyes started to sparkle. "I think maybe that once a woman has fallen in love with a dragon shape shifter, there's no going back to normal men. They just don't have it going on."

"You mean you'd give me another chance?"

"If you'll give me one. I'm sorry, Brandt."

Brandt took her hand in his. "I'm sorry, Kay. I'm sorry for everything."

"Don't be sorry for everything," she said. "There was so much that was good. Be sorry that we were stupid enough to let it go without a fight." Then Kay reached up and kissed his cheek. Her fingers were on his jaw. Her eyes were full of stars. His Kay was forgiving him, and Brandt couldn't believe his luck. Her chaste kiss started his world spinning again.

"We're going to be grandparents, Brandt," she said

with her usual brisk efficiency. "We're far too young for it, of course, but there's nothing to be done once the firestorm is consummated."

"I suppose not." He smiled despite himself, his heart beginning to thunder.

"I booked a flight to Oʻahu to see Brandon compete this week. Meet Liz. Surprise them both, undoubtedly." Her grip tightened on his hand and her eyes shone. "Why don't we go together?"

Brandt bent and kissed her thoroughly, trying to put twenty-five years of denied passion into his touch. "Are you really ready to live with a dragon?" he asked long moments later.

"I think I'm due a little adventure," Kay said with a smile. "And I've had some time to come to terms with the idea." She grimaced. "I'm sorry that I said what I did. I was surprised and frightened."

"Not without cause. I'm sorry I didn't tell you sooner."

Kay smiled again, her expression revealing that she'd seen to his heart, as always. "Are dragons supposed to be afraid?"

"Only when they have everything to lose."

Kay reached for him then, offering all he wanted and more, and it was a long time before their kiss ended.

Brandt glanced at the starry sky overhead, then back to Kay. "How about a ride to Hawaiʻi?" he asked.

Kay's mouth opened in astonishment. She looked between him and the sky, then back at him again.

"Really? Of course—you can fly! That sounds marvelous."

"It is. Trust me, Kay."

"Oh, Brandt, I do." She pulled his head down for another kiss, a kiss that seared his very soul.

Just the way the firestorm had done.

Liz wasn't really surprised that the *Pyr* congregated in Sloane's suite at the resort, or that they were proud of what had been achieved. They demanded the whole story be recounted three times, and they were clearly annoyed that they hadn't been able to contribute more. Liz knew that their generous sharing of their knowledge had been a key to their success.

They congratulated Brandon and thumped his back. Someone had ordered wine and Sloane was in the middle of everything, doing dragon first aid. The room was filled with conversation and relief, and sleeping children were nestled into several of the chairs. It was late afternoon.

What Liz didn't expect was for Erik's daughter to rouse herself from slumber on the couch. The little dark-haired girl couldn't be more than three years old, but she had a solemnity about her that was unusual in a toddler. She marched directly toward Liz, her green eyes as vivid in hue as those of her father, looking like a child on a mission.

Erik watched Zoë, so completely still that he could have been frozen in place.

Garrett also watched her progress, nodding approval.

Liz crouched down when Zoë stopped in front of her. The little girl didn't say anything, just dug in the pocket of her pink overalls. Liz blinked when Zoë presented her with a black scale, a dragon scale, that was edged in orange.

"It's one of Brandon's," Liz said, prickling with awareness that the *Pyr* were watching closely. "Where did you get it?"

"It fell off," Zoë said, and her mother caught her breath. Zoë looked Liz in the eye. "You have to fix it."

Then she turned and marched back to the couch, climbing into her former place and snuggling down to sleep. Liz looked around, knowing that there was import in the little girl's gesture. This couldn't be one of the three scales Brandon had given to Chen because Jorge had broken all of those scales.

She remembered then what Sloane had said about a *Pyr* losing a scale when he falls in love. "This isn't one of the scales Chen took, is it?" she asked, already knowing the answer.

Brandon grinned and caught her hand in his. "I didn't pull that one out." He leaned closer, his eyes shining, and dropped his voice to a theatrical whisper. "I guess the news is out that I'm in love with you."

His words made Liz's heart skip a beat, but she was worried. "But that means that you have another gap in your armor," she said. "That makes you vulnerable."

"Love makes everyone vulnerable," Erik said.

Eileen smiled at him. "I like that there's physical evidence of what's in a dragon's heart." The other women smiled in turn.

"But how can you be so calm about this?" Liz asked the women. "If they're missing scales, they're weaker."

"But we're not missing scales any longer," Niall said. He turned to the other *Pyr*. "Let's show her."

Erik flung out his hands and shifted shape in a glorious shimmer of blue light, becoming an ebony and pewter dragon. He reared back and Liz saw that there was a scale on his chest that was different from the others. It had a stone affixed to it.

"A rune stone," Eileen said. "It had belonged to Erik's father, but I gave it back to him."

Quinn shifted shape next, his powerful sapphire and steel dragon form making the large room seem small. He also reared back, displaying his chest to Liz. There was a scale that was different, as well, one that looked to be made of silver.

"Wrought iron," Sara said. "We repaired Quinn's armor with the material he loves best." She smiled at him, caressing his jeweled hide.

"Did you give it to him?" Liz asked, seeing a pattern.

Sara smiled. "Yes."

Niall changed shape next, the flash of pale blue making Liz wince at its brilliance. There was a scale on his chest that differed from the others, as well. She had to step closer to see that it looked different because it was transparent, and there was a tattoo on the flesh beneath it.

"My work," Rox said with pride. "Tattoos have been protective talismans since the very beginning." She touched the triple spiral on Brandon's shoulder. "That's why someone gave you this one."

"Really?"

"Really. I'm serious that I'd like to meet this artist."

Brandon smiled at her. "Consider it done."

Erik nodded at Sloane, who shifted shape in his turn. Sloane's scales were perfectly matched and Liz realized that he was the only one who didn't have a mate.

"I'll guess you haven't had a firestorm," she said, and Sloane inclined his head in agreement. His scales were all the colors of tourmalines, shading from green to gold to purple over his length. He was regal and elegant.

"Not yet," he said, and smiled. "Only once in a lifetime. I hear it's worth the wait."

They all looked at Brandon, who took a deep breath and shifted shape. His dragon was as black as night, the fiery edge to his scales making him look as if he were lit from within. Liz checked his scales when he reared back and gave a cry of delight. The scales that had been forcibly removed were already growing back over his wounds.

Sloane chuckled with satisfaction as he leaned closer to look. "My work is done," he said. "Although it couldn't have been done without Liz."

"But what does it mean?" Brandon asked.

"That the loves you have lost are returning to you," Quinn said.

"My mom?" Brandon asked, looking down at his chest and touching one of the new scales. He fingered the first spot that she'd healed, and even in his dragon form, Liz could see his grimace. "My dad?"

Erik nodded. "You know now that you are incomplete as long as he is out of your life."

Brandon rubbed his talon over the gap. "I don't blame him so much now. It's not easy, and we made different choices."

"Maybe he's changing that now," Sloane suggested.

"Maybe you should talk to him and find out," Erik said quietly. Their conviction was such that Liz realized they knew something about Brandon's father.

"I don't even know where he is," Brandon said. "I'd call him right now, but I don't know where to start."

"Keep your heart open," Niall said. "In case he comes to you."

Brandon glanced at Liz, and she smiled. "It can't hurt to hear his side of the story," she said, and he nodded agreement. He touched another healing scale. "My mom," he said, and the others nodded. He brushed his claw across the third, the one that Liz had most recently seared. "But what was the third loss?" He looked at the *Pyr* in confusion, but none of them had an answer for him.

It was Liz who stepped forward and put her hand

on his chest. She looked up into his eyes and saw the change in him. "Yourself," she said. "You despised yourself and the dragon within you when we met."

"But it wasn't my dragon. It was what Chen wanted my dragon to be."

"Exactly." Liz touched the newly exposed bit of skin with concern. "So, am I right that I have to give Brandon something to heal this fourth spot?" She turned to Quinn. "I thought the Smith repaired the scales of the *Pyr*."

"I do, but the repair of the scale lost in a firestorm will not take without the willing aid of the mate."

Liz looked at the dragons in the room with her. They all reminded her of jewelry, precious metals and precious stones. She wanted to give Brandon a magical token, something of herself that would become part of his armor yet still adhere to the expectations of the *Pyr*.

"Ginger gave Delaney her mother's amber earrings," Sara said softly, as if she guessed Liz's conundrum.

Liz smiled at the other woman and tugged her grandmother's jet earrings from her ears. "These were my grandmother's," she said, looking between Quinn and Brandon. "And I think they were her grandmother's before that. They are filled with the magic of my lineage. Will they do?"

"They will more than do," Quinn said with satisfaction. He accepted them and turned them in his claws, his eyes gleaming as he examined the hallmarks.

"Sterling," he murmured. "It is one of my favored materials for a repair."

"Thanks, Liz," Brandon said, his voice husky. "If you're happy to give them, I'll be honored to carry them."

Liz nodded, knowing that this solution was exactly right.

That was when she realized that Garrett and Zoë had joined the group of *Pyr*. The dragons stood around the perimeter of the room, forming a casual circle, and the toddlers were in the center. Garrett pretended to breathe fire beside his father, in obvious anticipation of the scale repair. Quinn seemed to inflate as he took a breath, becoming larger and more imposing. He lifted the lost scale in his claw, then loosed a torrent of dragonfire upon it. The scale heated in his grasp, glowing with inner fire.

Liz was enraptured. She felt the flicker of her own gift and knew from Brandon's expression that she was sparkling again.

She had to help. When Quinn heated the earrings in his other claw, Liz summoned the flame in her heart. She fed it with her ardor for Brandon and saw a tongue of flame leap from her own fingertips. Quinn pressed the earrings against the scale and Liz added her fire to his own to secure them there.

She heard his deep chuckle.

"I believe we have fire covered," he said, his eyes glinting with humor. He heated the back of the scale, then pressed it against Brandon's bare skin. Brandon arched his back and bared his teeth, exhaling smoke as the scale was seared into place. Quinn gave Liz a look and she added her healing fire to the scale.

"Fire," Quinn repeated with satisfaction. "And earth in the jet."

"Air," Erik commanded, and Liz blew on the cooling scale impulsively. She felt Brandon tremble beneath her touch and knew the repair had hurt.

"Water," Sloane added, and Liz glanced up. She saw the tear on Brandon's cheek and lifted it with her fingertip, touching it to the repaired scale. It sizzled on contact, emitting a puff of steam, and he shook from nose to tail in relief.

Liz reached up to kiss him, proud of what he had endured and accomplished. Brandon shifted shape and caught her in his arms, dipping his head for a very satisfying kiss.

Liz was starting to think that having a dragon baby wouldn't be so bad at all.

The *Pyr* had celebrated Brandon's victory in grand style. They were at the beach bar at the resort long into the night, talking and laughing, eating and drinking. The children had fallen asleep and the sky overhead was filled with stars. They were wonderful company, but Liz wanted to do some private celebrating of her own. She felt both tired and invigorated, back in balance after a long time of ignoring who she really was.

It was all because of Brandon.

And the firestorm. Like him, she now believed in its promise and in their shared future. Their child would be a boy, she'd been told by the *Pyr*, a dragon shifter who came into his powers at puberty. Liz didn't think it was out of the question that he'd also inherit some enhanced link to the elements from her side.

He smiled at her and ran a finger down her cheek. "You must be exhausted," he murmured, the wicked glint in his eyes telling her that she wouldn't be falling asleep anytime soon.

Liz feigned a yawn all the same, covering her mouth with her hand. "I am. Aren't you?"

"Beat," Brandon agreed, then winked. "Don't you have to teach at that symposium?"

"Tomorrow at nine. Maureen rescheduled everything because of delayed flights."

Brandon cocked a finger at her. "I'm coming to listen."

"You're interested in marine biology?"

"I'm interested in oceans and I'm interested in you." He grinned at her. "And I like the idea of our working together for a better future."

"So do I," Liz agreed and kissed him. She could lose herself in his kiss, even now, and she suspected that was never going to change. Brandon's fingers slid into her hair and he deepened his kiss, sparking the flame in her heart that was never going to die.

"Look at the two of them," Niall said.

"I think it's sweet," Eileen said.

"Get a room," Sloane teased, throwing the paper

umbrella from his drink at them. The other *Pyr* laughed as they cast an avalanche of paper umbrellas over Liz and Brandon.

Brandon broke his kiss, laughing as he tugged Liz to her feet. "You guys staying a bit? Liz is teaching tomorrow, but I'm going to surf the Banzai Pipeline on Tuesday."

"Wouldn't miss it for the world," Erik said with a smile.

"You'd better win," Quinn said, his voice a low rumble and a glint in his eyes. "Seeing as how we came all this way."

"He'll do his best," Liz said, but Brandon was more confident than that.

"I'm going to nail it," he said with a confident smile. "I've got a new sponsor, and a son on the way." He dropped his voice to a whisper. "Plus I've got to make sure Liz doesn't just think I'm her boy toy."

They laughed together, as comfortable with each other and as supportive as a family. "Sleep well," Sara said, drawing her shawl forward to nurse her son.

Garrett waved sleepily from his father's lap and Brandon urged Liz toward their room.

"I like them," she said, not sure what he was thinking.

"Yeah," he admitted, as if surprised. "It's like discovering you have all these uncles who are okay."

"Even when you thought they were evil."

His smile was rueful. "I guess you shouldn't believe everything you hear."

"Or maybe you need to remember the rule of three," a woman said from behind Liz.

Liz froze, not daring to hope it was who she wanted it to be. Brandon looked from her to the woman behind her, his confusion clear.

Liz turned, not truly believing that her mother could be with her again.

Her mother was there, in a way. She looked as if she were made of smoke and will-o'-the-wisp, her figure silvery and ethereal.

"Whatsoever you send out into the world returns to you threefold," her mother said softly. "Today's events proved that old adage clear."

"Mom!"

"Why are you surprised?" Her mother smiled. "Haven't you felt me with you every day and night, my Elizabeth?"

Liz shook her head, her vision blurred with tears. "But it was my fault...."

"No." Her mother touched featherlight fingertips to her lips. "No."

Liz's throat was tight. "I tried to forget what I was."

Her mother smiled serenely. "And I guarded you in darkness until you remembered."

"Mom!" Liz was overwhelmed to have this moment and felt blessed to be forgiven.

She bent and kissed Liz once on each cheek, her eyes filled with pride. "Congratulations, Firedaughter. You have mastered the final test." Her eyes glinted as she looked over Brandon and her smile broadened. "I knew that there was an unusual man in Liz's future. She's too special for anything less. I sensed that all would come together when you found each other."

"It did," Liz said.

"Absolutely," Brandon said, holding Liz close to his side. "Brandon Merrick." He held out his right hand with that confidence Liz so admired, his smile radiant enough to warm the sun.

Her mother smiled back at Brandon, nodding approval of Liz's choice. "Teach the young one all he needs to know," she said quietly, her gaze dropping to Liz's flat belly. "When worlds collide, it's not always clear how they'll mix."

"I thought it was the darkfire that made everything unpredictable," Brandon said.

Liz's mother nodded. "Darkfire in the hands of a Firedaughter is even more unpredictable."

Then she brushed her fingertips across Liz's collarbone, her touch as light as a spring breeze. Her skin tingled and Liz saw the completed pentacle glitter beneath her mother's touch. Liz looked up at her mother, but the shadowy vision of the woman she'd loved all her life was gone. She blinked back her tears as Brandon took her hand in his.

"You're not rid of me, Elizabeth," her mother murmured in her ear, her whisper filled with familiar humor. "I'm not an Airdaughter for nothing. I will appear to you, when I can and when you need me. I promise. You have only to look."

And that was more than Liz had ever expected.

She met Brandon's gaze and took his hand, her heart pounding with joy.

"Blessed be," her mother whispered, her voice already fading.

"Blessed be," Liz echoed, smiling because she knew that she was blessed beyond belief.

Epilogue

Kira had been right.

The surf broke perfectly on Tuesday morning, just as she'd forecast. Brandon was down on 'Ehukai Beach when the sun came up, watching the waves break on the reef. It was absolutely textbook. The waves had to be twenty-five feet high, the curl of the Pipeline exactly the way Brandon preferred it to be.

This would be his day.

He would succeed because of Liz and the firestorm.

He hurried back to his place and woke Liz with a kiss, then put on some breakfast, following his precompetition ritual to the letter. He did his warm-up exercises and tugged on the wet suit from Kira. His sense of anticipation was growing with every passing moment. They went back down to the beach, and the organizers had their staff ready. He registered and signed waivers, got his time slot, shook hands with the other competitors.

Matt, Dylan, and Rick were there early, each of them nearly as excited about Brandon's opportunity as he was. Kira fussed over the wet suit, Brandon's impetuousness forgiven, and gave him a kiss on the cheek in encouragement. Liz talked to them all, then gave a cry of pleasure when she spotted a familiar face.

Brandon could have told her that her friend Maureen would be there—he'd heard that diesel Mercedes pulling into town—but he hadn't wanted to spoil the surprise.

They both surprised him with the news that Liz had been offered a chance to collect samples at the reserve for her research. She'd made a good impression in her lectures and was optimistic—with Maureen's encouragement—that the research opportunity could develop into a job offer at the Institute. She was ready to move to Hawai'i to make that happen.

Everything was coming together perfectly.

Brandon was aware of the *Pyr* gathered on the beach, watching him with pride, and he waved to them all. Garrett and Zoë ran over to give him hugs, and Brandon felt as if he'd been welcomed into an extended family he'd never realized he had.

He watched the waves, welcoming their consistency. He'd wondered whether he should use his affinity with water to improve the surf on this day, but it turned out that he didn't have to decide. The ocean was cooperating all on its own, which suited Brandon even better. The sun got hotter and the beach got more crowded. Liz smeared lotion on them both and he felt the tension building. The Jet Skis pulled a couple of competitors out of the water, big names who had miscalculated the Pipeline, and the excitement on the beach grew.

Brandon surfed twice and made good showings, although he knew that he had to completely nail his third run. The international team organizer had already spoken to him by lunchtime, but there was no firm offer on the table.

It all depended on his last run.

He needed to be perfect in the Pipeline.

Finally the whistle blew and it was his turn. Brandon ran into the surf alongside the other competitor. They plunged into the water as one and started to paddle for the incoming waves. Although they were in competition with each other, a sense of camaraderie joined them. They were both really in competition with the waves. They punched through the break together, swimming with power into the trough. The other guy was on the inside.

"Your choice," Brandon said, because that was protocol.

"This one," the guy said. "I'll take this one."

"Looks like a beauty," Brandon said. "Have a good ride."

"You, too." They grinned at each other, exchanged thumbs-up; then the wave began to swell against the horizon. The other guy turned his board and started to paddle toward the shore.

"Go, go, go!" Brandon shouted, knowing the people on the beach would be shouting the same thing but that the other surfer wouldn't be able to hear them. The wave moved beneath him, gathering power and momentum.

"Get up!" Brandon cried as the wave's high point lifted the other surfer high. The other guy was on his feet, riding the curve toward the shore. Brandon could barely hear the applause on the beach. The other surfer ripped the face of the wave, much to the approval of the audience. He'd get points from the judges for his moves.

Then he tried to ride the Pipeline. Brandon saw immediately that he hadn't read the curl properly. He'd no sooner gotten the front of the breaking wave than it crashed over him, driving him down into the reef. The Jet Skis roared, but the other guy was up.

He looked pissed off when he began to paddle back out beyond the break. Brandon smiled. He knew what it was like to have the water get the better of you. He let the next wave pass, not liking it so much, and the other surfer joined him on the outside.

"Nice rip," Brandon said, and the other guy nodded.

"You going?" he asked.

Brandon eyed the wave swelling against the horizon. "Yeah," he said. "This one's mine."

"It's going to be big."

"That's the way I like them." Brandon turned and paddled toward the beach with powerful strokes. He felt the wave gaining on him, then matched his speed to it perfectly. The wave moved beneath him, lifting him high, higher than he'd expected. He heard the surprised cry of the surfer behind him and of the spectators on the beach. He had no time to be surprised. He had to concentrate.

He didn't rip the surf or try any fancy moves. He just rode it with control, positioning himself perfectly. The surf broke just as he'd anticipated, and the white curl of foaming water appeared right beside him. He let one hand trail in the deep turquoise of the roiling water and felt the spray of the Pipeline closing around him. He stayed right at the lip of the breaking wave, the white spray sparkling all around him, the roar of the ocean filling his ears.

Brandon was surrounded by a tube of swirling water, as if the ocean held him safe in the palm of her hand. It was exhilarating, as if he'd stepped out of time. He felt in tune with the world and her elements, in balance with his dragon and its awesome power, and filled with joy for his future with Liz. For this moment, there was nothing but him and the sea and the happy pulse of his heart.

Perfect.

And it seemed to last forever.

He soared out of the end of the Pipeline when it crashed to nothing on the reef, standing on his board and riding in to the beach on his own momentum. A roar of applause rose from the audience, and he saw that the judges were giving him perfect scores. Kira was shouting with joy, and the photographers were clustering around him, their shutters clicking. Liz was running across the sand toward him as the siren blared, signifying the end of the session, and he caught her up and swung her around in his arms.

"You were great!" she said with excitement.

"Because of you," Brandon said, and kissed her. He saw the organizer of the international team coming toward him with a big smile, and he knew exactly what he was going to say. He turned to the man with a grin and stretched out his hand in greeting, barely hearing the invitation to join the team that had been his goal for years.

Because he saw an older couple standing back from the crowd, their hands clasped.

His parents had come to watch him.

Brandon couldn't believe it. He looked twice, but they were still there.

Smiling at him.

In a daze, Brandon accepted the coach's offer and shook his hand, aware that Liz was practically bouncing beside him. "You did it," she whispered in delight.

But Brandon stared in astonishment at his parents. They were not only here and smiling, but together. Before he could make sense of it, his mom smiled and waved. Brandon opened his arms to her on instinct. She started to cry as she hurried toward him, then caught him in a fierce embrace.

"I had to meet this Liz of yours," she said when she'd kissed him a hundred times. She turned to Liz expectantly. Brandon introduced them, looking for his dad.

Brandt Merrick hung back, as if uncertain of his greeting. Erik stood behind him, one hand on the other *Pyr*'s shoulder. Brandon nodded, then strode to his father, offering his hand. "Hey, Dad. It's good to see you," he said, meaning every word of it. "I'd like to talk to you, if you have time."

"All the time in the world," Brandt said with a smile as he seized his son's hand. He looked into Brandon's eyes. "I'm sorry."

"Me, too." Brandon caught his dad in a tight hug, feeling his tears rise when he felt his father catch his breath. He looked up and met Erik's knowing gaze, then saw the leader of the *Pyr* smile with approval before he turned away.

He led his dad back to Liz and his mom, marveling as he did so that just a week before, he'd thought that his dragon would ruin his life. Now he had everything, everything he'd always wanted and a love he'd never dreamed of finding.

And he would defend it, both as man and as dragon, for all the days and nights of his life.

This was the gift of the firestorm.

Don't miss the bad boy of the *Pyr*!
Turn the page for a preview of Lorenzo's
story in Deborah Cooke's

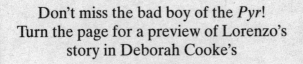

Available now.

Cassie had to hand it to this Lorenzo guy. The custom-built theater for his stage show, *The Trial by Fire*, was incredible even by Vegas standards. He hadn't skimped at all. There was nothing tawdry or tacky about it. The interior was gorgeous and elegant, far more luxurious than any of the other venues they'd visited or glimpsed.

The seats were cushy and upholstered in black velvet. They were scrupulously clean, as if they'd been upholstered just that day. The carpet was black and thick underfoot, unstained as far as she could see. There wasn't so much as a stray kernel of popcorn. The curtains on the stage looked like real velvet, black with a line of metallic orange along the hem. That line etched the glittering outline of flames.

Trial by fire. She got it.

There were sconces spaced along the walls, each looking like a brass bowl that held a flame. Of course, they couldn't have been real flames, not with fire codes, but they looked real. The temperature in the theater was cool but not cold. It felt like a refuge, both from commercialism and the noisy bustle of Vegas.

She listened to the audience as they took their seats and murmured to each other. She felt their wonder and knew that Lorenzo had them believing in him even before he began his show.

Cassie folded her arms across her chest, less willing to be persuaded. All of this magic stuff relied on trickery, on making people look left when things happened on the right, for example. She was determined to see the truth of whatever this guy did.

Her BlackBerry vibrated again and she glanced at it. Again they had doubled the price they'd pay for shots of those shape-shifting dragons. Melissa Smith's television show about the *Pyr* must have really good ratings. Cassie scrolled through the message, eyeing the specifications for what they wanted.

A suite of shots, documenting the change from man to dragon.

That would be tough to fake.

Of course, if the *Pyr* were real, the shots wouldn't be fake.

Cassie dismissed that possibility. She wondered what the editor would pay for proof that the *Pyr* were a hoax. Well aware of Stacy's disapproval, Cassie sent a message to ask.

Her BlackBerry received a reply almost instantly. This story was hot. She wasn't totally surprised that the editor would pay the same price for proof of a hoax, but was surprised that the price had increased again.

But where would a person find one of these supposed dragon shifters?

"Off," Stacy muttered. "You promised."

Cassie turned off the device and put it away. It would be enough money to retire. To leave the business of illusion for good.

She was surprised by how appealing that idea sounded.

Cassie was still thinking about that money as the lights began to dim and music started from all sides. The flames in the sconces leapt higher, and that line across the bottom of the stage curtains began to glitter.

As if it were burning.

A trick, but a good one.

If she were pretending to be a dragon shifter, where would she hide?

Maybe, just maybe, in a place where nothing was what it seemed to be.

A place like Las Vegas.

Hmm.

Lorenzo nodded at his staff and strode to his place at center stage, where he would await the rising of the curtains. He fought his awareness of the slow burn of the eclipse, teasing at the edge of his thoughts. He felt the firestorm light for some poor *Pyr* and ignored it, just as he had a hundred times before.

Even though it was close.

It was *not* his problem.

Lorenzo was in the act of donning his top hat when the music swelled. One pair of curtains swept back and the other curtain rose skyward.

Right on cue.

Perfect.

The audience stared at him in expectant awe. Lorenzo had a moment to think that everything would be just fine.

Then he raised his hand in a welcoming gesture, and the light of his own firestorm sparked from his fingertips.

Lorenzo was astounded.

His firestorm launched an arc of fire that illuminated the space between him and a woman in the front row. She was lit suddenly with radiant golden light.

The audience gasped.

Lorenzo wanted to swear.

The woman had been sitting with her arms folded across her chest, reluctant to be impressed. Her skepticism would have made his eye skip over her under other circumstances. The blonde beside her was more typical of the women Lorenzo took as lovers.

But the bright glimmer of the spark startled her.

And it compelled Lorenzo to look. Her bones were good. She could have been attractive if she'd chosen to do anything other than tug her hair back into a sloppy ponytail. She wore no makeup and was dressed in jeans, a cotton shirt, and hideous red cowboy boots.

Lorenzo couldn't stand cowboy boots.

Even on cowboys.

Women certainly shouldn't dress like cowboys, not if they wanted to show their glory to advantage. Women should wear skirts and high heels, lacy little bits of nothing, and lipstick. They had serious assets and they should use them.

This woman apparently didn't bother. Her hair was reddish blond, her skin fair. She jumped when the spark struck her shoulder, and the golden light revealed that she was young and pretty. There was intelligence in her expression, wariness and interest mingled together.

Despite that, there couldn't be a woman on the face of the earth whom he was less likely to find intriguing. She seemed to feel the same way about him. Lorenzo didn't find it promising that they had that one thing in common.

Meanwhile, he smiled at the crowd and bowed, as though everything were going according to plan.

Far from it! Curse the firestorm, its timing, and its choices. Curse his *Pyr* nature and everything that came with it.

Lorenzo was just going to have to work with the firestorm.

Somehow.

Cassie jumped when the spark struck her shoulder. She'd assumed it was an illusion, but the collision of that flame with her skin gave her the strangest sensation.

She was hot.

She was simmering.

No, she was *aroused*. The electric heat of desire slid through her body, turning her mind in earthy directions, making her fidget in her chair. She was consumed with lust, which was about as far from her usual frame of mind as possible.

She stared at Lorenzo, wondering what the hell he was pumping into the air in this place. He smiled at her as slowly as she'd anticipated. Like he knew what she was thinking. He was suave and confident, and she wondered whether he made love slowly, too.

In fact, she tingled at the very idea.

He was manipulating her, but she couldn't figure out how.

Lorenzo was gorgeous, but Cassie saw lots of hot guys up close and personal in her line of work. Genuine or augmented. She talked to them, she cajoled them, sometimes she even shared a joke with them. Not a one of them had ever made her feel like this. Not a one of them had ever made her mouth go dry or made her panties wet with a single glance.

She wasn't sure there had ever been anybody who had made her feel like this.

And she didn't like it one bit.

"Welcome, ladies and gentlemen, girls and boys." Lorenzo's voice was low and rich, the kind of voice a woman could listen to all day long.

Or all night long.

Cassie stifled a shiver and folded her arms more tightly across her chest. Charisma. He had charisma. Buckets of it. That was all. And he knew how to work a crowd. He had each and every one of them in his pocket already.

Maybe there were vibrators in these chairs.

Or just in hers.

"I hope you are prepared to be amazed!"

A flick of his wrist, and the stage erupted in flames. They were brilliant orange and waist-high, surrounding Lorenzo. He stood, smiling, in his tux, untouched by the fire. Maybe he was Faust, completely at ease with the heat of hellfire. Certainly there was something wicked in his smile.

With a gesture from him, the flames were all extinguished, the stage still looking like wooden boards.

Unburned.

The audience applauded wildly, but Lorenzo was already on the move.

"Yum!" Stacy whispered, and Cassie nodded agreement.

Okay, she wasn't just burned-out. She was going insane. Cassie felt like a besotted teenager, but she couldn't take her eyes off Lorenzo.

This was not good.

Also available

FLASHFIRE
A Dragonfire Novel

by DEBORAH COOKE

Master illusionist Lorenzo's dragon nature is his biggest
secret. It's also another detail to juggle, like ensuring each
of his Las Vegas magic shows is a true spectacle.
That is until he feels the burn of his firestorm and his
whole world shifts.

Lorenzo wants to satisfy the firestorm and put it behind
him. But photographer Cassie Redmond is hard to forget.
And when Slayers target the mate he didn't believe he
wanted, Lorenzo realizes he'll do anything to
keep Cassie safe...

Also in the series:
Darkfire Kiss
Whisper Kiss
Winter Kiss
Kiss of Fate
Kiss of Fury
Kiss of Fire

Available wherever books are sold or
at penguin.com

facebook.com/projectparanormalbooks

Also available

DARKFIRE KISS
A Dragonfire Novel

by DEBORAH COOKE

Rafferty Powell has resolved to destroy his hated
arch-nemesis, Magnus Montmorency. The pair have
exchanged challenge coins, and their next battle will be
their last. But Rafferty never expected to meet a woman
whose desire for Magnus's end matches his own—and
whose soul sparks a firestorm within him...

"Impossible to put down."
—Romance Reviews Today

Available wherever books are sold or
at penguin.com

facebook.com/projectparanormalbooks

S0318

Also available

WHISPER KISS
A Dragonfire Novel

by DEBORAH COOKE

The national bestselling Dragonfire series
continues to heat up...

For millennia, the shape-shifting dragon warriors known as the
Pyr have commanded the four elements and guarded the earth's
treasures. But now the final reckoning between the Pyr and the
dreaded Slayers is about to begin...

Niall Talbot has volunteered to hunt down and destroy all the
remaining shadow dragons before they can wreak more havoc.
But fate has placed him in the hands of Rox, an unconventional
tattoo artist who doesn't even flinch when a shape-shifting
dragon warrior suddenly appears on her doorstep. And as a
woman who follows her heart in matters of passion, she makes
the perfect mate for a firestorm with Niall...

Available wherever books are sold or
at penguin.com

facebook.com/projectparanormalbooks

S0181

Also available

WINTER KISS
A Dragonfire Novel

by DEBORAH COOKE

The mysterious Dragon's Blood Elixir gives immortality to
Magnus, the Pyr's greatest enemy, and his minions—so it must
be destroyed. Outcast from the Pyr because of his own
dangerous impulses, Delaney will do anything to vanquish
Magnus—and vows to complete a mission which will either
redeem him or end his suffering.

But his plans don't take into account his sudden firestorm—
or the hot-tempered Ginger Sinclair. The firestorm reforms
Delaney closer to his old self. And when Ginger learns about
Delaney's scheme, she cannot resist a strong man with a
noble agenda.

Available wherever books are sold or
at penguin.com

facebook.com/projectparanormalbooks